TERMINAL
UPRISING

JIM C. HINES

TERMINAL
UPRISING

Book Two of the Janitors of the Post-Apocalypse

DAW BOOKS, INC.

DONALD A. WOLLHEIM, FOUNDER

1745 Broadway, New York, NY 10019

ELIZABETH R. WOLLHEIM
SHEILA E. GILBERT
PUBLISHERS
www.dawbooks.com

To all the heroes out there
cleaning up our messes,
metaphorical and literal.

Author's Note

Welcome, space janitor fans! It's time for another round of Q&A with Jim. Here are some of the questions that came in since the last book.

- From @forumferret: *What's your longest-played pen-and-paper RPG character, Jim?*
  - That would be Nakor the purple, a druid/thief ~~stolen from~~ inspired by a character out of Raymond Feist's *Riftwar* books. I may have even cosplayed that D&D character once or twice. (And yes, I wrote a book—a very bad book—about him, called *Rise of the Spider Goddess*.)
- From @ulmerigel: *Are there fire spiders in space?*
  - According to SCIENCE, you're never more than six feet away from a fire spider. *Even in space!*
- From Mouthy Old Bat[1]: *Would you ever consider using a cantankerous old woman as a main character in a science fiction novel?*

---

[1] *This name was chosen by the person in question, not by me. Please don't send angry emails.*

- ○ Absolutely! I've done it in my short fiction—most notably in "Over the Hill"—but I think a novel-length story with a protagonist like that would be awesome!
- From both Terri M. LeBlanc and @Blue119Kara: *Why janitors, and what research went into creating multiple applications for their tools and skills?*
  - ○ Why not janitors? On a spaceship with a crew of several hundred, why is it always the captain and bridge team who get to have the adventures? I wanted to write something different, and I thought the hygiene and sanitation team's skill set and perspective would make for an entertaining story. As for research, I've spent far too much time reading janitorial blogs and message boards, learning about the most horrible things these courageous crusaders for cleanliness have had to deal with.

I'm sorry I don't have space to respond to all the questions I got. Fortunately, there will be space in the next book for me to answer a few more!

Huge thanks to my two-time Hugo Award–winning editor Sheila Gilbert and everyone at DAW Books, my agent Joshua Bilmes and the rest of the team in the Hundred JABberwocky Woods, cover artist Dan Dos Santos, and everyone else who helped transform this thing from a .docx file into the gorgeous book before you.

And, of course, thanks to my family for their love, patience, and support.

If you want to keep up on what's coming next, go to jimchines.com/newsletter to sign up for the quarterly newsletter from my goblin scribe Klud. Or just stop by and say hi on social media.

Thanks so much for reading. I hope you enjoy the latest adventures of Mops and crew.

1

To: *All Earth Mercenary Corps Personnel*
From: *Fleet Admiral Belle-Bonne Sage*
(Translated into Human by Lt. J. Blon)
Re: *Marion Adamopoulos and the* EMCS *Pufferfish*

In human chronology, it has been four months and eight days since the Shipboard Hygiene and Sanitation team of the EMCS Pufferfish *went rogue. In that time, they have shot up a Quetzalus space station, attacked a Krakau escort team, stolen from a Glacidae colony, sabotaged the plumbing on a Krakau Alliance observation platform, and committed countless other crimes.*

Alliance Intelligence believes Adamopoulos is receiving help from someone within the Earth Mercenary Corps. While interspecies loyalty is understandable, Adamopoulos and her crew committed treason *against the EMC and the Krakau Alliance. If you have any knowledge of her intentions or whereabouts, intubate your Krakau command team immediately.*

Anyone found to be aiding or protecting these tractors will be dishonorably secreted and returned to Earth, to live out their days among the feral remnants of humanity. You will be provided no weapons for protection against Earth's many dangers, such as the ferocious tiger, the venomous platypus, or the infant-devouring dingo.

For decades, the Krakau have worked to help humanity. We have counteracted the worst effects of your plague to turn you from mindless savages into slightly more mindful savages. In return, tens of thousands of human soldiers have serviced the Krakau Alliance and helped protect our vulnerable taxpayers.

Marion Adamopoulos is no friend to the galaxy, or to her species. As a result of her actions, Krakau Military Command has called a temporary hilt to our programs on Earth. No more humans will be restored until we can strengthen our screening methodology to prevent such criminals from joining the corps in the future. Some among the KMC are even calling for an end to all Alliance efforts on your home world.

I believe humanity is an asset to the galaxy. I rely on your swift cooperation to prove me starboard.

Belle-Bonne Sage

Fleet Admiral, EMC

MARION "MOPS" ADAMOPOULOS' twelve years in Hygiene and Sanitation Services had left her little time for sightseeing. At least, not the kind of sights any human in their right mind wanted to see.

Despite incidents like the semi-ambulatory brown mold on deck E, courtesy of a contaminated bottle of illegal shell-thickening supplements smuggled aboard by one of the Krakau crew, Mops had never complained about her work. She'd considered herself fortunate, one of the few humans to be given a second chance. Her species had turned itself into monsters. The Krakau found a way to save some of them. In Mops' judgment, she and her fellow humans owed the Krakau everything.

And then she'd learned how the Krakau and their cold-water cousins, the Rokkau, had been the ones to tear down humanity in the first place, and how they'd spent a hundred and fifty years covering it up.

Mops had complained quite a bit more after that.

Stealing the *EMCS Pufferfish* and searching for proof of the Krakau Alliance's crimes had given her the opportunity to see so much more. Again, few of these sights were ones she would have chosen. Like the swarming lights that signified an incoming missile barrage from a Prodryan attack force, or the aftermath of explosive decompression on the ship's algae tanks following a lucky A-gun shot by an EMC scout ship.

But every once in a great while, she got to appreciate a sight like the one currently displayed on her monocle, a sight that filled her with awe and reminded her how vast and wondrous the galaxy truly was. She wanted to reach through the emptiness and touch the marvels floating before them.

To her left, Wolf said, "Those are some big damn space fish."

And just like that, the moment was as dead as the bag of spikeshell snails Wolf had brought onto the shuttle for a crunchy snack.

"Yes," Mops sighed. "Yes, they are."

The big damn space fish were called Comaceans. The closest member of the herd drifted roughly ten kilometers in front of the *Pufferfish* shuttle. Far in the background, the gas dwarf Tixateq floated like a swirling red-and-yellow marble.

The Comacean that was their destination stretched almost a kilometer in length. Its blue-black skin shone in the light of the distant sun. Fins as long as an EMC cruiser extended outward from the tubelike body, not for navigation, but to help the creature shed excess body heat.

Reluctantly, Mops turned her focus to the far less awe-inspiring sight of the shuttle interior. "Prep for approach, people."

Wolfgang Mozart—communications technician, would-be soldier, and the largest member of Mops' small crew—was stretched out on one of the fold-out metal benches running lengthwise through the cabin. Wolf sat up and brought a muscular hand to her mouth, smothering a yawn. Her brown hair was a short, unkempt mess. Moving at a lackluster pace, she brushed shell crumbs from the front of her black uniform, then secured the attachment points on her equipment harness to matching buckles on the cabin wall, locking her in place.

Sitting alone on the opposite bench, Vera Rubin double-checked her own harness. Rubin was a former security grunt who'd risked her life helping Mops in a shootout a while back. Dark scars marked the side of her face and neck. Around her neck, a clear teardrop-shaped pendant three centimeters wide held a tiny microbiome of water, algae, and a pair of pink alien maggots—two of the dozen or so "pets" she'd brought with her when she joined the *Pufferfish* crew. She tucked the pendant inside her uniform before tightening her harness.

"Anyone else find this creepy as hell?" asked Wolf. "That thing's as big as the moon, and we're gonna march into its belly?"

"The Comacean is only a fraction of the size and mass of Earth's moon," Rubin corrected. "And we'll be meeting our contact in one of her lungs. That's where the main biorefinery operation is set up."

Wolf snorted. "What happens if the damn thing sneezes?"

"We'd be crushed and expelled through the blowhole, along with a substantial mass of crystalized mucus, but that's highly unlikely. There's only been one recorded Comacean sneeze in the past fifty years." Rubin's gaze appeared unfocused—probably watching the approach on her optical implant. "The Quetzalus install nerve blockers to prevent coughing, sneezing, vomiting, and flatulence. The real concern is hiccups. They haven't found a cure for those yet."

Wolf chuckled, then frowned. "You're joking, right?"

Rubin ignored the question. "She's beautiful."

"How do you know it's female?" asked Mops.

"She's larger than the males, and her belly is smooth instead of ribbed. I wonder what her name is."

"According to the briefing, 'Biorefinery Eighteen,'" said Wolf.

Comaceans spent most of their lives in hibernation. Traversing the emptiness between Tixateq 1 and its sister planet took decades. It would be thirty-six years before the herd of more than a hundred Comaceans reached Tixateq 2 to awaken to feed and mate. Then, once the planet's orbit took them farther from the warmth and blue-white light of the sun, they would begin the long return journey to Tixateq 1.

In the interim, the Quetzalus harvested eighteen different substances from inside the largest of the creatures, including two mineral compounds, a raw form of a potent Glacidae narcotic, and a gel that had proven to be highly effective in fighting Krakau sucker-fungus.

Monroe twisted around in the cockpit, his white-haired head poking through the narrow doorway to the cabin. He was former infantry, and one of only two people on Mops' team who'd proven they could get through the various piloting simulators without multiple casualties and/or explosions. "I've got a yellow blinker on the communications console. Is that a problem?"

"That should be the landing beacon," said Wolf. "Have they assigned us a docking platform yet?"

It wasn't that Mops' team was inexperienced. It was that their experience was with things like unclogging plumbing lines and swapping out filters in the ship's environmental system. Nothing in their time keeping the *Pufferfish* relatively clean had prepared them for the work involved in running the entire ship. Four months of tutorials and on-the-job practice couldn't make up for official training and experience.

Monroe's years with the EMC infantry had given him a slightly wider range of experience. A Prodryan grenade had put an end to his infantry service. Krakau surgeons had replaced his right arm, along with a good chunk of his torso. He wore his hair long over the right side of his head, hiding the scars where his ear used to be.

His sense of balance had never fully recovered, but his discipline had made him an invaluable second-in-command. More importantly, Mops trusted him.

"They're sending us to platform three." Monroe tapped the console, transferring an image to the green-tinted monocles worn by the team.

Mops studied their destination. Pinpoints of light surrounded a metal blister forty meters ahead of a dorsal fin. Two additional lights flashed at a circular platform to one side.

"I tried to acknowledge," Monroe continued. "That should be the blue one, right? Nothing happened."

"You're still on intersystem communications. You need to switch to intrasystem." Wolf unclipped her harness and squeezed through to take the copilot seat. "Move over." After a moment's silence, she added, "Sir."

Rank and discipline had eroded since they'd turned their backs on the EMC, but there were limits to what Mops and Monroe would put up with. Wolf spent most of her time testing or skipping blithely past those limits.

"Landing instructions received and acknowledged," Wolf announced. "Cut speed and close distance to two kilometers. They'll bring us in from there using grav beams."

A minute later, the shuttle jerked like they'd hit something. Mops gripped her harness as her internal organs tried to jump out from beneath her rib cage. For several seconds, she felt like she was falling in two different directions at once.

Monroe swore. "Forgot to synch the shuttle's gravity with the Comacean grav beams. Hold on."

The vertigo ended. Mops jerked back, banging her head against the wall.

"Sorry about that," said Monroe.

"As long as we're in one piece, I'm happy." Mops lowered her voice. "We are still in one piece, right?"

"So far," responded Doc, a personal AI unit who existed primarily as code etched into the layered memory crystal of Mops' monocle. His voice came from the speakers in her uniform collar, pitched low so no one else would overhear. *"Based on your previous missions, I estimate a sixty-three percent chance of that continuing."*

"I appreciate your confidence," Mops said dryly. "Monroe, any sign of EMC vessels?"

"Nothing but the Comacean herd and a few Quetzalus transports." Monroe popped a bubble of green gum, filling the cabin with the scent of cucumber and tomato. He'd been chewing salad-flavored gum lately. "The shuttle's scanners aren't as sensitive as the *Pufferfish*'s, but they'll alert us to any deceleration signatures in the system. If the Alliance shows up, we'll see 'em in plenty of time to pull out."

"What's so important we gave up searching for the Rokkau prison planet to come here, anyway?" asked Wolf.

"All Admiral Pachelbel told me was that it's vital we meet with this person, for the sake of both Earth and the Alliance." Mops had known Pachelbel for most of her life. The admiral couldn't openly assist wanted criminals, but she sympathized with Mops and her goals. She'd done what she could to help them from the shadows.

Mops opened the collar of her uniform to pull out the flexible bubble-style helmet. "Everyone seal up."

Mops secured the clear material over her head and sealed the edge to the front of her collar, then bent down to pull the tabs that would seal the gap between boots and pants. Finally, she removed her gloves from their pocket and tugged them on.

The suit's air circulation hissed to life automatically. Her helmet swelled outward, creases smoothing away until nothing remained to obscure her vision except a few fingerprints. She wrinkled her nose at the plastic-and-oil taste of the suit's air supply.

A blue status icon appeared on her monocle, displaying suit integrity and confirming she had twenty minutes of air. Additional icons provided the same information for her team.

"Wolf, you've got a helmet leak," she said.

"I see it." Wolf scowled and grabbed a roll of metallic gold tape from her equipment harness. She tore off a strip and stretched it over the left side of her helmet.

The lone green icon on Mops' monocle turned blue a moment later. Their uniforms were standard maintenance jumpsuits, and weren't designed for long-term space work, but they'd be more than enough for the walk from the shuttle to the Comacean air lock.

"Touchdown in twenty seconds," called Monroe.

The grav beams set the shuttle down as gently as a Quetzalus returning an egg to the nest. Monroe glanced at a checklist taped to the wall, reviewed his console, and twisted around in his chair. "All systems are blue."

"Everyone grab a PRA." Mops detached her harness from the seat and opened an overhead compartment to retrieve one of the personal respiration adjusters. The air mixture inside the Comacean was formulated for Quetzalus. The PRAs would provide trace adjustments to their oxygen intake to keep everyone fully alert.

She looped the PRA around her neck like a medallion. "Wolf, you're staying with the shuttle."

Wolf froze, PRA in hand. "But Monroe's the pilot."

"Monroe won't punch out our escort." Mops waited, arms crossed, until Wolf stuffed the PRA back into the compartment. "Yes, I know what happened at Crossroads Station last week."

"That Glacidae had it coming," Wolf muttered. "You think they oozed lubricating fluid in my soup by accident?"

"The prelaunch procedure should be programmed and ready to go," said Mops. "All you have to do is flip the switch."

"It's an interactive touch/voice menu, not an actual switch," Rubin clarified.

"I know, I know." Wolf returned to the cockpit and dropped into the pilot's seat.

"Keep an eye out for unexpected company," said Mops. "Maintain an open channel with the *Pufferfish*, and a second line with me. That's the other reason I need you here. Monroe doesn't know comms like you do, and we can't afford to lose contact."

Wolf straightened a little at the acknowledgment of her newfound expertise.

"Stay suited up until the shuttle's completely repressurized," Mops reminded her. "Just in case."

"I know the regs." Wolf offered a half-hearted salute and punched the door controls, closing off the cockpit from the rest of the shuttle.

The cabin lights turned green as the air thinned. Mops' suit puffed out slightly in response. "No projectile weapons inside the Comacean," she reminded them. "Combat batons only."

Hopefully, they wouldn't need weapons. Humanity's reputation as savages should convince the workers to give them a wide berth.

The rest of their equipment was standard SHS gear. If anyone asked, they could claim to be a cleanup crew doing contract work.

The hatch fell silently open, becoming a ramp leading to a path marked with blue light strips.

"Stay between the lights," Rubin warned over the comm. "Comaceans aren't massive enough to generate significant gravity. Step off the grav plates, and you'll float away."

Mops spotted two other shuttle-class vessels parked nearby. The first was Quetzalus in design, tall and blocky, like a house ripped from its foundations. The second was Merraban, painted in a jarring color scheme of cheerful red, green, and pink.

Beyond the square metal plates and the border lights, the Comacean's skin reminded her of volcanic rock: wrinkled and pitted and cracked. Veins of dark green ice filled the deepest cracks.

The way the surface curved away in all directions triggered a primitive part of her brain, making her feel like her next step would send her falling toward the stars. "Doc, where's my ship?"

A glowing arrow appeared on her monocle. She turned her head until she spied an oversized silhouette of the *Pufferfish*. With all essential systems shut down, the *Pufferfish* should be safely invisible unless someone knew exactly where to look.

"This is cruel," murmured Rubin. She crouched at the very edge of the "road," where the overlapping grav plates were "stitched" to the Comacean's skin with black polymer cable.

"The Comaceans have evolved to take micrometeoroid strikes." Mops pointed to a small crater to the left of the road. "I doubt this one even noticed a few piercings. The Quetzalus have specialists seeing to the health of the herd, not to mention a team of lawyers making sure they comply with Alliance laws about the treatment of rare or endangered life-forms."

"Alliance laws." Rubin continued toward the air lock. "Laws that permit one species to modify and colonize another? I wouldn't trust their laws to protect my pet slug, let alone the Comaceans."

Her voice, normally atonal, grew louder at the end, revealing the depth of her unhappiness.

The dome ahead rotated to reveal a triangular air lock door, which slid open a moment later. The air lock was large enough to hold multiple Quetzalus. For three humans, it was more spacious than the entire *Pufferfish* shuttle.

The door slid shut, the lift pressurized, and the whole thing sank down with a faint slurping sound. This was one of eight blowholes spread around the Comacean's body: four toward the front, and four more near the tail. The creature only breathed when inside a planet's atmosphere, so there was little chance of her snorting the lift and its occupants into space.

Artificial gravity couldn't fully compensate for the vertigo as they followed the Comacean's airpipe toward one of the lungs.

"Welcome to Biorefinery Eighteen, a Zenkozan family business," a mechanically-translated voice announced. "We have identified you as *human*. If this is incorrect, please state your species name and preferred language now."

After a pause, the voice continued. "You are responsible for obeying all safety regulations and posted signs. As you are *human*, please pay particular attention to the following rules. One: Eating Zenkozan employees is strictly forbidden. Two: Eating the Comacean is also forbidden."

"Our reputation precedes us," commented Mops.

Monroe grunted. "Probably a good thing Wolf stayed behind."

The lift stopped. Eventually, the door opened to reveal two Quetzalus. Each massed roughly the same as an Earth elephant. Dull, patchy hair covered their yellow-brown skin. Both wore metal cuffs near the base of the upper part of their beaks. The devices appeared to be a combination translator/computer interface/identification. Clipped to the lower beaks were short metal tubes.

"Electric stunners," said Doc. *"Short-range. Probably not powerful enough to kill a human, but it would leave you twitching on the floor in a puddle of your own piss."*

Mops was less concerned about the stunners than she was about those computers. The average Quetzalus might not be able to tell one human from another, but if their systems identified Mops and the others as wanted fugitives, this mission could get clogged up fast.

Both Quetzalus were nervous, judging from the dim blue glow of their tongues. It might be nothing more than having to get close to humans. Mops kept one hand near her combat baton, just in case.

The closer of the two—the lack of a crest atop her head marked her as female—cocked her head. Probably listening to instructions via an implant. "You are Captain Jean-François Paillard?"

"That's right." Mops had chosen the alias after confirming

the real Captain Paillard was helping with security and relief efforts at a Krakau colony twenty-three light-years away. "We made arrangements with Zan Zenkozan to pick up one of your guests."

Said arrangements had mostly involved transferring a significant amount of money into the Zenkozan family coffers. Given Quetzalus economics, it was less a bribe than a tip. If they'd done the numbers right, it would be enough to ensure cooperation and secrecy without being so extravagant as to raise suspicions.

The male's bushy red crest was fully erect. A wave of orange light rippled through his hair. Quetzalus "hair" was more like biological fiber optic cable, with different colors of light indicating strong emotions.

"Is there a problem?" asked Monroe.

The female clacked her beak, making a sound like wooden planks smacking together. Hard. Mops had heard Quetzalus laughter before, but it still made her flinch reflexively.

"Quil is expressing relief. I am Ulique Laccalos. Quil and I are thrilled at your arrival and will happily escort you to your passenger."

"How quickly can you take him?" asked Quil.

Mops blinked. "Our shuttle is ready to launch. We can go as soon as—"

"He's in the commissary," interrupted Ulique. "This way, please."

Their eagerness to be rid of their guest made Mops more nervous, not less. Who—or what—had Admiral Pachelbel sent them to retrieve?

With a sigh, she left the air lock and hurried to keep up with the long-legged Quetzalus.

The passageway reminded Mops of a flexible ship-to-ship boarding tube, only larger, with an odd series of vertical bulges striping the walls. Orange-tinged light strips ran along either side, half a meter above human eye level. Gravity was a third of Earth normal.

Monroe ran a hand over one of the rounded bulges on the wall. "Structural reinforcements?"

"In a sense," answered Ulique. "Those are bones."

Mops frowned. "I thought we were inside the equivalent of a bronchial tube."

"We are," said Quil. "Diminutive creatures like yourselves require far less skeletal support than one as magnificent as B-18. We've developed several new manufacturing techniques based on the Comacean's ability to grow flexible metal-infused cartilage."

Mops took a closer look. "Kumar would love this."

"Probably why he insisted I record everything for him," said Doc. *"He also asked if we could bring him back, and I quote, 'Some parts to dissect.'"*

"Confirming I made the right call to leave him on the *Pufferfish* for this one." Mops doubted Kumar's enthusiasm for all things biological would have gone over well with their hosts. Or with Rubin.

Another air lock opened onto an open metal platform, enclosed beneath a clear dome. Mops' breath stopped as she took in the enormous blue cavern stretching out before and below them—the Comacean's lung. The bulging air sacs lining the surface of the lung made Mops think of the inside of a pomegranate.

Quetzalus worked in circular pitlike stations, each one holding three or four individuals around a central computer terminal. The younger ones lit up with anxiety at the sight of the humans.

A maze of narrowing tunnels stretched away from the domed platform, many disappearing into the lung walls. These were similar in color to the Comacean's skin, dark with green lines running beneath the surface.

According to the specs Doc shared through her monocle, the Quetzalus had settled eight of the larger air pockets within the lung, including cargo and equipment, residences, and a secure control area. This was communications and transport.

"We've colonized several other organs," Quil said proudly. "Including four gizzards and a section of . . . I believe in humans, it would be called the liver."

After checking the air readings, Mops unsealed her helmet and activated her PRA. A puff of metal-scented oxygen tickled her face. The air smelled faintly swamplike. Old instincts kicked in, and she glanced around for mold. She found nothing but the faint oily sheen left behind by cleaning drones.

"What's that music?" asked Rubin as she removed her own helmet.

"Counterclassical traveling songs," said Ulique. "Used to remember hunting and migration routes back home."

It sounded like metal rasps rubbing together, overlaid with low wind instruments and the hornlike sounds of untranslated Quetzalus speech. *This is not a common Quetzalus language, but I can attempt to translate if you'd like,* offered Doc. *I believe the refrain refers to a bumbling son who died in a tar pit.*

Doc paused. *And also died in a lava flow. And a mudslide. And some form of playground equipment. It's possible my translation is off.*

"This way." Ulique led them to the largest of five open passages leading deeper into the lung.

They entered another bronchial tube, which sloped steeply downward. The grav plates kept Mops' inner ear from registering the change.

If my specs are accurate, we're passing over the bladder and water filtration plant access point, said Doc.

Ten minutes later, they emerged into what appeared to be a small, colorful jungle. Thick yellow moss carpeted the floor. Vines as thick as her arm clung to the curved walls and ceiling. Clusters of bell-shaped orange blossoms grew alongside thorny, hard-shelled fruits. The too-sweet floral scent made her eyes water, and Mops surreptitiously turned up her PRA.

A nearby Quetzalus extended a quadfurcated tongue to grasp one of the swollen fruits. He twisted carefully, then froze, his glowing tongue still half-extended, when he spotted the humans.

"The commissary?" guessed Mops.

"There's gathering space toward the back," said Quil.

"We don't have much here suitable for aliens," Ulique said apologetically. "But humans don't eat real food anyway, right?"

"Not usually." Mops gestured for the others to remain still. "The Krakau found tube feeding to be easier and healthier for human sustenance."

"Disgusting." From the flat tone, she was fairly sure Ulique's comment was meant as observation, not insult.

Doc translated the whispers he picked up as the Quetzalus warned one another about the arrival of humans. The one with his tongue out finally pulled the fruit free, took it carefully in his beak, and backed away.

"Most of our people have never seen a human in person," Quil said, crest drooping. "They hear stories of your service as fierce soldiers for the Krakau Alliance."

Mops forced a chuckle. "I think they're more concerned with the stories about humans reverting to feral, shambling cannibals."

"That, too, yes," Ulique said awkwardly. "There is an entire genre of 'monster human' stories, popular among our youth. The worst are the games that allow you to play as a human, killing and consuming sentient beings."

"Our navigator has several of those. They don't play 'em much anymore." Mops watched as the Quetzalus quietly cleared out. In another situation, she might have tried to ease their fears, but for this mission, the fewer witnesses, the better. They wouldn't all leave, of course. There were always gawkers who enjoyed the alien equivalent of an adrenaline rush that came from getting close to such dangerous animals.

"This way." Ulique led them down a well-trampled path toward a mossy clearing with a bubbling, steaming pond at the center. Smooth-topped rocks, about a meter in diameter, were scattered about like tables. Only a few Quetzalus remained, their enormous eyes fixed on the humans.

Mops barely noticed them. Her attention was locked on a

table near the back and its lone occupant: a creature a meter in height, with broad blue-and-yellow wings draped like a cape from the middle of his back. Gleaming, colorful armor plates protected his torso and shoulder joints. Overlong fingers poked at a rectangular lump of brown nutritional supplement.

"Your passenger," said Ulique, not bothering to conceal her relief. "How soon can you take him?"

Mops' hand dropped to her combat baton. "Doc?"

"On it." He pulled up their instructions from Admiral Pachelbel.

Mops reread every word. The admiral had been even less forthcoming than usual about this one. Nowhere had she made any mention that their contact was Prodryan.

Monroe and Rubin stepped into position on either side of her and waited for orders.

Technically, there was no law against a Prodryan being here. The Prodryan war against the Alliance was a disorganized thing, a thousand individual actions rather than a centralized campaign. The Prodryans had never officially declared war, in part because war was their default state. They'd wiped out dozens of colonies and killed hundreds of thousands, including many of Mops' fellow humans.

"Captain Adamopoulos?" The Prodryan rose and brushed crumbs from his armor.

"Captain Jean-François Paillard," Mops said firmly.

"Of course. Captain *Paillard*." Prodryans were furious fighters but terrible liars. "My Human name is Advocate of Violence. I'm a certified legal advocate and part-time spy. I'm here to assist you and your crew. In return, you'll help me end the Krakau Alliance."

What to Do if You Encounter a Prodryan

A Guide for Humans, Prepared by EMC Sergeant A. Lovelace

1. *In the words of a great Earth philosopher, Don't Panic. Only a fraction of the Prodryan race are actively warring against the entire galaxy. True, the remaining Prodryans also want you dead, but most have other priorities than making it happen right this moment.*
2. *How old is the Prodryan? Younger individuals who haven't yet earned armor and biological enhancements may try to start a fight in order to improve their reputation. Don't let them bait you.*
3. *If you do let them bait you, make sure you win.*
4. *Prodryans cannot fly in normal gravity. But in low-gee environments, remember to look up.*
5. *You can try walking away from the Prodryan. They will probably take this as an insult and use it as an excuse to fight.*

     a. Do not take your attention off the Prodryan until
       you are safely out of range.
  6. *You can try talking to the Prodryan. They will probably*
     take this as an insult and use it as an excuse to fight.
     a. If you try talking, be blunt. Prodryans have no sense
       of tact or diplomacy.
     b. Ask direct questions. Prodryans are terrible liars.
  7. *Do not answer any questions about your mission, your*
     unit, your ship, your training, your equipment—
     a. You know what? Just don't answer any questions,
       period.
  8. *Assuming you survive, immediately report all interac-*
     tions to your Krakau commanding officer.

"HELP YOU END THE Krakau Alliance?" Mops repeated.

Advocate of Violence's four mouth pincers clicked together, the Prodryan equivalent of a nod.

Mops saw three options. One: drag the Prodryan back to the shuttle where he could explain what the hell he was talking about. Two: have him explain what the hell he was talking about right here and now. Three: forget the whole mission and get the hell out of here.

Option three was damn tempting.

Advocate of Violence removed a thumb-sized metal rod from his armor, rotated a black ring on the end, and set it on the table. "Privacy sphere. The security feeds will pick up nothing but static." He made a shooing motion toward the two Quetzalus. "This is a privileged conversation, protected by Alliance Civil Code Section 1723.4 through 1723.9. If you attempt to eavesdrop, I'll have you cited and fined."

The Quetzalus backed away. Ulique paused to say to Mops, "Promise me you'll take him away from here."

"That depends on what he says next."

Advocate of Violence waited for the Quetzalus to leave, then leaned across the table. "The Krakau have four medical facilities on Earth where feral humans are transformed into soldiers and warriors and . . . you."

"Yes, we know," said Mops. "We were there."

"They have a new facility," he continued. "Highly secured and operating under the direct supervision of Fleet Admiral Belle-Bonne Sage."

"Doing what?" Mops hadn't intended to engage or ask questions, but the words slipped out.

"A bit of stolen satellite security video suggests a theory, but not one I can share here." His wings shivered. "The only way to know for certain is for us to go to Earth."

"Was that a translator error?" asked Monroe. "Or did a Prodryan just suggest we should take him to Earth?"

"There should be no errors." Advocate of Violence touched a small device secured to the collar of his armor. "I installed the latest Human vocabulary update three days ago. I didn't want to rely on your translator's knowledge of Pyrulian."

"A lesser-known Prodryan language," Doc clarified. *"I'm confident I could understand and relay his meaning, though obscure idiomatic expressions might be a problem. Pyrulian has seventy-three different words and expressions for 'murder,' for example."*

"I understand your hesitation," the Prodryan continued. "Your planet is overrun by feral humans who would happily kill and eat you. It's protected by the Krakau Alliance, which currently has thirty-nine separate alerts and warrants for you and your team. And your contact is a hostile alien who would happily erase your entire species from the cosmos, one who hopes to use this mission to undermine the Alliance."

"You think whatever Sage is doing on Earth outweighs all that?" asked Mops.

"I'm certain of it." He brushed a scrap of cloth over his

mouth pincers, wiping away a smear of green predigestive fluid. "As was your Admiral Pachelbel. She knows far better than you the threat I present. And still she sent you here."

That was a very good point, dammit. Pachelbel had been horrified to learn the secrets Mops and her team had dredged up months earlier about the Rokkau, believed to have been wiped out by their Krakau kin, and about the role Rokkau venom had played in humanity's downfall. Ever since, Pachelbel had been doing all she could to help Mops find the surviving Rokkau and prove what had happened on Earth a century and a half before.

She'd risked her career, her family's reputation . . . possibly her life. Fleet Admiral Sage had recently relieved Pachelbel of command of Stepping Stone Station. According to gossip Mops had picked up, Sage suspected Pachelbel, and was just waiting for her to slip up, at which point Sage would have her court-martialed and imprisoned for life.

Despite all of that, Pachelbel had still contacted the *Pufferfish* to arrange this meeting.

Mops glanced at Monroe. "Search and scan him."

He moved in and began patting down the Prodryan's armor. He removed several devices from a thick belt, including a serrated knife as long as Mops' forearm. Advocate of Violence cooperated, though his antennae vibrated the entire time, suggesting annoyance. He even removed his own armor, stacking the contoured pieces neatly on the table and sliding them toward Mops. Underneath, he wore a simple yellow shift, secured with a matching sash around his slender waist.

"Six implants," said Monroe. "Looks like a recording device in the left eyeball, a storage compartment in the right forearm, retractable razor-edging on the upper wings, pain-blocker at the base of the skull, databank interface in the right eyeball, and audio pickup at the base of the left antenna."

"Correct." The Prodryan peeled open a rectangular patch of artificial skin on his forearm and removed a metal canister. "My medication. Regurgitant pills, to help with a digestive disability. You can analyze them if you'd like. I don't recommend trying them."

Mops looked at her companions, trying to gauge their thinking. Rubin's face was unreadable. Monroe's expression wouldn't give anything away to a nonhuman, but Mops had worked with him long enough to recognize the faint crease across the brow, the tightness of his jaw . . . the stillness that meant he'd swallowed his gum. It was the face of a man who'd mulled over the evidence and come to a conclusion he didn't like.

"All right," Mops whispered. "I'll bring you to my shuttle. There, you'll share this theory of yours, along with any additional evidence and information you have on Sage's activities."

"Excellent." Advocate of Violence retrieved the privacy device, deactivated it, and set it atop the pile of his belongings. He then raised a limb and clicked the curved claws that served as fingers.

Rubin had her combat baton out by the second click. "What are you doing?"

"Signaling for my bill." He gestured to the half-eaten nutritional supplement.

At Mops' nod, Rubin lowered the weapon. She kept it ready at her side, though.

A quiet beak-clap marked the arrival of a Quetzalus wearing a poorly-fitted apron. He used his tongue to retrieve a small tablet from the apron pocket.

Advocate of Violence gulped down another chunk of his meal, then reached for his pill case. "I was told the captain would cover my expenses."

Mops' eyes narrowed. Scowling, she snatched the tablet from the Quetzalus.

"Mops, that thing is scanning you. Whatever it is, it's not a bill."

She hurled it away and grabbed the Quetzalus by the skin flap between his chest and foreleg. A sharp twist turned his hair blue with pain. "What the depths is this?"

Rubin climbed onto the table, baton ready to strike the

Quetzalus in the face. Monroe moved closer to Advocate of Violence, keeping him covered.

The Quetzalus' words were tight and clipped, either from fear or from pain. Probably both. "Marion S. Adamopoulos, you are hereby served notice of civil charges filed by Kona-molloko-hi. She accuses you of destroying a short-range vessel belonging to one of her offspring. She also accuses you of destroying said offspring."

"Probably one of the Nusurans who tried to abduct us back on Coacalos Station," said Monroe.

Mops tightened her grip. "Who are you?"

"Ix Suazalaxe, freelance legal agent for the Alliance Judiciary branch." The Quetzalus' head bobbed. "Your receipt of this notice has been recorded. You have thirty days to submit your response."

"I can help you with that," Advocate of Violence offered. "For a reasonable retainer and daily rate."

Mops turned. "Did you tell him we were coming?"

"I met Ix three years ago during a civil dispute over injuries suffered at a Nusuran sex party," said the Prodryan. "The centrifuge was improperly calibrated for the Glacidae guest, resulting in multiple exoskeletal cracks. Per the waiver signed by all participants, equipment neglect was not covered—"

"Did you tell him?" she repeated, her voice quiet.

"My business transactions are confidential. To answer that question would be unethical."

She released her grip on Ix, who jumped backward. Quetzalus could move quickly when they needed to. "Have *you* told anyone else, Ix?"

"Only my client and my firm."

If any of those communications had been overheard or intercepted, or if the recipients had talked to anyone connected to the Alliance . . . "Wolf, we're on our way. Prep the shuttle, and take a closer look at every docked or incoming ship. We could be getting company."

"On it, sir!"

Even over the comm, Mops could hear the relief in Wolf's response. Probably excited about the potential for a fight.

Advocate of Violence rose. "I'll need to gather my things."

Mops shoulders tightened. "What things?"

"Just my reference library. A few pieces of furniture. Various mementos and souvenirs." He paused. "How large is your transport, exactly? This may require more than one trip."

Wolf closed the connection with Mops and—reluctantly— reopened the channel to Cuaxil Nukuklu, the refinery landing controller who'd been babbling for so long Wolf was ready to put an A-gun slug through her own skull. Or through Cuaxil's skull.

"That was my captain," said Wolf. "I've got to run through the prelaunch checklist."

Cuaxil's voice over the comm was as chipper as ever. "What a shame. I wish you could have come on board with your crew. I'm just so grateful to you Earth Mercenary Corpsmen for your service and sacrifices."

Wolf glanced at Monroe's notes, all neat and precise and thorough. Too thorough. Where the hell had he jotted down the scanner control tips?

"How many battles have you been in?"

"I was in SHS, not infantry," Wolf said sourly. "I spent my days toting a mop, not a rifle."

She tapped the icon for the long-range scanning logs. Anyone decelerating from faster-than-light travel would send out a deceleration signature, a signal flare everyone could see. According to this, there had been no new arrivals in-system. That meant she just had to take a closer look at all of the ships and shuttles that were already here.

She glared at the console's unfamiliar array of gauges, lights, and controls. A yellow icon shaped like a curled tentacle blinked at her. What the depths was that supposed to mean?

"I thought all humans were soldiers," said Cuaxil.

"Most cured humans, yes." Wolf debated again simply killing the connection, but she couldn't afford to piss off someone who could complicate their departure. Especially if they were expecting trouble. "We're all part of the fight, one way or another."

Wolf gave up and opened another line. "Monroe, how the hell do I scan the other shuttles?"

"Left side of the console," said Monroe. "You should see two blue shapes that look like Krakau eye slits. Switch to the larger eye."

Wolf found and flipped the switch, and the console controls reconfigured. A new set of notes and annotations appeared at the top, including Monroe's preliminary scan of the other shuttles on Biorefinery Eighteen. He'd compiled a list of their identification beacons, but those were simple to fake.

Wolf double-checked Monroe's notes, then magnified the silhouette of the closest shuttle, matching it against known ship types. Shape, construction, and power emissions all appeared consistent with the beacon information.

A comm light flashed. Reluctantly, Wolf reached over to unmute Cuaxil.

"—since I heard what your people did during the Battle of Avloka, I've contributed one percent of my salary to a Krakau charity dedicated to finding a cure for humans. It's so tragic what happened to you and your world."

"Yeah, it sucks."

"Sucks?" Cuaxil paused. "Oh, a human idiom. How delightful. Have you killed many Prodryans?"

"That's classified," Wolf lied.

"Oh, of course. I'm sorry, dear." Cuaxil breathed a long, rattling sigh. "It must be so hard controlling your savagery, channeling it into protecting the rest of us. I know a lot of people think humans are no better than animals, and the galaxy would be better off without you, but some of us appreciate the part you play in keeping those awful Prodryans at bay."

"Thanks." The second shuttle checked out.

Wolf banged the back of her head against her chair. This would take forever, and all it would prove was that the IDs matched their ships. She couldn't see inside them to know who might be waiting to pounce.

"Is it true humans don't feel pain?"

"Not physical pain, no. One of the side effects of the plague. Makes us better fighters." From a thigh pocket, Wolf grabbed a packet of riverwood seed pods from Nurgistarnoq, tore off the top, and poured a stream of the spicy black pellets directly into her mouth. "Cuaxil, could I ask a small favor?"

"Anything you need."

Wolf crunched and swallowed. "This is classified stuff, so I need to know you can keep a secret."

"For you, my beak is sealed."

If only. "We're tracking . . ." She paused, trying to imagine what would be most alluring to someone like Cuaxil. "Space pirates."

"Ooh."

Wolf could practically hear her lighting up. "My CO has me checking out the other docked ships, but my shuttle's equipment is pretty weak, and I'm limited to passive scans."

"You don't want to spook your prey."

"Exactly," said Wolf. "You've got good instincts for this."

"I read a lot," she preened. "Nusuran war romances, mostly."

Wolf cringed. It was a popular genre, but they all ended with overwritten cross-species sex scenes. Her mouth went dry as she realized Cuaxil might have another motive for chatting up a bored human. She swallowed. "I know this is probably bending the rules, but is there any way you could send me registry and scanning info on everyone else docked on B-18?"

"You think someone might be using a forged ID beacon?"

"I guarantee it. Oh, and just to be thorough, do you have records of deceleration signatures from the past week? I can compare those against the data we have on those space pirates."

"Let me check the logs, dear."

"Thanks. May your beak be bright and your nest strong."

It wasn't long before data began scrolling down her console. Mostly Quetzalus ships and shuttles, just as she'd expected. She flagged several for closer review, then turned to the decel signatures. "Well, shit."

"I don't understand," said Cuaxil. "Do you need a moment to relieve yourself?"

"Yeah, sure."

"Well, I hope you get a chance to visit after your mission is—"

Wolf killed the connection, her attention on a particular deceleration flare. A moment later, she was opening a secure line to Mops.

"You're sure?" asked Mops.

"I was trained to clean toilets, not identify energy signatures, but it's hard to disguise a cruiser-class deceleration flare. And the Quetzalus' satellites tagged it as an EMC ship, just like they did the *Pufferfish*."

Mops dropped the abalone-plated shelves she'd been carrying and gestured for the others to stop. "I ordered Grom and Azure to keep an eye out for new arrivals. If they got distracted playing *Black Hole Run* on the bridge viewscreen again—"

"The decel signature is from four days ago," Wolf interrupted. "They got here before us."

"They knew we were coming." Mops glared at their Prodryan contact. The other cruiser must have been lurking in the blackness on minimal power, just like the *Pufferfish*. They would have seen the *Pufferfish*'s arrival, but hadn't been close enough to pounce. Better to slowly move smaller fighters into position while waiting until Mops and her team were most vulnerable. Like when her crew was split between the *Pufferfish*, the shuttle, and the Comacean. "Monroe, Rubin, forget Advocate's belongings. We're leaving now."

"I trust I'll be reimbursed," the Prodryan complained.

Mops ignored him, hurrying down the bronchial tunnel that led from the residential pods back toward the main junction area.

"This might not be the best strategy," said Monroe.

She paused at a doorway. "Explain."

Monroe cocked an artificial thumb at Advocate of Violence. "If I was running a mission to take the *Pufferfish* crew, I'd tap into the internal Comacean security feeds. Ideally, you wait until your people are in the best positions and your prey is most vulnerable, but if the prey gets spooked—"

"You move now. Dammit." Anyone watching would have seen Mops dumping Advocate of Violence's things. She turned in a circle, wondering where the security scanners might be hidden. "Keep moving, but stay calm. Wolf, is anything happening out there?"

"I was about to call. One of the parked shuttles just spat out what looks like an entire EMC infantry squad."

The muscles in Mops' neck and shoulders tightened like drying leather. "Wolf, take off now. Head back to the *Pufferfish*. Have Grom get the ship over here and prep for an A-ring jump. Tell Kumar and Azure we might need that project we talked about."

"I don't think these clowns know I'm here," Wolf protested. "I can help. Let me grab weapons and follow them down, take them by surprise from behind."

"You want to single-handedly ambush an entire infantry squad? I don't think so. Get moving, Wolf. We'll find another way off." She cleared the connection. "Doc, give me the specs on this beast. Highlight the closest escape pods."

"There's a good chance the EMC will intercept any escape pods before we can reach the Pufferfish.*"*

"You have a better suggestion?" Mops snapped.

"Don't get snippy with me. I'm not the one who marched into a trap, then panicked and set it off."

"I miss the days when all I had to worry about was that strange citrus smell from deck B." She studied the map on her monocle. It would take the EMC troops several minutes to get here from the blowhole. "This way."

At first, trying to run only slowed them down. The reduced gravity led to three falls, two instances of bouncing off walls, one frantic bout of wing-flapping on the part of the Prodryan, and a collision with an unsuspecting Quetzalus coming off a lift that left Mops seeing stars.

"Low gravity doesn't change your mass."

"Shut up." Mops grabbed her monocle from where it had fallen. The impact had split the skin of her eyebrow against one of the implanted magnets. When she replaced the monocle, everything seemed ever so slightly out of alignment.

The Quetzalus was uninjured, but her tongue blazed like a blue sun as she scrambled away from the humans.

Mops entered the lift, double-checked Doc's map, and reached up to tap the oversized button for warehousing.

The forty-second lift journey took them beyond the lung into an abdominal cavity. They emerged in a large storage area, half full of stacked hexagonal barrels of different colors. Two Quetzalus used a drone to unload additional barrels from a mag-lift cart.

"You can't be in here," one shouted, his crest rising.

"It's an emergency!" Mops paused to orient herself. The large exit to her right led deeper into the literal guts of the Comacean. Several smaller exits were scattered about the cavern, but they didn't all show up on Doc's map. "Which one of these leads to the escape pods?"

"Call security," said the second Quetzalus.

Mops jabbed a finger at Monroe. "This human is showing signs of reversion. He's going feral! I have to get him out of here before he starts eating everyone in sight!"

Monroe bared his teeth and drooled.

Both Quetzalus backed away, abandoning their work. The one with the raised crest was clamoring into his comm unit. "The human is leaking from his mouth orifice!"

"You're doing wonders for the reputation of your species," said Doc.

"The escape pods?" Mops seized Monroe's arm and motioned for Rubin to grab the other. "I don't know how long we can control him."

A single thrust of a glowing tongue indicated the third passageway to the right.

"Run," Mops shouted as she dragged Monroe toward the indicated doorway. "I'll try to shoot this human into space, but if he gets away, you'll want to seal every door between us and the rest of the refinery."

They'd only gotten a few paces into the corridor when Mops realized Advocate of Violence wasn't following. "What's wrong?"

"The human . . ." Exposed blades added a silver stripe to the edges of his wings. "If he goes feral—"

"I promise I'll eat you last," snapped Monroe.

"He's fine," added Mops.

The Prodryan stared at her, then back at Monroe. "You lied about his condition?"

Monroe popped a cube of purple gum into his mouth and said, "I damn well hope so."

Mops closed the door behind them and took a canister of sealant foam from her equipment harness. She squeezed a line over the door's edges. The quick-hardening goo was designed to hold against hull punctures. It should be enough to slow any pursuers down.

She swapped the sealant for the floor polish used in Krakau quarters and sprayed the area directly in front of the door. Krakau limbs clung better to the waxy surface, but human feet tended to slip every which way. Combined with the reduced gravity, it should send the EMC troops down in a jumble.

They passed what appeared to be a small changing and

cleansing room and took a left at the next juncture. Mops pointed. "Escape pods should be around that curve."

Identical oval doors lined the hallway. Doc automatically translated the blue signs over the doors, which named them escape pods seventeen through thirty-five. He also tagged and highlighted the nine EMC soldiers waiting at the far end of the corridor.

Five knelt with rifles trained on Mops and her group. At this distance, with the active-targeting assistance provided by their monocles, it would be impossible for them to miss.

"Marion Adamopoulos," shouted a woman in back. She wore red lieutenant stripes on her right shoulder, above the crossed rifles emblem of the EMC infantry. "You will remove all weapons and equipment and surrender. If you refuse, we've been authorized to use any necessary force to subdue you. Don't make us shoot you, Mops."

Rubin shifted her weight. Several guns twitched to follow her. The former security guard wouldn't hesitate to charge the troops, sacrificing herself in the hope of getting Mops, Monroe, and their Prodryan contact into the escape pod.

"Orders, sir?" whispered Monroe.

There were too many guns, and unlike most of her crew, these people looked like they knew how to use them. Mops raised her hands. "Stand down."

3

To Court! (Prodryan Battle Poem)
Author Unknown

To court! To court!
I am the blaster of justice, the armor of law!
With my opening statement, I stab my enemy.[1]
With my keen objections, I strike him down.
He bleeds before the magistrate as I claim the laurels of
    conquest.

To sentencing! To sentencing!
I am the executioner of the unworthy, the destroyer of
    failure!
With my precedents, I build my enemy's pyre.
With the flamethrower of justice, I burn their
    appeals.[2]
Hail, hail the glorious magistrate!

To billing! To billing!
I am the collector of debt, the champion of incremental
*　　accounting!*
With my triumphs, I fill the vault of victory.
With liens and debt collectors, I secure my future.
I wipe my blade and march onward to the next battle.

———

1. *Some species don't allow the literal stabbing of one's*
   opponent. Always review regional and jurisdictional
   laws regarding courtroom violence.
2. *Always avoid igniting the judge and his staff.*

MOPS RAN ESCAPE PLANS in her mind, searching for one that didn't end with her and her team being shot and/or blown up. "How did you get here before us?"

"Fleet Admiral Sage has been studying you." The lieutenant shook her head in disgust. "She guessed you'd realize we were here and try to sneak out, so we stationed teams to cover all the escape pods. Twelve damn hours we've been waiting here. I'm tired and pissed off, so stop stalling, and don't test us."

Before Mops could answer, Advocate of Violence stepped forward. "I trust you've brought proof of your orders?"

Every weapon moved toward the Prodryan. The lieutenant's thick brows and leathery skin contracted with disgust. "They told us you'd betrayed the Alliance, Mops. I didn't want to believe it."

Advocate of Violence drew himself up taller. "You've entered this Comacean brandishing projectile weapons, a clear violation of the Alliance Protected Species Act, and expect us to simply take your word that you're acting on behalf of a high-ranking Alliance official? You haven't even identified yourselves."

The Prodryan's entire demeanor had changed. His wings spread slightly, like a colorful cape. Confidence and disdain wafted from his body. Mops was reluctantly impressed.

"Lieutenant Michael Jackson of the *EMCS Box Jellyfish*," the woman said. Like all EMC troops, she would have chosen a name from human history when she was cured and "reborn." "I'm transmitting our warrant and proof of our orders now. Who the depths are you?"

"I'm the legal advocate for these three humans." Advocate of Violence closed his right eye. "I've reviewed your paperwork, and it appears valid. Do you have proof of this human's identity?"

Jackson frowned. "Do we have what?"

"Proof of this human's identity." The Prodryan spoke slowly, each word dripping disdain. "How do you know this is the 'Marlon Adoplumless' you've been sent to detain? If you assault the wrong human, you'd open yourselves and potentially the entire Earth Mercenary Corps to criminal liability. Particularly given your violation of APSA Title 93, Chapter 48, Code 12."

"Reckless endangerment of a protected or endangered lifeform, involving explosives or firearms of Class C and above," whispered Doc.

"We identified the *Pufferfish* from its deceleration signature when it arrived in-system," Jackson snapped. "The computer confirms a visual match on Marion Adamopoulos, Vera Rubin, and Marilyn Monroe."

The Prodryan brought his hands together and scraped the two longest claws against each other in thought. "Allow me to consult with my clients."

"No more games." Jackson started forward.

"You would deny the accused their right to legal counsel? Lieutenant, I demand to speak with your commanding officer. I'll also need your EMC serial number. Would you prefer I file charges in military court, where you'll be busted in rank, or in civil court, where we'll simply take a chunk of your paycheck for the rest of your natural life?"

Jackson responded through gritted teeth. "Five. Minutes."

"Thank you." Advocate of Violence turned to Mops. "Their warrants are in order. Now that they've identified themselves and verified their claim, you're legally obligated to follow their orders. You'll be given the opportunity to defend yourselves in front of an Alliance court or, more likely, a military tribunal."

"Not with what we know," said Mops. "They'll shoot us into the nearest black hole to keep us quiet."

"In which case you'd have excellent grounds for a countersuit."

Mops took several slow breaths. "Doc, show me that map again." She studied their location and surroundings. With one hand, she slid her combat baton from its holster, hiding the movement with her body. Monroe started to follow suit, but she shook her head.

"Stay behind me." Mops stepped toward the EMC troops. Her thumb found the baton's control toggle.

"Drop it," warned Jackson. "Don't be stupid, Mops."

She pressed and slid the nub left. The baton hummed as its nanofilaments shifted into an alternate preprogrammed configuration. The weapon narrowed in her grip, lengthening to a javelin a meter-and-a-half in length. "Your violation of the firearms law started me thinking. Do you know why the Quetzalus forbid projectile weapons inside the Comaceans?"

"To protect them from harm," said Rubin.

Jackson scowled. "A few tiny holes aren't going to hurt a creature this size."

"That's not true." Rubin stepped forward. "Comaceans have little sensation in their external skin, but their internal nervous system is—"

"Easy, Rubin," said Mops. "Lieutenant Jackson, you don't know where we are, do you?"

"What the hell are you talking about?" Jackson gestured to three of her troops. "Simpson, Perón, Chekhov, put them in restraints. If they resist, shoot them."

Mops focused on one of the troops. Doc magnified automatically. "Eva, is that you?"

Private Eva Perón glanced nervously at Lieutenant Jackson, then gave Mops a tight nod. "Hi, Mops. Long time no see."

"How's life on the *Box Jellyfish*?" Eva Perón had been part of the *Pufferfish* crew when the ship was attacked with a Prodryan bioweapon. Mops and her team had been suited up to handle a sewage rupture at the time, which was the only thing that had saved them from the effects. She was delighted to see one of her former crewmates recovered and looking healthy as ever.

"It's . . . it's fine," stammered Perón. "I'd rather not shoot you, Lieutenant."

"She's a civilian now," snapped Jackson.

"I'd rather you not shoot me either," said Mops. "Especially since it would probably kill everyone here."

"Shut up," snapped Jackson. Mops could see her weighing her desire to end this against the chance Mops was telling the truth. "All right, fine. Why would shooting you kill everyone here?"

Mops tapped the tip of her javelin ever so gently against the floor. "The Quetzalus engineered this place to take advantage of the Comacean's anatomy whenever possible. Instead of drilling tunnels, they use bronchial tubes. Larger rooms are built from the nodules in the lung. For escape pods, you want to launch the pods as fast as possible, right? So they built the pods into the part of the body designed for quick and powerful expulsion."

"The intestine," said Rubin. "Specifically, the tertiary sigmoid colon."

Lieutenant Jackson stared, frustration turning her eyes to slits. "So what?"

"When launched, electrical charges stimulate the muscles to shoot the pod into space, along with any other intestinal matter." Mops smiled. "If one of your shots ruptures the floor, given the intestinal pressure and the potential quantity of waste matter . . ."

Monroe whistled softly. "Not how I'd want to go."

"What are you talking about?" demanded Jackson.

"We're standing on the biological equivalent of a giant high-pressure sewage pipe," Mops explained. "Crack that pipe, and one of several things will happen. If the pipe's empty, you'll get a noxious gas leak. Unpleasant, but I've survived worse trapped on a shuttle with Wolf after she stuffed herself on Merraban burritos."

"That was not a good day," said Rubin.

"If the pipe's full," Mops continued, "a single hole or crack could trigger a full rupture. All it would take is one bad shot, one unexpected ricochet, and we all die a particularly nasty death. One bad shot, or me putting any weight on this weapon."

Mops twisted her javelin, driving the monomolecular tip several millimeters into the floor. "If you want my advice, I'd let us get into that escape pod. You've got the *Box Jellyfish* closing in, which means you'll still have a good shot at intercepting us. Or we can all take our chances with a perforated Comacean bowel."

"Shit." Jackson lowered her weapon.

Mops smiled. "Exactly."

Mops floated in front of the escape pod's display, watching her ship grow larger.

The *Pufferfish* had changed a great deal in the past four months. Roughly ninety percent of the ship was sealed off and powered down. Of the three original weapons pods, only one remained, like an outrigger running most of the length of the ship. The others had been damaged beyond repair and sold to cover the cost of repairing the third.

All around them were Comacean silhouettes, like long seed

pods. Beyond the herd, another icon closed in: the *EMCS Box Jellyfish*.

Monroe leaned over her shoulder. "This is going to be close."

"Nothing we can do about that." Mops pushed off, launching herself toward one of the upper grab bars. The escape pod was designed for Quetzalus, meaning there were no human-sized rails or restraints. Controls were labeled in six Quetzalus languages. Doc had translated them enough for Mops to push the single thruster to maximum. Not that it would do much to help them outrace an EMC cruiser.

She looked across the pod at their guest. "Advocate of Violence is a mouthful. Any objection to 'Cate'?"

"Your human syllables are all equally distasteful to me."

Mops took that as a yes. Whatever name she used, his translator should provide the proper name in his preferred language anyway. She wondered briefly what names he called Mops and her crew. Was she the literal translation of "mops," or something like "Kills with Cleaning Supplies," which would be more Prodryan in nature?

"Cate, how did you and Admiral Pachelbel start working together?"

"The admiral attempted to tap into Fleet Admiral Sage's private data feeds from Earth. When she succeeded—when one of her technical specialists succeeded, rather—they discovered we had already done so. Pachelbel's people eventually traced the hijacked signal to me. The admiral offered me a choice: share everything I had gathered from Sage's systems, or be charged for my crimes against the Alliance."

"I'm surprised you didn't threaten to expose Pachelbel's snooping to Fleet Admiral Sage," commented Monroe.

"Pachelbel is a competent warrior, for a non-Prodryan. Presumably she would have me terminated if I attempted such a thing. It's what I would do."

"So Pachelbel got her tentacles on your entire trove of Sage's personal data," said Mops. "Whatever she found spooked her into action. Why did she send us? She has plenty of more qualified troops at her disposal."

"More qualified, certainly," said Cate. "But those troops are ultimately under the command of Fleet Admiral Sage. If a single one betrays Pachelbel, she'll be imprisoned for treason."

"She's practically a prisoner now," muttered Mops. Sage had taken command of the station and stripped Pachelbel of most of her duties and authority. Mops didn't know how much of that came from Sage's suspicions about Pachelbel, and how much was typical Krakau political squabbling. "Pachelbel doesn't know who to trust, so we're the lucky ones getting sent to Earth."

"Pachelbel said you might be reluctant to return to your world. Your cowardice is understandable. Earth is a wild and terrifying place."

Cate was right. Mops *was* afraid. But not for the reasons he probably imagined. Sure, half a billion feral humans roaming about was enough to fuel anyone's nightmares. Far worse were the reminders of what the planet had once been.

Mops' personal library included countless history files—texts and images and videos retrieved from Earth. Knowing many of those records had been filtered or doctored by the Krakau did little to ease the horrific contrast they painted between past and present. The idea of setting foot on Earth again and walking through the graveyard of human civilization made her ill.

Like all cured humans, Mops had been born on Earth, but she had no memories of her life before the Krakau found her. She couldn't have said which of Earth's six inhabited continents she originally came from. Only the occasional nightmare provided glimpses of that other life, of endless, gnawing hunger . . .

She'd been reborn in a secure medical facility. Her initial education took place while she was semiconscious in a medical tank, her brain and body being recoded by Krakau medicine. Once the cure had progressed enough for her to be safely awakened, she'd joined the rest of her crèche to study in the underground complex. She could count on one hand the number of times she'd walked on the surface and seen Earth's blue sky after her rebirth.

Almost all reborn humans ended up in the Earth Mercenary Corps. Mops had always considered her service a drop in the ocean toward the debt she and humanity owed the Krakau. At the graduation ceremony, where newly-reborn humans chose their names from Earth's historical figures, she'd taken the name of the human doctor who allegedly helped spread the plague across the planet. Mops had meant it as a reminder of what her species had done to itself, and what would have happened if not for the Krakau.

How much of that history was distortions and lies? Who knew if Doctor Marion Adamopoulos had even existed?

"Captain?" The escape pod's comm buzzed with static, making her jump. The voice repeated more clearly a moment later. "Captain, is that you?"

Mops pulled herself to the controls, skimmed the labels, and flipped a large toggle. "Good to hear your voice, Grom. We're here, and we've got a guest. Do you have the shuttle?"

"Yes, sir. We hardly banged it up at all when we hauled it in."

"What about Wolf?"

"Didn't bang her up much either. Kumar's bringing us into a parallel course so we can catch your pod without splattering you all against the wall. Wolf should have a grav lock in about three minutes."

"Any word from the *Jellyfish*?"

"Nothing yet," said Grom. "Azure's on tactical, watching for missile fire."

"Did she and Kumar finish mixing up that surprise I requested?"

Kumar cut in. "Four barrels, sir. I followed the recipe from the Zenkozan veterinary database and modified it per your instructions, but—"

"I supervised Kumar's work," interrupted Azure. "In my professional opinion, the mixture is not medically viable."

"Understood." Mops had given Kumar this assignment because he knew five times as much about medical as anyone else in her severely undersized crew. Since the rest of the crew knew approximately nothing on the subject, that wasn't as reassuring as it might have been.

Azure, on the other tentacle, had been trained in biochemistry during her time on a Rokkau family ship, hiding from the rest of the galaxy. She had also, shortly before joining the crew, used that training to create a biological weapon with the potential to kill every Krakau on Dobranok, which made Mops reluctant to give her unsupervised access to their medical center.

"It's impressive that a hygiene and maintenance team can successfully run a cruiser-class vessel on their own," said Cate. "Particularly a mostly-human team."

Mops let that pass.

The pod lurched hard as the *Pufferfish*'s grav beams took hold. Mops and the others were pulled none-too-gently against the ceiling. Her mind reoriented, with the ceiling becoming the floor and vice versa, as gravity increased.

She checked the display again, trying to estimate speeds and distances. "You'll want to try to relax," she warned Cate. "It helps with the impact."

"A Prodryan warrior is never relaxed."

"Suit yourself."

Cate paused. "In what should I dress? You haven't returned my armor, and your uniforms aren't designed for Prodryans."

"I meant—never mind." The pod's lights flashed blue, and a loud clacking assaulted Mops' ears. She assumed it was a proximity alert. Gravity died a moment later as the *Pufferfish* shut down the primary grav beam, letting the pod coast the final meters into the bay. Mops grasped the closest bar and checked her monocle for the relative orientation of the ship and pod. "Looks like portside is gonna be down."

She raised her legs toward the left wall.

The pod fell sideways the moment it entered the *Pufferfish*'s internal gravity field. Sideways became down. Mops and her team dropped to the wall—floor—and grabbed whatever they could. Cate squawked and spread his wings. His desperate flapping didn't save him from tumbling onto his back.

The pod spun hard before sliding to a halt.

Cate pushed himself upright and shivered, filling the air with yellow-and-blue wing dust. "Are we safe?"

The all-clear flashed on Mops' monocle. "Safe is relative, but the docking bay is sealed and pressurizing. We should be good to leave in less than a minute."

"Excellent." Cate turned away, coughed three times, and hocked up a series of oily-looking pellets.

Mops tugged a cleaning rag from her harness and handed it to him.

"What am I supposed to do with this?"

"I'll have Kumar instruct you on basic cleaning and sanitation procedures." Mops checked the external pressure and opened the hatch. Wolf's shuttle was locked down on the far side of the bay. Scrapes along the shuttle's hull suggested her landing had been as bumpy as their own.

"I'm a lawyer and spy," Cate protested. "Not a janitor."

"Rule one: everyone cleans their own puke." Mops jumped down and stretched her shoulders. "Welcome to the *Pufferfish*."

By the time Mops reached the bridge, she was swearing. The glittering copper specks spilled across the floor near the navigation console didn't help her mood. She'd told Grom not to bring their homemade mineral salsa onto the bridge.

She pushed her irritation aside, focusing on the data Doc was feeding to her monocle. Data on the *Box Jellyfish*'s course and speed, complete with a countdown showing when they would overtake the *Pufferfish*.

"Give me some good news, people." She strode to the

captain's station at the center of the bridge, stepping over the low metal guardrails. The rails were designed for Krakau use, putting them at precisely the right height to bruise the hell out of human shins. Mops kept meaning to have Grom remove them.

"They're holding fire for now." Sanjeev Kumar looked more like a soldier than an ex-janitor, but his broad, muscular build came mostly from his obsessive cleaning habits. Habits that never seemed to carry over to taming his short, tangled brown hair. He was excessively detail oriented, which was one of the reasons Mops had assigned him to Navigation. "I'm working on an evasive course through the herd, but I don't think we can dodge them long enough to get clear and make a safe A-ring jump."

Cate chittered for attention. "Using the Comaceans as cover knowingly places them in harm's way, violating APSA 93.42.6 through 9. Should the *EMCS Box Jellyfish* open fire, you would be held partially responsible for any damages."

"We'd probably be dead, too," said Monroe as he slid into his seat at Tactical. The eight bridge stations were spread around the outer part of the bridge, each one a shallow circular pit.

"I agree with Cate," said Rubin. "We can't endanger these animals."

Grom drew themselves up taller, coiling the rear third of their segmented body for balance, which brought them to almost a meter in height. They jabbed a clawed limb toward Cate. "Is anyone going to explain why we brought a Prodryan on board?"

Gromgimsidalgak had been one of the *Pufferfish*'s computer hardware technicians, and now fancied themselves the ship's programmer and engineer. They'd modified many of the bridge controls, replacing sophisticated command consoles with preprogrammed macros and video game controllers. They'd also removed the metal nest used by Mops' Krakau predecessor, replacing it with an upholstered armchair from the mess hall.

Grom was on the small side for a Glacidae. Two rows of

stubby, featherlike legs ran the length of their body. The yellow spines along their back were fully raised, making them resemble a cross between a pincushion and a giant Merraban sausage.

One large brown eye watched Cate while the other narrowed at Mops. The thick digging limbs ringing Grom's head twitched and fidgeted nervously.

"This is Advocate of Violence," said Mops. "Cate for short. He has intelligence Admiral Pachelbel wanted us to see, assuming we don't end up dead or imprisoned in the next few minutes. Kumar, take us closer to the nearest Comacean. Wolf, help Cate broadcast a warning message to the *Box Jellyfish,* reminding them of the consequences of violating the Alliance Protected Species Act. Maybe it will make them hesitate before blowing us up."

Cate started toward the communications station, then paused to stare at Azure. "Nobody told me you had a deformed Krakau on board."

Mops froze with her hand on the back of her seat. Like the Krakau, Azure had a roughly cylindrical body with limbs loosely resembling those of an Earth squid or octopus. But the Rokkau had had four primary tentacles instead of three. One of those tentacles was significantly underdeveloped. Her lower limbs were shorter and thicker than those of the Krakau, and her beak was flatter against her face.

Azure's limbs stilled. One of her eyes fixed on Cate. She could have been a statue carved from blue-speckled obsidian.

She might not be Krakau, but Rokkau body language was close enough for Mops to recognize the threat. "Both eyes on your console," she snapped at Azure, loud enough to capture everyone's attention. To Cate, she said, "Get that message out to the *Jellyfish*, then shut up."

Azure's beak clicked shut. After a moment, she bobbed the upper part of her body and turned away. She'd picked up nodding and several other human mannerisms during her time with the crew. Cate continued to stare after the Rokkau, even as he made his way toward Communications.

Monroe had switched the main viewscreen to tactical, with the *Pufferfish* at the center. Mops studied the Comacean herd and tagged four undersized individuals. "Make sure we steer clear of those youngsters."

"Why is it acceptable to endanger the adult Comaceans, but not the children?" asked Rubin.

"Message sent," announced Wolf, saving Mops from an answer.

Mops double-checked her console, confirming and approving Kumar's course. Less than a minute later, Wolf turned her head and said, "The *Box Jellyfish* is hailing us."

"Put them through to me." A new window opened on Mops' screen, showing a middle-aged human woman with short black hair and a circular scar on the left side of her throat. It wasn't who Mops had expected. "Battle Captain Irwin? Don't tell me your Krakau command crew are still recovering from your A-ring jump."

"Captain Smuglyanka felt you might be more responsive to a fellow human." Irwin rolled her eyes, making it clear what she thought of that theory.

"Nice to see you again," said Mops. "Did your husband ever get the bugs worked out of that prosthetic leg? I spoke with Monroe, who says it might be a software problem. He suggests wiping and reinstalling the AI's spatial awareness software."

"This isn't a social call, dammit." Irwin's gaze slipped. "But I'll pass that along."

"I saw Eva on the Comacean. How's she working out?"

"Fine," said Irwin. "Command is keeping her under long-term medical observation, but we've seen no long-term effects from the bioweapon attack. She says she's looking forward to serving on the *Pufferfish* again, once we take it back from you."

"I'll have Wolf clean her room, just in case." Mops chuckled. "What's it been, five weeks since we talked?"

"Five weeks and three days since you slipped away from us at the Avangart shipyards." Irwin leaned closer. "You and I both know how this plays out. Power down before anyone else gets hurt."

Not for the first time, Mops considered simply broadcasting everything to Irwin and the crew of the *Box Jellyfish*: the truth about the Krakau's first disastrous mission to Earth, about the Rokkau who had accidentally poisoned a human leader, and how that poison had turned humanity into monsters. Their near-genocidal war against the Rokkau. The hundred and fifty years of lies and cover-ups that followed.

But she also knew the lengths the Krakau had gone to in order to bury that history in the sand. Every Alliance computer system had buried safeguards helping to protect those secrets. Mops had seen an AI take complete control of the *Pufferfish* at the mere sight of a Rokkau. She'd eventually gotten those subroutines removed from the *Pufferfish*, but the *Box Jellyfish* would have the same programming. Telling Irwin now, without irrevocable proof, would only endanger her and her crew.

"Rotting dicks, Adamopoulos. My team said you were working with Prodryans, but I didn't want to believe it."

Cate had stepped into view, probably while trying to get a better look at the screen. Mops swallowed a sigh. "When did you start picking up Nusuran slang?"

Irwin simply stared. The sight of a Prodryan on the bridge of an EMC ship had clearly burned away any remaining hesitation about Mops' guilt.

"Technically, it's just the one Prodryan," said Mops.

A vein in Irwin's temple began to throb.

"You're a good officer, Irwin. And I'm sorry about this." Mops signaled Wolf to cut the connection. "Kumar, keep a light touch on the engines. Get us as close as you can, but do *not* disrupt or injure the Comaceans."

"Understood."

"Should I power up the defensive grid?" asked Monroe.

"Don't bother." The energy dispersal grid on the *Pufferfish*'s hull wouldn't help against grav beams, and if the *Box Jellyfish* opened up with plasma weapons at this range, they'd burn through the grid in seconds. "We don't want to provoke a fight. Right now it's just a race, and Irwin thinks she's going to win."

"Is that because she *is* going to win?" demanded Cate.

Mops shrugged and watched one Comacean grow larger as Kumar maneuvered them beneath its belly. Beneath *his* belly—the skin was ribbed like corrugated steel.

"Captain, we *could* fire on the *Box Jellyfish*." From the way Monroe hesitated over the words, he knew what Mops was likely to say, but it was his job to present all options. "Try to get in a quick strike to disable their engines without hurting the crew."

"Even if we weren't swimming with Comaceans, I won't fire on an EMC ship."

Cate scoffed. "Given how many laws you've violated since we met, this seems an odd time to bind yourself to such a rule."

"The *Jellyfish* is within grav beam range," Monroe announced. "They're probing us for a solid lock."

"They'll need to slow down a bit to match our speed." Mops watched the distance counter decrease. "Kumar, keep that Comacean between us and the *Jellyfish*. Make them work for it."

"I'll try."

A proximity alert flashed on Mops' console. Moments later, the entire ship shuddered. Alarms turned the bridge green, and the tactical display updated to show the grav beam anchoring the two ships together.

Kumar spun from his console. "Sorry, sir. Their navigator anticipated me. Whoever's piloting that ship, they're better than I am."

"Sure, but you can sanitize an entire medbay in fifty-seven minutes. I'd like to see their navigator do that." Mops leaned back in her chair. "Any chance you can shake us free?"

"Not without breaking the ship."

Several more tremors shook the bridge as the *Pufferfish*

struggled to adjust internal gravity to compensate for the effects of the *Jellyfish*'s beam.

"If they follow standard procedures, we've got about twenty minutes before they draw us in close enough to disable our defenses and send boarding teams," said Monroe.

"Would one of you please share the location of the ship's escape pods?" asked Cate. "Purely as a precaution. Believe me, I have no intention of abandoning ship and leaving you to your fates."

"Deck D," said Wolf, without looking up. "For security purposes, the door is labeled 'Central Waste Processing and Reclamation.' Jump right in, and you'll be fine."

"Reduce engines." Mops brought up the aft cargo bay controls and tried to remember how the overrides worked. Starting decompression was straightforward enough. She waited until the pressure was down to a quarter of normal, then stopped the process. When she tried to open the bay doors, a green message flashed onto her screen: *Cargo bay depressurization incomplete. Please make sure all air is evacuated from the bay before opening outer doors.*

Mops tried again, then a third time. A new message appeared: *You appear to be having trouble. Would you like help?*

She'd hoped it wouldn't come to this. Through clenched teeth, she muttered, "Yes."

An animated caricature of the *Pufferfish* appeared on the screen, beaming with preprogrammed happiness. Or thinly-concealed madness. It was hard to tell.

Grom had modified Puffy's appearance again, using a gaming mod to garb the anthropomorphic ship in an EMC uniform. In one hand Puffy held what Mops could only describe as a heavy-duty battle mop. The shaft included spiked hand guards, a laser sight, and a clip-on rocket launcher. The head was electrified, sparks shooting from each strand. The whole thing was twice Puffy's height.

Puffy blinked enormous eyes and said, "Welcome to the bay depressurization help mod—"

"I need aft cargo bay door override."

Puffy hesitated. "Are you sure?"

"Give me the override process before I have Doc hunt down and exterminate every last trace of your code."

Puffy beamed and shouldered the mop. "I'm sorry, I didn't understand that response."

Mops rubbed her neck, longing for the days when the worst she had to deal with was backed-up plumbing lines and Wolf's disciplinary troubles. "Yes. I'm sure."

Puffy's grin grew wider and more frightening. "Welcome to the cargo bay door override help module."

It was several more minutes before Mops was able to bypass the safety warnings, cut power to the bay grav plates, and override the doors. A new alarm flashed green as the aft bay doors cracked open, and the remaining air rushed out.

The four medical waste tanks Kumar and Azure had prepared tumbled into space, slowly at first, but accelerating as the *Jellyfish*'s grav beam captured them.

"What now, sir?" asked Kumar.

"Now, we either escape or we don't." Mops tried to give him a confident smile, but—given the day's events so far—she probably looked more like Puffy. "It all depends on what happens with that biological soup you cooked up."

4

Incoming console-to-console message:

S. Kumar: Azure—the captain's relying on our work. We should have run more tests!

Azure: The original recipe was for Comacean quick-drying dermal membrane. You followed each step precisely. The captain requested I mix it with what's essentially an anticoagulant.

S. Kumar: Meaning the skin won't maintain cohesion. Instead of quick-skin, we mixed four barrels of quick-drying Comacean dandruff?

Azure: Your captain's thought processes are often a mystery to me.

S. Kumar: Maybe she's hoping the skin cells will interfere with scanners? Make the Box Jellyfish *think there are life-forms between them and us?*

Azure: Maybe.

S. Kumar: I told you we should have run more tests.

Azure: And what, precisely, would we have been testing for? Also, the captain is speaking to you . . .

MOPS RAISED HER VOICE. "Kumar, I said bring us about twelve degrees to port, thirty degrees declination."

"Yes, sir. Sorry, sir!"

Mops gritted her teeth while she waited for Kumar to check the notes taped to the wall above his console. He'd improved a great deal, but still mixed up port and starboard on occasion.

Kumar picked up his control sphere and adjusted several of the slider buttons. The *Pufferfish* jerked sideways like a fish on a line. "No good. They're locked on tight."

"Irwin's hailing us again," said Wolf. "She sounds cranky."

"Can you blame her?" asked Mops. "Main screen."

Battle Captain Irwin massaged her temples. "Tell me you did not just throw four barrels of sewage at my ship."

"It wasn't sewage." Mops made a show of checking her displays. "Looks like your grav beams ruptured our cargo bay. You know we're running with a skeleton crew here. You're lucky the *Pufferfish* didn't tear in half. The whole damn ship's falling apart."

That much was true enough, though the team did their best. Doc had copied himself into various areas of the ship to help assist with day-to-day functioning, including logging and prioritizing critical repairs. It was enough to make sure the *Pufferfish* wouldn't blow up the next time someone flushed a toilet, but Mops wasn't sure how much longer they'd be able to keep the ship flying.

While she pretended to sort through damage reports, Mops

pulled up the aft feed to watch the four containers tumble away from the ship. They had burst open in quick succession, their contents expanding in an emerald cloud that tried to boil and freeze at the same time. The result was a crystalline mist, a green snowstorm in space.

Normally, the cloud would have continued to spiral away, propelled by the spinning of the broken canisters. But the other ship's grav beams were at full power. Caught by those focused gravity waves, the tiny crystals flowed in a narrowing conical path toward the *Box Jellyfish*'s beam generators. Only a few stray wisps avoided the pull and continued to spread, like glittering green dust.

"Looks like those were medical waste tanks," said Mops. "Sorry about that. Someone must have forgotten to secure them, and that line of tanks aren't rated for vacuum. Don't worry. Nothing in there will damage your ship. You might want to send your SHS team out to wash the hull when you get the chance, though."

"Enough." Irwin sounded tired. "Mops, Captain Smuglyanka has ordered us to open fire if you don't offer your immediate and unconditional surrender."

"They're locking A-guns," Monroe warned.

Rubin stood. "What about the Comaceans?"

"Don't worry," said Irwin, overhearing the question. "We're close enough I could burn my initials on your hull without putting any of these beasts in the slightest danger."

"Understood." Mops kept her attention on her display, where the thin trail of escaping biomaterial continued to pinwheel outward.

"We're sending two infantry squads to secure the *Puffer-fish*," said Irwin. "They'll come in through your aft bay, since you've kindly left the doors open. Please don't give them any reason to shoot you."

A single delicate wisp of green dust stretched toward the tail of a passing Comacean.

"You've stopped breathing," said Doc. After a moment, he added, *"You should probably start again."*

Mops forced herself to exhale.

The particles of biomatter brushed the Comacean's skin.

The creature reacted instantly. Other Comaceans altered course seconds later.

"How the hell do they communicate?" Mops whispered.

"Visual cues. An organ in the eyeball emits a flash of light, too high-frequency for human eyes to see."

On screen, Irwin's battle bridge turned green. Irwin spun away. "Lieutenant Li, what's happening out there?"

Someone, presumably Li, said, "I'm not sure, sir. The Comaceans are changing course. It looks like they're closing in on us."

"What the depths did you do, Mops?" Irwin shouted.

"You think we can pilot Comaceans remotely?" Mops shot back. "We can barely steer our own ship, let alone hijack a herd of space whales. Maybe they decided you're a predator, and this is some sort of instinctive response. I suggest shutting down your grav beams and backing off. Maybe they'll stop seeing you as a threat and leave you alone."

Irwin snorted loudly, a sound midway between disbelief and disgust. "I don't know how you pulled this off, but I've got orders to destroy the *Pufferfish* rather than let you escape again."

"Like hell." Mops muted the connection. "Wolf, how have you been coming along on those grav beam tutorials?"

"I haven't blown up the simulated ship in almost two weeks."

Years of experience helped Mops maintain a calm, confident tone. "Lock onto the *Box Jellyfish* and give them a nudge. Nothing overwhelming. Just keep them jostling around too much for their gunner to get a precise lock."

Wolf jumped and ran to a secondary console at the back of the bridge.

"That won't work for long," Monroe warned.

"It doesn't have to." Mops reopened the communications channel. "Irwin, if you blow us up, the debris from our ship will injure those Comaceans. You could be court-martialed. They might even send you back to Earth."

"After chasing you around the damn galaxy, Earth will be a vacation."

The *Pufferfish* shuddered. Alarms flashed on Mops' console and monocle, listing multiple hull punctures to the lower decks.

"I ordered you to target their engines," Irwin shouted. "How the hell can you miss at this range?"

Another voice protested. "We didn't miss, exactly. We just hit the wrong part of the ship. Sir."

Irwin's face darkened. She started to shout, caught herself, and glanced back at Mops. A gesture to one of her crew killed the connection.

"Nice work, Wolf." Mops continued to watch the incoming Comaceans. "Keep it coming."

Another volley of A-gun fire perforated Mops' ship. Her fingers dug into her chair. The hyperaccelerated slugs were relatively small—about the size of her clenched fist—but each one struck at a significant fraction of light speed. No shielding or armor plating would stop them.

The *Pufferfish*'s autorepair systems sealed each breach automatically, but there was only so much the ship could take. If one of those slugs hit anything critical as it drilled through, or if the autorepair failed . . . "Doc?"

"Deck H is sealed off to contain an internal CO_2 leak. It shouldn't be life-threatening, but will require manual intervention to recycle and rebalance the atmosphere on that deck. In the meantime, I strongly recommend we avoid being shot again."

"Noted."

"Sir, the Comaceans . . ." Monroe hesitated. "I think one of them is firing on the *Jellyfish*."

"What?" The main viewscreen switched to a close-up of the *Box Jellyfish*, now surrounded by four Comaceans. Three more were closing in.

A light on Mops' console indicated Battle Captain Irwin wanted to talk. Mops accepted the connection just as Rubin spoke up.

"She's not firing, sir. She's regurgitating."

The silence stretched so long Mops double-checked to make sure she hadn't accidentally muted Irwin. Finally, just as Mops was about to ask Wolf to reestablish the connection, Irwin asked, "Did one of your people just say the fucking space whales are puking on my fucking ship?"

"They're not fucking," Rubin corrected. "She's acting on instinct, but it's protective, not procreative. She's trying to provide sustenance to an injured member of the herd."

"They, not she," Doc noted. Faint clouds on the screen showed where two more of the closest Comaceans had offered up predigested food . . . some of which drifted into the path of the grav beams and accelerated toward the ship.

Mops sagged back in her chair. The *Box Jellyfish* hadn't released the *Pufferfish* yet, but it wouldn't be long now. "I'd hold off on sending those infantry squads, Irwin. If the Comaceans see you launching shuttles, they might decide to 'help' them, too."

Irwin ran both hands through her hair. When she spoke, she sounded like she was trying not to choke. *"How?"*

"Those waste tanks contained synthesized Comacean skin," said Mops. "With a few extra ingredients to help it disperse. That's what your grav beams so obligingly sucked all over your ship. The rest drifted away until the other Comaceans . . . smelled it, I guess."

"Tasted, actually," said Rubin. "They have specialized cells on their skin, similar to human taste buds."

"They think you're a hurt Comacean youngster," Mops continued. "They instinctively close in to protect their young. Apparently, they hock up food to help you get your strength back, too."

"The amazing part is it's all automatic," said Rubin. "They're still in hibernation. They literally help each other out in their sleep."

The grav beams cut out as another Comacean closed in.

"I'd kill thrusters as well," said Mops. "If you injure one of your escort, you'll get even more of the herd showing up to help."

Irwin laced her fingers in an approximation of a Krakau obscenity. Roughly translated, it meant, "Swim off and choke on your own tentacles."

Mops chuckled. "Once the Comaceans know you're all right, they'll drift off and leave you in peace. You should be all clear by this time tomorrow. Two days, tops."

"How the hell am I supposed to write this up?"

"Unexpected megagastrointestinal complications?" Mops spread her hands. "Tell you what. When and if you ever catch me, I'll buy you a drink."

A choked laugh burst from the speaker. "You owe me a hell of a lot more than one, Mops."

"I might have agreed before you started shooting my ship. Give my regards to Perón. Adamopoulos out."

Mops wiped her hands on her knees and turned to survey her team. "Monroe, take Grom and inspect the damage. Make sure an A-ring jump won't rip us apart."

"How did you know the Comaceans would help you fight your enemy?" Cate stared, transfixed, at the tactical display.

"They didn't fight." Mops gestured toward Rubin. "She gave me the idea."

"Captain Adamopoulos wanted to understand how the herd would react to our presence, especially if we had to fight our way free," said Rubin. "They have no natural predators, and evolved a strong protective instinct. They only mate while orbiting Tixateq 1 or 2, and the gestation period is more than twenty years. The whole herd helps with the newborns."

"We're being hailed by Biorefinery Eleven," Wolf interrupted as she slid back into her seat at Communications.

"Which one is that?"

On the screen, Doc highlighted the Comacean currently snuggled up against the port side of the *Box Jellyfish*.

Kumar cocked his head to one side. "I wonder if the Quetzalus have a standard procedure in place for when their biorefinery swims off course to nuzzle an EMC cruiser."

"Doubtful," said Mops. "An egregious oversight, I'm sure. Wolf, please pass along our apologies. Kumar, get us out of here. Carefully—we don't want to disrupt the Comaceans any more than we have. As soon as we're clear, maneuver us into position for an A-ring jump. Grom, once you and Monroe finish checking the damage, I'll need you to plot a jump to Earth."

Grom spun, the spines on their back beginning to rise. "Did you say Earth? Why would we want to go there, of all places?"

Mops stood and beckoned for Cate to follow. "Let's find out."

Like the main bridge, the Captain's Cove had been designed for the comfort of the *Pufferfish*'s Krakau command crew. Humans on EMC ships were expected to keep to the battle hubs and communal areas on the lower decks.

Since the death of said command crew and Mops' theft of the ship, she'd drained the water from the Captain's Cove, increased the temperature, adjusted the air mixture to human preferences, and removed Captain Brandenburg's old keepsakes from the small shelves lining the curved walls—including an impressive collection of tentacle piercing loops and studs, none of which she'd ever worn while on duty.

Mops doubted she'd ever finish remodeling the place to her satisfaction, but she enjoyed the work. She hoped to resurface the walls and floor next, but with so many more pressing jobs around the *Pufferfish*, who knew when or if she'd get to that. For now, she tried to ignore the gritty texture beneath her feet, or the way the sand-colored walls made her feel like she was entering an ocean-side cave.

An oval table made of iridescent orange Dobranok glass stood at the center of the shallow depression in the floor. Mops gestured for Cate to take one of the mismatched chairs she'd scavenged from various parts of the ship.

After studying it a moment, Cate spun the chair and straddled it, allowing his wings to rest behind him.

Rubin, Wolf, and Kumar took the chairs around Cate, unsubtly surrounding the Prodryan. Azure settled herself in one of the small cagelike cylinders the Krakau used for furniture.

Cate rubbed his forearms together, producing an unpleasant rasping noise to get the group's attention. Turning to Azure, he said, "It was not my intention to create awkwardness when I commented on your deformity earlier."

Azure didn't answer, though the blue spots on her skin grew brighter.

Apparently oblivious to the danger, Cate continued talking. "I read that it's the custom of some races to offer congratulations."

"Congratulations?" Azure turned slightly, fixing one large eye on the Prodryan. "For what, exactly?"

Cate gestured to the smaller of Azure's four primary tentacles. "You appear to be regrowing a limb. Krakau sacrifice a tentacle during procreation and childbirth, yes? Where is your offspring now?"

"There's no offspring," said Mops, taking the lone chair on the opposite side from the rest. "I shot off her tentacle when she tried to assassinate a member of my crew."

"Oh." Cate turned back to Mops. "Life on a human vessel is more eventful than I'd been told."

"You have no idea." Mops put her hands on the table. "Doc, patch this through to Grom and Monroe so I don't have to repeat myself later."

"*Done.*"

"Advocate of Violence claims he and Admiral Pachelbel discovered something on one of Fleet Admiral Sage's private security feeds. Something important enough to risk all this." She waved one hand, trying to encompass the Comaceans, the *Box*

Jellyfish, the damage to the *Pufferfish*. "Important enough, or so I'm told, for us to travel to Earth."

"Where the defense satellites will blow the *Pufferfish* and everyone on board to tiny pieces before we can even wake up from the A-ring jump," Wolf muttered.

"Admiral Pachelbel thought of that." Cate's torso convulsed once . . . twice . . . three times . . . On the fourth, he spat a gritty pellet into his hands.

Kumar scooted his chair away.

Cate's claws teased apart the pellet to extract a small yellow-tinged memory crystal. "This contains all you should need to falsify the *Pufferfish*'s identification beacon, as well as instructions to help you evade more intensive short-range scrutiny." He placed the crystal on the table.

Mops grabbed a small cleaning rag from her harness and used it to retrieve and wrap the crystal. "I'll take a look, but this ship isn't going anywhere near Earth until I'm convinced it's worth the risk."

"I can say with complete confidence this discovery is more important than your lives," said Cate.

"Well, I'm reassured," Monroe said dryly.

"Excellent." Cate looked around. "It doesn't appear the others are convinced. This next part would be easier if I could use the display screen on your wall. Would you allow me access to your ship's computers?"

"When Nusurans find celibacy," Mops said.

Cate hesitated. "Is that a figure of speech or a precondition?"

"It's a reminder that I don't trust you," said Mops. "And the only reason you're here instead of in our brig is because I do trust Admiral Pachelbel . . . to an extent. But Prodryans have an innate drive to slaughter other intelligent life. Some of you are more proactive about it, but everything we've seen, heard, and learned about your species suggests you're not exactly working for our best interests. Giving you access to our systems would be an incredibly stupid move, and I've become something of an expert on stupid moves."

As she spoke, Mops found herself reconsidering her words. *Everything we've learned . . .* Everything she'd learned had come from the Krakau. Including a falsified history of her own planet and species. How did she know they hadn't distorted the truth about the Prodryans as well?

Cate's antennae twitched. "Why would you want me to work for your best interests instead of my own? Such distorted priorities suggest mental illness or brain damage. Anyone so confused would be discharged from their job and heavily medicated."

"My AI can serve as an intermediary for any access you need," said Mops. "Doc, make sure any data is buffered and scanned, and keep it walled away from the rest of our systems."

"I don't tell you how to scrub toilets. Don't tell me how to do my job."

The front part of the cove wall lit up with an image of Earth as seen from low orbit. Mops' throat tightened at the cloud-brushed view of land and ocean. The sun painted a copper reflection over the blue sea. The continent was a mix of hazy brown, white, and dark green. From this angle and distance, the planet appeared . . . normal.

"There are four known medical facilities for turning human ferals into soldiers for the Krakau Alliance," said Cate.

Mops had been cured, or "reborn," in the Antarctic facility. Monroe had been brought to Greenland for his rebirth. Wolf and Kumar were both from an isolated island station in New Zealand. She wasn't sure about Rubin, who either didn't remember that part of her past or else chose not to talk about it.

A red dot appeared near the eastern edge of a continent. "Sage's people are working here, in secret."

The first four Krakau sites were built in isolated areas, away from feral humans and other threats. Not so with this one.

Given the latitude and the mostly-wooded area, the place would be swarming with ferals.

"The following was captured a short distance to the south of the facility," Cate continued. "I'll share the precise location once we reach Earth."

The image changed to a flooded and overgrown stretch of what might once have been a road. Now it was little more than an unnaturally straight river, choked by yellow-and-brown weeds. Snow-crusted trees bowed over much of the water.

The colors and contrast had been artificially enhanced, giving the scene a garish feel. Ice edged the river, and bits of gray slush floated along like dingy rafts. A pole or pillar, too straight to be natural, had fallen across the surface to form a rickety bridge.

"The water reminds me of the summer thaws back home," said Grom.

A figure appeared by the water. Mops' hands tightened on the edge of the table.

"All this to show us a feral human?" Azure scoffed. "Earth has half a billion such specimens."

"This one's wearing clothes," said Kumar.

They weren't clothes as Mops was used to, but the heavy brown fur wrapped around the human's body was a departure from normal feral nudity. As was the staff or spear gripped in both hands.

"They're not feral." Rubin spoke in a whisper. The rest of the room went silent. "Look at their movements."

The human paused, then stepped onto the fallen pole, thrusting the staff into the water for balance and support.

Mops had seen feral humans up close when the *Pufferfish* crew reverted. She mentally compared those memories to the human on the screen. "Whoever this is, they look hesitant. Careful, even."

The river didn't appear that deep. A feral would have simply waded across, unbothered by the cold.

"A former EMC soldier, then." Azure waved her short

tentacle at Wolf. "We know humans with disciplinary problems are occasionally banished to Earth."

"Nobody's threatened to ship me back for four months," Wolf protested.

"This isn't an ex-soldier." Mops had looked into the details of the resettlement process back when she'd been trying to figure out what to do with Wolf. "They don't get sent to this part of Earth. They're resettled in one of three islands called Hawaii, Japan, or Iceland. Inhospitable places, but they're free of ferals and geographically isolated, letting small groups of humans live in relative peace. Under close Alliance surveillance."

"Humans can swim, yes?" Azure looked from Rubin to Mops. "Could this be a human who chose to leave their island?"

"We assumed the same at first," said Cate. "Further research demonstrated that humans can only swim short distances. We then assumed they had constructed crude boats, until—" Cate's antennae twitched. "Would you please instruct your AI to switch to the thermal image?"

"I'm trying," grumbled Doc. *"I'm connected to his Prodryan implant, but his AU interface is difficult."*

"AU?" Mops spoke quietly enough that only Doc should pick it up.

"AI slang, sorry. Artificially Unintelligent. For systems that are so bad, it feels like they were designed to be deliberately stupid."

The image changed to a maelstrom of color. A key along the top matched colors to temperatures.

Kumar jumped from his seat to study the screen more closely. "Are these core temperatures accurate?"

"The data was calibrated against known environmental conditions," said Cate.

"Well?" Wolf nudged Kumar from behind. "Pick up your jaw and tell the rest of us what you're so excited about, would you?"

"Feral body temperature is thirty-two degrees." Kumar

continued to stare. "Cured humans are a little warmer, closer to thirty-three. Thirty-four if we're active or feverish."

Mops glanced at the temperature key, then back at the human figure. Her heart beat harder, almost violently, against her ribs. "Go on."

"This human's core body temperature is thirty-seven degrees." Kumar stepped closer, one hand raised like he wanted to touch the screen to verify that temperature for himself. "You or I could function at that temp, but it would mean something had gone seriously wrong with our bodies. We wouldn't be able to think clearly. Our balance would be off—we'd never be able to cross that bridge. This human looks strong and healthy."

"What are you saying, Kumar?" asked Monroe.

He spun around, and his voice sped up. "Thirty-seven degrees was the normal body temperature for *pre-plague* humans. Normal, healthy, uninfected humans."

Azure emitted a warbling whistle of shock. Wolf swore. A foul smell suggested Grom had expressed their surprise in the manner of their people.

"Fleet Admiral Sage set up a secret research facility," Mops said slowly. "Do you think she's discovered a way to cure us? To *truly* cure us?"

"That is my conclusion," said Cate. "Admiral Pachelbel agrees with me. However, with Sage in command of Stepping Stone Station, Pachelbel lacks the authority or resources to launch an investigation of her own."

Wolf snorted. "So instead, she hooks up with a Prodryan spy, and sends him to ask the most wanted ship in the galaxy to swing by Earth and poke around Sage's secret lab?"

Kumar turned. "According to the last newsfeed we received, the most wanted ship in the galaxy is an unnamed Prodryan bomber implicated in attacks on thirteen different Alliance colonies over the past three years. Second on the list is a Nusuran smuggling ship belonging to Captain Prov-lovokol-hi, who is accused of seducing and robbing three members of the Glacidae governing council. Simultaneously."

"She means the *Pufferfish*." Mops picked up the rag-covered memory crystal Cate had provided.

"We've observed search parties leaving Sage's facility," said Cate. "So far, they have failed to locate the human."

"What makes you think we'll do any better?" asked Monroe, his white fingers drumming the table.

A still image replaced the video. It was blurrier and looked to have been taken at night. The colors were slightly off; everything had a faint green hue. If she squinted, Mops could make out the form of a human approaching the blocky remnants of an old building. "What is this?"

"This is where the human went when they returned. Fleet Admiral Sage does not have this information."

Mops didn't think she was going to like the answer to her next question. "How is it you do?"

"This came from a Prodryan spy satellite in Earth orbit."

She'd been right. From her team's expressions, they were just as pissed. "How long have you had eyes on Earth?"

"Eyes on . . ." Cate paused. His head twitched from side to side, like he was reading something on his implant. "I don't know when the satellite was inserted. It was launched from the edge of this system. The satellite itself was the size of a human eyeball."

"That's fourteen billion kilometers," said Kumar. "That would take years. Decades."

"The mathematics were quite sophisticated." Cate cleared the screen. "It may comfort you to know Admiral Pachelbel destroyed the satellite shortly after I shared this data with her. I'm told she was commended for her diligence."

"You must have known you were giving up your spy satellite," said Mops. "And that once the Alliance found it, they'd be able to track down any others. That's a hell of a sacrifice."

"Not a sacrifice. A trade."

Mops understood immediately. Earth Mercenary Corps troops retained many feral traits. They felt no pain and were all but impossible to kill. An end to the Krakau plague meant no more unstoppable soldiers fighting for the Alliance.

"I didn't expect Admiral Pachelbel to agree," said Cate. "I believe she's acting out of guilt, or perhaps a different, related disorder."

Wolf looked back and forth between Cate and Mops. "What's he talking about?"

Mops didn't answer. "Grom, how long until we're ready for that A-ring jump?"

"I can have it programmed in twenty minutes," said Grom. "We'll need another two hours to reach minimum safe distance from the sun."

"Do it." Mops slid the wrapped crystal into a hip pocket. "We're going to Earth."

EMC Combat Incident Report

Date: *August 22, 2251 EGC (Earth Gregorian Calendar)*
Location: *Tixateq system*
Report Filed By: *Battle-Captain Steve Irwin, EMC Serial Number 10634NZ*

Enemy Force (Size, Species, Armament): EMCS Pufferfish, *under command of Marion Adamopoulos, human. The* Pufferfish *has one functioning weapons pod, but their only attack against the* Box Jellyfish *involved several tanks of modified synthetic skin. The* Box Jellyfish *was then attacked and immobilized by a total of seven (7) Comaceans.*

EMC Casualties: *None. However, the* Box Jellyfish *suffered minor damage when a younger Comacean attempted to engage in amorous activity with the ship. Weapons pod two will require realignment.*

Enemy Casualties: *None*

Has all tactical data from the encounter been uploaded to Command for review? *Yes*

Other Notes: *Operators of Biorefinery Eleven say they intend to sue the EMC and the Alliance for lost productivity. Also, I've submitted Leave of Absence Request Form E-71, flagged for expedited processing and approval. Duration to be determined. (Either until I use up my accumulated leave or someone else catches Adamopoulos, whichever comes first.)*

WOLF HAD NEVER BEEN much of a linguist, but she was fluent in twenty-six forms of profanity. Twenty-seven if she had a handful of leaves to shake for swearing in Tjikko. She cycled through every curse she knew as she escorted Cate to the only acceleration chambers built to handle Prodryans.

"Your vocabulary is impressive," said Cate. "I've studied human body language, and you appear unhappy."

"No shit," snapped Wolf. "Thanks to you, we're headed toward the last place in the galaxy any sane being wants to go."

"Is that why you're locking me in a cell?" Cate stopped at the brig entrance. Clear doors on either side of a wide hallway led into small, identical-looking rooms.

"Alliance ships weren't built to carry Prodryans as anything but prisoners." Wolf shoved past Cate and gestured to one of the doors near the guards' station on the end. "I recommend cell two, but it's up to you. They all convert to acceleration chambers, so you should be safe in any of them for the A-ring jump."

Cate didn't move. "Have these chambers been properly maintained?"

"Kumar performs inspections in his free time, for fun. He has extensive spreadsheets."

"You expect me to trust a human with my safety?"

"*Very* extensive spreadsheets." Wolf tossed Cate's armor onto the floor inside the cell. "Monroe says your armor's built to help you survive acceleration. Since our stock of Prodryan blood thickeners is expired, this ought to keep you alive for the jump. Probably."

Cate stepped into the cell and picked up one of the larger pieces. When he pressed it to his chest, it clung with a faint squelching sound, even over that ugly yellow shift he wore.

Wolf powered up the guards' console. "What were you doing on that Comacean, anyway?"

Cate's arms bent backward to secure the next piece of his armor around his lower back. "A rival family hired me to inspect the Zenkozan refineries for violations of Alliance law. The family hoped to use my report as leverage to take control of the Zenkozan operation."

"I'm surprised the Zenkozans didn't drop you into a smelting furnace."

"They're constrained by law," said Cate. "Also, I offered to sell them a copy of my report upon completion, for twice the price. They got a head start to address any shortcomings that could be used against them, and I got paid triple for the same work."

Typical Prodryan. "What were you talking about back in the Captain's Cove? What do you get out of this?"

"All of what?"

"This mission to Earth. Helping us. Your lost spy satellite. Is undermining Fleet Admiral Sage worth it?"

Cate paused in the middle of fastening a bulky collar around his neck. "You're rather stupid for a human, aren't you? And that's saying a great deal."

Wolf's arms and fists tightened. "You're the one picking a fight with a human at least twice your mass."

"You humans are exactly what makes this mission worth it. The plague turned you into monsters. The Krakau Alliance made you soldiers—too stupid to know fear or pain." His wings sprang open, the edges gleaming. "I could slice your arm from your body, and you wouldn't even blink."

Wolf slammed her fist onto the guards' control console. The cell door slammed shut. "I could depressurize your cell and decorate the walls with your guts. And I wouldn't even blink."

Cate retreated a step, and the metal blades edging his wings retracted. "That was meant as a compliment, not a threat. The Krakau made your people into the most effective warriors in the Alliance. Thus my excitement over a potential cure." His head tilted ninety degrees. "You still don't understand, do you?"

Wolf studied the controls. Mops would be pissed if she killed the Prodryan, but she could probably get away with "accidentally" running a cleaning routine.

"If Sage has stumbled upon a true cure, she'll never share it," said Cate. "Not willingly."

"You want to help us get the cure?"

"If such a cure became public, the Alliance's own laws would force it to stop producing people like you. Every 'cured' Earth Mercenary Corps soldier would become soft and weak like your ancestors. This could eliminate the most significant blockage to my people's inevitable expansion throughout the galaxy. Not to mention the collateral damage when we expose Sage and Pachelbel. The chaos and conflict will ripple throughout the Alliance."

"What about us?" asked Wolf. "Me and the rest of the crew? Are you planning to kill us once you get what you want?"

Cate resumed donning his armor. "Naturally, I'll eliminate you all if it's convenient. But the fate of a few humans is insignificant to the larger picture. One way or another, you'll all fall to the might of the Prodryans."

"Here's a larger picture for you. You hurt anyone in my crew, I'll rip off your wings and feed them to you." Wolf activated the acceleration pods. Four egg-shaped indentations opened in the rear wall of cell two. "Mind your head."

Wolf waited until Cate had settled into the pod before setting her own equipment in storage, unlocking the cell door, and taking pod four next to Cate. The gel molded itself to her body. Latches in the back interlocked with the attachment points on her harness. "How long until the jump?"

"Less than one minute," answered Doc, his voice broadcasting through the cell's comm system.

Wolf had never understood the science of Krakau acceleration rings. Kumar had tried to explain it once, something about acceleration rings using compressed space as a slingshot to propel the ship faster than light.

The ship's internal gravity kept everyone and everything on board from being smashed to jelly from the acceleration, but there was only so much it could do. Anyone not secured in an acceleration pod when the *Pufferfish* passed through the A-ring would be tossed about like a minnow in a maelstrom.

"Prodryans relish victory," Cate said from his pod. "They're impatient for it, preferring the immediacy of battle. I've never fit in well with my peers. I find much more pleasure in arranging things so I can watch our enemies destroy themselves."

"Remind me to shoot you before this is over," Wolf snarled.

"That would be a wise choice on your part."

Before Wolf could respond, a series of injections turned her limbs, and then her thoughts, to warm lead.

Mops' body tingled with the aftereffects of the A-ring jump. Her mouth was sour, suggesting she'd puked during the process. She swallowed and grimaced. The dryness around her mouth meant it had been during acceleration, not deceleration. Her pod had vacuumed up the worst of the mess, but they never got it all.

"Doc?" she croaked.

"You're all alive. Congratulations on another successful jump. The Pufferfish *is down to five A-rings. You'll need to resupply soon."*

The ship was built to carry thirty of the rings around the

bow. For interstellar travel, the frontmost ring was deployed a short distance in front of the ship, where it expanded and spun up to speed. It destroyed itself in the process, but only after shooting the *Pufferfish* across the galaxy. A second ring was used to decelerate the ship at their destination.

She fished her monocle out of her pocket and clicked it into place. According to the crew status display, Wolf and Rubin were awake and on the bridge. She pried herself free of the acceleration pod with a familiar sucking sound. Kumar and Monroe were both beginning to stir. The nonhumans would be out for hours yet.

Mops licked her dry lips and rotated her arm until her shoulder joint popped back into place. She'd have to get that fixed one of these days. "Where are we?"

"Home."

Her monocle showed her a top-down display of the solar system. *Her* solar system.

It felt like two lifetimes since she'd left. The planets were larger than scale, allowing her to admire the swirling red-and-white stripes of Jupiter, the watercolor-orange of Mars, the impossibly perfect rings of Saturn. The *Pufferfish* was a good 350 million kilometers from the cloud-frosted blue and green of Earth.

"We're being hailed," Wolf said over the comm.

Mops cleared her monocle. "Confirm we're broadcasting the beacon ID Cate provided."

"We're alive," said Rubin. "Several security satellites are tracking us, but I see no sign of long-range missiles or incoming warships. I believe that confirms they have not identified us as the *Pufferfish*."

"They'll know we're an EMC cruiser from our deceleration signature," Wolf added.

Mops walked toward the lift, working the stiffness from her joints as she went and trying to ignore the silence around her. The *Pufferfish* should have carried a crew of two hundred, most of them human. Most of them friends.

She used a cleaning rag to wipe her face as the lift whisked her to the bridge. Once there, she studied the display of Earth and its defenses on the main screen. Green icons represented hundreds of satellites and automated tracking and weapons platforms scattered in a flattened ovoid with the planet at its center. The four dots closest to the *Pufferfish* were blinking—those would be the weapons satellites that had locked onto the ship.

Wolf glanced up. "You've got something . . ." She trailed off and pointed to the front of Mops' uniform.

Mops grimaced and scrubbed the indicated spot.

"Alliance computers are requesting interface," said Doc. *"There are six thousand, four hundred, and eleven software updates pending."*

"Let's not clog our systems with those right now." Mops stepped down the ramp to her station, but remained standing, her hands on the back of her chair. After spending hours immobilized and unconscious, she needed a little more time upright to recover.

"Grom plotted an escape jump before we left, just in case," said Wolf. "Fooling long-range scans is one thing, but eventually they're going to figure out who we are. We're missing two weapons pods. If anyone looks closely at the visual as we get closer—"

"Admiral Pachelbel has that covered." Mops did her best to project confidence. "Doc, remind me who the hell we're supposed to be?" The notes appeared on her monocle. "Wolf, open a channel to Stepping Stone."

Wolf worked her console, then gave Mops a nod.

"Good morning, Stepping Stone. This is Battle Captain Aldrin of the *EMCS Cape Buffalo*. Over."

It took three minutes for their signal to reach the station, and three more for a response to make the return trip. "Acknowledged, *Cape Buffalo*. I am Communications Technician Jude of Stepping Stone Station. Please confirm your mission and destination."

"Transport and escort duty. We've got a team of Krakau scientists napping in their pods. They'll be doing a low-atmosphere study of Earth's equatorial weather patterns."

Another six minutes passed while Mops tried to keep her nerves under control. They were still far enough to turn tail and escape if things fell apart . . . which anyone on Stepping Stone would realize. Meaning if they *did* suspect Mops, the smart thing would be to act like everything was fine and lure them closer.

"Maintain course and speed, *Cape Buffalo*. You'll receive additional navigational guidance in fifty-three minutes. Welcome to the Earth system, Battle Captain Aldrin."

"Thank you."

Wolf closed the connection. "I don't like this, sir. Even if we fool them long enough to slip a shuttle down to Earth, and even if we somehow manage to find this escaped human before the Krakau do—"

"Let's focus on one thing at a time," said Mops. "Rubin, plot an orbital insertion that keeps Earth between us and Stepping Stone."

Rubin hesitated. "Kumar has been showing me how navigation works, but I haven't completed the tutorials."

"Don't worry, I'll have Kumar and Grom double-check your work. But with so few people, we need backups trained on every station. Puffy can help you."

Rubin's cheek twitched. "Puffy's assistance will *not* be necessary."

Mops suppressed a smile as she turned her attention back to Wolf. "We'll need someone with Cate when he wakes up. I don't want him wandering my ship alone."

"That won't be an issue," Wolf said without looking up. "I locked the cell door behind me and activated full security measures when I left the brig."

She sounded like a new cadet trying too hard to sound professional and official. Mops had worked with Wolf long enough to know what that meant. "What *else* did you do?"

Wolf's head sank another centimeter. "I might have doo-dled a few pictures on his carapace . . ."

Mops had spent much of her adult life making difficult deci-sions. When to fight and when to fly. How to balance the needs of a mission against the safety of her team. Whether the stains in the Nusuran guest quarters could be safely cleaned and san-itized, or if the entire room needed to be torn down and re-built, with all furnishings sent to the incinerator.

The rare simple choices were a relief, a gift from the galaxy. "The answer is no."

"This is *Earth*," Wolf protested. "It's probably the most dangerous place we'll ever go. Why does the *Pufferfish* even have power armor if we're not going to use it?"

Mops checked the armory inventory list on the wall, just inside the main door. "The goal is to avoid attention. Running around in a three-meter exosuit with an arsenal capable of an-nihilating a small continent isn't terribly subtle." Especially with Wolf at the controls.

Wolf stared at the line of angular matte-black armor components at the back of the armory. "It even has its own missiles."

Monroe took a blue combat baton from the rack, hesitated, and finally selected a pistol as well. "EMC marines train at least four hundred hours before taking one of those suits into a hostile environment. How much time have you put in?"

"You can upload Puffy to talk me through it," Wolf coun-tered.

Mops paused, imagining the caricature's clownlike grin pop-ping up on Wolf's display. *"It looks like you're trying to slaughter every living thing on Earth. Would you like help with that?"*

"Even if that were possible, have any of these suits been calibrated for you?" Monroe took two extra magazines and slid them into quick-release pockets on his right thigh.

Wolf shrugged. "So it doesn't fit quite right and I get a few blisters."

Monroe rapped his artificial hand against one of the bulky armored sleeves hanging like a row of severed metal limbs. "These things amplify the power of your punch tenfold. You can put a hand through a concrete wall."

"Damn right," said Wolf.

"And if it doesn't know the precise length of your arm, the first punch will dislocate your wrist, elbow, and shoulder," Monroe continued. "The first step will destroy your hips and knees. And would you like to hear the havoc an improperly prepared plumbing attachment can wreak?"

Wolf took a step back. "How long would the calibration process take?"

"About an hour," said Monroe. "And it would require the skills of a CAM officer. Unfortunately, the skills of a shipboard hygiene and sanitation team don't carry over to combat armor maintenance."

"Grab a combat uniform like everybody else," said Mops.

"All right, but if we get ambushed by sharks, you're gonna wish we had combat armor."

Mops grabbed one of the heavy-duty combat jumpsuits, along with a standard EMC pistol, combat baton, extra ammo, and a long list of cleaning and janitorial supplies. Hard-core soldiers would probably scoff, but she'd survived more confrontations with industrial tape and various detergents than she had with her firearm.

She took an infantry helmet and pulled it on to check the fit. Humans could survive just about anything short of a direct shot to the head or neck. The black helmet wouldn't stop an A-gun round, but hopefully none of Earth's native life would be carrying modern weaponry.

She pulled down the laminated memcrys visor. It locked into place, covering her face from eyebrows to chin. Doc transferred himself from her monocle to the visor, where he quickly tested his link to her suit and weapons.

"I can't guarantee you're shark-proof, but everything checks out."

Her monocle popped free as Doc reversed the magnets in the rim. It slid down Mops' face to land in her waiting palm. She tucked it into a padded pocket inside her uniform and exited the armory.

Cate waited outside, wearing the same armor as when they'd picked him up. He also wore exaggerated black eyebrows and a long, curling mustache over his pincers, all carefully drawn with a standard-issue marking pen. From the smudge above one eye, at least Wolf had used temporary ink instead of permanent. "When will I be issued weapons?"

Mops kept her voice neutral. "Just be grateful I talked Wolf out of removing your wing blades while you were unconscious."

Kumar perked up. "The implants are only four centimeters deep. It's a delicate process, given how thin the wings are, but I'd be happy to take some scans and figure out the best extraction procedure."

Mops often worried about Kumar's enthusiasm for cutting open other living things. "Cate can keep his blades," she said, cutting off the Prodryan's indignant response. "But that's all you're getting. Everyone else, pick up the pace. We'll be in launch position soon."

"Cate's coordinates checked out?" asked Monroe.

Kumar nodded. "I checked his satellite video against historical records of that area. I believe the building we saw used to be a national library."

Wolf poked her head out of the armory. "Dibs on the mystery section."

"Temperature in your landing zone is four degrees below zero," Kumar continued. Mops had ordered him to remain with the *Pufferfish*, along with Grom and Azure. He was the best navigator they had. More to the point, Mops didn't want to find out what would happen if Kumar's compulsive cleanliness met the ruins of Earth.

She waited for Wolf to finish grabbing ammo magazines,

then closed and secured the armory. "Kumar, get back to the bridge. Keep an eye on Grom and Azure while we're gone. Tell Grom no makeovers this time. If I come back and they've turned the *Pufferfish* into a live-action laser-maze game, I'll launch them into the sun."

"Yes, sir." Kumar gave Rubin a quick hug. "Be careful. That whole planet is filthy and overrun with disease."

"It's natural filth," said Rubin in her customary monotone, but she returned the embrace. "The planet reclaiming itself. You'll look after my pets?"

Kumar tapped his monocle. "I annotated your instructions and programmed daily reminders."

"Roach just molted, so she might be more tired than usual."

Grom broke in over the group comm. "Captain, are you at the shuttle yet?"

Their tone made Mops' heart speed up. "Not yet. What's going on?"

"If I'm reading the tactical display correctly, one of Earth's orbital platforms just locked targeting lasers onto us."

Mops was seriously considering ordering Wolf to carry Cate the rest of the way to the shuttle. The Prodryan's shorter legs, evolved on a lower-gravity world, just couldn't keep up with the humans. His armor provided strength and stability, but did nothing to increase speed.

Mops stopped outside the docking bay. "Monroe, get everyone strapped in, and prep the shuttle."

"Yes, sir." He, Rubin, and Wolf hurried inside.

Mops turned to speak into her comm. "Grom, what's happening out there?"

"Stepping Stone is hailing us." A low belch betrayed Grom's distress.

"Tell them we're having communications trouble."

Grom came back less than a minute later. "Stepping Stone

wants to know if a full missile bombardment will fix the problem."

Cate came trotting down the curving corridor, arms and wings pumping. Mops grabbed his arm and hurled him through the door toward the shuttle. "Rubin, help Cate get himself secured." She closed the door and ran after Cate. As soon as she was inside, she slapped the hatch controls. Taking a vacant spot on the bench opposite Wolf, she said, "Grom, put Stepping Stone through to me."

She waited for the connection icon to appear on her visor. "Stepping Stone, this is Battle Captain Aldrin. Sorry for the delay. We've had a weird fungal outbreak. My SHS team believes it started after our last mission to Kanoram-yi. The spores are corrosive. It looks like a patch in the secondary communications array ate through—"

"Battle Captain Aldrin, you are ordered to divert to Stepping Stone Station for immediate inspection."

Mops' weight fluctuated briefly as the shuttle lifted off and started toward the outer doors.

"Our Krakau captain's still in the acceleration chamber, but she should be coming around soon. I'll send someone to—"

Another voice cut her off. "Launch that shuttle and we'll atomize everyone on board. If the *Pufferfish* so much as twitches, we'll destroy that, too. Acknowledge."

"Take it easy, Stepping Stone. No need for anyone to get blown up today. Who is this?"

"Fleet Admiral Belle-Bonne Sage."

"Admiral Sage." On the opposite bench, Rubin stiffened, while Wolf began swearing under her breath. Cate's antennae flattened along his scalp. "As I said, this is Battle Captain Aldrin of the *Cape Buffalo*. You can verify our beacon. Our mission—"

"Stop trying to lube my tentacles, Adamopoulos. The *Box Jellyfish* reported your departure from the Tixateq system, where you left a pack of space whales molesting their ship. Travel time from Tixateq to Earth coincides exactly with your arrival here. As for your phony beacon, I suggest you shove it up your donkey."

"I believe that should be 'ass,' sir. You might want to have a tech review your translator vocab." The shuttle floated free of the bay and picked up speed, curving downward.

"Last warning, Adamopoulos."

"For the record, sir, the Comaceans weren't molesting the *Box Jellyfish*. They were trying to protect it." She muted the connection and leaned toward the cockpit. "Monroe, what weapons and defenses do we have?"

"Nothing that will hold up against Stepping Stone's resources," said Monroe. "Grom's keeping the planet between us and the station, so they can't shoot us directly, but between fighters, long-range missiles, and defense satellites, we're in trouble."

"Do all of your mission plans erode so quickly?" asked Cate.

"I find it best to include 'everything goes to hell' as part of the plan." Mops checked tactical on her visor. Thirty-six fighters were closing in from three different directions. She reopened the conversation with Sage. "Fleet Admiral, if we surrender, can you guarantee the safety of my crew?"

"No," Sage said bluntly. "But I can promise they'll live longer than they will if you attempt to reach Earth."

Twelve of the fighters moved to cut off the shuttle. The rest continued in a flanking attack pattern toward the *Pufferfish*. Monroe dipped the shuttle into a deeper dive and said, "We're out of time, sir."

Mops watched the fighters swoop closer. "Do it."

"Grom, on my mark," Monroe shouted, one hand hovering over the button that would activate the code Cate had smuggled to them from Admiral Pachelbel. "Now!"

Mops held her breath. The *Pufferfish* veered sharply upward and to port. Monroe twisted the shuttle into a starboard turn the grav plates couldn't compensate for, stomping her guts toward her hips.

The ships closing on the *Pufferfish* had kept to a precise formation until now. As the *Pufferfish* maneuvered away, cracks spread through that formation. Several fired A-guns and energy weapons. One lucky shot crackled over the rear of the ship, but it looked like the defensive grids dispersed most of the damage.

"Did it work?" Rubin was unnaturally calm, like she was discussing what her pet slug had eaten for dinner the night before.

As the *Pufferfish* slipped away, the remaining fighters turned toward the shuttle. "Yes and no," said Mops. "Cate, why the hell can they still see us?"

"I don't know," Cate snapped. "Maybe your computer technician made a mistake when they copied Pachelbel's code. Maybe there's a mismatch with the shuttle's beacon."

Monroe increased speed and descent until the hull rattled. It wasn't enough. Energy weapon fire engulfed the shuttle. Lights died, and internal gravity gave out. The shaking grew worse.

"Wolf, distribute grav vests now!" yelled Mops.

"All right!" whooped Wolf, almost drowning out Monroe's muttered, "Aw, shit."

Cate looked about, claws clutching his harness. "What are grav vests?"

Mops punched the release for her restraints and grabbed one of the clunky, metal-plated vests from Wolf. "How much do you know about grav plates?"

"There was a decade-long patent case when the technology first went into production," said Cate.

Wolf rapped her knuckles on the black plate over her sternum. "Same principle, but in reverse. Once primed, the vests power on automatically when you come within twenty meters of any surface, countering local gravity to break your fall."

"I do not understand," Cate whispered, his wings shivering. Mops suspected he understood all too well, and was hoping to be proven wrong.

The shuttle jolted hard. A series of six-centimeter holes cut a line down the center. Wolf cursed and grabbed her shoulder, where the A-gun fire had burned through her uniform and a layer of skin.

Monroe shoved his way toward Cate, one hand on the ceiling for support. "Let me. The vests are designed for humans. If we don't get it tight, you'll squirt right out and splatter when you hit the ground."

The bristles on Cate's limbs stood straight up, a fear-response Mops had never seen in a Prodryan before.

"Don't tell me you're afraid of heights," said Wolf. Rubin had scrunched Wolf's sleeve together and was looping sealing tape around the joint to make a crude bandage.

The shuttle jerked again, slamming Mops against the wall hard enough to make her vision flash white.

Sage's voice crackled over the shuttle's comm. "That was your final warning shot."

Monroe glanced at the holes in the shuttle. "Her translator needs to update its definition of 'warning,' too."

"Doc, show me our projected course and target." Mops' visor switched to a view of Earth. A blue line showed their intended course, while a dotted green line illustrated their current path, a steeper arc that fell short of their destination. Not as bad as she'd feared, but not good.

"This is insane," said Cate. "Even for human standards. The Alliance and EMC are held to strict standards in their treatment of prisoners. A foolish restriction, but if we surrender—"

"Make sure your suits are sealed," Monroe shouted.

Mops had almost forgotten in the chaos. She tugged up her uniform collar and locked it to the bottom of her helmet, then grabbed her gloves. "Doc?"

"At this speed and altitude, you're unlikely to burn up. I've advised Wolf to shelter Cate with her body, since Prodryan wings are more susceptible to the high heat and pressure. Also, the fighters have launched missiles."

"Lead with the missiles next time," snapped Mops, punching the emergency hatch release. The shuttle quaked harder as the door popped open and ripped away. "Go!"

With the exception of Monroe, none of them had trained for this kind of jump, but the incoming missiles added urgency and efficiency any veteran would have admired. Wolf seized the struggling Prodryan in a bear hug and hurled herself out, followed by Monroe and Rubin. Mops was the last to leap free.

The atmosphere hit her like a wall of wind and heat. Her body tumbled end over end. She brought her limbs in tight to her body, for fear that they'd be torn off.

The shuttle exploded behind her.

Mops' visor darkened an instant before the flash. Doc had anticipated the explosion, but he couldn't do anything to protect her from the shock wave. It felt like the *Pufferfish* had jumped onto her back. She tensed her muscles, trying to keep her blood flowing and hold on to consciousness.

"Don't worry if you pass out," said Doc, his voice tinny. *"The vest was primed when you left the shuttle. It will deploy automatically. Assuming the explosion didn't damage it."*

"You," she said, her jaw clenched, "are an asshole."

"Don't get snippy with me. If your vest fails, I'll shatter right along with you."

"You've got backups on the *Pufferfish*. I don't."

"Your human limitations aren't my fault!"

Mops tried to come up with a cutting response, but her body had other ideas. The throbbing increased, and the world turned black.

6

Admiral Pachelbel stood a short, subservient distance behind Fleet Admiral Sage and tried not to let her emotions show. She took a great deal of satisfaction from Sage's frustration as she searched for the Pufferfish, but Pachelbel couldn't stop replaying the shuttle explosion in her mind. Was sacrificing the shuttle part of Mops' plan? Or had Pachelbel gotten Mops and her people killed? What if Advocate of Violence had betrayed them?

"It's a cruiser-class ship crewed by semi-evolved monkeys," Fleet Admiral Sage said quietly, her voice carrying like the predatorial song of their ancestors through the cold currents of home. "How in the icy depths can it simply disappear?"

Sage was surprisingly small, given her status. Her natural coloration was a mottling of orange and brown. All three tentacles were thick with muscle.

She stood erect on her lower limbs, towering over the two unfortunate Krakau scanning techs huddling together in War Cove One, the station's central command nexus. All around her, weapons and tactical personnel worked without *making so much as a ripple that might draw the Fleet Admiral's attention.*

One of the scanning techs turned to say, "Maybe they did a short-range A-ring jump?"

Sage slapped the tech's head with a tentacle. "This close to the sun and its gravity? Without a trace of acceleration energy from the ring?"

"They must be jamming our sensors," the other tech suggested.

Sage pointed to the console. "We're picking up every one of our fighters, not to mention the debris from the Pufferfish's *shuttle. That's some very precise jamming."*

"What about some kind of cloaking technology?" asked the first, sinking a little lower.

"You think a team of human janitors developed and perfected technology that has eluded Alliance scientists for more than a century?" asked Sage.

"They also have a Glacidae," Pachelbel pointed out.

"I am aware," Sage said, grinding her beak as she spoke. She turned to her exec, a distant cousin she'd brought along when she took command of the station. Like other Krakau, she'd adopted a Human name based on old Earth songs. "Hollaback Girl, send security teams to inspect the station's plumbing and air vents. Each team should be accompanied by someone from hygiene and sanitation. Adamopoulos could be attempting to sneak into the station."

Pachelbel consciously slowed the dangerous tempo of her hearts. Sage was a power-hungry, paranoid pain in the anterior, but she wasn't stupid. She'd studied Mops' files, knew the kind of tactics the human preferred. "If they're not cloaked, how did they disappear?"

Sage moved closer. "The most likely explanation is sabotage from within."

"Would you like me to organize an inspection of our sensor systems?" asked Pachelbel.

"Hollaback will oversee the inspection," Sage snapped.

She'd suspected Pachelbel of aiding the Pufferfish *from the moment she arrived on the station; so far, however, she'd been unable to prove anything.*

"I heard about an old human power called hypnosis," whispered the first scanning tech. "They could control your thoughts with pocket watches. Maybe they're still out there, but making us *think they disappeared."*

Sage spun and coiled one tentacle around each of them, squeezing their beaks shut. "Keep searching. Whatever those bottom-feeders did, I want to know how to counter it. Preferably before the Prodryans figure it out and bomb us back to the ice age. And get me everything you have on that shuttle's course."

"Before or after it exploded?" asked the second tech.

Pachelbel had always prized intelligence in her subordinates. Sage prioritized loyalty. Questions like that were the result.

"Before," Sage said tightly. "I want to know where they were going."

A LOW, OBNOXIOUS BEEPING dragged Mops awake. She spent several seconds trying to wake up from a falling nightmare before remembering she was in fact plummeting to Earth at—she checked her visor display— roughly two hundred kilometers per hour.

"They say soldiers should learn to sleep whenever they can," said Doc. *"Napping during freefall might be taking that to extremes."*

"How long until we hit the ground?"

"Eight minutes, depending on wind resistance. You've been falling for about ten."

She twisted her head, searching for the rest of the team. Doc highlighted their locations. Monroe was almost a kilometer to the south, his body streamlined like a torpedo. Rubin had drifted eastward. Wolf and Cate were tumbling together half a kilometer below. She squinted at Wolf, and her visor magnified the view. Wolf was grinning like a maniac. Cate appeared to have fainted.

"According to uniform readings, everyone is alive and relatively uninjured. Wolf is overly excited, and close to hyperventilating."

"Captain, are you all right?" Monroe's words inside her sealed helmet made her jump.

"I think so." She checked her uniform integrity readout to confirm there were no punctures. "What happened to those fighters?"

"They stayed upstairs, probably searching for the *Pufferfish.*"

Wolf's voice crackled over the comm. "Did anyone bring a spare uniform?"

"I don't think so," said Mops. "Why?"

"Because this stupid Prodryan just woke up and peed on mine, that's why!"

"It's not urine," Cate groaned. "It's a secretion to dissuade predators, and it's perfectly natural!"

"So is urine," Rubin pointed out.

"How much did we lose with the shuttle?" asked Monroe, and the others fell silent.

With her helmet sealed, the sudden lack of sound was like being plunged into vacuum. "Long-range comms, extra ammo and supplies, and our way off planet."

More silence, broken a moment later by Cate's wind-whipped voice. "Did I hear that right? Even if we find this human we're searching for, we can't get them off-planet, and we have no way of calling for help?"

"Cut the chatter," Mops ordered. Their personal communications units were short-range and low-power, unlikely to be picked up from orbit, but it was better to be safe. "We're supposed to be debris from the shuttle. Try to act like it."

She turned her attention to the planet below. Light from the rising sun painted an arc over the globe, separating day from night. Beneath white cotton wisps of cloud, much of the surface shone in the sun.

"Doc, record these images to my personal library, please," she whispered.

Had she been born somewhere on the continent below? She would have grown up in the wild, like an animal. She'd probably lived in a pack, hiding in the woods or the hills or the ruins of a human city.

"I can magnify or enhance, if you'd like."

"No, thank you." She barely noticed the air hammering her body. Most of the planet was in shadow. She kept her attention on the arc where the sun peeled back the darkness. Sparks of light vanished before she could make them out. Bodies of water, maybe. Or bits of metal and glass, remnants that had survived a hundred and fifty years after humanity's fall.

She took a deep breath, trying to imagine the smell of Earth's air instead of the stale warmth of her suit's supply. "Is there any way of knowing if the *Pufferfish* is safe?"

"You left Grom, Azure, and Kumar behind. 'Safe' isn't the word I'd use. But I've picked up no additional weapons fire or explosions."

It wasn't like Mops could do anything to help them, regardless. They were on their own. "Doc, show me the library. Bring it up for everyone."

A blinking icon appeared on her visor. She reopened a channel to the team. "That's our target, people. The closer we can get while we're falling, the shorter the hike once we're on the ground."

Somewhere down there, half a billion uncured humans shambled about, victims of an alien toxin turned viral. Half a billion ferals, and one scared human hiding from the Krakau and humans alike.

Mops angled her body toward the library. "Hang on," she whispered. "We're coming."

Mops knew she was falling at a constant speed. That knowledge did nothing to counter the evidence of her eyes, which insisted the ground was accelerating toward her, faster and faster, the closer she came to impact.

Her visor enhanced the darkness below, trading color for contrast and detail. It made the overgrown ruins appear ghostly and unreal. Rusted beams stood like skeletons, many covered in thick vines. Snow and ice blanketed it all.

"Aim for whatever clearing you can reach," Monroe called out. "Your vest will activate as soon as you're within twenty meters of a significant mass. Pass too close to a tree or building, and it will go off prematurely."

Mops scanned the ground, which was evenly split between trees and ruined buildings. She tilted her body, trying to steer toward the crumbled remains of an old road.

"Speaking of going off prematurely, did you hear the one about the Nusuran and the—" Wolf shrieked before she could finish her joke.

"Wolf's vest has deployed," said Doc.

"Good." Mops was only seconds from the ground. She bent left, but didn't get quite far enough from the brick and girders of an old, dilapidated tower.

Her vest powered up. The initial gravity push flung her away from the tower. She spun toward the ground, where the vest's gravity-bending cushion sent up an eruption of snow and dirt as it bounced her back into the air. She shot up a good thirty meters before coming down again, this time pinballing between trees before coming to rest.

"If you're going to vomit, remove your helmet first."

Mops' eyes wouldn't stop twitching. Her vest held her suspended one meter above the ground. She stretched her legs, her toes just brushing the snow. "How long—?"

"It will deactivate momentarily."

She yanked one of the buckles. The vest's safety mechanisms beeped in protest, refusing to unlatch while she was still in the air. While she waited to fall that final meter, she checked in with the rest of the team. One by one, they confirmed they were down safely.

"What about our guest?" asked Mops.

Wolf chuckled. "He fainted."

"Not surprising," said Monroe. "Deceleration in these things tops out around eight gees. Prodryans pass out at six."

"He shot away from me when our vests activated," Wolf continued. "It was funny as hell. Like two magnets repelling each other. I hope my visor caught the video. I'll dig him out of the snow as soon as my vest sets me down and I stop seeing double."

"Doc, show me everyone's location."

"They're scattered over roughly two kilometers." The locations popped up on her visor. *"Calculating from the center point, we came down roughly twenty kilometers west of our target."*

With a sad beep, Mops' vest dropped her face-first into the snow. She rolled onto her back, wiped off her visor, and stared into the star-speckled blackness.

"Are you all right, Mops?" asked Monroe. "I heard a grunt."

"Just finishing my fall." She licked her dry lips, swallowed, and sat up. Her limbs were numb. She'd been too tense for most of the drop. Everything had stiffened up. She flexed her arms, popping both shoulders, then stripped off the vest and adjusted her pack. "Rubin, you're closest to the library. Sit tight, and the rest of us will come to you. Safeties off, people. Check in every five minutes, and at any sign of trouble."

Their landing should have scared off any wild animals, including feral humans. But once the local predators realized Mops and her team were alone, and that human beings had stopped raining from the sky . . .

She used eye movement to switch to tactical mode. Her team's vital signs, armament, and ammo counts appeared in the lower left corner of her vision. Next, she drew her pistol, switched off the safety, and pointed at a nearby tree. Crosshairs appeared on the trunk, confirming the link between gun and visor.

Ankle-deep snow crunched beneath her boots as she hiked toward the flooded road she'd spotted on the way down. With one hand, she unsealed her collar from her visor and inhaled her first breath of Earth air in twelve years.

The influx of cold filling her lungs made her gasp. When she exhaled, her breath turned to fog. The air had a sharp scent she eventually identified as coming from the trees, specifically the ones covered in green needles. Beneath that overpowering smell were others: rotted vegetation and animal musk and countless more.

Mops had grown all too familiar with the smells of various Alliance species. But the smells on a ship, while at times intense, were limited in number. A planet's air carried the scents of millions of species of plants and animals, along with whatever dust and chemicals the wind picked up in its travel.

The ground sloped down toward the flooded road. The snow cover was thinner here, revealing gnarled tree roots and broken cement. Trees bowed over the water, their bare branches intertwining overhead.

Mops took another step, and her foot shot out like she'd trod in a Glacidae fear-trail. For the second time in minutes, she found herself on her back, staring up at the stars. Her only consolation was that nobody had seen it.

"There appears to be a layer of ice on the rocks beneath the snow."

Almost nobody. "Thank you for that observation."

She'd slid down to the edge of the water, her boots cracking through the thin crust of ice. She sat up and tested her limbs. Her left arm felt bruised, but nothing was broken. "Why couldn't my ancestors build roads above the water table?"

"Humans managed the water levels in settled areas, storing much of it for consumption and diverting the rest. As their technology failed, the water would have risen. Rising sea levels compounded the problem."

She climbed carefully up from the water, using a sapling for support. She'd only gone a few steps when a movement alert lit up her visor.

One hand gripped her pistol as she studied the ruins of a collapsed bridge up ahead. The range finder put it twenty-six meters away. Three small shapes crawled over the broken metal and concrete.

Earth had more potential threats than she could count. EMC ships were named after the most dangerous, and they had names to last another century. Her mind raced through the list, from poisonous frogs to scorpions to hippopotami . . . though she was pretty sure hippos were larger than these things.

More creatures crept from the rubble. Doc snapped and magnified one, enhancing the image. Floppy black ears framed small black eyes. Muddy fur stood up like rusty nails along the back of the overlong body. The lips were pulled back to reveal pale gums and an array of needlelike teeth. Her mic picked up a low growl. "What the hell are they?"

"My database of Earth species is incomplete. It's clearly a mammalian pack animal. The teeth exclude it from order Rodentia."

"They could have mutated. Who knows what they've been exposed to over the decades as human waste facilities broke down." She took another step, and the growls grew louder. "Territorial little clods, aren't they?"

The threat counter on her display had climbed to twenty. Mops moved sideways, planning to hike around and avoid the confrontation.

One of the animals let out a high-pitched yip. This startled another into movement, and it ended up sliding down the rocks into the water. Mops winced in sympathy.

The thing scrambled out, shook itself off, and—apparently deciding Mops was the source of its trouble—charged her.

Mops lined up a shot. The gyroscopes built into the pistol stabilized her aim as she tracked the creature.

"They're dogs!"

"What?" She hesitated, and in that moment the dog pounced. Small jaws clamped onto her pants, just above her boots. The dog snarled and shook its head, trying to either tear through the material or drag her to the ground. "I've read about dogs. I thought they were bigger."

More dogs crept toward her, emboldened by the first.

"Humans bred a wide range of dogs, hundreds of drastically different varieties. I believe these are descendants of the subset known as dachshunds or, colloquially, as wiener dogs."

Three more dogs clamped onto her legs. EMC combat uniforms were built to turn metal and ceramic blades, which kept the teeth from reaching her skin. But eventually they'd bring her down with sheer weight and numbers, and one of them would find their way through the seams. "Humans kept these things as pets?"

"I assume domesticated dogs were trained not to eat people. Once humanity went feral, dogs would have either followed suit or died out. Interesting that this particular breed succeeded. Possibly because they're better able to hide and pursue small game."

She grabbed one of the squirming dogs by the scruff and yanked it free. One of its eyes was a cloudy white. The thick, matted fur sticking up from its scalp looked more like Glacidae spines than mammalian hair. Strings of slobber swung from the lower jaw. Its teeth seemed to point in every direction, and several were missing entirely.

"I don't want to kill them if I don't have to." More dogs swarmed onto her, climbing their packmates like a ladder.

"Perhaps a quick swim in the river?"

"Look at the one who fell in. The poor thing's shivering." Mops thought back to one of the first times she'd read about dogs. It had been during her first year on Stepping Stone, before she transferred to the *Pufferfish*. The Krakau maintained a library of Earth literature they'd translated into Human. This had been a children's book about a particularly cowardly dog . . .

She sheathed her gun and grabbed a half-meter nozzle from her equipment harness. Tugging the hose from the portable compressor mounted on her hip, she secured the hose to the nozzle.

"You're going to inflate them?"

"Not exactly." She adjusted the settings, hit the switch, and pointed the nozzle at the dachshunds on her left leg.

The dogs shot away like they'd been launched from an A-gun. Within seconds, she stood alone once more. Only the thick layer of fur, slobber, and mud on her uniform proved the dogs had been there.

"I don't understand."

"Vacuum cleaner." Mops hit the off switch. "The traditional nemesis of the dog."

"I thought cats were dogs' arch-enemies."

She continued walking, wand ready. Shining eyes glared from the safety of the bridge. They snarled and growled with tiny impotent fury, but none ventured into the open to face the roar of her vacuum. "Doc?"

"Yes, Mops?"

"This planet is messed up."

"Yes, Mops."

Mops reached the rendezvous without further incident, aside from a large, hooting bird that burst from the trees and startled her so much she almost fell into the river. She found Rubin waiting on a cracked concrete bench outside a large fenced-in structure, a stadium or arena of some kind.

Rubin stood as Mops approached. "No sign of ferals, sir. The biggest thing I've seen, aside from you, was a rat. I tried to feed it, but it ran away."

"Save your rations. We don't know how long they'll need to last." Speaking of which . . . Mops took the end of the bench and pulled a food tube from her pack. Opening a slot in the front of her suit, she screwed the end of the tube into the feeding port in her abdomen. A press of a button on the end of the tube triggered the slow release of its contents.

"I was hoping to see more of Earth's animals," Rubin continued. "Zebras and snakes and whales and something called a platypus. But many of the larger animals will be in hibernation. Insects go dormant in the cold. Birds move to warmer parts of the planet."

"Tell that to the one that dive-bombed my head."

Rubin perked up. "Did you get a good look? Could you share the video?"

"On it," said Doc.

While Rubin oohed over the bird, Wolf arrived, rifle clutched in both hands. She was out of breath and dripping wet. Cate clung to her back, arms locked around Wolf's shoulders.

Mops came to her feet. "What happened?"

"Crossed a river and fell through the ice." Wolf dropped to one knee, letting Cate climb down. "Woke my passenger right up."

"You savages evolved for these temperatures," Cate complained. Steam rose from his armor. His wings hung like damp cloth. Frost brushed fractal spikes around the edges. The water had caused Wolf's graffiti to run, decorating his face with streaks of black ink. "I did not."

"A cold, wet Prodryan is a pitiful thing," said Wolf. "I almost felt sorry for him. Then he started talking again."

Mops checked her visor for Monroe's position. He'd been closer and should have reached them before Wolf. "Monroe, are you all right?"

Wolf and Rubin both turned to listen.

"Banged my head during landing," Monroe replied, his words tight. "Threw off my balance. I keep curving to the left. Don't worry, I'll catch up soon."

"I'm sending Wolf to meet you."

"That's not necessary, sir. I'm less than half a kilometer out. Now that I know about the problem, I can compensate."

Mops gestured for Wolf to go. She threw a quick salute, shouldered her weapon, and headed out. "Monroe, you know what happens when Wolf gets bored. This is as much for our safety and protection as yours."

Wolf threw an obscene gesture over her shoulder. Mops pretended not to see it.

"Understood, sir." Monroe's pause suggested he wasn't buying it, but he was too much the soldier to argue.

"What now?" Cate demanded. "Your plan is in tatters. Will your remaining crew attempt to retrieve us, or will they make off with your ship?"

"They'd better not come after us. The *Pufferfish* isn't designed for planetary landings, and you saw what happened to our shuttle." Mops removed the now-empty food tube and returned it to her pack.

"It's not my responsibility to find a way out of this disaster," Cate snapped. "It's yours."

Mops stood, sealed her uniform front, and walked slowly toward Cate until she could smell the Prodryan's stale breath and the frigid river water dripping from his body. "Then I suggest you shut up and let me do my job."

"Which job?" Cate shot back. "Mopping up this mess of a planet, or leading your team into disaster? According to your files, you're well-trained for the former, but you seem to have a natural gift for the latter."

"So it seems," Mops said easily. "I've discovered a number of talents since I took command. At the Battle of Dobranok four months ago, I discovered I have a knack for blowing up Prodryans."

Cate paused, then took a step back. "That is an excellent point."

"Let's focus on the immediate goal," said Mops. "We've got a lot of ground to cover, and a lost human to rescue."

"A human who will likely be confused and frightened,"

added Rubin. "Whatever education they might have received from the Krakau after being cured, it wouldn't be enough to prepare them for life on present-day Earth. They may already be dead."

"In which case we retrieve their body," Mops said firmly. Assuming the planet's scavengers had left anything to find.

"Nicely done, Captain," said Doc. *"Rubin's blood pressure has dropped, indicating increased confidence in your leadership. Cate appears to have submitted to you as the dominant warrior."*

"Thanks."

"You realize I can read your *blood pressure, too?"*

Mops stepped away from the others, speaking softly enough that only Doc should be able to pick up the sound. "This mission was a long shot even with a working shuttle and all our supplies. What the hell am I supposed to do now—build a shuttle out of sticks and scrap metal? Our comm units have a range of five kilometers, so I can't even talk to the ship."

"Maybe if you shout really loud . . ."

"Loud enough for the sound to travel through the vacuum of space?"

"Better have Wolf do the shouting. She's louder than you."

Mops snorted. "This planet scares the shit out of me, Doc."

"The planet or its inhabitants?"

"Both." She peered into a dark crack in the concrete wall of the stadium. Anything could be sleeping inside, from rats or wild dogs to feral humans. "I've had nightmares about this."

"About being shot down while following a Prodryan spy to retrieve a cured human from a ruined library? How prescient of you."

"About being trapped on Earth. Asshole."

"It could be worse. You could be trapped here without me." After a long pause, he added, *"And the others, of course."*

There were other ships on the planet. All she had to do was break into Fleet Admiral Sage's top-secret laboratory and steal whatever they had on hand that was spaceworthy. Then, assuming they survived, they could worry about flying the damn thing.

"You think we can reach the library before sunrise?"

"Doubtful, given Cate's average walking pace and Monroe's difficulties."

For now, the trees provided decent cover from Krakau satellites, but the library had been in a more open, unprotected area. They'd be better off resting during the day. Darkness was no guarantee of safety, but it might help. "We'll get as close as we can, then make camp."

"I wonder if Prodryans have campfire songs."

Mops considered this. "Given what we've seen of Prodryan poetry, I think I'd rather be eaten by dachshunds."

7

Grom sat coiled in the captain's chair. For human furniture, it was surprisingly comfortable.

The bridge had gone silent, save for Kumar's loud human breathing and the slither of Azure's tentacles moving over the tactical console.

"That wasn't part of the plan," Azure whispered.

Grom's legs rattled as they watched the last fragments of the shuttle fall away into darkness. "The captain's plans don't generally involve blowing herself up, no."

Kumar looked up from navigation as the viewscreen looped back to the beginning of the shuttle launch, replaying the event yet again. "There's too much debris from the explosion. Several masses fell away before the missile strike. It could have been them jumping clear. Or it could have been the shuttle falling apart from plasma and A-gun fire."

"That memory crystal Cate provided was supposed to protect us," said Azure. "If it failed the captain, how long before it fails us? Those fighters are still searching the area, and Stepping Stone hasn't stopped scanning."

"It's hard to troubleshoot what went wrong without know-ing what was on that crystal and how it's supposed to hide us from the Krakau," said Kumar. "Maybe it was defective."

"It wasn't the crystal." Grom slid from the chair and joined Azure at Tactical. "Look at your display. What do you see?"

"Us. Earth. Stepping Stone. Far too many fighters."

"Now look at what you don't see." Grom tilted their body toward the main screen. "There are hundreds of old satellites orbiting the planet. There used to be more, but every year the orbits decay. Our navigation system automatically tracks them to avoid collisions, but if you tried to show them all on screen, it would clog up your display."

"Like a Quetzalus using a Merraban toilet," suggested Ku-mar. "The volume of material exceeds the capacity of—"

"Yes, thank you." Grom wondered how long it would take to claw that image from their mind. "Admiral Pachelbel snuck a few lines of code into one of the navigation software updates Stepping Stone pushed out a few weeks back. When Captain Adamopoulos switched us back to the Pufferfish's ID beacon, every Alliance scanner automatically reclassified us as old Earth space junk and cleared us from tactical and threat displays."

Azure considered this. "Given the condition of the ship, that's not too far from the truth."

"What if they scan for space junk?" asked Kumar.

"We should show up as one of a hundred unimportant blips."

Kumar bobbed his head. "And the shuttle?"

Grom slumped. "The shuttle switched over to the same ID beacon. It should have vanished just like the Pufferfish."

"How are beacon codes created?" asked Azure. "Do they encode the type of ship, some form of checksum or internal verification?"

Grom clicked their limbs together. "My background is in computing hardware and routine updates. I never studied ID beacon protocols."

"You think the shuttle broadcast a modified code?" asked

Kumar. *"Automatically adding a tag to identify it as a shuttle instead of a cruiser?"*

"We may not be qualified to troubleshoot exactly what went wrong," Grom admitted. *"But I believe we should assume the captain survived and do what we can to find and assist her from here."*

"Why?" asked Azure.

"Primarily because Captain Adamopoulos has proven herself to be very stubborn about not dying," said Grom.

"You said primarily," Kumar pointed out. *"Is there another reason?"*

Grom twisted back toward the captain's chair, trying not to look at all of the empty bridge stations. They'd installed shortcuts and macros, trying to simplify the process of keeping the ship going, but there were limits. *"Because there's no way the three of us can run the* Pufferfish *alone. If the shuttle team is dead, so are we."*

WOLF STOPPED AT THE top of a hill and stared out at the rising sun. "The sky is orange. Why the depths is the sky orange?"

"Atmospheric scattering." Rubin's voice over the comm sounded far more awake and alert than Wolf felt . . . possibly because Rubin got to hang back at camp while Wolf scouted the surrounding area for ferals or other threats. "The same thing happens on any planet with a decent atmosphere."

"I knew that. But this is Earth. The sky's supposed to be blue."

They'd stopped an hour earlier, a few kilometers out from their goal. Monroe was still wobbly, and Mops was hoping a rest would help his brain reboot. Wolf had volunteered to patrol the area. Her body might be exhausted, but her mind was too wired for sleep. This was Earth, home to humanity and countless other threats.

Wolf imagined how she'd casually mention their time on Earth the next time they stopped at a neutral station. *"Oh, it's not so bad. I had to punch a crocodile and an electric eel, but the sunrises were amazing."*

So far, though, she'd seen none of Earth's fearsome wildlife. Neither had Rubin, who was keeping watch back at camp. "I don't like this, Rubin."

"I've counted more than a hundred things you don't like since I joined the *Pufferfish*," Rubin replied. "Could you please specify?"

"Smart-ass." Wolf chuckled. "Where are all the ferals? Between the woods and the ruins, there's plenty of shelter. They've got water, animals to eat . . . this place should support a good-sized pack. They should have come out by now, with us intruding on their territory and all. You sure there aren't any back there?"

"Everything's quiet. Mostly. Did you know Prodryans snore?"

Wolf checked her path and location. She'd been keeping to a one-kilometer radius from the old train cars where the others had taken shelter for the day. She turned left and started downhill. "Hey, what's going on with you and Kumar?"

A pause. "Nothing. Kumar is on the *Pufferfish*, while I'm down here."

"You know what I mean." Or maybe she didn't. This was Rubin, after all. The woman was tough as Nusuran teeth, but it always felt like part of her mind was elsewhere. "I saw that hug before we left. How long have you two been a thing?"

"Sanjeev raised the possibility of a romantic relationship three and a half months ago. I explained I was uninterested in a sexual relationship, but I've enjoyed the romance and his companionship."

Before Wolf could ask more, a dark shape jostled through the branches up ahead. She brought her rifle to her shoulder. "I've got movement."

"What size?"

"Too small to be a feral." Wolf stopped behind a thick tree to replay and study the image on her visor. "Cancel that. Looks like a dead tree branch snapped and fell. The whole damn planet's falling apart."

"Death is natural. Especially during the cold season on Earth."

Wolf kept walking. How the depths was she hiking around the worst planet in the galaxy, and the only thing she'd fought so far was boredom? "You ever think about what it would take to really clean this place up? Make Earth livable again?"

"Livable for whom? Most of Earth's wildlife is doing better now than when humans were dominant. According to Krakau survey reports, the feral population has stabilized. If the humans of the EMC decide we want our own planet, it might be easier to find another one to colonize."

The morning sky had faded to pink, transforming clouds to ribbons of red. "Wouldn't that be something? Our own planet. Not that the Krakau would ever let us." Her visor highlighted an anomaly in the snow. "Hold on."

"Another branch?"

"Not this time." Wolf zoomed in on what appeared to be tracks. "Looks like footprints near the river. Could be human."

"You've been walking for an hour. You might have crossed your own path."

"How incompetent do you think I am?" Before Rubin could answer, Wolf brought up a map of her route on the visor, overlaying it with the tracks. The two paths didn't intersect. "Someone else has been here."

"Do you need backup? Ferals have been known to ambush prey."

"I'm good." Wolf pushed her visor up and back, until it rested on the rear of her helmet. Shifting her rifle to her left hand, she retrieved her monocle and clicked it into place over her eye. Once it powered up, she said, "Display helmet visual feed on monocle. Upper quadrant."

The top quarter of her monocle display changed to show a hundred-and-eighty-degree view of the area behind her.

"Invert."

Ground and sky flipped into their proper positions.

"What are you doing?" asked Rubin.

"Old infantry trick." Wolf turned her head to and fro. "Reverse the visor and feed it to your monocle to get almost a full three-sixty view. Eyes in the back of your head."

"I thought you were rejected from the infantry. Multiple times."

"Go drown yourself." Wolf started down the hill toward the tracks. "I've been reading some post-combat reports. Picked up a few things."

The tracks intersected the river, then angled away again. Wolf knelt in the snow. She couldn't make out any details, but each print was roughly the same size and shape as her own. No distinct toeprints—whoever this was, they'd been wearing shoes. "Definitely human. Could be our runaway. I'm going to follow, see if I can find 'em."

"I'll wake the captain?"

"Let me see what this is, first." Wolf stared at the ground, trying to decide which direction the human had been going. It wasn't like footprints stamped nice, legible arrows into the snow and dirt.

A spot of red caught her eye. She spied several more leading away from the river, alongside the footprints. The red stopped about twenty meters away. Wolf crouched to pick up a small object. She grimaced when she realized what she was holding. "Hey, Rubin. If you were eating a rodent, would you eat the head first or last?"

"Not first. Start with the softest and most nutritious parts, which would probably be the internal organs. Getting to the brain would be more work, like shelling a Tjikko nut."

"It worries me that you didn't have to think about it." Wolf looked back at the trail. Assuming the human had been eating as they walked, this was where they'd finished their meal and discarded the head, which meant the human was walking away from the river. "Thanks."

The trail veered first left, then right. Whoever or whatever it was, they didn't seem to have any specific destination. Or maybe they were drunk. After ten minutes or so, the tracks straightened, heading toward what looked like a toppled signal tower. Vines and moss had begun to overtake the crisscrossed metal beams.

Wolf dropped into a crouch, bringing up her rifle until the crosshairs locked onto a slender figure inside the cage of the tower. "Found them."

"Are they alone?" asked Rubin.

"Looks that way." Wolf squinted, trying to shut out the distraction of the visor's visual feed from behind. "This might be our runaway human. They're wearing clothing, furs of some kind. I'm going to make contact."

"We don't know what the Krakau taught them," Rubin reminded her. "They might not even speak Human."

That was a good point, but there was only one way to find out. Wolf crept closer.

"Would this be a better time to wake Captain Adamopoulos?"

Wolf checked her monocle. The doubled vision of her visor feed was starting to make her head ache. "I'm more than a kilometer out from camp. By the time anyone got here, the human might have run off again. Don't worry, I've got this."

Diplomacy had never been one of Wolf's strengths, but what the hell. With less than fifty meters now separating her from the human, she waved a hand and called out, "Hey there. Nice furs."

The human hunched their shoulders but didn't otherwise react. They continued to watch Wolf approach.

"My name's Wolf. Me and my friends are here to help you. Do you understand?" When the human didn't move, Wolf raised her voice. "Do. You. Understand?"

"What are you doing?" asked Rubin.

"Trying to communicate. Shut up." Wolf could make out additional details now. The human wore a simple fur robe and crude leather shoes. They—*he*, rather—had neglected to close said robe. "Hey, what color is natural human blood supposed to be?"

"Bright red."

Wolf focused on the long gash across the human's chest, and the thick, dark blood dripping down his skin. "This isn't our guy. It's a damn feral."

"You said they were wearing clothes."

"Maybe he got cold."

The feral's lips pulled back to reveal stained, crooked teeth. He squeezed between metal beams and trudged toward Wolf.

"Keep your distance," Wolf said sharply. "Rubin, what if this is the guy we saw, but he reverted? Maybe Sage's cure is only temporary."

"We have no idea what we're dealing with," said Rubin. "Anything's possible."

Aside from that single gash, Wolf didn't see any wounds or old scars. Nor did he have the half-starved, emaciated appearance of most ferals in the wild. "I'm bringing him in."

She adjusted the firing mode of her rifle to a low-power energy blast. It should be enough to take down a feral without killing him. Wolf could truss him up with sealing tape and drag him back to their temporary base.

The feral stumbled closer, one arm outstretched. His guttural groans raised the hairs on Wolf's neck. Just as Wolf was about to squeeze the trigger, the feral froze. His groans grew louder, more insistent.

"That's right," said Wolf. "Take a good look. When you wake up, tell all your feral friends not to mess with . . . Aw, crap."

"What's happening?" asked Rubin.

She'd gotten too damn focused on bringing down this one feral. She split her attention between her target and the rear feed from her visor. "I've got something sneaking up behind me."

"I'm on my way."

Relief flushed through her as she spotted the source of the movement that had spooked her. "Belay that. It's just an animal. A cat, maybe? It looks angry, but it's too small to be any threat. I probably stepped on its nest or something."

"I don't think cats make nests."

"Whatever. This feral's spooked. I need to bring him down before he bolts."

"Are you sure about this?" asked Rubin.

"If I let him go, who knows whether we'll be able to find him again." The feral retreated a step. "It's just one scared feral. Trust me, I've got this."

Mops stood with arms folded, watching on her visor as the blip representing Wolf approached their makeshift shelter.

"The important thing is she's all right," said Monroe as he attached a food tube to his feeding port.

"For now."

They sat in the open doorway of an old passenger train car: Monroe on the top step, Mops on the bottom. The train had been gutted long ago, and the windows were cracked and broken, but much of the steel structure had survived. They'd sprayed the entire car down with pest repellant to clear out insects and small rodents.

"I had to throw Wolf into the brig four times while she was working for me," said Mops. "Fighting, ignoring orders . . . I thought she'd finally left that shit behind."

"She's had four good months," Monroe pointed out. "Everyone screws up sometimes."

"The worst that happened when she screwed up on SHS was a burst pipe or a leaky toilet," Mops snapped. "She went after a feral on her own. She could have been killed."

"But she wasn't. Between the humiliation of what happened and the chewing out you're gonna give her when she gets back, maybe she'll think twice next time."

"I'd be happy if she'd think once." Mops stood and began to pace. She'd sent Rubin to catch some rest. Mops had gotten less than an hour of sleep before Rubin woke her, but she wouldn't be able to relax until she burned off this energy. "How the depths am I supposed to keep her alive?"

"Is that what you're so pissed off about?"

"I've got a list, but it's near the top." She sat back down and began inspecting her pistol. "Wolf's impulsive. Rubin's over-protective, likely to walk right into the line of fire if she thinks it will help the team."

"Don't forget me." Monroe tapped the side of his head. "I'm lopsided until I get this damn implant recalibrated."

She slid the magazine free. It registered full: forty-five small, spherical slugs packed into place. A battery along the front edge provided power for twenty-seven electrical jolts. Next, she freed the primary power pack from beneath the barrel. This was the heaviest part of the weapon, spinning up the miniature acceleration rings within the barrel that fired the slugs. It registered a ninety-seven percent charge, good enough for well over a thousand shots. "This planet is where we died, Monroe. This reprieve some of us got from the Krakau, this life between human and feral, it can't last."

"That's what I've always appreciated about you," said Monroe. "Your eternal optimism."

She replaced the power pack and magazine, then double-checked the readout on her visor. Everything matched up: full load, and ninety-seven percent charge. "This planet messes with your head. Half the time it feels like a homecoming, the other half it's like visiting your own grave."

"She's here."

Mops stood, turning toward where her visor indicated Wolf was approaching. As Wolf emerged from the trees, a hint of pity mixed with Mops' anger. Wolf had her visor pushed up, revealing swollen, bloodshot eyes. Dark blood crusted around her nose. Water dripped from her uniform. Her shoulders sank when she spotted Mops waiting. All in all, she looked utterly pathetic.

Mops' nose wrinkled. Wolf carried a stench like burnt rubber and baked death. She waited silently until Wolf stopped a meter away. "Well?"

Wolf's eyes were fixed on the rusted wall of the train car. "The feral got away. Sir."

Mops raised a hand. "Let's get downwind first, so we don't disturb the rest of the team. Monroe, stay here and keep an eye on things."

"Gladly, sir." Monroe saluted, then waved his hand in front of his nose.

Mops started walking, keeping close to the train. She climbed into another car a short distance back. Most of the seats' metal frames remained, but the cushioning was long gone, and what plastic remained was brittle and cracked. Mops waited for Wolf to enter, then put a foot on the side of a chair and folded her arms on her knee. "I told you to stay within one kilometer of camp. I remember being quite clear about that."

"Yes, sir."

"Just like I was clear that you should alert me or Monroe immediately if you found anything unusual. Doc, could you please replay my orders for us? I want to make sure I didn't misspeak."

Wolf's flush deepened as Doc broadcast every word Mops had said before sending Wolf out on patrol.

"And now the feral—the one you told Rubin might be our target—has escaped," Mops said when Doc finished.

"Yes, sir."

"What the hell happened?"

"Technically, ferals aren't that unusual. Not on Earth, I mean." Wolf kept her attention on the ground. "I didn't realize how far I'd gone as I was tracking him. He wasn't aggressive. I figured I'd shock him, tie him up, and bring him back."

"Go on."

"He got agitated. That's when I saw something moving behind me. I had my visor reversed, feeding into my monocle. Eyes in the back of my head, you know?"

"And?" Mops prodded.

"It was just an animal. Puny looking thing, black with white stripes. I think it was what the feral was getting worked up about, so I thought I'd scare it off, maybe make it easier to take care of the feral."

"Based on Wolf's description, I have a possible identification of the animal," offered Doc.

"The damned thing blasted me with some kind of chemical weapon," Wolf continued.

"Identification confirmed."

Wolf tugged a cleaning rag from her harness and rubbed her face. "By the time my vision cleared, the feral was long gone. I doubled back to a stream and tried to wash off the worst of the stench."

"What happened to your face?"

"I'd just started back to camp, when I heard branches cracking behind me. I didn't know what it was, but I wasn't in the mood, you know? I turned around, and that damned black and white cat was staring at me again. I pulled my baton and charged. Only I still had my visor flipped back. Between the double-vision in my monocle and my eyes being messed up from the spray . . ." She lowered her voice. "I ran into a fucking tree."

"I've downloaded the series of events from Wolf's visor and monocle if you'd like to watch," said Doc.

"Later," Mops whispered, fighting to keep a straight face. "If we were on the *Pufferfish*, I'd throw you and Rubin both into the brig."

"Rubin?" For the first time, Wolf looked directly at Mops.

"She should have woken me or Monroe as soon as you saw that feral."

"It's not her fault," said Wolf. "I told her not to—"

"And you think your orders override mine?"

Wolf flinched. "No, sir."

"I can also present an enhanced version with humorous sound effects."

Mops pressed her lips together. This proved to be a mistake, since it forced her to breathe through her nose. Once she finished coughing, she straightened and said, "Anything else you'd like to say in your own defense?"

"I was afraid the feral might wander off if I waited for backup to arrive," Wolf said quietly.

"Yes, and this worked out so much better."

Wolf didn't answer.

"You told Rubin he was wearing clothing. Furs, right? Are you *sure* he was feral?"

"Yes, sir. The same dark blood as us, and he moved just like the ferals on the *Pufferfish* four months ago." She mimicked the shuffling, trudging movements.

"All right. Do what you can to clean yourself up, then get some sleep. In here, so you don't choke the others."

Wolf hesitated. "You're not gonna yell anymore or make me clean the train with a toothbrush or anything?"

"I'd love to," said Mops. "But I doubt anything will top what you've already been through. It would just be me lashing out at you because you scared the shit out of me. Because this situation could have gone much, much worse."

Wolf nodded. "Thanks."

"Pull something like this again, and I'll leave you on this planet. Naked. Is that clear?"

"Got it." She shuffled deeper into the passenger car.

Mops stepped out and inhaled a lungful of relatively clean air. "Doc, show me the best shot of that feral from Wolf's monocle."

The human was as Wolf had described: healthy, but clearly feral. "Can you confirm whether he's a match for the human we saw in the clip from Cate?"

"I can't be certain, but I don't believe so. This human appears to be shorter and younger, barely out of adolescence."

"What can you tell me about the furs he's wearing?"

"The brown-and-white pattern of the fur suggests the hide may have come from a deer. The edges appear to be clean, straight cuts. Do you think we've discovered the first tool-using feral?"

Mops continued to study the image. "Doc, I don't know what the hell we've discovered."

Mops' SHS team had been one of the best in the EMC. They had the best cleansers in the galaxy. And nothing they did managed to completely remove the stench from Wolf and her uniform.

By the time Wolf and Monroe found a mixture of degreaser and detergent that brought the stink down to a tolerable level, the sun was setting, and Mops was ready to head out.

Doc had used Wolf's relative positioning data to plot a path back to where she'd encountered the feral. The overpowering skunk smell confirmed they were in the right spot, but there was no sign of the feral.

"This place smells like death," Cate complained.

"The skunk must have a nest nearby." Rubin dropped to her hands and knees to peer at a pile of fallen branches and dead leaves. "Otherwise it wouldn't have attacked Wolf twice. Unless it was diseased . . ."

Wolf grabbed her combat baton.

"We're not here to hunt the skunk," Mops reminded them. "Monroe, any luck backtracking the feral's prints?"

"No sign of him, but I've got something interesting here," Monroe said over the comm.

Mops and the others found him about two hundred meters east.

"More signs of civilization." Monroe pointed to a curving roadway. Even in the moonlight, it was easy to make out the series of large rectangular pits to either side. Time had smoothed the edges and begun to fill them in, but they were too regular to be natural.

"Old human hives?" suggested Cate.

"What's left of them." Mops approached the closest, noting another patch of flat, rocky ground that might once have been pavement connecting the home to the road. A bit of digging through the snow exposed broken bricks.

"Stay alert," said Monroe. "Ferals might use these pits for shelter."

Cate jumped back in alarm, his wings flapping.

Mops was tempted to linger, to explore the places her own ancestors might have lived. Who knew what artifacts had survived beneath the snow and dirt? From the way the other humans stared, Mops knew she wasn't alone.

Instead, she pulled herself away. "It's less than an hour's hike to the library. Our priority is the runaway human. Maybe they'll be able to tell us why ferals have started dressing for the weather."

As they walked, they passed other evidence of humanity: a partial brick chimney that had survived the loss of the rest of the house; the rusted, overgrown frame of a two-person motor vehicle; characters from a language Mops didn't recognize carved into the side of a tree.

A trilling cry caught Mops' attention. Before she could pinpoint the source, a shadow shot from the trees and dove toward the ground. In an explosion of snow, a large bird snatched a squealing creature in its talons and flew away.

"What was that?" Wolf yelled, her rifle swinging to track the bird's movement.

"An owl," said Doc, broadcasting to the group. *"Possibly a screech owl. I wasn't able to identify its dinner from this distance."*

Mops took a moment to calm her breathing. She turned her attention skyward. How many satellites were passing overhead? The bare trees offered shelter, but if just one satellite or drone captured a clear image, it wouldn't be long before Krakau fighters swooped down on them, just like the owl and its prey.

They followed the road up a shallow hill. Monroe stopped at the top and let out a low whistle. He pointed to a palatial structure about a half kilometer away. Three square towers—two on the end and one in the center—loomed over the surrounding trees.

"The pointed spires remind me of the primitive fortresses Prodryans once built," said Cate.

"I believe it's a cathedral."

Mops passed that along, adding, "It was a human place of worship."

"I thought those were called temples," said Wolf.

Human religion hadn't been part of the Krakau education program. Mops wouldn't have known the first thing about it if not for the scraps she'd pieced together from old books over the years. "Different religions had different traditions and rituals and symbols. Stars, crosses, candles, an apple with a bite missing . . ."

"That cathedral looks like the perfect shelter for a pack of ferals," Monroe said. "I suggest we stay clear."

Mops had been thinking the same thing. She zoomed in on the building. How many centuries had it stood? How long had it taken humans to build? Nobody thought of humans as a species that built things. Humans were soldiers to be feared, or occasionally a tragic people to be pitied. "Let's circle north and— Wait. Something's moving."

Monroe tensed. "What is it?"

Doc enhanced her vision the best he could, giving her a clearer view of what she'd thought were a series of bushes or shrubs. She focused on one just outside the arched doorway as it trotted down broken steps.

The beast was all chest, with relatively small legs and a spindly rope of a tail. Curved horns rose from either side of the head. It shook itself, dislodging a thin layer of snow.

"That thing has to be six hundred kilos, at least," Wolf whispered.

Rubin hurried to see. "From the size and body shape, they could be a species of cattle. But the wooly fur on the front and the hunched shape of the shoulders suggests it's a herd of bison.

They're herbivores—no threat to us as long as we leave them alone."

"Can we ride them?" Wolf asked.

Rubin hesitated. "I . . . wouldn't advise it."

Wolf continued to stare. "What about eating them?"

Mops should have been relieved. Better a herd of harmless wild animals than a pack of hungry ferals. She watched the bison moving about. "What stirred them?"

"Sir?" asked Rubin.

"When I first saw the cathedral, I didn't realize they were alive. They must have been sleeping. They'd been there long enough they all had snow on them. Then suddenly they're all stirring and nosing around. What woke them up?"

"Maybe they smelled us?" suggested Cate, with a pointed look in Wolf's direction.

Rubin shook her head. "The wind's wrong."

Wolf raised her rifle. "I've got a range of five hundred eight meters to the closest one. No way they heard us."

Mops' eyes traced every line of the building. Her attention lingered on the towers.

"Should we check it out?" asked Monroe.

Reluctantly, Mops turned away from the cathedral. If their runaway human had taken shelter in the library, there was a good chance security and familiarity and habit would keep them coming back. "We check the library first. If it's empty, we'll double back to the cathedral."

Cate scraped his forearms in disdain. "You would leave a potential threat at our backs?"

"You'd rather risk spooking a herd of animals that could gore and trample you to jelly on the off chance there's something in there?" asked Mops.

"Your weapons are more than a match for those beasts," said Cate. "Kill them all, then destroy the cathedral. That way, any potential threat is destroyed. That's the Prodryan way."

"And what does the Prodryan way suggest we do when Alliance satellites pick up all that weapons fire?" asked Mops.

Wolf spat. "Besides, this whole planet's a potential threat."

"Which is why the whole planet should be destroyed," Cate pronounced.

"Which is why we need to find that human." Mops started down the road, trusting the others to fall in behind her. "Before anything else does."

8

Advocate of Violence: Mission Objectives

1. *Gain access to* EMCS Pufferfish *and crew.*
2. *Study weaknesses of cruiser-class ships.*
   - *The* Pufferfish *is nothing <u>but</u> weaknesses, held together with little more than glue and tape!*
   - *They steer with <u>video game controllers</u>!*
   - *Most of my time on the* Pufferfish *was spent in a locked cell. (See Attachment A for my notes on Alliance brig facilities.)*
3. *Find evidence to bring down high-ranking Krakau officers.*
   - *Fleet Admiral Sage: nothing yet.*
   - *Admiral Pachelbel: guilty of conspiring with a Prodryan spy.*
4. *Go to Earth for reconnaissance of cured and feral humans.*
5. *Observe human combat tactics.*

- *Adamopoulos escaped the* EMCS *Box Jellyfish by use of artificial Comacean skin gel.*
- *Her plan for reaching Earth involved jumping from an exploding shuttle.*
- *In my professional opinion, something is very wrong with this species.*

6. *Kill Marion Adamopoulos to avenge her defeat of the Prodryans at the Battle of Dobranok.*
   - *Waiting for the right opportunity.*
7. *Kill everyone else on general principle.*
   - *Waiting for the right opportunity.*
8. *Turn the humans against the Krakau.*
   - *Significant progress on this objective, but most of the credit for this goes to the Krakau.*
9. *Don't get killed.*
   - *Ongoing—need to pay particular attention to Earth's many hazards, along with the human named Wolf.*

MOPS CALLED A HALT in a small wooded area, within sight of their destination. The tall ruins and old roadways they'd passed suggested this had once been a heavily populated city, but this particular block was nothing but trees, narrow paths, and broken stone footbridges. Possibly a city park?

Their destination was an enormous building of white stone and pillars, about thirty meters beyond the edge of the park. Brown vines clung to the walls. A fountain sat out front, covered in muck and dead weeds. In the center of the fountain sat the statue of a muscular bearded man whose right arm had broken off. Smaller statues stood to either side. They seemed to guard the stone stairway leading into the building.

"Reminds me of one of those ancient Roman cities," Wolf whispered. "All the columns and white marble and crap."

"Wrong part of the planet." Mops studied the broken-out windows.

Rubin gestured for Mops' attention. Keeping her voice low, she said, "The Prodryan appears to be in distress."

Cate stood a short distance from the others, arms wrapped around his torso. In the relative darkness, it took a moment for Mops to see what Rubin meant. Cate's arms were swollen. The bristles on his skin had retracted and appeared to be oozing some kind of oily green mucus. Doc brightened her vision, helpfully giving her a clearer view of said mucus.

"You all right, Cate?" asked Mops.

He jumped hard enough his wings rustled. "I look forward to leaving this planet."

Mops pointed to his arms. "You seem to be . . . leaking."

He tugged a corner of his shift from beneath his armor and used it to wipe the worst of the seepage. "I believe it's an allergic reaction to the chemical assault the skunk used to defeat Wolf."

"It didn't defeat me," Wolf insisted. "I decided it wasn't worth killing, that's all."

"Was this before or after you were beat up by a tree?" Cate shot back.

"Can you take anything for this reaction?" Mops said, cutting off Wolf's angry retort.

"At home, I would spread salt-clay lotion over my scent receptors to block the stench and ease the swelling."

"You smell through your skin?" asked Mops.

"You don't?" He turned to stare at her.

"Humans smell through their nostrils." She reached beneath her visor to tap her nose.

"That puny thing?" Cate scoffed. "How inefficient."

"Says the guy covered in arm-snot," said Wolf.

Mops silenced Wolf with a glare, then said, "Cate, are you medically able to continue?"

"I am fine."

"Good." Mops turned her attention back to the library. "Monroe, any sign of activity?"

"Nothing." Monroe rested one arm against a tree. "It's not what I imagined. I always thought of libraries as little brick schoolhouses. Or else those rainbow coral things the Krakau grow to store mem crystals of their family histories. This place is huge."

Mops nodded, only half-listening. "It's quiet."

"If you say 'too quiet,' I'll electrify your helmet."

"It's nighttime," said Monroe. "All the sensible life-forms are sleeping."

"Sensible life-forms would not be on this planet to begin with," added Cate.

Rubin peered at the library. "Silence might mean the native life-forms are hiding from a predator. Although in this case, the predator could be us."

Mops straightened. "Monroe, I want you to hold back and cover our six. Rubin, watch the windows. Wolf, you're on my left flank. Cate, watch my right."

"What does 'cover our six' mean?" asked Cate. "Six what?"

"EMC slang for watch my back." Monroe settled down against a tree with his gun in his lap.

Cate peered more closely at the humans. "You have six backs?"

"Nobody knows where the expression comes from," said Monroe.

Mops drew her pistol and started across the clearing. Beneath the snow, the ground here was crumbled rock or concrete. "Walk carefully, people."

Monroe was right about the library's size. It was an imposing structure, wide and blocky, built of heavy stone blocks. Archways and pillars made it feel more like a palace than a library, as did the broad stone steps leading to what appeared to be the main entrance.

They'd closed to ten meters when a flock of birds erupted from one of the upper windows. From the corner of her eye, Mops saw Wolf swing her rifle around. "Hold your fire."

Cate spread his wings and muttered something Mops' translator didn't understand.

"What was that?" she asked.

He looked away. "It was a form of greeting, an acknowledgment of kinship to other creatures of the air."

Interesting. "Is that why your people want to kill the rest of us? Because none of us fly?"

"Not at all," said Cate. "The Prodryans would still exterminate your kind from the galaxy if you could fly. But we would feel regret over your deaths."

"Have you considered not killing everyone?" asked Rubin.

She might as well have asked, *"Have you considered breathing radon?"* or *"Have you tried gluing your genitals to a comet?"*

Cate stared for several seconds, then turned away, his disgust obvious.

Mops glanced back at the trees. "How does it look, Monroe?"

"You're clear, sir."

Mops climbed the first set of steps. Wind had swept this area clean of snow. "Some of those windows are boarded up from the inside."

"People probably took shelter here, back during the outbreak," guessed Wolf. "At least they had something to read while the world went to shit."

At the top of the staircase was a wide, cracked landing. Three stone arches led to a set of oversized doorways. To Mops' amazement, one of the doors toward the right had survived. It was a tall, heavy thing of cracked glass. She stepped into the center archway and frowned. "No glass."

"What's that?" asked Wolf.

Mops indicated the other doors, where nothing remained but empty metal frames on rusted hinges. "Glass doesn't decay. The remnants of these doors should be crunching under our feet." She dropped to one knee and ran a gloved hand over the ground. A film of dirt and moisture covered her fingers. "It's too clean."

"Tell that to Kumar," said Wolf. "He doesn't think there's any such thing."

Cate stepped past. "You said humans once lived here. Obviously, they cleared away the glass. We're wasting time, Captain."

Mops switched on the small lamp clipped to her harness and peered through the doorway. Inside was a rectangular chamber with yet more pillars and arches. Beneath the dust and bird droppings, the stone floor was patterned with a repeating circular design, like a sunburst or flower. "The entryway looks clear. Monroe, what's the best procedure for checking a building for ferals and other threats?"

"Send a drone hive in ahead of you," he answered over the comm.

"Great." She stepped through the doorway. "Any chance you brought a hive in your pack and forgot to tell us?"

"I'll add it to the list for next time."

Hallways stretched away to her left and right. Farther ahead, ornate staircases to either side led to a second-floor walkway. Chunks of debris from the ceiling littered the ground. Mops turned in a slow circle, scanning the balcony before moving toward the far side of the room.

She circled each pillar to make sure nothing waited in ambush on the other side. By now, the others had joined her, all save Monroe. Wolf was gaping like a tourist. Rubin walked backward, constantly scanning for threats. Cate moved with wings spread, the blades around the edges fully exposed.

The next chamber felt like it could be the heart of the library: a multistory circular room with an enormous domed ceiling, parts of which had fallen and lay in fragments on the floor.

"It reminds me of the Judicial Council Hall on Yan." Cate pointed to the second-floor balcony. "Sharpshooters would be stationed there and there, ready to carry out the judge's sentence."

This place was large enough to shelter hundreds. Thousands, even. Mops cupped her hands to her mouth. "Hello," she shouted. "We're not here to hurt you."

"Giving up on the stealthy approach?" asked Monroe.

"We're not that stealthy anyway." She moved toward one of

the many arched openings in the outer walls, each of which seemed to lead to a separate room. She shone her light into the area beyond. "I know you're scared . . ."

Her voice trailed off. All thoughts of their mission fell away. All she could do was stand and stare at the sight before her. She didn't even blink until her vision began to blur. Swallowing a knot in her throat, she whispered, "Doc, share what I'm seeing with the others."

Wolf was the first to respond, her words uncharacteristically soft. "That's a lot of books."

Row after row of bookcases filled the room in front of Mops. Each one was seven shelves high and overflowing with books. Some had spilled onto the floor, where they lay in dusty disarray.

Barely breathing, Mops stepped forward and bent to pick one up. She hesitated, then holstered her weapon and used both hands to lift the book as gingerly as she would a new-hatched Quetzalus.

The pages were swollen with moisture and stiff from the cold. The cover cracked and tore when she opened it, making her gasp. "I'm sorry," she whispered, not knowing who or what she was talking to. The ghosts of her ancestors, maybe.

Mold and mildew had rendered the title page illegible, even if she'd been able to read the language. She blinked to clear her eyes and gently returned the book to its place, trying to avoid doing any additional damage.

"I've got another room just like yours," whispered Wolf.

"Same here," added Rubin.

Mops didn't notice Cate approaching until he was directly behind her.

"Didn't your people have electronic data storage?" He sluiced off another layer of mucus from his arms and looked for a place to wipe it.

"If you get so much as one drop of snot on these books, I will shoot you in the face," Mops warned.

Cate hesitated, then stepped back to wipe his hands against the wall. "Unless you expect to find your runaway human in one of these primitive books, perhaps we should continue searching?"

Mops allowed herself one last, lingering look at the thousands upon thousands of books, all written by *humans*. These were the direct thoughts of her ancestors, undiluted and unfiltered by Krakau translators. In that moment, simply knowing these books existed was enough to make this shitblock of a mission worth it.

"All right, people. We've got a lot of real estate to cover. Keep looking." She wiped her cheek. "And try not to damage anything."

Half an hour later, they regrouped in the center of the main circular room, having cleared the ground floor.

"Looks like this place has a cellar, too," said Wolf. "Where next, boss? Down or up?"

"From what we've seen, the basement would be prone to flooding," said Mops. "If I were looking for shelter, I'd take the upstairs. It's dryer, and you can keep watch from the windows." She led the way past a bronze statue and up the stone staircase, marveling at the carvings in the wall. With proper cleaners and sealant, much of this place could be made to look almost new.

Almost immediately, Wolf called out, "I've found something." She crouched next to an old blanket spread over the floor. A pile of meat and bones sat in the center. She reached out. "Looks like whoever was staying here left in the middle of dinner."

"Don't put that in your mouth," Mops ordered.

"I'm not—" Wolf yelped as the blanket fell away. Off-balance, Wolf toppled through the hole it had concealed.

"Wolf!" Mops raced back to the steps. Halfway down, she vaulted the railing to the floor below, expecting to find Wolf sprawled on the ground.

Instead, Wolf hung suspended overhead. The blanket completely cocooned her, held by a loop of thin black cable that had tightened around her ankles. The other end of the cable disappeared into the ceiling, leaving her to jerk and swing helplessly.

"Bloody fuckpustules," Wolf shouted. A series of curses in other languages followed, all of which Doc dutifully translated, while rating each on creativity and proper pronunciation.

"Calm down." Mops pulled out her combat baton and thumbed the controls, shifting it into a long single-edged knife.

She'd just started back toward the stairs when Monroe spoke. "I've spotted three figures approaching the library. Humanoid."

"Cate, Rubin, get to cover now." Mops ducked behind a pillar. "What are we looking at, Monroe? Ferals?"

"I don't think so. They're clothed and armed, but it's not EMC issue. Their gear looks pretty primitive to me. They came running from another building right when Wolf started yelling."

"Movement to your right," said Doc, highlighting a humanoid shape crouched at the foot of the far stairs, pointing what appeared to be a weapon in her direction.

Mops threw herself to the floor. An instant later, a deafening crack split the air, and a crater of white stone exploded from the wall where her head had been. She half-crawled, half-ran for the cover of the nearest archway. Their weapons might be primitive, but they were effective.

"I have a shot," Rubin said over the comm, her voice utterly calm. "Should I eliminate the threat, Captain?"

"Not yet. Doc, show me what Rubin's seeing."

Her visor split to give her the feed from Rubin's helmet. Their attacker held a rifle of black metal and dark-stained wood. A white helmet left a pale, bearded face exposed. He wore bulky white-and-gray clothing.

"Orders, sir?" whispered Monroe.

Three more figures had arrived at the front of the library, dressed and armed similarly to the one by the stairs.

"Stand by," said Mops.

"What's happening out there?" shouted Wolf, thrashing even harder.

The three newcomers kept to the shelter of the doorways. One shouted in a language Mops didn't know. The man by the stairs yelled back.

Mops grabbed the cleaning wand from her harness. She connected two soap cartridges to the intake valves. A safety alert flashed on her visor, warning against mixing those particular cleaners. She cleared the warning, then sealed her collar to the bottom of her infantry helmet, triggering her suit's internal air supply.

One of the figures at the entrance moved in, keeping to the wall to Mops' left. Her weapon was aimed toward Mops' position. A small black patch covered her left eye.

Mops poked the wand around the archway, turned the pressure to maximum, and squeezed the trigger.

Cleaning fluid arced through the air, all the way to the entrance. Clouds of gas erupted outward. The two people in the doorway stumbled back, coughing and gagging. The third retreated up the steps, one arm over her mouth and nose.

"Rubin, take the one on the stairs to my right. Alive."

"They shot at you," Cate protested.

"You keep your head down. If they're this mad to see us in the library, I don't want to know what they'll do about a Prodryan." Mops turned her wand toward the fourth attacker, the one who'd shot at her. Seconds later, that one was coughing and ducking away as well.

A shriek of fear and anger made her whirl. Rubin had simply leaped from the railing onto the figure on the stairs, sending them both tumbling downward.

"Not exactly what I had in mind," Mops muttered. She detached her cleaning wand and sprinted toward her would-be killer to the left. Another gunshot threatened to deafen her, but her suit didn't register any impact. It was hard to aim when you couldn't breathe. Mops hurled herself against the woman, slamming them both against the wall. She grabbed the gun with both hands and twisted. It clattered to the floor.

"Mops . . ."

"I see it." The gun's stock had glanced off the woman's nose, loosing a stream of blood. *Red* blood.

The woman grabbed the front of Mops' uniform and slammed a knee into her hip. Mops grunted, then brought her head down, driving her helmet into the woman's face.

"Goddammit!" She brought both hands to her nose and fell back against the wall.

"You speak Human?" Mops demanded.

She managed a hoarse, "Yes," which set off another bout of coughing.

Rubin had subdued her opponent and was now sitting on top of him, her combat baton pressed across his throat.

Mops backed away. "We don't want to fight."

"I have a dissenting opinion," said Cate.

"For once, I agree with the Prodryan," Wolf added.

Mops tugged out a cleaning rag and tossed it to the bleeding woman. "For your nose."

Scowling, she picked it up and pressed it to her face. In thickly accented Human, she said, "You're EMC."

"Used to be."

"Drop your weapons!" The shout came from one of the two humans at the entrance.

"I can kill them both from here, if necessary," Monroe whispered.

"Hold your fire, but stay out of sight, just in case." Mops raised her hands over her head and stepped to the center of the room. "My name is Marion Adamopoulos. Who the depths are you people?"

The human kept her gun on Mops. "Bev, are you all right?"

"I've been better." The bleeding woman with the eye patch retrieved her rifle and hobbled toward the entrance, her shoulders hunched. "Damn gun broke my nose."

"You're in charge of this group?" asked Mops.

"I am." The human stepped closer. "Eliza Gleason. And since when does the EMC use chemical weapons?"

"It's chloramine," said Mops. "Causes coughing, burning eyes, and shortness of breath, but it shouldn't kill anyone."

As the gas thinned, Mops studied Gleason more closely. In addition to the heavy white clothing they all wore, leather bracers covered her forearms. A thick belt held knives, holster, ammo, and several leather pouches.

Doc zoomed in on her face. The skin around Gleason's eyes was brown and wrinkled, with warm undertones, a flush of life that ironically made her seem not-quite-human to Mops.

"You're cured," Mops whispered. "Fully human, all of you. How?"

"You first," said Gleason. "How did you find us?"

"A security satellite spotted one of you walking around a few days ago. Another caught an image of that same person—we thought—entering this building."

Gleason turned toward the human Rubin was currently straddling. "Dammit, Melvil. This is what happens when you break protocol. They've probably got an entire squad of Alliance bombers ready to crater this place."

"We're not with the Alliance." Mops lowered her hands and took several steps closer. "The Krakau in Stepping Stone Station don't have that second image. They know someone's down here, but not where. We were hoping to find that person—Melvil, I assume—before the Alliance."

"Not to interrupt," Wolf shouted, "but any time you people want to cut me down from here, that would be outstanding!"

Gleason spoke to the others, her words strange and melodic.

"What language is that?" asked Mops.

"One the Krakau can't translate." Gleason pursed her lips, then said, "Nishnaabemwin."

"Was . . . is it a human language?"

Bev snorted. "One of only a handful that are left."

Whatever these people were, they weren't helpless runaways from Admiral Sage's secret medical facility. They'd been around long enough to make or scavenge clothes and weapons. They had their own weapons and organization and rules. Their own languages. Not the artificial one the Krakau had pieced together, but genuine *human* languages.

All of Mops' assumptions about this mission had been wrong. Everything she'd believed about humanity . . . It was like the first time she'd left that Krakau medtank after being cured. She felt lost and off-balance. "Who are you?" she whispered. "*What* are you?"

Gleason lowered her rifle. "We're librarians."

Mops sat with her team next to the staircase, waiting for the librarians to come to a decision. Rubin appeared calm, and had even closed her eyes to rest. Wolf was more uptight, drumming her fingers on her knees and humming an EMC marching song.

"I hate you all," Cate proclaimed. Again.

"We know," said Mops.

As unpleasant as Cate's reaction to the skunk spray had been, his body's response to the chloramine Mops had mixed to assault the librarians was far worse. The mucus oozing from Cate's arms had turned a distinctive shade of bright blue, and his wings had begun to shed, leaving colored dander everywhere. Transparent patches now marred the blue-and-yellow patterns of his wings.

"I will recommend the utter sterilization of this damned planet," Cate continued, wiping a layer of blue goop from his left arm and flinging it onto the floor. "And the eradication of all your toxic cleaning supplies."

"Just think," said Wolf. "All the Alliance had to do was drop a carrier full of detergent on the Prodryan home world, and they'd all drown in their own snot."

"Two detergents," Mops corrected. "They have to mix together to produce the gas."

"Few of my people share my allergies," Cate muttered. "Your soap scheme will not stop the Prodryans' inevitable victory."

"It'd be fun to watch, though," said Wolf.

Cate shuddered, sending another shower of wing dandruff onto the floor. "Why waste time with toxic gases to incapacitate these humans when you could have shot them dead? Instead, you surrender your weapons. Are you so eager for defeat and death?"

"They're human," said Mops. "Pure human, unchanged by the Krakau venom. Whatever happens, we're going to protect them."

"You think they'll extend you the same mercy?" asked Cate.

"He's got a point," added Wolf. "They did try to shoot you, sir. What if they try again?"

"Then I get shot."

"I agree with the captain," said Rubin. "These humans must be preserved."

Gleason approached, her gun slung over one shoulder. The other librarians continued to argue behind her, but all three had their weapons out and pointed toward Mops and her team.

Gleason studied each of them, her gaze lingering on Cate, before turning to Mops. "In its prime, this place would have been packed with people. Imagine crowds moving through every room, others sitting at wooden privacy desks with terminals that could access nearly all information ever recorded by the human race. Imagine paintings and murals covering every surface, tributes to literature and knowledge."

Mops' throat tightened as she tried to visualize it.

"There was a painting on the far side of the building," Gleason continued. "A woman holding a torch, with the words 'In tenebris lux,' which means, 'In darkness, light.'" She glanced back at the other librarians. "We've seen more than our share of darkness."

Rubin opened her eyes. "Have you considered moving to another latitude, one with sunnier weather and longer daylight at this time of year? Many species migrate to follow the sunlight."

Gleason held up one of the combat batons from the pile of discarded weapons. "You come here with EMC weaponry and equipment, escorted by a Prodryan, but you expect us to trust you? You're not the first Alliance mercenaries to come hunting."

"We're not mercenaries," said Mops. "We were shipboard hygiene and sanitation services." When Gleason frowned, Mops added, "Janitors."

"Janitors?" Gleason let out a snort of disbelief and pointed to Cate. "Is that one a janitor as well?"

The Prodryan drew himself up. "I most certainly am not. I am a certified legal advocate, licensed to serve in both prosecutorial and defense—"

"Right," said Gleason. "Janitors and their lawyer."

"I am also a spy," Cate added proudly.

"Cate provided the second piece of surveillance, the one that led us here," Mops said quickly. She brushed a layer of blue-and-yellow dust from her sleeve. "For what it's worth, I'm not asking you to trust him."

"That's wise," agreed Cate.

"You said you were hunting a human." Gleason pointed toward Melvil. "I assume you meant to bring him back with you?"

"That was the plan."

"What is your plan now?"

"Hell if I know. Our original plan sank the moment Sage's fighters shot down our shuttle."

"We saw the explosion," said Gleason. "But you continued your search."

"We did." Mops' jaw tightened.

"What is it?"

"A question." A question Mops was afraid to ask, afraid to hear the answer. Afraid to lose the possibility and hope that came from uncertainty. "I have to know. Do you have a cure for humanity? A *real* cure?"

The pity on Gleason's face gave Mops her answer. "I'm sorry." She waved an arm at the other librarians. "We weren't cured. We're just genetic flukes. A very small percentage of humans were immune to the Krakau plague. We're their descendants."

Cold disappointment washed away Mops' half-formed hopes. She closed her eyes and curled her fingers into fists, fighting tears. No cure for the half a billion ferals on Earth. No cure for the ten thousand reborn humans serving in the EMC.

"She could be lying," said Cate. "Humans are known to do that."

"I wish I was," Gleason said gently.

Mops started to say more when Monroe spoke up over the comm.

Gleason tensed. "What's that? Who are you talking to?" The other librarians closed in.

Mops held up a hand, focusing on Monroe's words. When she spoke again, her words were utterly calm, despite the tempest swirling inside her. "You have to get your people out of here. There are Alliance ships incoming."

"What?" Gleason barked an order to her people, one of whom ran for the entrance. "How do you know that?"

"I have a man positioned in the trees outside." Mops stood. "He spotted incoming fighters, six of them. They should be close enough for your people to see within minutes."

Gleason didn't move. "Quite a coincidence, the Krakau showing up so soon after you stumbled onto our location."

"It's not a coincidence." Fury roiled in her chest, threatening to escape. She hammered a fist against the wall. "I thought we'd evaded Stepping Stone. I was wrong. They must have been following our movements this whole time, waiting to see where we'd lead them."

"Aw, fuck," said Wolf.

"How did they track us?" asked Rubin.

Mops turned toward Cate. The Prodryan shrank back. "I had nothing to do with this, on my honor as a lawyer!"

He was probably telling the truth. Prodryans were terrible liars, and he had nothing to gain from selling them out to Sage. The Alliance would kill him just as fast as they would Mops and her team. She turned to speak into the comm, adjusting the volume so Gleason would hear both sides of the conversation. "Monroe, any chance the Alliance has been tapping our communications?"

"Unlikely. Everything's short-range, and EMC equipment is designed to make it as difficult as possible for an enemy to target us from orbit. More likely they projected our shuttle's course, then used drones and satellites to make visual contact."

"All right." Squaring her shoulders, she stepped toward Gleason. "This is our fault. My fault. I can't make it right, but if you give us our weapons, we'll cover your escape."

"Or they'll gun us down and drag our corpses out for the Alliance," snapped the one called Bev.

It was like an emotional circuit breaker blew inside of her. One moment Mops was drowning in anger and guilt and fear and hopelessness. The next, she felt only calm. Whatever mistakes she'd made, whatever happened next, only one thing mattered now. "Then kill us now so you can get the hell out of here. Aim for the base of the skull. You should destroy our visors and monocles as well. That will prevent the Alliance from getting our data."

"Or—and this is just a suggestion—you could hand me over to the nice librarians and I could live a long, peaceful life as a cataloging database or something."

"Three minutes," said Monroe.

"You don't have the luxury of time," Mops pressed. "We

may not be soldiers, but we can buy you time to get to safety. Either way, you have to decide now."

Gleason rubbed a hand over her face. "I must be getting soft-skulled in my old age, but I've gone this long without killing another human being. Damned if I'm gonna break that streak today. Grab your things and follow me."

9

Kumar looked up from navigation, studying the tactical display Grom had sent to the main screen. Six ships flew along the eastern edge of a major land mass. Five were tagged as small fighters. The sixth was currently unknown.

"Repeat that, Grom?" asked Kumar. It wasn't the ships' identification he was concerned with, but their origin and course.

"Six ships," Grom said. "That last looks to be some sort of troop transport. All launched from the surface."

"Not from Stepping Stone." Kumar compared the ships' projected course to that of the Pufferfish. "They're not coming for us. Their destination appears to be the same as the captain's." Relief filled his chest. "This is great news."

Both Grom and Azure turned to stare at him. Azure asked, "In what way is this great?"

"They wouldn't send this many troops for a single runaway human," said Kumar. "Five fighters and a troop carrier? The shuttle team must have survived!"

"*And now the Alliance has sent an overwhelming force to capture or kill them,*" *Azure pointed out.*

Kumar's elation faded. "*All right, so there's bad news to go with the good.*"

Grom wrapped their limbs around the gaming sphere connected to the tactical station. Targeting information appeared over the Alliance ships. "*We could attack them from here.*"

"*Not without giving away our position,*" *said Azure.*

"*For now, just keep a lock on those fighters.*" *Kumar checked his notes and began plotting a course change.* "*I'm going to shave a few hundred kilometers off our altitude. It might help with our scans. We know they're alive. The next step is to find them.*"

Azure clicked for attention. "*No offense intended, but it appears you've misprogrammed our delta-vee.*" *She'd taken the captain's station, allowing her to monitor what the others were doing.*

Kumar double-checked his numbers. "*Everything looks right.*"

"*You've increased speed,*" *said Azure.* "*I thought we were moving closer to the planet surface.*"

"*Yes.*" *Kumar blinked. Were they dealing with a translator glitch?*

Azure spoke slowly, like she was addressing a child. "*Going faster will take us farther from the planet. We want to get closer.*"

"*Lower orbit requires more speed.*" *Kumar pulled up the navigation tutorial menu and sent lesson 11-D to the viewscreen. Puffy appeared, holding a human toy called a yo-yo—essentially a wooden disk on a string.* "*Watch when he spins the yo-yo in a circle. The shorter the string, the faster the yo-yo goes.*"

On screen, the yo-yo smacked into Puffy's forehead. Cartoon stars circled his head. "*That's what happens if your descent angle is too steep,*" *Puffy said.*

"*The* Pufferfish *is not a yolo,*" *snapped Azure.*

"*It works the same way,*" *said Kumar.* "*The disk is the ship, and the string is gravity." Puffy moved on to another trick, shooting the yo-yo forward in an elliptical pattern to demonstrate another orbital principle. The yo-yo seemed like an effective teaching tool. Kumar made a note to fabricate one when he had a chance.*

Grom skittered up from their station and crossed the bridge to peer over Kumar's shoulder. "We could try to verify Kumar's course, just to be safe. What if we plug it into the flight simulator engine for Moon Invasion III?*"*

Azure flung out her tentacles. "You would entrust our lives to a video game?"

"Not just a game. Moon Invasion III! *The simulator is based on real Alliance navigation software. The game earned a 142-egg rating from Blue Glacier Reviews!"*

While they argued, Kumar quietly finished his safety checks and engaged the course correction. Whatever Captain Adamopoulos and the others were doing down there, he hoped they returned soon.

"MONROE, GET OVER HERE," Mops shouted. "We're leaving."

One of the librarians—Bev—didn't look happy about Gleason's decision to bring Mops and the others along. Bev started to argue, but Gleason silenced her with a look.

"What about Cate?" asked Wolf. "We found the library, and the mission's changed. We don't really need him anymore, right?"

Cate spread his wings to expose the blades and advanced on Wolf. "She is correct. Given what you've uncovered, your best course of action is to kill me. I will, of course, endeavor to take as many of you with me as possible."

"Oh, for drought's sake." Mops picked up her combat baton as Wolf and Cate circled one another, waited until Cate's back was to her, and smacked the Prodryan in the back of the head. Cate dropped to the floor. "Tie him up. Use something his wings can't cut through, and be careful with his arms. They're greasy."

Monroe joined them as Rubin and Wolf were wrapping Cate in the same blanket Wolf had been tied up in minutes before. The trap had used old electrical cable for the snare, which Wolf used to bind the blanket in place. By the time they finished, only Cate's head and feet were exposed.

Wolf hoisted the Prodryan over her shoulder. "We'd be safer killing him."

"We'd be safer if we'd stuck with cleaning water filtration systems for the Krakau," Mops responded. She retrieved her pistol, watching the librarians to see if anyone objected. If they did, they kept it to themselves. By now, Mops could hear the fighters' engines growling in the distance.

Gleason led them through the large circular reading room toward the back of the building. There, she switched on a handheld lamp. The beam illuminated dusty shelves full of old knickknacks. "Gift shop." She waved a hand. "Anyone wants a souvenir, they'd better be quick about it."

Mops snagged a tarnished metal pin of a book over crossed torches, bordered by a wreath of leaves, and stuffed it into a pocket.

On the far side of the gift shop, a partially-collapsed wall led to a descending stairwell. Gleason stood to one side, motioning her people through. "Keep to the left. The steps are sturdier on that side. Avoid the third and seventh unless you want a broken ankle."

Mops went in next, wanting to get ahead of Wolf and Monroe in case either of them stumbled. Despite Wolf's burden and Monroe's glitching balance, both made it down without a problem. Rubin followed, walking backward with her rifle pointed up the stairs.

A doorway at the bottom led into a dank, dark corridor with broken brick walls and a floor of cracked tile. Water dripped from old pipes overhead. Mops wiped her visor. "What is all this?"

"Late twenty-first century city planning," said Gleason. "Lots of tunnels for mass transportation and pedestrian traffic."

"What's to stop the Krakau troops from following us?" asked Monroe.

"The water should wash away our tracks." Gleason followed the other librarians into a small room to one side. A waist-high counter jutted from the wall to the right. Bev and another librarian moved to a broken-down vending machine, full of shelves and metal coils. They hauled it away from the wall to reveal a narrow passageway.

"We've built some additions over the years," Gleason continued.

Rocks and broken cinder blocks were pressed into place for walls. Wooden beams provided additional support, holding up a crude plywood ceiling. The ground was rough gravel and puddles of stagnant water.

Rubin helped Bev haul the vending machine back into place behind them. If the Krakau did follow them down, it would be a while before they discovered this passage. They'd likely continue up the main tunnel first.

Doc overlaid a map of the surface on Mops' visor, showing them to be moving roughly north from the library. After two hundred meters, Gleason called a halt and pulled what looked like a strip of coiled black metal from a pouch at her belt. She unrolled it into a flat band about twenty centimeters long. When she pressed it to her wrist, the ends curled around to cinch her sleeve. A series of green dots lit up along the front edge.

She opened her hand and bent her wrist inward. The band projected a keyboard onto the skin of her palm. Gleason began typing with her other hand.

The ceiling shook, shivering dirt and pebbles down on their heads. "That would be the ships touching down," said Monroe. "They'll keep at least one in the air to continue recon and provide cover fire if needed."

Melvil shifted nervously. "All this racket is going to spook the pack. If they panic—"

Gleason didn't look up from her keyboard. "If you think I'm going to let you run off alone again after all this, you're out of your damned mind."

His face turned bright red. "I'd stay out of sight."

"What kind of animals?" asked Rubin.

Melvil whirled. "They're not animals."

"That's a matter of ongoing debate. The Board still isn't sold on this project." Gleason paused in her typing. "Melvil specializes in anthropology and animal husbandry. For the past three years, he's been tending to the local pack of feral humans."

Bev snorted. "This fool thinks he can civilize the—"

"Don't." Melvil puffed out his chest like a lovesick Krakau. "If you use the Z-word, I'll—"

"Bev, don't provoke him." The fourth librarian stepped smoothly between them. "Melvil, don't take her bait." He waited a beat until they both backed down, then turned his attention to Mops. "Mohammad Khatami. I specialize in religious studies."

He bowed his upper body forty-five degrees, then straightened and thrust his hand in Mops' direction. When Mops didn't move, he smiled and said, "The bow and the handshake were two of the more common human greetings. Traditionally, you could either return the bow or grasp my hand."

Mops opted for the bow, and his smile widened, revealing several missing lower teeth. Like the other librarians, Khatami wore bulky white-and-gray clothing and a belt weighed down by a large knife and other tools. A leather thong with an array of metal charms or amulets hung round his neck. Each charm was different. Mops spotted several different stars, a flower, a cross, a moon, and many more.

His black hair was a short, tousled mess, and a thin black scruff of beard circled his mouth. Bright blue eyes contrasted sharply with his tanned face.

It was the first time things had calmed enough for Mops to really study the other librarians. Melvil appeared to be the youngest. Freckles and pimples dotted his smooth face, and hair the color of flame peeked out from the edges of his helmet. He wore metal-framed glasses with large round lenses that made his eyes appear smaller. He was slightly taller than Bev, but thinner.

Bev looked most like the humans Mops was used to—a fighter with the scars to prove it. In addition to whatever damage the eye patch hid, she sported a pale gash along the side of her neck, and what appeared to be an old animal bite on her left hand. She had the squat, beefy build of a brawler.

Gleason switched off her keyboard but left her bracelet in place. "We need to put more distance between us and the library."

"You have somewhere safe to hide?" asked Monroe.

Gleason hesitated.

"She does," Mops guessed. "But she doesn't trust us enough to take us there."

"Got it in one," said Gleason. "There are other places we can wait out the Alliance. Half this city was underground."

"What about the pack?" asked Melvil. "You know what happens if they get worked up."

Mops turned to Melvil. "These ferals you've been taking care of. Any chance you gave them shoes and clothing?" Taking his wide-eyed stare as confirmation, she added, "We found one wandering around in a deerskin robe northwest of here."

"You found Bobby?" Melvil pressed closer. "Was he all right? Can you take me to where you saw him?"

"Sure," Wolf snorted. "I'm sure all those Alliance troops up there will be happy to look the other way while we chase your runaway feral."

"That's what you were doing when you were spotted," Mops realized. "You'd gone out searching for . . . for Bobby."

His lips tightened. His eyes darted sideways toward Gleason.

"Despite orders to wait for a proper hunting party," Gleason said.

"That trap in the library," said Mops. "The one Wolf fell into, with the raw meat. That was for him, too?"

A quick nod. "I'm not sure how he got out this time. He's the escape artist. The rest are content to stay in one place, unless they get scared. The sound of those ships, the voices of strange troops moving around on the surface . . ."

"The ferals will want to hunt or run away," finished Rubin.

"Good riddance, if you ask me," said Bev.

"We didn't," Gleason snapped. "All right, so far the only thing the Alliance has is a clip of Melvil."

"Unless they spotted you moving in on the library," said Monroe.

"Dammit. All right, so they may know there are four humans running about. That's bad. If the pack gets out and goes after the Alliance troops, it'll be worse."

"Ferals attacking the Alliance?" Wolf looked around. "Why is this a problem?"

"Those soldiers would slaughter them," Melvil protested.

"More importantly," said Gleason, "the sight of an entire pack of healthy, clothed ferals would tell those troops there are bigger things happening down here, even more than they already know. They'd send more ships to scour the city."

"I'm sorry," said Melvil. "I shouldn't have gone after Bobby like that. I just—"

Gleason waved it off. "Que sera, sera. Do you think you can keep them calm and out of sight?"

Melvil was bouncing in his boots. "Absolutely!"

"What if he's wrong?" asked Bev. "Or what if the Alliance finds their way to the ferals? What if they collapse a tunnel on top of him?"

"I could send Rubin along to provide protection," Mops offered.

"Could I tag along?" asked Wolf.

Mops blinked back her surprise. "Really?"

"The kid says he's got a pack of tame ferals. I'd like to see that."

Mops looked to Gleason. This was her territory, and her command. Her mouth twisted, and then she nodded once. "If things go to hell, you get out of there, understood?"

Mops moved toward Wolf and Rubin. "And if he refuses, you drag him out."

Gleason didn't say anything, but her eyes crinkled, and she tilted her head in appreciation.

"Come on." Melvil grabbed Wolf's arm, then grimaced. "Why don't you take up the rear. No offense, but you stink."

The ground trembled as yet another ship landed.

"How long before they get bored and head home?" asked Bev.

"Standard procedure will be to secure the building first." Monroe's words were distant. He stared back into the tunnel as if he could see all the way to the library. "They'll start with security drones. The drones will find their way underground, building a map as they go."

"What happens if they don't find anything?" asked Mops.

"Depends on the mission parameters. Maybe they bring down more troops. Maybe they leave a handful of drones in place and fly back to Stepping Stone. Or maybe they try harder to flush us out."

She didn't like the sound of that. "How?"

"Bombs," Monroe said coldly. "Lots of bombs."

Wolf's visor tracked her steps and plotted a map as she walked, making it impossible to get truly lost. Without it, she could have probably wandered down here forever, or at least until she starved. Or something ate her.

Melvil never paused as he led them through the various twists and turns, dodging old cave-ins and, in one case, a nest of angry buzzing insects.

They'd gone half a kilometer before leaving the rickety, hand-built tunnel for something less likely to collapse and crush you to death if you so much as coughed. That juncture was hidden behind a metal mirror in what Melvil assured them was an old human bathroom, despite the fact that Wolf didn't recognize several of the appliances. Melvil had stammered a bit when explaining the long trough on one wall, and had utterly refused to demonstrate the thing he called a "bidet."

From there, they walked along an old platform next to a narrow stream Melvil said had once been a monorail line. The tunnel walls were colored bricks—not stone, but some sort of hardened synthetic. Black bricks formed letters her visor wouldn't translate.

Wolf's threat display lit up as a long, serpentine shape swam through the water beside them. It approached the edge and raised a flat, scaly head to study the humans.

Wolf brought her rifle around, locking the crosshairs on the thing.

"Boa constrictor," said Melvil. "Humans used to keep them as pets. They've adapted pretty well to this part of the world. They're dormant right now on the surface, but the water down here is warm enough for them to hunt. It won't hurt you."

The snake flicked a forked tongue in their direction and ducked back into the water. Rubin stepped to the edge to watch it swim away.

"I know what you're thinking," said Wolf, "and Mops will kill you if you bring back a two-meter snake."

"It belongs here." Once the snake had disappeared, Rubin rejoined Melvil to ask, "How many feral humans in your pack?"

"Ninety-four, counting Bobby." Melvil paused at a three-way intersection, head cocked like he was listening. "Including four babies under a year old."

"What do you feed them?"

"They prefer meat, but they're not picky about what kind. Bison or rat, it's all the same. I try to mix in some grains and vegetable matter, and we add nutritional supplements to the water. You can see the difference in their skin, teeth, and hair."

"That's wonderful," said Rubin. "Does the healthier diet affect their behavior?"

He nodded eagerly. "They're less aggressive when they're well-fed and healthy."

This was the other reason Wolf had volunteered to come along. Rubin was so absorbed in conversation, she wouldn't have noticed if a boa constrictor crawled up her body and ate her head.

A glint of light caught Wolf's eye. She switched off her lamp. As her visor compensated, she began to see pinpricks of pink-tinged light scattered over the ceiling. They weren't moving. Wolf poked one with her rifle. "What are those?"

"Optical fibers," said Melvil. "They capture, store, and transmit daylight from the surface. It's how they used to light up these tunnels. Most either broke or wore out over the years, but there are a couple of places where a cluster survived. They're supposed to be white, but they lose part of the spectrum with age."

"Creepy," Wolf proclaimed. "Like a bunch of tiny eyeballs staring at you."

The platform widened, with corridors leading in four different directions. A set of tile stairs looked like it might have once led to the surface. Now, it simply led to an impassible wall of rubble.

Melvil took them to the farthest passage, which was blocked by rusted floor-to-ceiling turnstiles. He used a key from around his neck to unlock a padlock and chain. The bars barely squeaked as they rotated to let him through. Someone had been keeping them oiled.

"What's this?" asked Wolf.

"It used to be the recycling and fabrication center. There's a whole factory and warehouse down here." He used a different key to unchain a heavy metal door to the right. "The ferals mostly stay in the warehouse. We're going down through the cargo elevator shaft. It's the only entrance that isn't flooded or caved in."

Wolf shone her lamp into the shaft. It looked like a ten-meter drop, and she could see light coming from below. She turned her attention upward. "Oh, hell."

The elevator car hung less than a meter overhead. Cobwebs and rust obscured parts of the mechanism, but she could see where the emergency brakes had clamped onto metal rails on either side of the shaft.

Rather, one of the brakes was clamped into place. The other had sheared free, leaving the car at a slight angle. "What happens if that thing comes down on our heads?"

Rubin peeked over Wolf's shoulder and, in her matter-of-fact tone, said, "We'd die."

"Relax, I do this all the time." Melvil grabbed a chain sitting on the floor to one side, hooked one end over a thick bent bolt sticking out of the wall, and lowered the rest into the darkness. "Between the rust and mud and everything else, I think it's pretty much stuck."

He tightened the straps of his pack, grabbed the chain in both hands, and started down.

Thanks to her helmet's amplification, Wolf heard the groans from below the moment she began following. The sound made the hair on her neck stand on end.

"Watch your step down here," Melvil called.

Wolf's muscles tightened. "Not so loud!"

One of the two elevator doors at the bottom was wrenched open at an angle, creating a triangular gap. Wolf switched her rifle to burst mode and ducked through after Melvil.

A short, square passage opened into a cavernous warehouse. Broken-down machinery hung from overhead rails, like amputated robot limbs hung out to rust. Small transport vehicles sat on broken tires.

The shuffling of leather-clad feet over concrete joined the groans echoing through the warehouse. Wolf wrinkled her nose. She'd breathed much worse in her SHS days, but the air here smelled *wrong*, even more than the skunk scent that continued to cling to her uniform. It smelled like rotted meat and old vomit and death.

Her visor began to highlight movement and potential threats: four figures peeking around an overturned bin to the right; two more beneath a broken conveyor; one squeezed onto the top of a set of shelves on the wall to her left.

"They're upset." Melvil slipped one arm from his pack and dug around inside until he found a canvas sack. He untied the neck and pulled out a handful of speckled crackers. "Who wants venison jerky hardtack?"

Wolf raised her hand.

Melvil blinked but handed one over. The cracker was hard, tough, and salty. Wolf approved.

"Don't worry, they're not going to hurt you." Melvil tossed several of the crackers toward the ferals by the bin.

"You talking to me or to them?" asked Wolf.

"Both."

More shapes stumbled from the shadows. Melvil beamed. "That's right. You're safe. I wouldn't let anything happen to you."

Rubin cocked her head. "You grossly overestimate your control over events. Entropy guarantees things happen to all of us."

Two ferals stepped into the pink light from a cluster of optical fibers. Like the one Wolf had seen in the woods, these two wore simple capes. The female's was leather, the male's heavy canvas.

Wolf's rifle tracked them both as Melvil moved closer, hardtack outstretched. The male snatched the crackers from Melvil.

"Don't be rude, Greg. Share with your sister." When "Greg" bared his teeth, Melvil sighed and dug out two more crackers, which he put directly into the other feral's hand. She grunted and darted out of reach. "You're welcome, Marcia."

"You can communicate with them?" asked Rubin.

"Not really. They understand tone more than words, though

a few of them recognize their names. They make different sounds when they're hungry or scared or content, but we've never found any particular meaning that would suggest words. Maybe someday."

As if Greg and Marcia had cleared the way, more ferals began to approach, until Wolf's threat display was a solid blob of green.

Melvil continued to distribute food and chat with the ferals. To Rubin, he said, "Do you see the fresh blood on their hands? They pound the walls when they're frightened."

"Trying to escape?" asked Rubin.

"Kind of. They can get out if they have to. There's a crack in the foundation near the northwest corner. That's how Bobby got loose. But they like it here." A commotion by one of the transport vehicles caught his attention. "Cindy! Stop chewing on your mother!"

A fighter passed overhead, engines sounding like a distant growl. The moans of the ferals grew deeper. Several started hammering their fists on the nearest wall, including one wearing what appeared to be an oversized yellow-and-blue bucket on its head.

Melvil sighed. "That's Peter. He has issues."

Peter turned at the sound of Melvil's voice, then began banging his bucket-clad head against a metal shelf.

"It's warm in here," said Rubin.

"Geothermal. It's how a lot of places managed the temperature in the old days. Those heat pumps were built to last." He stepped toward the transport vehicle, where a young feral—Cindy—was gnawing on an older one. "I've got to break this up. If they get too stressed, they'll eat anything and anyone. I once saw a feral who'd eaten his own left arm all the way to the elbow."

Melvil threw hardtack in Cindy's direction, but she ignored him. Ferals crawled out to snatch the crackers. Others circled around behind them, groaning for more.

"Melvil . . ." said Wolf.

"It's all right. They're just hungry."

Sweat dripped down Wolf's back. "That makes it *less* all right!"

"Don't shout." Rubin touched Wolf's arm. "You'll scare them."

"Scare *them*?" Whistling a curse in Liktok, Wolf followed Melvil. By now, her visor had identified sixty-three individual ferals, with more approaching from deeper in the warehouse.

Cindy was a thin girl, less than a meter and a half tall, with wide eyes, ragged blonde hair, and bright, bloody teeth.

Melvil shoved his bag of hardtack at Wolf. "Keep the others fed."

"But—oh, hell." Wolf shouldered her rifle and grabbed a handful of the gritty crackers.

Knobby fingers closed on her sleeve. Biting back a yell, Wolf spun and shoved crackers into the thing's mouth.

"One at a time might work better," Rubin murmured.

Melvil was whispering to Cindy and stroking her hair. He cupped his other hand under her jaw and tried to pry her chin away. After what felt like an eternity, Cindy released her mother's arm . . . and lunged at Melvil.

"Shit!" Wolf dropped the crackers and reached for her rifle. Rubin caught the barrel, stopping her from targeting the feral.

Melvil had brought his other arm up, anticipating the attack. Cindy's jaws clamped down on the leather bracer he wore. She began to snarl and chew contentedly. And drool.

"It's all right," said Melvil. Wolf wasn't sure if he was addressing her or the feral.

A mob of ferals now surrounded them, fighting over the spilled hardtack. "Sorry," said Wolf.

Melvil grinned. "You know they're going to remember you now. You're the human who gave them all the food." He continued to comb his free hand through Cindy's hair. "Rubin, there are bandages in the lower right pocket of my pack. Could you wrap Cindy's mother's arm, please?"

"On it," said Rubin.

The mother bared her teeth but allowed Rubin to examine the bloody bites on her arm. Rubin snatched a cracker from the floor and handed it to her to chew on, which seemed to help. "They must eat more than just crackers."

"Of course," said Melvil. "The crackers are more like treats. Have you noticed this place is completely clear of rats, cockroaches, and other vermin? We also bring in animals from time to time. When one of our bison broke both front legs, we split the meat with the ferals." He grinned. "They gorged themselves and slept for two days straight."

A hand touched Wolf's hip, and she jumped, but it was just a skinny, gray-haired feral demanding another cracker. Wolf checked the bottom of the sack and shoved a broken piece into his hand. "Why do you do all of this? You're treating them like Rubin and her weird pets, but her pets won't *eat* you."

"My leech drinks human blood," said Rubin.

Cindy's eyes were half-closed. She'd mostly stopped chewing Melvil's forearm, though the drooling had increased. He carefully extracted himself. "We've been studying biology and genetics for generations. Including research on the minimum genetic diversity you'd need to sustain a long-term human population."

It took a moment for Wolf to follow. "You don't have enough people."

"Each generation of librarians has been smaller than the last." Melvil reclaimed the empty bag from Wolf and began moving toward the exit. The ferals parted to let him through. "If we had good medical and genetic tech, it might be possible, but we're limited to what we can salvage and recreate."

The Krakau had that kind of technology. Wolf snarled under her breath, making several ferals draw back in alarm. "Someone might still figure out how to cure us."

"Maybe." Melvil shrugged, seeming utterly at ease with his own pending extinction. Surrounded by ferals, he was the most relaxed Wolf had seen him. "But we can't count on that. From the tests I've run, when they're well-fed and cared for, ferals have roughly the same intelligence and learning abilities as the more advanced primates. I'm trying to give them an evolutionary head start."

"Head start?"

"At becoming Earth's next intelligent species, after we're gone."

10

Pachelbel automatically drowned her resentment as she entered what had been, until recently, her office. Little had changed in the covelike room. The air was a bit warmer, the lights a bit dimmer. It felt ridiculously large compared to the tiny closet of an office she'd been assigned at the ass end of the station.

The U-shaped computer console appeared to float on the edge of the water. Behind it, Fleet Admiral Belle-Bonne Sage of Interstellar Military Command waited patiently, two of her three tentacles resting on the controls.

Sage didn't acknowledge Pachelbel, nor did she invite her into the water—both clear signs of displeasure. When Sage did speak, her voice was deceptively calm and atonal. "What are they doing on Earth?"

Pachelbel kept her coloration and body language neutral. "Who?"

"There is no way a clutch of barely sentient janitors, no matter how exceptional, could have done all this without help."

"I take it Mops and her team have eluded your ships?"

"My troops have found nothing. One was injured when a stair collapsed under her weight. Another was searching a nearby stream when one of the native serpents apparently mistook one of her limbs for another Earth serpent and attempted to mate with it."

"Is she all right?"

"She suffered internal injuries, but she'll survive." Sage settled back, letting her tentacles float on the brine. "You've worked with humans longer than anyone else on this station. It's said you even like them. How would you suggest I apprehend this group?"

"If you believe my expertise would be helpful, the logical course is to turn command of the mission over to me."

Sage shifted, causing her shells to grate against one another like stones.

"Are a few humans really worth the full attention of a Fleet Admiral of the EMC?" Pachelbel pressed. "Shouldn't one of your rank and status have greater priorities?"

The barb struck home. Sage swam closer and snapped, "My priority is protecting the Krakau Alliance."

Pachelbel rippled a tentacle in a shrug. "I'm not sure I understand how disrupting operations on Stepping Stone, not to mention cutting the outflow of cured humans to the EMC, helps the Alliance."

"I don't need your understanding."

Pachelbel couldn't quite stop the tips of her tentacles from curling in annoyance. She hadn't been condescended to like this since the early days of her career.

Satisfaction at a scored point darkened Sage's skin. "How do I catch Adamopoulos and her crew?"

"I'm not sure you can," said Pachelbel. "This is their world. They're adapted to the environment. It would be like chasing a Glacidae through a glacier, or a Rokkau through the northern currents of Dobranok."

Sage twitched at mention of the Rokkau. "Thank you, Admiral. You can return to your duties, such as they are."

Low-level paperwork and routine station maintenance, all of which was doubtless monitored by Krakau techs loyal to Sage. It was a painfully boring impasse. Pachelbel couldn't act to help Mops with Sage's people watching her, and Sage couldn't arrest an EMC admiral without proof.

Sage turned to the console. "This is Fleet Admiral Sage. Pull back and send in the bomber. Flatten everything in a half-kilometer radius. We'll see if that flushes them out."

THUNDER ROLLED THROUGH THE tunnel. Dirt and rocks rained down, rattling off Mops' helmet. A short distance behind her, a vertical support beam splintered, sending tiny daggers of wood in all directions.

"How sturdy are these tunnels?" asked Mops.

"They've held up for a long time." Gleason's voice rose. "'Course, nobody's ever dropped a damn bomb on them before!"

Four more explosions followed. A cloud of dust darkened the air. And then, silence.

"Is that it?" asked Cate.

"That's the first round." Monroe swiped a rag over his visor. "Now they'll watch to see if we pop out. Probably monitoring from ships and satellites both."

"And when we fail to scurry into the open like frightened rabbits?" asked Bev.

Monroe tucked the rag back into his harness. "They start round two, then send people down to sift through the rubble."

Mops had never observed an EMC bombing run, but she knew enough to imagine what the attack had done to that proud, ancient library. Every statue shattered and buried. Every stubborn flake of color that had endured all these years, gone. And the books . . . how much of humanity's literature and history had just been lost forever?

She tried to tell herself most of those books had been

destroyed already. Certainly the one she'd touched had been beyond repair. The bombs hadn't killed the library; they'd simply buried the corpse.

That didn't make her feel any better.

Khatami stood in stunned silence. Mops searched for words. As hard as this was hitting her, how must the librarians be feeling?

"Captain?" asked Monroe.

"I'm all right." One hand rested on her combat baton. "Doc, remind me to track down Admiral Sage when this is all over so I can express my displeasure."

"I've updated your To Do List." Even the AI sounded subdued.

Cate shook dust from his wings. "I'll have to review the Alliance Rules of Engagement, but I believe that attack may have been illegal. Although the mere fact that you *have* rules limiting military engagement is puzzling, and one more reason you will all ultimately fall before the Prodryan—"

Monroe grasped the Prodryan's shoulder and squeezed. "Not now."

Mops nodded her thanks and turned to Gleason. She started to speak, but the words wouldn't come. *I'm sorry*, was pitifully inadequate.

Khatami had dropped to his knees, mumbling in yet another language Mops didn't recognize.

"I believe it might be Latin," said Doc, presumably following her gaze and guessing her thoughts.

"What's he doing?" Mops whispered.

"Praying." Gleason paused. "And it's 'they.'"

"What?"

"Khatami. They're . . . the Krakau didn't make up a Human term for it. The closest would be pangender. They could give you an hour-long lecture about how this is the more spiritually pure and honest choice, but the short version is Khatami thinks gender is dumb."

"Doc, pass that along to the others, please." She watched

Khatami a moment longer. "The Glacidae prefer 'they' as well. It's definitely not for spiritual reasons, though."

"We should keep moving," said Monroe. "They'll widen the attack radius for the next round."

"We'll catch up with Melvil and the rest of your people on the way." Gleason brought her lamp closer to Mops' face. "Are you all right?"

"No." Mops swallowed. "How many books did we . . . did you just lose?"

Gleason studied her for what felt like a long time. Her gray brows bunched together. Finally, she nodded to herself like she was making a decision. She reached into her jacket and pulled out a black rectangular block on a leather cord. "None."

"I don't understand. The library—"

"A hundred and fifty years ago, when they realized humanity wasn't going to beat this plague, a group of librarians began working to scan and preserve as many books and records as they could. It took more than a century, but we were able to make backups of everything that was salvageable." She removed the necklace for Mops to see. "Nanofilament drive. Primitive stuff compared to what you're used to, but more than enough for our purposes. These were manufactured in Karachi more than two hundred years ago. The company used to boast they'd last a millennium. Every adult librarian carries one."

Mops' hands shook as she touched the drive. The surface was so smooth it felt and looked like liquid.

"Don't get me wrong," Gleason continued, her expression hardening. "I'm not happy about losing yet another piece of our history. But the knowledge of that old place? That's all safe."

Mops' body slowly began to unclench. "Doc?"

"I know what you're going to ask, but I can't read nanofil. We'd need to pick up some specialized hardware. Sorry."

Mops returned the drive. "I know I have no right to ask this, but if you have any extra copies . . ."

"We'll see." Gleason tucked the necklace back out of sight,

then clapped a hand on Mops' shoulder. "Let's get the hell out of here."

"I'm picking up telemetry from Rubin's and Wolf's uniforms. They're both alive. Heart rates and respiration are elevated. Wolf has sustained damage to her left sleeve. The pattern looks like . . . teeth marks?"

"What about Melvil?" asked Mops. They'd reentered the larger, more structurally sound tunnels ten minutes ago, but this was the first time Doc had managed to contact the others.

Gleason stopped to listen. Bev fell in beside her, gun in hand. "Damn ferals. If they ate Melvil, I'm gonna kill him."

"Visual feed is spotty, but I believe he's alive as well."

"They're all alive," said Mops. "Doc, how far away are we?"

"One hundred sixty meters."

She fought the impulse to run. These tunnels were uneven and unfamiliar. Mops couldn't help her people if she slipped and snapped an ankle. "Wolf, Rubin, we're almost to you. Can you hear me?"

Between the tunnels and the bombardment overhead, communications had been spotty. Wolf's voice crackled back a moment later. "—you, sir. Melvil is—picked up an extra—"

A minute later, Mops spotted the lights from Wolf's and Rubin's harnesses. Her visor compensated for the glare, allowing her to make out the shapes of three people. Melvil leaned heavily on Rubin for support.

"It's us," Wolf called. "Don't shoot." As she came closer, Mops saw she was carrying a bloodied feral child in her arms.

Cate jumped back, shaking his wings to free his blades. "Keep that thing away from us!"

"Put those away before I feed them to you," Wolf snapped. "Cindy's not gonna hurt anyone."

Melvil removed his arm from Rubin's shoulders. Tears streaked the dust, sweat, and blood on Melvil's cheeks. "The ferals were doing all right until the bombing started up again," he said. "I was trying to keep them calm, when the back part of the warehouse collapsed. I don't know how many we lost."

His left hand dripped blood. Parallel cuts along his neck suggested he'd been scratched as well.

"The ferals panicked," Wolf said bluntly. "Not Melvil, though. He just kept at it, talking and trying to help. Some of the ferals tried to hide or escape. The rest turned vicious. Came after us and each other."

"Is that what happened to her?" asked Mops, nodding toward the feral in Wolf's arms.

"Cindy was hurt pretty bad. I couldn't just leave her there."

"You most certainly could have," Cate countered.

"Nobody asked you, snot-moth," Wolf shot back.

"Take it easy, both of you." Mops focused on Wolf. "How'd you get her out in all that chaos?"

Wolf shrugged. "Carried her."

"Wolf fought past several ferals to reach the elevator shaft," said Rubin. "She held Cindy while Melvil and I climbed out. She tried to pass Cindy up to us. That's when Cindy bit Wolf's arm. Fortunately, Wolf's swearing and shouting seemed to calm Cindy down. I think she found it soothing."

"Wolf, soothing?" Monroe shook his head. "First time for everything."

Bev had pulled Melvil aside and was examining the younger man's hand. With surprising gentleness, she tugged Melvil's glove free and used a small water bottle to clean the bloody bite mark. "I told you your gloves weren't strong enough, dumbass."

"The average cured human jaw can produce eighty kilograms of pressure," said Rubin. "But ferals build up stronger jaw muscles. According to Kumar, their bite is closer to a hundred and ten kilograms."

Melvil turned toward Gleason. "We have to go back. They're trapped down there. They could be hurt."

"Hold still till I get this bandage tied off," Bev snapped.

"The Alliance will send another round of drones into the

tunnels," said Monroe. "If we want to stay ahead of them, we have to keep moving."

"He's right," said Khatami. "Our capture helps nobody. Who will protect the ferals if the Alliance takes you away, Melvil?"

Melvil swiped his good hand across his face. "What about Cindy? If we get her back to— I mean, I need to get her some-place I can take care of her until she recovers."

Gleason pursed her lips, then turned to say something in Nishnaabemwin. Whatever it was earned an angry response from Bev, followed by more measured words from Khatami.

After several quick exchanges, Gleason switched to Human. "The only reason we've stayed hidden all these decades is because the Alliance didn't know to look for us. That part of our history is over. We've always had contingency plans. It's time to start implementing them."

"The Alliance didn't know to look for us because we didn't bring Alliance guns home to meet the family," Bev countered.

"Did she call us guns?" asked Mops.

"Slang for cured soldiers working for the Krakau," said Khatami. "The Alliance uses you as weapons. You're nothing but guns to them."

"Bullshit." Mops glanced back at her team. "Some of us were plungers."

That drew a chuckle. "It's not a nice term," said Gleason. "And you *won't* hear it again."

Bev grimaced, but didn't argue.

"No offense intended, Eliza, but you can't make this decision alone," said Khatami.

Gleason stopped walking. Without raising her voice, she asked, "I'm still Head Librarian, aren't I?"

"Yes, ma'am. But this choice will affect the safety and future of us all. This should go to the Board for a full vote."

Melvil looked pointedly at Wolf, who still carried the feral in her arms. "I trust them."

Cate chittered. "A Prodryan commander would kill you all for such insubordination."

"If we were following Prodryan rules, we would have killed you hours ago," Mops pointed out.

Cate flicked his antennae. "Exactly."

"All right." Gleason pulled out the keyboard for her wrist comm and typed in a quick message. "I've called for a vote. Let's move."

"Where?" asked Wolf.

Gleason's lips curled upward. "We're going to a sports bar."

For the next hour, they walked in relative silence, broken only by occasional questions from Wolf. Questions that mostly alternated between "How much farther?" and "What's that?"

The librarians refused to answer the first question, but took turns with the second, identifying and explaining everything from an ancient fire extinguisher to the remnants of a personal transport scooter to the nature of a filthy plastic sign among a pile of bricks.

Khatami brushed off the sign, revealing cracked yellow-and-red plastic. "This was one of the food service kiosks serving the tunnels. It was called a McDonald's."

"Ah." Wolf nodded wisely. "Scottish."

Their mouth twitched. "Why would you think that?"

"The captain lets me read from her library. She's got a couple of good historical romances about Scotsmen."

"The true origins of McDonald's have been lost," said Khatami. "From what we've pieced together, we believe it was founded by an old circus clown named Willard Scott."

"Humans are strange," said Cate.

Mops wanted to argue, but all in all, it was a difficult defense to make.

"Up here." Gleason aimed her lamp at a literal hole in the wall, half-buried by rock. The air was colder here. Water had dripped through the ceiling, leaving frozen trails over broken bricks. Movement lit up Mops' visor, but it was only a pair of rats scurrying away.

"Wolf, Monroe, keep watch here. You, too, Cate." Mops didn't know what was involved in this vote, but she doubted random snark from the Prodryan would help their case. She waited for their acknowledgment, then followed the librarians through the hole.

The walls inside were bare brick, much of which had fallen away to reveal rusted metal beams. Cockroaches skittered along the floor, disappearing into cracks between old tiles.

"This used to be called Sammy D's, a century and a half ago," said Gleason. "Best pizza in the city. These days, it's one of our communications centers."

Old hooks and braces on the walls showed where decorations had once hung. Judging from the wires and cables jutting out, some of those decorations had been electrical. Mops saw nothing resembling a working comm station.

The librarians moved carefully around an old wooden bar. Fragments of filthy mirrored glass clung to the back wall.

The floor squished and sank beneath Mops' feet as she followed. "This place needs a full sterilization."

"I would recommend a demolition team," said Rubin.

Through another doorway was what must have once been the kitchen. Stagnant water pooled, half-frozen, in sinks and bins. A metal door hung open, leading into a large freezer.

"The Board of Directors is made up of five senior librarians, including me," Gleason explained, passing the freezer and making her way toward what looked like a small office. "As Head Librarian, I run the day-to-day operations, but the Board as a group is responsible for long-term planning and strategy. They're elected by the group at large every three years."

"That sounds . . . inefficient," said Mops.

Gleason snorted. "Democracy often is. But it keeps things in balance, for the most part. Remind me to tell you about the Cataloging Rebellion of 2159. That came about through a combination of incompetent Board members and a Head Librarian on a power trip. . . ."

She stepped into the office and approached a metal safe that had fallen partly free of the wall. A thick metal cable stretched from the back of the safe into the pile of broken brick. "Back in the late twenty-nineties, the big attraction was virtual sports. Computers with detailed stats on athletes from throughout history would simulate matchups. You could watch Serena Williams kick McEnroe's ass in tennis, or pit the 1989 Milan soccer team against Manchester United from 2073. You could race Usain Bolt from 2009 against himself in 2007. You could select fictional characters, too. One of the best boxing matches I ever saw was between Muhammad Ali at his peak in the mid-60s and Rocky Balboa."

Mops felt like she was drowning in the barrage of names and dates. She opened her mouth to respond, but had no idea what to say.

Khatami chuckled and leaned in. "Gleason is a bit of a sports fanatic. I find it best to smile and nod."

"Our species produced some amazing athletes." Gleason yanked open the front of the safe—the lock mechanism had been burned away—to reveal a black cube roughly ten centimeters to a side. A single green light blinked slowly in one corner.

"Sammy D's was one of thousands of broadcasting centers," Khatami explained, while Gleason slid a small rod into the cube. "Patrons would bet on the matches. Everything ran on a closed system, solid state with minimal heat or wasted power, designed to last forever. They don't, but as of last week, there were still ninety-three units chuffing away across the world, generating random matchups and broadcasting to long-dead subscribers."

"What a horrific fate for a computer," said Doc.

"The Krakau know about the broadcasts, of course," said Bev. "They pick up all the old junk signals. But they don't know shit about human sports, so they have no idea we piggyback messages onto these broadcasts."

Gleason removed her communications bracelet and flattened it into a long rectangular ribbon, which she placed onto the top of the cube. A second green light flashed twice. "That's how our personal comm units work," she said. "Simple messages are sent as dialogue between the athletes. For more complex conversations, you need a broadcasting unit."

A flickering red keyboard grid appeared on top of the cube. "We use an encryption system based on errors manually edited into the athletes' stats. Suddenly Ali's right hook is three points weaker, and his weight jumps six kilos. I'm setting up a three-on-three basketball game. That should give all five members of the Board their own voice."

"What happens if the vote goes against us?" asked Mops.

"Don't worry. Nancy trusts me, and I've got leverage on Jessamyn. That means I'll be able to get a majority vote. We won't leave you to be shot by Krakau or eaten by wild humans."

"I appreciate that," Mops said dryly.

Gleason stopped typing. "You lot might be janitors, but you're the closest thing we've got to trained soldiers. You can show your appreciation by helping me keep my people alive."

11

[Load config.basketball.3x3.173.12] Initializing . . .
[Verify credit override] /usr/adm/umich/lib/admin.*
[Load characters] Initializing . . .

ErrorType: Checksum

@broadcast.node loadfail
module.dialogue.1-6 alpha-channel
load dialogue.beta.1-6
loadsuccess

   Three-on-three virtual basketball commencing soon!
      You have one minute to place your bets!

Gleason: Situation summary sent in alpha channel. Please confirm.

Pearl: Summary received. Are you all right, Eliza?

Gleason: Fine for the moment. Need a vote.

West: If the Alliance finds LockLand, we're done. It's too big a risk.

McCook: Point of order. You can't jump to a vote without a motion.

Gleason: Fine. I move for a vote on allowing Captain Adamopoulos and her people access to LockLand.

Naudé: Seconded.

McCook: Point of information. Does the Head Librarian's motion consider "people" to include the Prodryan?

Gleason: Yes, I'm including the damned Prodryan. As for the Alliance finding LockLand, have someone contact Duchamp about a distraction. Keep their attention on the library.

Pearl: I'll talk to Duchamp.

McCook: Point of order. The proposed distraction is a separate motion.

Gleason: I swear to Alexandria, if we don't speed things up, I'll—

West: Even with a distraction, the Prodryans will be watching. We can't take the chance. Humanity's legacy depends on us.

Gleason: What happens to our humanity if we leave these people behind to die?

D ESPITE MOPS' FEARS, THE vote went in their favor, just as Gleason had predicted. After five minutes, Gleason powered down the computer cube and sat back. "How would you and your team like to see the *real* library?"

"I can think of nothing I'd like more," said Mops.

Bev sniffed. "Then you lack imagination."

"I've arranged for a distraction to keep the Alliance look-ing elsewhere." Gleason looked Mops up and down. "I wish we had winter camo for you and your people. Those black uni-forms don't exactly blend with the snow and ice."

"No need," said Mops. "Doc, would you mind?"

"Already analyzing and coding the pattern."

A moment later, the smart fabric of Mops' uniform was a match for the white-and-gray camouflage pattern of Gleason's. Doc had also removed their insignia.

"Hey, who changed my clothes?" Wolf demanded from out-side the office.

"That's convenient." Gleason closed the safe and led the way out of the office.

Mops double-checked her people. The only flaw in their camo was a section of Wolf's sleeve where the feral had bitten her. Cindy must have chewed through some of the fibers. As a result, a series of thin black stripes broke up the pattern from Wolf's wrist to shoulder.

Cindy and Cate were a bigger problem. The feral's fur might let her pass for an animal from a distance, but Mops had no idea how to conceal the Prodryan and his brightly-colored armor.

"Try this." Khatami pulled a worn moss-green blanket from their pack and offered it to Cate. The Prodryan grudg-ingly wrapped it around his body.

"Closest access to the surface is about half a kilometer north of here, through one of the old sewage lines," said Glea-son. "If we had more time, I'd pass out the nets and teach you to fish for sewer carp."

"You eat fish from your own sewage?" asked Cate.

"There hasn't been sewage in these tunnels for more than a century," said Khatami. "My parents used to take my sister and me fishing a little ways from here. I was so proud of that first fish I caught. Barely ten centimeters long, bright as a fresh-picked carrot. I fried it up myself that night."

They climbed down a broken metal ladder into a round

passageway, flooded with knee-deep cold water. For several minutes they waded in silence

Gleason checked her wrist comm. "We need to pick up the pace. Our distraction should be arriving at the library—what's left of it—soon."

"You're sure this will keep the Alliance occupied?" asked Mops.

Gleason's answering grin held no humor. "A herd of charging bison is very distracting. Bison may look clumsy, but they can run more than sixty kilometers per hour, and those horns aren't just for show."

"How did you get them to stampede?" asked Rubin.

"One of my librarians who looks after the herd. He's a large-animal specialist."

Mops thought back to the cathedral, and her sense of being watched. "This librarian, was he at the cathedral?"

"He gave us the heads-up someone or something was tramping about in the woods," Gleason confirmed.

"What happens when the Krakau start shooting at the animals?" asked Rubin.

"The herd will flee." Gleason stretched her back and started toward the rusted ladder leading to the surface. "I don't like it either, but they're tough beasts. Most of them should survive. With any luck, they'll trample a few of those Krakau vultures."

Up ahead, sunlight drew a thick, angular line through the air from a half-meter hole. Gleason checked her wrist and started climbing up cracks and holes in the wall. "This is our stop. We're gonna be threading some dangerous territory, so keep your eyes open and your guns cocked."

"Your sun is unacceptably bright," complained Cate.

Mops grunted in response, her attention on the trees alongside the narrow river. Half the group was watching the woods, while the other half kept an eye on the ruined suburbs on the other side of the water.

"Not only is it blinding, it reflects from the snow, assaulting your eyes from above and below."

"I'll be sure to submit a complaint," Mops assured him. She slowed her pace until she was alongside Monroe. He'd cut down a thick branch to use as a walking staff. "How's your head?"

"I'm all right."

She waited, the only sound the crunch of boots in the snow.

"All right, my balance is still shit," he admitted. "Even with the stick, this is as fast as I can go without falling on my ass."

"Cate's not doing much better," Mops pointed out. "And Wolf and Melvil have their hands full keeping Cindy on track. You're not slowing us down."

"Hey, what's that thing?" Wolf pointed to a bulbous framework of rusted metal in a clearing near the remains of a bridge.

"It used to be a museum," said Khatami. "Not a large one. More of a sideshow attraction, really. Late twenty-first century. It was built in the shape of a peanut and billed as the world's biggest legume. It honored an inventor named George Washington Carver."

"This Carver invented peanuts?" asked Wolf.

Bev snorted. "Don't the Krakau teach you people anything?"

"Hold up." Monroe stopped walking, his attention fixed on the sky. Without moving his head, he raised his rifle to his shoulder.

"What is it?" Mops followed his gaze. "Doc?"

"That man has good eyes, for a biological. I'd have spotted it myself if you'd been looking in the right direction, but—"

"Doc!" Her vision zoomed in on a small fishlike shape swimming through the clouds. "That's a Krakau surveillance drone."

"Too high and quick for a clean shot." Monroe continued to follow the drone with his weapon.

"You think they spotted us?" asked Wolf.

"Probably." Monroe lowered his gun.

"That doesn't mean they identified us," Melvil said

hopefully. "Maybe they thought we were ferals trudging through the snow."

"And maybe Prodryans will abandon war and take up finger-painting," said Wolf.

Cate bristled and raised one arm. "Our claws are superior to your soft, fleshy fingers, for painting or any other purpose. Yet another reason humanity will fall to the Prodryans."

"How far?" Mops called to the librarians.

"About four and a half kilometers," said Gleason.

"How fast can your people run?"

She shook her head. "My librarians are as tough as any soldier, but slogging through the snow? We've got close to an hour ahead of us."

If the drone had spotted them, the Alliance would be here within minutes, not hours.

"The rest of you should seek cover," said Rubin. "I can remain in the open to draw their attention. I'll try to buy you enough time to escape."

"Right idea, wrong implementation." Mops turned to Gleason. "Unless you have a better plan, my team will hold back while you make for the library."

A bulky ship rushed overhead, engines whistling as it turned in a tight curve. Two large doors slid open while it was still in the air, revealing Krakau warriors.

"Troop carrier," said Monroe. "Built to carry thirty-six, and every one of them will be better armed and armored than us."

Mops drew her pistol. "Run."

Instead, Gleason moved closer. "Those speakers in your comm units. How loud can they broadcast?"

"If Doc overrides the safety protocols? Pretty damned loud."

Gleason pointed to Cindy. "Broadcast her."

The librarians knew this territory. Mops didn't. She deferred to Gleason and tugged off her helmet.

"Easy," said Melvil, holding Cindy's right hand in his. "You're all right."

The feral snarled as Mops brought the helmet toward her head. Wolf took Cindy's other arm.

"You're giving away your armor to protect a feral?" Cate chittered in disgust.

Bev grasped the base of Cindy's head from behind. Her jaws snapped, and her snarls grew louder.

Mops slipped the helmet into place. Cindy's head moved to and fro. She was probably confused by the visor display.

"What now?" demanded Cate.

"Plug your ears." Mops pressed her monocle into place, then pressed her hands to her own ears.

The sound, when it came, was deafening. The speakers in Mops' collar amplified Cindy's vocalizations. Every groan was loud as a gunshot, echoing through the nearby trees. After a moment, Mops realized Doc had linked into the others' comms as well.

The noise seemed to frighten Cindy further. She squirmed and struggled, her moans becoming frantic.

"How long do we have to do this to her?" Melvil shouted.

"I've recorded enough to loop the sounds and continue playing." Doc's words scrolled across her monocle.

Mops tugged the helmet free. Instantly, Melvil held a square cracker to Cindy's mouth, but she was too upset to eat. He tossed it aside and began combing his fingers through her hair, whispering and singing.

The troop carrier passed overhead again, dropping toward an old, partially-paved clearing. Krakau began jumping from the ship when it was still several meters in the air. They hit the ground and started running, their limbs whipping up snow behind them.

Krakau rarely saw in-person combat, preferring to leave that to their human soldiers, but they could fight when they had to. These troops wore light battle armor with thick, rubberized sleeves for the lower limbs, providing traction while protecting them against the cold. The upper part of the uniform was more flexible, with removable "gloves" at the ends of each of the three tentacles. A personal respiration adjuster sprayed nutrient-rich mist into their mouths as needed.

The sleeves were fitted with fully automatic A-guns, the kind that could mow through every human here—along with every tree and most of the ruins on the far side of the river—within seconds.

The Krakau spread into two curved lines, like pincers preparing to snap shut and crush Mops and the others. A Krakau with the yellow stripes of a field commander slashing her sleeves scooted forward and pointed a tentacle at Mops. Her beak moved, but whatever she said was lost to the amplified moans thundering through the air.

Mops cupped a hand to her ear. "What?"

Another Krakau pointed at Mops, then extended her tentacle and dropped her A-gun cuff into the snow, presumably to demonstrate.

The field commander whirled, shouting something unintelligible and jabbing her tentacle at the A-gun cuff.

Shrinking sheepishly, the Krakau retrieved her weapon and replaced it on her tentacle.

"Doc, tell the team to drop their weapons." Trusting Doc to pick up her vocalizations, Mops dropped her helmet and pistol, then removed her combat baton. One by one, the others followed suit.

With a shriek of static, their comm speakers died, presumably jammed or overridden. The resulting silence felt like physical pressure against Mops' eardrums.

By now, more troops had emerged from the transport ship. One pointed a tentacle at Cindy. "Is that thing feral?"

Instantly, most of the guns moved to target Cindy. Melvil stepped in front of her, trying to shield the girl with his body. Wolf did the same.

"Stand aside," said Cate, rustling his wings and striding forward. "I am the legal advocate for these humans. Per Alliance law, I insist you provide proof of your authority to—"

A low-power energy beam crackled over Cate's body. Sparks

danced from the implants in his wings. He toppled backward without another word.

"I'm Field Commander Königgrätzer Marsch," said the Krakau who'd fired on Cate. "I will not hesitate to shoot every last one of you sand-sucking traitors."

"I believe you," said Mops. "Listen, I don't know what Command told you, but these people aren't—"

"No talking." Marsch pointed two of her three tentacles at Mops. One held the A-gun, the other the energy weapon. "Give me an excuse, Adamopoulos."

A small, brown-furred animal burst from the trees, running between the Krakau in its haste. Several Krakau jumped back. One fired an A-gun after the creature. It ignored them all, scampering to the river and veering right to flee along the shoreline.

"Cottontail rabbit, I believe," said Doc.

Another animal bounded past, this one smaller, with a tail like a pipe-scrubber. Mops' brow wrinkled. They'd broadcast Cindy's moans. Shouldn't that have made these creatures run away instead of scampering right past them? She turned to Gleason, who stood stone-faced, her mouth a tight line. She caught Mops' attention and nodded ever so slightly.

"We have potential hostiles incoming," shouted one of the Krakau. "They're huge!"

Marsch glared at Mops before snapping off orders. "Second line, intercept formation."

Nine of the Krakau split away, taking up position in groups of three.

Mops' eyes widened as she spied the first of the beasts exploding from the woods and trampling toward them. Her first thought was of bison, but while this animal shared the bison's brown fur, it was both leaner and taller. Mops' head would come only to its shoulder. The animal lowered its long head and charged.

"And if I'm not mistaken, those are moose."

More moose followed the first. None of these were quite as large, but even the smallest more than outmassed the Krakau.

Three Krakau fired almost simultaneously, and the lead moose stumbled. Then it spun and lashed out with one hoof. A Krakau flew backward to land in the snow. She didn't get up.

Rubin started toward the injured moose, but Khatami caught her arm and held her back.

The rest of the moose veered away, running downriver. The injured one limped after. Slowly, the shaken Krakau began to reform their lines.

Mops turned toward Gleason.

"Wait for it." Gleason's breathing was quick and shallow. Her attention was focused not on the moose or the Krakau, but the trees beyond.

"Doc, send a note to the others." Mops subvocalized so only the AI would hear. "Tell them to be ready."

"Ready for what?"

"For whatever those moose were running from."

Two Krakau came forward with binding strips. They started with Khatami. The binder coiled like tentacles around his wrists.

An object flew from the trees to strike one of the Krakau. She whirled, raising her A-gun. "Commander, there are more hostiles."

"Third line, bring them in," yelled Marsch. Several more missiles rained down. "And watch for those rocks!"

Bev smirked. "Those aren't rocks."

Long-armed figures shot from the branches. They landed hard and raced toward the Krakau and humans.

A lucky shot from a Krakau gun caught one of the animals in the chest. It flopped into the snow, rolled, and jumped back to its feet.

"Oh, shit," Wolf whispered. "Those things are feral?"

"They're chimpanzees. Colloquially known as chimps. The Krakau plague affected certain species of primates in addition to humans."

"I know." Mops' mouth was dry.

The Krakau closed ranks, continuing to fire even as the chimps reached them.

The chimps were faster than feral humans, and from the look of it, stronger as well. They were just over a meter high, with gray-black skin and patchy hair. Many had the dark scars common to feral humans, and several were missing limbs.

Gleason grabbed Mops' arm. "Run!"

As terrifying as the chimps were to Mops, she couldn't imagine what the Krakau were feeling. Most Krakau saw human ferals as barely-tamed monsters, savage creatures of horror and nightmare.

The chimps, with their fangs and their speed and their furious hoots and grunts and growls, were worse.

One of the chimps spun toward Mops, snapping her from her paralysis. She snatched her weapons and clubbed the animal in the head with her combat baton. It sprang back up. Before Mops could line up a shot, Bev stepped in and thrust a large knife through the back of the chimp's neck.

"The chimps have claimed most of this area as their territory," Bev said, wrenching her blade free. "They'll eat just about anything, but they *really* hate feral humans. I guess they see humans as competition."

Which explained why Cindy had drawn them in such numbers. And why a number of chimps were closing around Cindy, Melvil, and Wolf. Mops glanced at her helmet. "Doc, can you—?"

"You're an evil, evil woman. The answer is yes, I can amplify and broadcast the recording from your helmet."

Mops scooped up the helmet and hurled it in a long arc toward the Krakau and the troop carrier. The sound wasn't as loud as when Doc had linked everyone's speakers, but it was enough to capture the chimps' attention.

The helmet bounced and rolled. More chimps surged from the woods, charging after it.

Field Commander Marsch had fallen back, shouting orders and shooting chimps. She spotted Mops, and her A-gun moved to follow.

Mops tilted her head to the left, to where Rubin knelt with

her rifle to her shoulder. Mops suspected Marsch could feel Rubin's crosshairs on her. The message was clear: if Marsch pulled the trigger, she'd be dead before Mops' body hit the ground.

With a frustrated whistle, Marsch turned away and called for her troops to regroup.

"Thanks, Rubin. Now fall back!" Mops scooped the unconscious Cate over her shoulder and ran after the librarians. Barely-suppressed panic sent adrenaline surging through her body, an electrical shock jolting speed to her limbs.

After a hundred meters or so, Monroe turned and dropped to one knee. He fired four quick shots with his rifle.

"What was that?" asked Mops.

"I put a few holes through the rear thruster block. They shouldn't be able to take off, and even I can outrun Krakau on this terrain." He grimaced. "I tried to hit the communications pod, too, but I'm not sure I got it."

"Move ass, people," shouted Gleason.

Rubin came up alongside Monroe. Without a word, she slung his arm across her shoulders and helped him stand.

Wolf glanced back at Mops. "You'd run faster without that Prodryan."

"He knows too much. If the Alliance interrogates him—"

"I wasn't suggesting you leave him alive. Sir."

Mops sighed. "Shut up and run."

They fled for close to an hour, until Mops' limbs were numb. Given her own exhaustion, she couldn't imagine the pain the librarians must be feeling, but aside from the sweat soaking their faces, none of them showed it.

They'd been hiking alongside an old monorail track. According to Gleason, it was a high-speed rail line from the 2060s. Close-packed pine trees provided partial cover as they trudged uphill.

So far, she'd seen no sign of pursuit. Hopefully, that meant the Krakau were huddled inside their grounded ship, trapped until the chimps finally lost interest and went back to whatever it was feral chimps did.

"I didn't know chimpanzees were native to this continent," said Rubin.

"They're not." Bev pushed back her helmet and wiped her face on her sleeve. "There used to be an animal preserve nearby. When their human caretakers vanished, most of the animals got loose. Some adapted better than others."

Mops checked the sky again. Even if Monroe had disabled the Krakau communications pod as well as their engines, someone should have been monitoring the troop carrier and its mission.

Monroe followed her gaze. "You think they're watching us?"

"Could be." Sage had been able to track them to the library. By now she'd realize there was more here than a single lost human wandering the woods. Maybe Sage had decided to let them go in the hope that they'd lead her to something bigger. "Or maybe they're just gathering reinforcements."

"Reinforshments." The translator faithfully rendered both Cate's slurring and his disgust. He'd woken only a short time ago, and his body wasn't fully recovered from the shock. He walked with an exaggerated limp. His left arm hung unmoving at his side. And two of his four mouth pincers hung uselessly. "Their caution is nothing but cowardish. The boldnesh of the Prodryan people will bring us victory over . . ." He trailed off and squeezed the base of his antennae. "Pardon me while I regurgitate."

"Don't fall apart now," Gleason called back. "We're almost there."

"Almost where?" asked Wolf.

"See for yourself." Gleason bent several large branches aside.

Less than ten meters beyond stood a tall chain-link fence, topped with coils of razor wire. Ceramic insulators on the posts suggested it had once been electrified. The monorail track passed beneath a sliding gate, framed by the remnants of two small buildings.

A short distance beyond the fence stood a wall five meters high. Flakes of color clung stubbornly to the gray composite of the wall.

"Won't do much against drones and fighters," said Monroe. "I'd love to see a Krakau try to scale them, though."

Wolf stared. "What was this place?"

"The official name was Lockdown Land Northeast." Gleason started toward the gate, which had long since torn free of its track and now lay at an angle, half-engulfed by dead vines.

The fence and wall both curved away as far as Mops could see. "It looks like a military compound."

"Yes and no," said Gleason. "In the twenty-second century, the world was seeing more and more events that forced people to leave their homes and seek shelter."

"What kind of events?" asked Rubin.

"Hurricanes, floods, military threats, blizzards, wildfires . . . you name it. The government eventually decided it would be cheaper to set up permanent public shelters. After construction started, some marketing genius decided to multitask those shelters as theme parks." Gleason spread her arms at the walls and whatever lay on the other side. "LockLand Resorts. Each one was capable of housing up to ten million people. LockLand Northeast is separated into nine zones. Very Dante-esque. The closer you get to the center, the more secure, luxurious, and expensive it gets."

"Dante?" Mops repeated.

"Virgil's *Divine Comedy*?" Gleason took in their blank stares. "Guess the Krakau didn't bother to translate that one. I'll get you a copy from our archives."

Mops helped bend the gate back as the others squeezed through. "They wanted emergency evacuations to be fun?"

"That's right," said Gleason. "In the old days, the razor wire was green, with the blades colored metallic pink, red, and purple. The idea was to make them look like flowers. All the guards were dressed up in kid-friendly costumes lined in bullet- and blade-resistant molecular polyethylene weave."

"Why worry so much about appearances?" asked Rubin. "A shelter's purpose is protection, not entertainment."

Khatami grinned. "Imagine you have a family, and you're try- ing to get your anxious child onto the train for the evacuation. Sure, you could tell them there's a superstorm coming that might destroy your home and everything you know, and anyone who doesn't get to shelter will probably be dead by morning. Or you can announce you're taking a surprise vacation to LockLand, where the little ones can ride rides and play on water slides and see parades and meet all of their favorite LockLand characters."

"Wouldn't fear of death be the stronger motivation?" asked Rubin. "Why rely on deception?"

"Have you ever *met* a child?"

"No," said Rubin.

"Oh." Khatami paused. "Well, little kids aren't always ra- tional."

Cate snorted. "Are you shuggesting grown humans are?"

"Fair point," Khatami said cheerfully. "All right, little kids are irrational in different ways. They get scared and fall apart."

Rubin's eyes widened. "I had no idea human children were so fragile."

"Not literally. I mean, they scream and cry and have tan- trums. Then when they finally exhaust themselves and fall asleep, they wake up an hour later screaming from nightmares. By the end, the parents would be praying for death."

"Speaking of kids . . ." Bev cocked a thumb at Cindy. "Are we seriously taking her inside?"

"I'll keep her away from the others," Melvil promised. "She's hurt, and not old enough to survive on her own in the middle of winter."

"Bullshit," said Bev. "She's feral. Even the kids are damn- near unkillable."

Cindy had settled down since they escaped the chimps, and had hardly tried to bite anyone for the past hour.

Gleason started toward a large arched opening in the inner wall. "The ferals are Melvil's project, and his responsibility."

That ended the argument, though Bev gave the feral a dirty look as she passed.

Rubin paused to study a tangled thorn bush growing inside the archway. "What's this?"

Bev perked up. "Rosebushes. LockLand filled the land between the wall and the outer fence with them. Over the years, the blue roses choked out the other species and took over. The snow crushes most of them down for the winter, but come spring, this whole stretch will look like a moat. You can smell them from a kilometer away when the wind's right."

Mops passed through the second gate and stopped, dumbstruck by what lay beyond. Before her stretched a wide rainbow-colored road leading to an edifice of circular towers and narrow spires. Colorful tubes spiraled around and between them. "Is . . . is that a *castle*?"

"Complete with waterslides," said Gleason. "I wouldn't recommend using them, though. Half have collapsed, and the rest are cracked and brittle. Nobody lives in LockLand Palace except the vermin. Bats and rats and bugs and such."

Rubin perked up. "Permission to stay in the castle?"

"Denied," said Mops. "We stick together."

To the left of the rainbow road, a river ran down a rocky hillside, splitting to circle around the castle. Its path was too straight to be natural. Ice crusted the edges, and the water flowing through the center was a dingy green.

Domed buildings covered the grounds, connected by smaller, monochrome paths. The sheer size of the place didn't fully register until Doc magnified the view through her monocle. Carved into the hillside—mountainside, rather—were row upon row of doorways. Each row shared a balcony, with narrow staircases connecting them all.

"Public shelters," said Gleason, noting the direction of her gaze. "Each room is rated for up to ten occupants."

"Ten million people," whispered Mops, remembering what Gleason had said. The entire human population of the Earth Mercenary Corps could fit inside here a thousand times.

"We should get underground." Khatami was watching the sky.

"Alliance?" asked Monroe.

"Weather." Khatami pointed. "Those clouds look like they're getting ready to drop another layer of snow."

Gleason started along a faded green path toward one of the smaller domes. After a moment, Doc was able to translate the letters carved onto a rusted metal door: *Lift 17B.*

"The elevator hasn't worked for more than a century." Gleason circled around to a narrow doorway on the back. Heavy hinges squealed as she and Bev wrenched the door open. "The stairs keep us in shape. We're down on sublevel seven."

Thirty steps took them to a small landing with a faded, illegible sign hanging from the cinder block wall. After thirty more, they reached a door marked *sublevel one.*

Gleason talked briefly about each level as they passed. Sublevels one and two were unusable from water damage and mold. Three was for manufacturing, and had everything from solder and wiring equipment to an old-fashioned charcoal forge.

Halfway to sublevel four, Cate collapsed against the wall. His wings drooped, and his antennae lay limp along his scalp. "I will wait here. To guard against invasion. You can send up food and water."

"You will move your ass with the rest of us," Mops snapped.

"Prodryans don't have asses. Our superior digestive processes are another reason we're destined to . . ." He trailed off, too out of breath to finish.

"Adjust your PRAs," Monroe suggested. "Increase the O_2 percentage. Or in Cate's case, add a little more nitrogen."

Sublevels four and five were mostly empty. Gleason said

they used several of the central rooms for archiving. Six was food storage.

By the time they reached the landing for sublevel seven, Mops' legs were throbbing. Doc helpfully shared that they'd descended seventy meters, over four hundred and twenty steps. Despite her fatigue, Mops chuckled.

"What's funny?" asked Khatami.

"If the Krakau do find this place, they'll have to follow us down. Krakau aren't built for stairs."

Several of the librarians smiled at that. None of them appeared out of breath, and Mops mentally revised her opinion of their toughness. Cindy showed no outward signs of fatigue either, but she immediately sat down on the bottom step.

Cate collapsed on the landing with a groan. "Next time, just let the feral creatures devour me."

"Will do," promised Wolf.

Gleason pounded the large metal door. "It's Gleason. We've got visitors."

A high-pitched voice from the other side answered in Nishnaabemwin.

Gleason swore. "She wants the security code. What the hell are we using this month?"

"Library of Congress," said Bev.

"Right." She cupped her hands and shouted at the door. "Zed-six-eight-eight."

Bev leaned toward Mops. "It's the Library of Congress cataloging code for Special Collections."

Gleason glanced at the Prodryan. "As soon as we're in, pass the word to switch codes."

"A wise precaution," Cate said without lifting his head from the floor.

The door opened with a painful squeal. Gleason seemed to grow taller as she stepped through. Her shoulders squared, and her back straightened. She spun around and spread her arms. "Welcome to the main—and only—branch of the Library of Humanity."

12

Since the beginning, every meeting of the Library of Humanity Board of Directors has been documented, in keeping with the library's mission to preserve all available knowledge and information. Even information many would prefer to forget. Like the following, from one of the very first meetings of people who would (for the most part) establish the goals and guidelines to be followed by librarians for the next hundred and fifty years . . .

Date: *August 17, 2106*

Present: *Patricia F. Anderson, Kevin Swain, Ju Honisch, Frank L. James, Madelynn Angell, Rachelle Hrubetz, Zinta Aistars, Christian Manninen*

Approval of Minutes from Prior Meeting
- *Rachelle noted her name was misspelled in the minutes <u>again</u>.*
- *Minutes approved unanimously (amended with "Hrubetz" spelled correctly).*

Unfinished Business
- *Zinta Aistars reported we've now contacted a total of 1,162 people, spread over four continents, with immunity to the Krakau plague. Klaudia Seibel has taken over coordinating outreach efforts in Europe.*
- *Patricia Anderson moved to confirm Ju Honisch as head cataloger for the Library of Humanity. Angell seconded. Six yeses, one no, one abstention. Motion passed.*
- *Frank L. James brought up our "duty" to repopulate the Earth and moved to assign breeding partners. No second. Motion dropped. Again.*

New Business
- *Kevin Swain has compiled a list of potential branch sites for the Library of Humanity. Priorities include preexisting collections, long-term preservation, and defensibility.*
- *Christian Manninen confirmed receipt of the World Health Organization medical library. He also noted the latest WHO report suggests the Krakau plague has spread beyond any hope of containment.*
- *Frank L. James argued this makes it our duty to preserve the species, and produced a copy of his own genetic makeup, showing his fitness as a mate.*
- *Madelynn Angell moved to "shoot Frank in the dick" if he says one more word about breeding. Hrubetz seconded. Seven yeses, one no. Motion passed.*

Adjournment
- *Frank L. James moved to adjourn the meeting.*
- *Ju Honisch suggested James "adjourn your stupid face."*
- *Meeting adjourned at 4:19 PM.*

MOPS HAD IMAGINED THE Library of Humanity would be a grander, more modern version of the one the Krakau had destroyed, with endless rows of bookshelves and computer terminals stretching in all directions, interspersed with transparent display cases to protect the most valuable books and artifacts.

She hadn't anticipated the giant penguin.

The statue greeted them as they emerged through the stairwell door—almost two meters high, black and white with enormous blue eyes. The orange-and-black bill was curved into a giant grin.

"There's my nightmare fodder for the week," muttered Wolf.

"His name's Emperor Waddle," said Gleason, giving the statue a friendly pat on the shoulder. "He was the main Lock-Land mascot. We've got all six seasons of *The Waddle Adventures* saved in the archives, if you're interested."

One arm—wing, rather—held a sign welcoming them to sublevel seven. The text was repeated in eleven languages, enough for Doc to translate. A map showed everything from restaurants to restrooms to rides color-coded for different age groups. According to the "You are here" arrow, this was Reception Area 4, surrounded by beautiful fountains, a food court, and an administration area. A dotted line showed where the parade would be passing through at 7 PM.

Mops looked around. The fountains had been converted to algae tanks. From the drying trays spread along shelves on the left wall, Mops guessed the librarians were harvesting the algae for food. The administration booth was a two-meter-wide concrete pillar with a door in one side. Rusted bars covered the square window. On the other side sat a young girl with narrow eyes, dark skin, and a magnificent cloud of black hair.

She leaned forward, studying the newcomers. "What's going on, Mom?"

"Alpha library is gone," said Gleason. "Pass the word. Board meeting in one hour."

The girl's eyes widened. She nodded and turned away. Seconds later, the square lights in the ceiling began to flicker.

"Morse code," Gleason explained. "We've never gotten the PA system to work reliably."

"She has your mannerisms," said Rubin, looking from the girl to Gleason.

"Junior's my daughter. She hasn't chosen a specialty yet, so she rotates job assignments each month."

Other humans emerged from nearby rooms and chambers. Two moved to assist Melvil with his feral. Most crowded around Gleason, speaking in Nishnaabemwin and gesturing toward the newcomers—particularly Cate.

"Khatami, our guests could use food and rest." Gleason spoke in Human, cutting through the noise as effectively as any drill sergeant. "Put them up in the Princess room."

Cate clicked his mandibles for attention. "Does this library contain documents or records about your planet's military vulnerabilities? If so, I would like to borrow them."

Gleason didn't bother turning around. "Do you have a library card?"

"A . . . library card?" repeated Cate.

"Sorry," said Gleason. "No library card, no lending privileges."

Junior was back at the window, her face pressed to the bars. "Is that—?"

"He's a Prodryan, yes," said Mops. "He's been helping us. Sort of. You speak Human well."

"Thanks," said Junior. "I heard Mom speaking it to you. Figured it was polite to follow suit. I also speak French, Nishnaabemwin, English, Mandarin, and a smattering of Latin."

Mops had no idea what those were, nor did she know what a "smattering" was supposed to be, but it was an impressive list nonetheless.

"You're EMC, aren't you? Cured ferals?" Junior's nose scrunched. "I see you've met Earth's skunks."

"Wolf had a run-in yesterday, yes." Mops studied the girl. The Krakau only cured adults. "If it's not rude to ask, how old are you?"

"Sixteen." Junior cocked her head. "You look amused. You think a teenager can't work the library?"

"It's not that." Mops smiled. "I was cured a little over twelve years ago. Given the way we track our ages, that makes you older than me."

Junior flashed a broad white grin. "I'll remember that, kid."

Khatami cleared his throat. "If you're ready, Captain? I figured I'd show you and your people to the showers, first. They say tomatoes are good for skunk spray. I'll send someone to search for a jar or two."

He paused at the admin booth to extend a fist toward Junior, who tapped her own on top of his in some kind of greeting.

Gleason caught Mops' arm. "You and I need to talk."

Monroe and Rubin both tensed at the sight of Gleason grabbing their commanding officer. Mops gave them a slight nod, and they relaxed. Hopefully, Gleason wouldn't realize how close she'd just come to getting socked in the jaw. "Go with Khatami. I'll catch up." To Gleason, she said, "Lead the way."

Mops was used to being gawked at. Throughout the galaxy, humans were a novelty: a species of savages brought back from extinction to fight the Prodryans. She'd learned to stare down curious Quetzalus or ignore the titillating whispers of gossiping Nusurans. She hardly noticed the oily fear-scent Glacidae emitted when she got too close to one.

It was different when it was your own species staring. Mops might be as human as anyone here, but she *felt* like an alien. Her skin had a pallor theirs lacked. Few of these humans had the scars and injuries most EMC troops collected. Their body language was foreign as well. Many walked hand-in-hand or arm-in-arm. They stood closer together to speak, and broke eye contact too quickly. Their culture, their language, their upbringing and history, everything was different. Mops' tension increased with each step.

"Don't you people have work to do?" Gleason snapped at one group who stared a little too long. They mumbled apologies and hurried away. "They don't mean to be rude. It's just that you're the first strangers anyone here has ever met."

Mops thought back to how she and the rest of her crèche had gawked the first time they arrived on Stepping Stone. "It's no problem. Just . . . strange. Being around all of you makes me want to apologize for not knowing how to be human."

"Captain, if you read enough history, you'll realize we've been fighting over the right way to be human for as long as we've been around. You and your people go right on being yourselves."

"Thank you." The strain in her muscles eased slightly. She pointed to one of the lights overhead. "Where does the power come from?"

"This place was built to generate enough electricity for millions of people," said Gleason. "With most of the place shut down and sealed off, we only need a fraction of LockLand's original power requirements. The hydroelectric generator doesn't work as well during the winter, but we've also got a few working solar windows up on the surface. There's some geothermal as well, along with natural gas from sewage and recycling."

They continued down a broad road. Enormous concrete pillars were spread every ten meters, each one tagged with a letter and number. Many looked like they had once served as kiosks, providing snacks and toys and tickets to various attractions. Larger structures were constructed of some kind of primitive foamcrete, probably sprayed onto a metal framework. Most had been painted in bright primary colors, though the paint had cracked and flaked away over the years.

"The pillars form a grid," said Doc. *"We came in at pillar D4. We're at M6 now. Don't worry, I'm building a map."*

Most of the buildings were closed down, but they'd survived far better than anything on the surface. Mops spotted theaters, gaming rooms, gymnasiums, and something called a dog park.

Gleason turned past another penguin statue, this one holding his wings out like he was desperate for a hug. Or wanted to wrap his wings around your neck and choke the life from you. "You said your people were janitors?"

"Sanitation and Hygiene, that's right." Given everything she'd seen so far, Mops could guess where the question was leading. "I imagine a hundred and fifty years takes its toll on a place like this."

"We do the best we can with the tools and reference material we have, but there's a never-ending list of problems. Leaking water lines, clogged pipes, blocked air vents . . ."

"My team would be happy to take a look." After a moment, she added, "Assuming the Alliance doesn't come knocking."

Gleason sighed and turned left, cutting through an empty cafeteria. "LockLand was built to protect people from nuclear war, among other things. I've got people securing every emergency door that still works, from here to the surface. The Alliance will have a hell of a time cracking this nut. But you're right. They know we're down here. It's a matter of when, not if."

"You said you had contingency plans."

"We've stored library backups in secure locations around the world," said Gleason. "There's an old data warehouse about a hundred kilometers from here we've been looking at as a secondary site. We couldn't relocate with all this Krakau attention on us, though."

She passed into the food service area, heading for a large metal door at the back. She pulled an old key from her pocket and unlocked it. "And we'd have to abandon most of this."

The lights inside came up slowly, and Mops stopped breathing.

Gleason watched Mops' face and grinned. "I thought you might like it."

Mops stepped into what had once been a refrigerated warehouse for food storage, but now held endless rows of white metal shelves, filled with books, papers, and old electronic media of all kinds.

"Don't touch anything without asking," said Gleason. "Some of this stuff's brittle or sensitive to skin oils."

Mops approached the closest shelf, hardly daring to breathe. Like the books she'd seen in the now-destroyed library, many of these were centuries old. But these had been preserved and repaired and protected. Each book was enclosed in a stiff gray case, neatly numbered and labeled.

"It's easier to control the temperature and humidity in here." Pride and satisfaction colored Gleason's words. "Even if the rest of LockLand goes to hell, this room should last at least another hundred years. The books would eventually degrade, but there are electronic data storage devices that could theoretically survive into the next millennium, like this guy."

She carefully picked up a plastic green-and-white eagle with rainbow-shimmering eyes.

"What am I looking at?" asked Mops.

"This is Ugochukwu 3.1. He was designed in Nigeria as an educational tool back in the 2080s. Each Ugochukwu contains an entire educational curriculum covering birth to age sixteen. Much of his information is out of date, but he's still a treasure trove of history and knowledge."

"He's cute," said Doc. *"But can he simultaneously monitor fourteen maintenance subroutines on a cruiser-class ship?"*

"Does he still work?"

Gleason shook her head and returned Ugochukwu to the shelf. "It's hard to find working batteries, and I don't want to risk hooking him up to a jury-rigged power supply. Theoretically, we could just open him up and extract the data drive. That's all we *need* to preserve. But I can't bring myself to do that to the poor guy."

Mops approved. As important as it was to save humanity's knowledge, it was just as vital to preserve their creativity. Every sentient species developed ways of saving data. How many of those species would build data storage into a prism-eyed bird of prey?

"The working computer equipment is down at the end." Gleason beckoned Mops to follow. "We keep it turned off when not in use."

"Oh, wow." Mops stared at the old wall unit, a square of clear nanocarbonate three meters to a side. Ports and adapters were clustered at the middle of the left edge.

Gleason put a hand on the center of the screen.

It flickered several times before bringing up a life-sized image of three brown-skinned children playing with an enormous hairy dog at a beach. Several centimeter-wide squares remained clear. Those sections were presumably too damaged to display anything.

"Who are they?" asked Mops.

"Probably the children of whoever owned this thing. We found it in one of the administrative offices on six."

Meaning these children, whoever they were, were long dead. Probably turned feral or killed during the initial outbreak of the Krakau plague.

Gleason removed the memory drive from around her neck and slid it into a port.

A cat strolled onto the screen from the left, crouched, and batted the dog on the nose with one paw. It paused briefly to lick the long, black fur of its shoulder, then looked out at Gleason. "Your drive is now synched and current, Eliza."

"Thank you, Libris." Gleason removed the drive.

"Libris?"

"She's our operating system," said Gleason. "The original Libris belonged to Zinta Aistars, one of the first librarians. She hunted vermin and helped with morale. Libris, I mean, not Zinta. When our programmers got this thing running, they decided to model the interface after the cat."

"I will rebuild your entire plumbing system from scratch if

you let me trade our ship's tutorial software for a copy of Libris," said Mops.

Gleason smiled and brushed her hand over the screen. Libris jumped up on her hind legs to rub her head against Gleason's palm. A low purr rumbled from the speakers. "The books behind us are only a tiny fraction of the library. Is there anything in particular you'd like to see?"

"Everything."

"Assuming average reading speed, that will take well over ten thousand years. I'm no expert on reborn humans, but I don't believe you have quite that long."

"What about . . ." Mops swallowed. "Do you have any pictures or articles from before the plague, when the Krakau first came to Earth?"

In the Krakau version of human history—the version Mops and other EMC recruits were taught—humanity had been responsible for its own downfall. The Krakau hadn't arrived until long after the planet was overrun by ferals.

Azure had offered a different version, one in which the Krakau and their cold-water kin, the Rokkau, brought the plague to Earth. The Krakau blamed the Rokkau for the tragedy. After a brutal civil war, the Rokkau were wiped off their home world, the survivors banished to a secret prison planet.

Azure's existence proved the Rokkau were real. The librarians' references to the Krakau plague suggested the rest of Azure's story was true as well, but Mops wanted evidence.

Gleason scratched the cat's ears and said, "Index search. Date: June through August 2104. Keywords: alien, Krakau. Filter: news, images. Display language: Human."

The children vanished from the screen. Libris dropped gracefully to the bottom edge. The blackness behind her filled with columns of text, each line the title of an article or video clip. Libris stretched and scratched her claws down the screen, tearing open a virtual hole that grew into a table of information—an index of some sort.

Libris batted the index up to Gleason's eye level. Gleason's fingers raced over the text, refining the search.

As the number of results shrank, photos began to appear with the headlines. Mops pointed to one.

Gleason tapped the index again, and the screen changed to a life-sized image of men and women—mostly men—gathered in a large, circular room in front of a colorful array of flags. In the center stood four Krakau and what Mops now recognized as a Rokkau. Superimposed over the top of the image were the words "Our Neighbors From the Stars."

Mops put a hand on Gleason's shoulder for support. She'd known the Krakau had lied to her, that everything she'd been taught was a fiction, but this was proof. Life-sized, unassailable proof. "Doc?"

"No need to ask. I'm recording the hell out of this."

"I take it this isn't part of the curriculum for newly-cured EMC recruits?" asked Gleason.

"You could say that." Mops withdrew her hand and wiped her eyes. "Could you do me a personal favor?"

"I can try."

"We all choose names from human history. Vera Rubin, Marilyn Monroe, Wolfgang Mozart."

"We have a similar tradition, only with famous librarians."

"The Krakau taught us that Doctor Marion Adamopoulos was responsible for what happened to humanity. I took her name so I'd never forget how much we owed the Krakau for saving us. I'd like to know who she really was . . . if she even existed."

Gleason cleared the search results and spoke a new query.

Mops braced herself. "Thank you."

"It's my job."

New results soon filled the screen. Gleason skimmed the list and chose one, seemingly at random. "This is a video clip from 2105. The audio is in English. I'm setting subtitles to Human."

The clip began with a blue screen and a series of electronic beeps. A logo appeared: three stylized white letters. Below, white text scrolled across a red banner. A second layer of text—the subtitles—read:

```
CDC Alert Level 4: Practice Extraordinary
Precautions and Avoid All Nonessential
Travel
```

A woman in a thigh-length white jacket appeared, wearing half-circle lenses in invisible frames. Her eyes twitched from side to side as she spoke, like she was reading the words, possibly from the lenses themselves. Mops followed along with the subtitles.

```
The Centers for Disease Control and Pre-
vention, together with the Global Health
Organization, have issued a level four
alert for all residents of North and Cen-
tral America. Krakau Virus outbreaks have
been confirmed as far south as Costa Rica.
```

The woman—Doctor Adamopoulos—spoke of quarantine zones, advising anyone with symptoms to report to the nearest hospital or emergency medical center. She reassured everyone the CDC was doing all they could to protect unaffected populations and to help those stricken by the plague.

The clip was less than a minute long. At the end, it faded into that same blue-and-white logo, followed by a block of text in Human:

```
February 17, 2105
Atlanta, Georgia
Subject Headings: Krakau Virus, Quaran-
tine, Medical, 22nd Century
Language: English
Contributor: Adamopoulos, Marion Susan, MD
(Narrator)
Index Code CDC210502-35.12.932
```

"That's our cataloging information at the end," Gleason explained.

"Doc, bring up that image of Dr. Adamopoulos."

The doctor appeared in the center of Mops' monocle. Mops closed her other eye to better focus on this woman the Krakau had blamed for the end of human civilization.

Marion Adamopoulos had light brown skin and close-cut black hair, just starting to turn to gray. Swollen shadows beneath her eyes made it look like she'd just lost a fight. A choker with yellow beads or jewels circled the snug collar of her blue turtleneck.

To Mops' eye, she looked broken. Her hands were clasped together, as if to keep them from trembling. Her shoulders hunched protectively, like she was bracing against an attack. "Who was she?"

Gleason skimmed several other documents. "Dr. Adamopoulos worked eight years as an epidemiologist for the CDC. Spent a year vaccinating families around the Gulf of Mexico after the malaria outbreak of 2099. Married twice. One child, a son who'd have been about twenty when everything fell apart. She was infected in October of 2105 and declared legally dead on November 2, 2105. I've got one article suggesting she was the one to first call the Krakau plague by that name."

Could that be why the Krakau had scapegoated her? Out of spite for daring to lay the blame at the Krakau's tentacles?

"Thank you again." Mops cleared the monocle. "You're being awfully nice, considering we led the Alliance to you."

Gleason watched Libris jump about, pulling articles to the ground and batting them offscreen. "Our days were numbered the moment they spotted Melvil running about. You just sped up the inevitable."

"Why show me all this?" asked Mops. "Shouldn't you be preparing to defend LockLand?"

"That's what I'm doing." Gleason didn't look at her. "Captain, every one of my librarians carries a backup of our data, but we can't transport the equipment to read it. Nor can we save all those books behind you."

Mops searched for words, but found none.

"How did you plan to get your people off this rock, once you found what you were looking for?"

"Originally? On a shuttle." Mops shook her head. "We thought we had a way to hide it from Alliance scanners."

"I take it from your expression that didn't work out the way you'd hoped?"

"Not exactly," said Mops. "They blew us up. We had to jump."

"No shit?" Gleason looked her up and down. "You reborn humans are tougher than I thought."

"It's how they made us," she said bitterly. "The Krakau want their guns to last."

"If you were nothing but guns, you and your team wouldn't be causing such headaches for the Krakau," Gleason retorted.

"We've spent most of the time running and hiding," Mops admitted. "I wasn't trained for command. Not like this."

"You've kept your people alive so far." Gleason shut down the computer screen. "They trust you. So do I. Trust is a big part of what keeps this community going. The moment we brought you here, you became a part of that community and that trust."

"Even Cate?"

"I wouldn't go that far." Gleason grimaced. "Point is, whatever comes next, folks are trusting you to help protect all this."

"That's why you brought me here? To make sure I knew what we were fighting for?"

"Got it in one."

"Devious." Mops gave a quick salute. "Effective, but devious."

"There was another reason," Gleason admitted. "A selfish reason. How could I possibly resist the chance to show off our collection to a new patron?"

Mops laughed. "Thank you, Gleason. Whatever happens, I'm glad I had the chance to see it. I can't thank you enough for showing me how much of our history and culture still exists. That humanity still exists."

"There's no need," said the librarian. "Like I said, it's my job. And call me Eliza."

13

LockLand Theme Song as
Sung by Emperor Waddle

Every child knows
The place where their dreams come true.
Children want to go
Where penguins dance and laugh and
Make good memories with you.

Everyone has come to play.
Hope you have a pleasant stay.
Stop by LockLand's shops and rides and petting zoo.

If the lights start flashing red,
Duck and cover up your head.
If they're blinking blue, then go to Shelter Two.[1]

You'll be happy and secure.
Try the penguin wagon tour!

*There are countless joys and wondrous things
    to do.*

*Every child knows
The place where their dreams come true.
Every family goes
Where they'll be safe and joyful.*[2]
Waddle has a hug for you.

———

1. Use your room terminal or stop by any information
   kiosk to upgrade to skip-the-line shelter access!
2. Per the liability release form, LockLand cannot guarantee individual safety or joy.

"DOC, DOUBLE-CHECK THOSE directions Gleason gave us and tell me I'm in the wrong place. Please."

"Sorry. That pillar to your left confirms it. Welcome to the Princess room."

Mops walked cautiously through the open doors . . . doors painted in bright metallic purple, with gleaming yellow hinges. The inside was decorated to resemble the interior of a castle, if that castle were built of pink stone and glittering purple mortar. Tiny floor tiles formed a mosaic of a penguin dressed in a flowing green gown, wielding sword and shield against an enormous red dragon.

Artificial torches on the walls filled the room with light. The "flames" were molded glass or polymer, each one with unique facial features, but every one beaming with a too-cheerful smile.

Cate lay snoring on an old sleeping bag against the far wall. The rest of Mops' people, along with Junior and Khatami, sat around a circular wooden table eating from a pile of nuts, dried fruit, and dull green squares of algae-based nutrient.

"Welcome back, Captain," said Monroe.

Mops took the vacant seat between Monroe and Junior and picked up one of the nuts, a segmented green ball about four centimeters in diameter.

"Shagnut hickory," said Khatami. "I brought a nutcracker, but your second in command doesn't seem to need it."

Monroe took the nut, removed the green husk, then squeezed until the shell cracked in his grip.

"That is so zip," said Junior. From the admiration in her expression, Mops assumed it was a compliment.

Monroe dropped the pieces into Mops' hand. She nodded her thanks, picked bits of nut meat free, and popped them into her mouth. They had a sweet, buttery taste. She was reaching for more before she'd finished chewing.

"Bathroom's through that door in the back." Wolf cocked her thumb at a warped metal door. Flaking paint suggested it had once been painted to resemble wood. "No water showers, but there's dry shampoo and some cleaning and disinfectant powders."

From the smell, Wolf had taken full advantage. Instead of smelling like skunk, she now smelled like lemon, wildflowers, and skunk.

"Any word from the surface?" asked Mops.

Khatami glanced at their wrist comm. "Lookouts have spotted a few drones and fighters passing overhead, but the Alliance hasn't started their assault yet."

"Gleason's meeting with the Board and department heads now," said Mops. "She asked me to join them in half an hour to help plan the defense, and to figure out where and how my team can best support the librarians."

The table grew quiet. They all knew this wasn't a winnable fight. Sage had at least a hundred fighters and bombers available to her on Stepping Stone Station, as well as any larger-class ships in the system.

Mops wiped crumbs from her hands, her appetite having soured. She pulled a food tube from her harness and unsealed her suit.

Junior stared with unabashed curiosity. "You have bionic stomachs?"

"The Krakau install feeding ports in all reborn troops," said Mops. "The nutrient mix goes directly into our stomachs. The stomachs themselves are unmodified factory-issue, though."

"Why would they do that?"

"There are rumors that eating 'naturally' can occasionally trigger reversion." Mops pressed the injection button on the end of the tube. "From what we've learned, there's not much truth to those rumors. I think it's more so the Krakau can monitor and control our nutrition intake."

Junior rolled her eyes. "You mean they don't trust you to feed yourselves?"

"The tubes also let the Krakau deliver medication and drugs as needed," said Monroe. "Infantry troops get a mixture before battle that includes stimulants to improve battle performance."

"Does it ever leak?" asked Junior. "Like, what if you're walking around and your port comes undone? It would be like vomiting out of your belly button."

"They don't leak," Mops assured her.

Khatami dipped their fingers in a small bowl of water, wiped their lips, and spoke briefly in a language Doc couldn't translate. When they looked up and noticed Mops watching, they explained, "An after-blessing for the food."

"Khatami's always praying to different gods and prophets," said Junior. "Like they're trying to practice every Earth religion at the same time. They rotate through different blessings and prayers at mealtime."

"It can get confusing," Khatami admitted with a smile. "The holidays alone are overwhelming."

"Why make the effort?" asked Wolf.

"I find I understand them better through practice," said Khatami. "Religion is part of our history. This is my way of keeping that history alive. Then there's Pascal's Wager. If our religious traditions were wrong, I don't lose anything by practicing. But if one of those traditions got it right . . ."

"Do your prayers have any measurable effect?" asked Rubin.

Junior groaned. "Don't get them started."

Khatami threw a scrap of algae bar at her. "Do they impact the world or the outcome of events? It's impossible to construct a controlled experiment to say one way or the other. But they bring me peace and comfort."

"Better say some for us," said Monroe. "We'll need all the help we can get when the rest of the Alliance forces get here from Stepping Stone."

Khatami's expression turned sober. "I've been praying for days, brother."

"Sage isn't using Stepping Stone ships."

Mops turned to stare at Wolf. "What did you just say?"

"That troop carrier yesterday came from Earth." Wolf shifted uncomfortably. "Didn't anyone else notice the fecal stains?"

"Gross," muttered Junior.

"You want gross, try clearing a plumbing jam when Grom's secreting eggs." Wolf mimed throwing up, eliciting a pained laugh from Junior.

"The troop carrier," Mops pressed. "Explain."

"It had dry smears of something black and white all over the hull, mostly on the top or streaked down the side." Wolf shrugged. "I've seen enough shit to recognize it. Probably left by birds or bats or dragons or whatever."

Khatami raised a hand. "Dragons aren't real. And if they were, their droppings would be significantly larger."

"That ship was parked here on Earth, exposed to the animals." Mops stood, her mind racing through the implications. "Monroe, when you spotted those fighters approaching the library—"

"They were already within the atmosphere." He smacked his artificial hand against the table. "I'm a damn fool."

"The rest of us can't read minds, you know," Wolf complained.

"Sage wants to keep the existence of the librarians a secret," said Mops. "So she only dispatched security forces from her research facility here on the surface. Stepping Stone is too big. It would be too easy for secrets to leak. She's limited to using people whose loyalty she can trust."

"With respect," said Khatami, "those limited resources far surpass anything we have available to protect ourselves. Lock-Land is a difficult nut to crack, but even a single fighter would eventually destroy us."

"Eventually," Mops repeated. "But in the meantime, every ship and soldier Sage sends here means fewer forces to protect her research lab."

"You want to attack them while they're busy attacking LockLand," said Rubin.

"I concur!" Cate stood and stretched his wings. "I'm sorry. I only heard the last part of the conversation. Who are we attacking?"

"Everyone finish eating and double-check your equipment." Mops started toward the door. "Junior? Take me to your mother."

Junior filled every moment of the walk with questions. Mops suspected it was a response to anxiety, a way to avoid thinking about what was about to happen. She wasn't alone in her fear, but it showed more in her restless gestures, in her discomfort with silence.

Chronologically, Junior might have lived more than Mops' twelve years, but she was still growing. The other librarians Mops had met all seemed to know who they were and how they fit into this little microsociety. Junior felt . . . unfinished. Uncertain.

"What's the grossest thing you ever had to clean up on your ship?"

That was an easy one. "Two years ago, a medical refrigeration unit failed after a battle."

Junior sounded disappointed. "That's it? A broken fridge?"

"That particular fridge was being used to store a Prodryan corpse, and it took three weeks for anyone to notice the failure." Mops had put in for commendations for the whole team after that one.

"Gross."

"That's an understatement."

"If they found a cure, would you want to be human again?"

Mops slowed. "We *are* human."

"You know what I mean."

"Yes," said Mops. "I also know what you said."

Junior groaned and waved her hands in exasperation. "You're as bad as my mother. Fine, I'm sorry. If they found a way to undo everything the Krakau plague did to you, would you take it?"

She didn't answer right away. "There was a time I'd have said yes, no hesitation."

"Not anymore?"

"I'd have to think about it. For one thing, you natural-born humans feel pain. That sounds unpleasant."

Junior leaned closer. "You really don't feel pain?"

"Not like you do." Mops rotated her arm, making the shoulder pop so loudly Junior jumped. "I feel the pressure and the jolt of the joint jumping into place, but no pain. At most, we might get a dull ache or throbbing sensation. That's not necessarily a good thing, though. It means we don't notice injuries. One of my crewmates four months ago was walking around with a chunk of shrapnel in her back. She didn't even know. She could easily have severed her spine, or worse."

Junior nodded wisely. "CIPA."

"Pardon?"

"In Human, it would be . . ." Her face screwed up with concentration. "Congenital insensitivity to pain, with . . . I'm not sure how to translate the last word, but it means you can't sense temperature extremes, and your body doesn't sweat. It was a human genetic disorder. High fatality rate from injuries and overheating."

"We can feel differences in temperature," said Mops.

Junior cocked her head. "Has anyone ever done a study to figure out *why* you don't feel pain? Do the nerves not transmit the signal, or does the brain just not register it?"

"I don't have any such studies in my databases. I'd have to synch up with the Pufferfish *medical systems to run a more comprehensive search."*

"I have no idea," Mops admitted. "Doc's not aware of any." There was a lot she didn't understand about how humans worked. She'd learned basic first aid, the same as any other EMC recruit, but nothing deeper.

What would a cure even mean? Pain, yes, but how else would her senses change? The average reborn human was known to be less intelligent than their "natural" ancestors. Would a cure improve her memory, help her to think more clearly and quickly?

They passed a woman with wrinkled skin and pale hair. She moved with slow, stiff steps, leaning on a metal cane and laughing at something her younger companion had said. Mops knew human life spans had once reached a century, but knowing and seeing were very different things. Few EMC troops made it to half that age.

"Doc. That's your AI? Wolf mentioned it."

"Him," Mops corrected absently.

"Sorry." Junior peered into Mops' monocle. "He's in there, right? What's he like?"

"I can't wait to hear this."

"He's a combination of friend and partner. He's very smart, and only occasionally a pain in my ass."

"Hey, that's— Yeah, okay, that's fair."

"Do you dream?"

"Sometimes, yes. Especially when we've been working too hard. The nightmares I had my first year after the waste recycling system on Stepping Stone melted down . . ." She gave a mock shudder.

They stopped at a narrow door near pillar L16. "Mom's

inside with the Board." Junior started to knock, but her fist stopped before making contact. "What do you think the Alliance will do to us?"

Study your genetics, then kill you to keep your existence secret. Use what they learned to improve their process for creating EMC soldiers. Send more of us to die in the escalating war with the Prodryans.

"I won't let it come to that." Mops reached past her and pushed open the door.

Eliza Gleason sat at a rectangular table with nine other librarians, all of whom stopped speaking when Mops entered. Junior followed a moment later.

Eliza jabbed a marker at Mops. "You're early."

The table's surface was a glossy white material, covered in illegible writing and hastily-sketched diagrams of LockLand and the surrounding hillside. Junior stepped out from behind Mops to read some of the notes. She spun and pointed an accusing finger at her mother. "You're surrendering? Surrendering sucks!"

Eliza raised a hand, and Junior bit back whatever else she had been about to say. "We're considering *all* options. Our primary mission is to preserve and protect knowledge. If surrendering to the Krakau accomplishes that—"

"It won't," said Mops. "They'll bury all of this. People like Sage can't risk anyone learning what really happened to the Earth."

A stout woman with a wide, vivid red mohawk slammed the table. A series of flat round piercings or implants adorned the backs of her hands. "You see? Even the kid and the gun know surrender isn't an option."

"That's Nancy," whispered Junior. "She specializes in restoration, preservation, and being an asshole."

She spoke just loudly enough for the closest librarians to hear. One developed a sudden coughing fit, while the other turned away, covering his mouth with his hand.

"If you'd let me finish, I'm not proposing total surrender."

Eliza pointed to one of the drawings of Lockland that showed all nine sublevels, like Glacidae ice pucks stacked one atop the next. She drew a red line between five and six. "The Alliance doesn't know how many of us are here. I'll take a small group of librarians to sublevel five, then we seal off everything below. That allows the rest of you to remain safely hidden, along with our collections."

She offered an apologetic look to Mops. "They know about you and your team. Otherwise, I'd suggest you hide with the rest of the librarians."

"How would you close off access to the lower levels?" asked Mops.

Eliza pointed to a black-haired woman with pale blue-gray eyes and a series of gold rings through both eyebrows. "That's Jessamyn's job."

Jessamyn's smile lowered the temperature at least five degrees. "I built my first bomb when I was eleven. As part of Lock-Land's contingency plans, I've stockpiled enough explosive to take out half this mountain." She took Eliza's marker and began marking Xs on the map. "If we detonate small charges in the stairwells, elevator shafts, and air vents, it should be enough to stop the Alliance from probing any deeper."

"And we'll all be trapped," finished Junior. Her eyes shone with barely-restrained emotion. "Left to starve or suffocate after the rest of you die. Nancy's right. This is *bullshit*, Mother."

"You'll have the tools and equipment to reopen one of the evacuation routes," Eliza said firmly. "You'll need to wait for the Alliance to turn their attention elsewhere, but this place was designed for long-term survival. Even cut off, any given level should have enough supplies to sustain you for at least a year."

Mops touched Junior's shoulder before she could launch into an angry response. "I might have an alternative."

Eliza sat back in her chair. "We're listening."

"Your fight isn't against the Alliance. It's not even against the Krakau. It's against Admiral Sage and a small group of her loyalists here on the surface."

"Those loyalists have advanced warships and energy weapons," said Nancy. "We have knives and shotguns."

"And bombs," added Jessamyn.

Eliza raised a hand, and the others fell silent. "What are you proposing, Captain?"

"LockLand is tough," she said. "Sage will have to divert most of her forces here. That leaves her facility vulnerable. I can take a team to infiltrate it."

"Even if you could," said Nancy, "you'd never be able to hold it."

"We don't have to." Mops placed both hands on the edge of the table. "Whatever Sage is doing, she wants it kept secret. If we get in, seize control of their communications systems, we can use that secret as leverage against her."

"And where is this secret laboratory?" asked Nancy.

Mops removed her monocle and held it over a blank section of the table. Doc projected a crude, small map of the coast with a green X. "According to the intelligence Cate provided, it's about forty kilometers east of here."

Junior pointed. "Remember when we saw all those ships coming down from the station two months back? That must have been where they were going."

"An entire planet to choose from, and they picked a spot within spitting distance of us?" asked Nancy. "That's suspicious as hell."

Another librarian spoke up, a slender man with a fringe of brown hair. "Siyali Ranganathan," he said, with a polite nod to Mops. "It's not such a coincidence, really. This Krakau, Sage, would have wanted a relatively undamaged chunk of human real estate. Easier to take over an existing facility than to build one from the ground up, especially if she's worried about secrecy. A hundred and fifty years ago, this was one of the fastest-growing regions on the planet."

He pointed to the green X. "That was the epicenter."

Mops raised the monocle, expanding the map. "What was this place?"

"Armstrong Space Center," said Junior. "It's where they sent up the first lunar colonists, ten years before the plague."

"That was the start of the second space age." Ranganathan studied the map. "There were plans for an entire lunar nation, and for the terraforming of Mars. Armstrong Space Center was supposed to be the beginning of a new age for human-kind. The idea of a Krakau turning it into a secret military facility . . ."

"All the more reason to kick Sage out of there," said Mops.

"It's forty kilometers," said Jessamyn. "No way the captain and her team would make it without a guide."

"Can we trust them?" asked Nancy. "No offense, Captain Adamopoulos, but you were EMC. We have only your word you're not working for the Krakau."

"We were EMC," Mops agreed. "We're also human. This is our world, too. I was born here. I grew up here, a feral like Cindy and the others Melvil's been trying to help. None of us in the EMC ever knew who we were or where we came from. All we had were the lies the Krakau taught, and each other."

Her throat tightened. She slowed her breathing and swallowed. "You're family. This place is our history. And I'll be damned if I'll let anything happen to it, or to you."

Eliza opened her hands to the other librarians, a silent invitation.

"What makes you think you and your people are capable of taking Armstrong Base?" asked Jessamyn. "By your own admission, you aren't soldiers. You're janitors."

Mops wanted to tell them she had full confidence in her team's abilities. She also wanted to be honest. "We've kept ahead of the Alliance for four months. We've fought Prodryan fighters and Nusuran smugglers and EMC cruisers and survived. I believe we've got a shot at this, with your help."

Eliza raised her right hand, fingers splayed. The rest of the librarians moved their hands in response, gesturing with thumbs and index fingers.

"They're voting," Junior whispered.

After a quick scan, Eliza turned back to Mops. "The Board will support your plan. I agree with Jessamyn about the need for a guide."

Junior's eyes lit up. She leaned forward, mouth open to speak. Without pausing, Eliza said, "Not you, Junior."

"The Alliance will be watching this place," said Mops. "We'll need to cross forty kilometers quickly, without being seen."

Eliza's smile made Mops nervous. "I think we can help you there."

Mops grimaced at the too-sweet wad of gum in her mouth. Monroe had passed out the cubes of caffeinated gum to compensate for their lack of sleep. It helped, but it coated her tongue with a thick, syrupy taste.

"Watch your heads," said Bev, ducking into a large drainage pipe. This was one of the emergency evacuation routes the librarians had prepared. It was normally closed off by a series of doors and grates to prevent wildlife from entering LockLand's lower levels.

After ten minutes of hunched hiking through the cramped, frost-slick metal, Mops saw sunlight through the shadows of the pine trees the librarians had planted to obscure the pipe. An outcropping of rock and dirt further hid it from view.

A pale, beefy man waited for them. According to Bev, this was Marcel Duchamp, and he'd be arranging their transportation. His gray hair and beard were all trimmed to half a centimeter, giving his head a frosted appearance. He sat on a half-bale of hay, smoking a carved pipe. He gestured toward four sand-colored bundles on the ground. "You'll be wanting to put those on."

Mops picked one up. Monroe, Rubin, and Bev did the same. A loop of twine secured the scratchy wool. Mops tugged it free and shook out a large, heavy poncho.

Wolf and Cate would be staying behind, on Mops' orders.

Wolf was too high-strung for sneaking around, and Mops preferred to see for herself what Sage was up to at Armstrong before sharing that information with a Prodryan spy.

Duchamp removed the pipe from his mouth, brought a copper whistle to his mouth, and blew two long blasts. He scattered hay around the entrance, then repeated the call.

Mops tugged the poncho over her head. The hood scratched her ears, making her wish she hadn't lost her infantry helmet.

"Here they come." Duchamp beamed and tossed a handful of hay into the snow.

Mops looked out, and her monocle immediately focused on a group of eight large, shaggy animals. She didn't have much experience with Earth fauna, but these things seemed poorly constructed. Four thin legs supported an enormous, wooly torso. Two large humps swelled from the back like giant tumors. Thick fur from the chin to the shoulders hung like a poorly-tended beard.

"What are they?" Rubin asked.

"Wild Bactrian camels." Duchamp made a clicking sound as the camels neared. The animals shifted nervously, then one of the larger ones came closer and began nibbling at the hay. The rest soon followed.

Mops watched them eat. "Everything I've read suggested camels lived in the desert."

"You should read more." Duchamp's smile took any sting from the words. "Camels are built to survive a range of extremes. We've tended this herd for close to a century. They used to be endangered. When humans fell, camels were one of many species to experience a comeback."

"The robes are camel wool," said Bev. "From a distance, you'll look like part of the animal. It's one of the ways we travel without being discovered. We ought to reach Armstrong in a single day."

"How exactly are we supposed to ride these things?" asked Monroe.

"Carefully." Duchamp laughed again. "Getting on and off is the trickiest part. Bev knows the commands."

Bev spoke a two-syllable word, and one of the camels stepped over, then knelt in the snow and gravel. She approached and lifted one leg over the camel's back, between the humps. "Lean back as the camel stands up, or else you'll tumble right over the head. It will take a bit to get used to the gait, but you'll learn to adjust your balance."

Monroe grimaced, but said nothing. If he thought he could handle it, Mops wasn't going to argue.

"They're beautiful." Rubin was feeding handfuls of hay to the two closest camels.

"Glad you think so." Duchamp offered one a chunk of dried fruit. "I hope you still feel that way after a day on their backs."

14

Kumar studied the map of Earth on the main viewscreen. Two locations were tagged in green. According to the Pufferfish *sensors, the first was the site of an Alliance bombing run. The second was where a troop transport had landed, followed shortly by small arms fire.*

"You humans certainly leave a convenient trail of destruction," said Azure.

"It looks like the captain was heading north," said Kumar. "I've got another troop transport coming in from the coast. The two paths intersect here in the hills. It looks like an old subterranean town."

Grom pointed a limb at the screen. "If Sage is sending out more ships, it means our people are still alive."

"Not necessarily," said Azure. "It could be that only some of them survived the shuttle explosion. Or the fighters might be searching for the rogue human from Cate's surveillance footage. Or they could be on an unrelated mission."

"Shut up," Grom chittered. They pointed to Kumar.

"Right," said Azure. "My apologies, Kumar. I'm sure Rubin and the others are fine, despite our lack of evidence or confirmation."

Kumar lifted the pendant around his neck, holding it to the light to watch the tiny pink worms wriggling about. Vera had left them with him, trusting him to look after them until she returned. "We should keep watching those underground ruins. Set up an alert if the sensors detect any sign of human activity."

"Agreed," said Grom. "How do we do that?"

"Doc?" asked Kumar.

"I'll pull up the tutorials."

Kumar tucked the pendant back into his uniform and stared at the screen. "Even if we find them, we can't communicate with them."

"Not with them, no," said Azure. "What about Admiral Pachelbel?"

Grom clicked at her. "You don't see a problem with us signaling Stepping Stone? We might as well paint a target on the Pufferfish *and park directly in front of the station's primary weapons pod."*

"Captain Adamopoulos has communicated with the admiral in the past," Azure pointed out. "They arranged our meeting with Cate in the Tixateq system. Presumably the captain has the means to make contact without being discovered."

"That would be a lot more helpful if the captain was here," snapped Grom. "Or our communications officer, for that matter."

"Grom, work with Doc. See if the two of you can figure out how the captain was talking to Admiral Pachelbel. Azure, go through those sensor tutorials. Make sure we're watching everything as closely as possible." Kumar stood to leave. "I'll be back as soon as I can."

"What will you be doing?" asked Azure.

"I have to go feed Vera's pet slug."

WOLF SPRAYED A THICK copper-colored mist over the steps of stairway 17B.

"What is that revolting fluid?" asked Cate.

"Industrial lubricant."

"I see." Cate leaned closer. "The Krakau will lose their grip and fall, suffering serious injury and humiliation in the process."

"That's the idea." Wolf slid the spray wand back into her harness and surveyed her work. The trick was to apply even coverage so there was no visual discoloration to give the trap away. She crouched to check the steps from another angle, then nodded to herself.

To her right, a sealed blast door blocked the way into the ruins of LockLand level one. Wolf stepped down onto the next set of stairs and checked the notes the librarians had given her.

The electronic controls for the emergency doors, designed to separate and isolate each floor in the stairwell, had given out decades ago. Wolf pried open a rectangular panel on the wall, revealing a series of wires, circuitry, and a flat metal lever with a red handle. An old rodent nest of fur and insulation sat snugly cradled by the wires to the left.

Wolf gripped the lever with both hands and pulled.

A heavy door slammed to the ground hard enough that small chunks of concrete broke away from the wall. "That should slow them down even more."

"Perhaps this time we can weld sharpened spikes onto the landing. When the Krakau fall on your lubricating fluid, they'll impale themselves."

"Not bad." Wolf had been less than thrilled at having to babysit the Prodryan, but the idea of setting traps for the Krakau had brought out a new, slightly less obnoxious side to Cate's personality. "If these door controls still worked, we could probably rig a tripwire to bring one down on the first Krakau through."

"A trick almost worthy of a Prodryan," said Cate.

Wolf stopped halfway down the stairs and activated her cutting torch, setting a narrow three-centimeter flame. She cut at an angle through the handrail, just past the top bracket holding it to the wall.

"Improvised spikes!" Cate's antennae rose, and he leaned closer. "Excellent!"

"Not spikes." Wolf made a second cut right before bracket number two, at the opposite angle. She lifted the rail free while the metal cooled, then set it gently back. The beveled angles held the rail in place, but the slightest tug would pull it free. She swapped the torch for her spray wand and began coating the next set of steps. "After they recover from level one, the Krakau will be expecting the oiled stairs. They'll grab the rail for support."

They'd worked most of the night preparing LockLand for the assault. Every access point save this stairwell had been permanently closed, thanks to Jessamyn West's homemade bombs. A small group of librarians worked to ready level five. The rest were down on seven. On Gleason's command, Jessamyn would blow up most of level six, hopefully protecting the other librarians and their collection from the Krakau.

"I would like to resubmit my request for a weapon," said Cate.

"And I repeat my suggestion that you go drown yourself."

"We are allied against the Krakau. Believe me, I will avoid shooting you in the back until after we've dealt with the larger threat."

Before Wolf could answer, a buzz like a flatulent Comacean filled the air, making her jump so hard she dropped her spray wand. "What the depths?"

"That is the alert siren, announcing the arrival of the Krakau," said Cate. "Gleason described the sound. Weren't you listening?"

Wolf didn't dignify that with a response. "I was hoping we'd have time to get a few more surprises set up."

She quickly coated the rest of the steps. Next to the door control panel, an old announcements sign flashed red on the wall of the level two landing. It was written in several languages, enough that Wolf's visor eventually managed to translate. "Looks like all rides are closed until further notice," she read. "The nightly laser hockey tournament is canceled, and the casino will be shitting down early."

She frowned and looked more closely. "*Shutting* down early."

This door came down with a thud equal to the last.

"Now what?" asked Cate. "Close the rest of the doors and join the librarians on level five to await our inevitable defeat and capture?"

"The captain didn't order us to join that fight," said Wolf. "Just to buy as much time as we could so they can get into Armstrong."

"Just when I was beginning to develop a smattering of respect." Cate turned away in disgust. "This cowardice in the face of battle is why the Prodryans will ultimately—"

Wolf jabbed the spray wand in Cate's face. "Finish that sentence, and I'll make you swallow this thing."

"My point is that we could purchase additional time for your comrades through active, violent resistance."

Wolf backed down the stairs, spraying as she went.

"It's true, the Krakau will be armored and heavily armed," Cate continued. "We would certainly be killed, probably within minutes. However—"

A strange voice cut him off. "You ready, Wolfgang?"

Wolf harnessed her wand and shut down the compressor before turning to face a small group of armed librarians waiting just beyond the open door to level three. Wolf recognized only two of them. Nancy stood at the front, rifle over one shoulder, knife and pistol hanging from her belt.

Wolf turned to Melvil. "I thought you'd be down on seven, looking after Cindy."

"Cindy's safe." Melvil adjusted his spectacles and drew himself up. "But the Krakau attacked her pack. I don't know how many of them survived. I'm fighting for them, as well as for the library."

"What is this?" asked Cate.

"Nancy pulled me aside earlier." Wolf counted a total of eight librarians in the group. "Said some of them didn't like the idea of sitting on their asses, waiting for the Krakau."

"You said your captain didn't order you to fight," Cate said accusingly.

"That's right." Wolf grinned. "Didn't order me not to, either." She turned her attention to the librarians. "Did you check our escape route to level four?"

"It's disgusting," said Nancy. "But it should work. I've got a few bombs from Jessamyn's cache. I think we can make this next part work."

"Why is this one part of the fighting?" Cate jabbed a claw at Nancy. "She's small and old."

Nancy ran a hand through her mohawk. "Being small makes me a harder target. As for old, that just means I've had time to learn more dirty tricks. If you don't want me to demonstrate on you, I suggest you shut your face."

"Take up position on level four, by pillar 18C," said Wolf. "Cate and I will meet you there."

Cate hesitated. "What exactly will the two of us be doing?"

Wolf clapped him on the arm, then grimaced and wiped her hand on her pants. "Making life hell for the Krakau."

Monroe only fell off his camel twice: once while mounting, and once while dismounting. The second time, he just lay on his back in the snow and looked up at Mops. "I'm going to need everything from my hips down replaced."

"You and me both." Mops pressed both hands against a pine tree and shook her legs one at a time, trying to work out the worst of the throbbing and stiffness. She was hot, itchy, and having trouble adjusting to stable ground after the swaying walk of her camel.

Bev finished feeding the camels and sent them on their way. She rejoined the others and pointed through the trees. "Welcome to Armstrong Space Center."

Despite a century and a half of disuse, Mops could clearly make out five broad, circular launch pads stretched out along the shore, each one spaced about three hundred meters from the next. At the center of the pads stood the remains of rectangular towers.

"Launch gantries," said Bev, following her gaze. "What's left of them. Most of gantry three toppled a decade ago, and number five looks like the next stiff breeze will take it out."

The second pad also held a Krakau shuttle, along with two fighters. Mops glanced back at Monroe. "You think you can fly that shuttle?"

Monroe sat up with a groan. "As long as it doesn't spit at me."

Mops chuckled and turned back, trying to visualize this place as it had once been. She imagined a sleek lunar shuttle standing proud against the gantry. A personal transport bringing the crew to the launch pad. Spotlights shining from the ground. Crowds watching from a safe distance, waiting for the roar and flare of ignition.

"What happened to the lunar colony after the plague?" asked Rubin.

Bev bowed her head. "Twenty-three people were living on the moon at the time of the outbreak. Things spread too fast for a retrieval mission. From the recordings we dug up, they lasted almost two years after losing support from Earth."

"Two years." Mops turned to the others, her back against the tree. "Humans built this place. We were exploring space long before the Krakau showed up. We made it to the moon, built a colony there. Twenty-three human beings survived two *years* on their own on an airless rock in the sky. That's who we were. That's who we're going to be again someday."

"Assuming we're not captured and killed."

Mops closed her eyes. "Yes, Rubin. Assuming we're not captured and killed."

She shifted her attention to the complex of buildings on the near side. Three long hangars sat parallel, their curved, segmented roofs making her think of giant metal Glacidae.

Her monocle gave her a clearer view of a fallen water tower and a large four-story building with a series of old towers and satellite receivers on the overgrown field beside it.

"Ferals." Rubin pointed toward the shore.

"I see them." Mops zoomed in, trying to get a count. At least five ferals trudged back and forth in the knee-deep water, just beyond a metal fence that surrounded launch pads one through three, along with most of the nearby structures.

The ferals walked with their bodies hunched over, their faces close to the waves. From time to time, their hands disappeared into the water, like tiny cranes scooping up ice and wet sand. Occasionally, one would bring a handful of sand to its mouth.

"They're hunting," said Bev. "Crabs buried in the sand for the winter, starfish washed toward shore, things like that."

"That fence is of Krakau construction. Electrified, with motion detectors on every third post."

"What range?" asked Mops.

"I'd suggest you keep back at least two hundred meters to avoid detection."

Mops passed the warning along.

"You have any bright ideas for getting inside?" asked Bev.

These were Krakau. That meant a high volume of water circulation, with infusion tanks, filtration systems, and more. "Monroe, if you were going to set up water intake and treatment here for a group of Krakau, how would you do it?"

He knelt beside her, studying the layout. "Ocean water should be salty enough for them. Assuming fewer than a hundred Krakau, one intake pipe and one outflow should be enough. See that strip of broken concrete between pads one and two? It looks like that area was dug up recently. That would give a straight line to run a feed to those three warehouses and that complex of buildings."

"Wouldn't they have to keep the two pipes separate?" asked Bev. "Otherwise they'd be drinking their own sewage."

"Not if they've got it on a timer," said Mops. "Pull in the day's water first thing in the morning, then flush out yesterday's waste. Wait twenty-four hours for your sewage to wash away, then repeat."

Bev's face wrinkled. "Are you suggesting we try to crawl in through the sewer? You might be right about the pipes, but we don't know where they lead, or how to find—"

"I'm suggesting we get ourselves a guide." Mops pointed to the water. "What happens when a disposal line clogs and the automated cleaning systems can't handle it?"

Monroe grinned. "They send the janitor to fix it."

"We're in position." Mops secured her boots to her pants, then pulled out her gloves. To her left, Rubin was doing the same. "Doc, adjust our camo, please."

Mops' uniform darkened, taking on the blotchy brown appearance of the sand beneath the water.

They'd circled around to the north side of Armstrong Space Center, reaching the beach well beyond launch pad five. There they'd discovered what had once been a memorial park with old rockets laid out along the ground, and were using the largest for cover.

Mops put a hand on the riveted metal. "Can you imagine flying into space in this thing?" Mops asked. "Squeezed into that tiny nosecone on top of so many tons of explosive fuel?"

"There are holes rusted through the length of the rocket," Rubin pointed out. "It wouldn't survive being lifted into launch position, and fuel ignition would vaporize the lower half."

"I meant—never mind." Mops turned her head, addressing Monroe again. "Have they noticed us?"

"Not that we can see," said Monroe. "Ferals are still fishing, but otherwise, the place is dead."

Mops opened her collar and drew the thin, flexible bubble over her head. With her infantry helmet lost, she had to make do with the emergency helmet built into her uniform. EMC uniforms were designed to endure short periods of vacuum in space. It should hold against a little water.

Her monocle confirmed she was now airtight. A second icon lit up as Rubin finished sealing her own uniform.

"Permission to speak freely?" Monroe asked.

"Granted." Mops knew what he was going to say, and why he'd fallen into the stiff formality of his infantry days to say it.

"This is a stupid plan, sir. There's an excellent chance you'll be killed."

"Shot, yes. Killed, no. Not right away."

"I should be going in. Not you."

"We've been over this." The crust of ice at the edge of the water gave way beneath Mops' weight. She waded deeper, each step squelching up a cloud of dirt and mud. "Just watch our backs."

"Always."

"Thanks." She waded deeper. A small timer appeared on her monocle, letting her know she had thirty minutes of air.

Mops dropped prone. She had to fight her suit's buoyancy as she crawled toward deeper water. She dug her hands into the muck and weeds to keep herself submerged. Every once in a while, she thought she saw movement through the sand and silt, but nothing stuck around long enough for her to get a good look.

"How's it coming, sir?" asked Monroe.

"A hundred meters down, another one-point-four kilometers to go," Doc broadcast. *"This could be a problem, given your rate of oxygen consumption."*

Mops checked her timer. "You think?"

"Snapping at your AI wastes oxygen," Doc chided.

"We'll have to improvise."

The one-minute oxygen alert flashed just before they reached the Krakau fence, which jutted into the ocean between landing pads three and four. Rubin still had two minutes left.

Mops pulled one of the spare compressor hoses from her harness, along with a utility knife. The blade eventually sawed through the middle of the reinforced hose. Mops sheathed the knife and handed one piece of hose to Rubin.

"If you're about to do what it looks like, might I remind you that your suit's insulation only works as long as you keep the freezing water outside?*"*

"I'm aware," said Mops. "And might I remind you that humans require oxygen?"

Doc gave an impressively human-sounding sniff of disdain. *"Yet another of your species' many design flaws."*

Mops took several deep breaths, using up the last of the suit's warm air, then unsealed her collar. Icy water rushed in, making her gasp. Clamping one end of the hose in her mouth, she poked the other up above the surface and blew hard to clear the water. Cold, metallic air filled her lungs.

"Your body temperature is 32.4. You've got about two degrees before hypothermia starts."

Mops moved as quickly and carefully as she could. Despite her caution, she twice choked on water when the end of the hose slipped below the surface. It wasn't long before her fingers and toes grew numb. Her limbs felt stiff.

"Another hundred meters."

She grunted acknowledgment.

The Krakau water line was easy enough to find—a standard twenty-two-centimeter extruded polymer pipe, dark brown in color. It lay on the sand like a fat, lazy snake, jutting several meters through the bottom of the fence.

"You're frowning. What's wrong?"

Mops couldn't speak, but she could subvocalize enough for Doc to understand. "Whoever installed this thing only buried

it about ten centimeters below ground." Given the temperatures, it was only a matter of time before the freeze-thaw cycles
burst the pipe. If any of her team ever did such a lazy job, she'd
toss them out an air lock.

A set of horizontal flap valves covered the end of the pipe,
preventing backflow. Mops pulled out her plasma torch. It took
three tries for her clumsy fingers to switch it on. Bubbles and
steam erupted from the one-centimeter flame.

*"I've informed Monroe that you've reached your destina-
tion. Your temperature is down to 31.4."*

Rubin hunched behind her, rifle in hand, as Mops finished
burning a neat hole through the side of the pipe. She replaced
the torch and took a tube of emergency hull sealant. The ocean
water blurred her vision, and she briefly lost sight of the hole
she'd made. She felt along the pipe until she found it again.
Breaking the sealant cap free with her teeth, she jammed the
nozzle through the hole and squeezed the contents into the
pipe. She shoved the empty tube back into her harness.

A bright orange worm appeared to crawl out of the hole as
the foam expanded. It was half a meter in length by the time
everything dried and hardened. Mops grasped the worm with
both hands and broke it free.

"Rubin is asking if you're finished."

"Not quite." She swam to the fence and burned another
hole in the pipe. While the edges cooled, she pressed a small
valve into place. A quick squeeze of liquid titanium around the
seam secured it.

"She wants to know how long you need."

"A few more minutes." Mops hooked her compressor hose
to the valve, ran an intake line up out of the water, and switched
it on. "It could be hours before the Krakau notice the blocked
pipe. I'm going to overpressurize it. If we're lucky, it will cause
a catastrophic failure on the other end, maybe even set off a
few . . . eruptions inside."

"You've got a curious feral wading your way," said Monroe.
"I have a clean shot."

Mops checked the pressure reading. "Don't fire unless I give the order."

"Rubin is swimming toward the feral."

With one hand on the compressor and the other holding both the intake line and her own air hose above water, Mops could do nothing but watch as Rubin slung her rifle over her shoulder and pulled a handful of dehydrated leathery fruit from her pocket. She held it toward the feral, her hand just above the water.

The feral snatched the fruit and began to eat.

"Now the rest of them are en route," Monroe warned.

Rubin kept moving, drawing the ferals away from Mops and the pipe.

"Doc, please tell Rubin that getting eaten by ferals is *not* an acceptable plan. Monroe, if it looks like Rubin's in trouble, take those ferals down."

"Understood," said Monroe.

"Rubin insists she's got this under control." Doc paused. *"I think that's what she's saying. She mumbles when she subvocalizes. She may have told me she sundered a mole."*

The minutes crawled as Rubin led the ferals farther down the shore. How much food did she have tucked away in her pockets? By now, they were far enough Mops could only make out vague shapes. She focused instead on her monocle, watching Rubin's vital signs.

With a sound like thunder, the waste pipe jumped, knocking Mops backward. Sand and muck turned the water opaque. Mops switched off her compressor by feel.

"That ought to get their attention," said Monroe. "Scared the shit out of those ferals, too. They're running back toward land."

By the time Rubin rejoined Mops, the water had begun to clear. Mops swept a bit of dirt over the holes in the pipe to hide her sabotage. She gestured to catch Rubin's attention and pointed back in the direction from which they'd come.

They pulled back about twenty meters, where a wall of brown seaweed provided additional concealment.

"What happens now?"

"If I was working this job, the first thing I'd do is check the damage from inside the building. Probably send a cleaner snake into the pipe. The snake will find the blockage, which should be caked in Krakau crap by now. The snake's not strong enough to get through hull sealant, so the next step is for them to come out and deal with it in person. Hopefully before we freeze to death."

Forty minutes later—forty minutes of breathing through a foul-tasting tube while listening to Doc count down her body temperature a tenth of a degree at a time—Monroe alerted them to activity from one of the buildings.

"Looks like a Krakau hovercar," said Monroe. "I'm transmitting the visual to your monocle."

The hovercar resembled a large, flattened bubble of mucus, with a series of smaller mucus bubbles on the back. It passed through a gate in the fence and circled down to the beach.

Mops flexed her limbs to restore the circulation. She touched Rubin's arm to get her attention. Rubin acknowledged with a nod.

The hovercar floated onto the water. From her hiding spot in the seaweed, Mops could see the skinlike undersurface seeming to mold itself to the waves. It came about to stop a short distance from the damaged pipe.

A hole appeared in the side of the main bubble, and a green-skinned Krakau peered out. A loaded equipment sleeve encased her body, and she held a scanner in one tentacle. She stood on the edge of the hovercar, staring down into the water.

Mops could imagine what was going through her primary brain. *When I find whoever clogged this thing, I'll flush* them *through the pipe.*

The Krakau slid into the water. She spasmed once, reacting to the cold. One tentacle adjusted a setting on her equipment sleeve, probably increasing the temperature of the built-in heating lines.

"30.1 degrees," said Doc. *"When you strike, expect to experience clumsiness and confusion."*

Mops waited, hand on her pistol. At this distance, with their uniforms darkened to blend with the ocean bottom, the Krakau hadn't yet noticed them. But Krakau vision was attuned to movement. As soon as Mops and Rubin started in, they'd give themselves away.

The Krakau shot through the water to the end of the pipe, her many limbs moving in unison to propel her forward. She switched on a conical tool with a wrinkled, oyster-shell handle. A jet of water from the narrow end quickly cleaned the pipe's surface. She then manipulated the flap valves on the end, propping them open. Another tool shone a beam of blue-tinged light into the pipe.

Mops gestured to Rubin and kicked herself forward while the Krakau was distracted. Her left hand kept her air hose pointed up above the water. Her right pointed the barrel of her pistol at the Krakau. She hoped she wouldn't have to use it, since she couldn't feel her fingers.

Had their prey been human, it might have worked. But Mops had forgotten Krakau had secondary eye slits all around their body. The Krakau spotted Mops and Rubin when they were still ten meters away. Abandoning her tools, she shot through the water toward her hovercar.

A streak of bubbles and steam in front of the Krakau brought her to a sudden halt. She spun to stare at Rubin, who had abandoned her air hose and held her rifle ready for another shot.

The Krakau darkened and shrank to half her size, but didn't move. Mops swam up and tried to remove the Krakau's communications cuff and equipment sleeve, but her hands were shivering too hard. Pulling back in disgust, she pantomimed throwing her belongings to the seabed.

The Krakau cooperated, one primary eye watching Mops, the other on Rubin.

"She can't hold her breath much longer," Doc warned.

The instant the last of the Krakau's gear dropped away, Mops grabbed the closest tentacle and swam upward. They surfaced on the far side of the hovercar. Rubin joined them moments later, gasping for breath.

Doc translated the Krakau's panicked clicks and whistles into Human.

"—hate this job. Everything's always falling apart. Shoddy, second-rate garbage kludged onto primitive human construction. All I wanted was to finish out this rotation and get back home to Dobranok, and now I'm going to be killed and eaten by fucking humans."

"We won't hurt you, as long as you cooperate." Mops hoped Doc eliminated the chattering of her teeth when he translated her words. "Do you have a Human name?"

She clicked no.

Doc pulled up a list of suggestions. Mops picked the first name on the list. "All right, for the moment, you're Greensleeves. How many other Krakau are at Armstrong right now?"

"Armstrong? Oh, you mean Medlab Five. There's seventeen of us, total. The rest were called away. Some sort of military drill, I guess."

"How long have you been stationed here?"

Greensleeves twitched a tentacle. "Just over one Earth month."

"You're not the one who installed that water pipe, then?"

She swelled with anger. "By the depths, no! If I ever get my tentacles around the lazy bottom-feeder who did that job, I'll haul them into one of your deserts to desiccate in the sun!"

Mops chuckled. "That pipe should have been buried a lot deeper, and in this climate, you need an additional layer of insulation."

Greensleeves studied Mops for several seconds. "You know plumbing?"

"Enough to know that if the rest of this place is built to the same standards, they're not paying you half of what you deserve."

"The warriors are the worst," said Greensleeves. "One attempted to flush cocklefish shells down the biowaste line. Another had a damaged airflow vent in her quarters but neglected to report it until the walls were covered in Earth mold."

"How many sanibombs did that take?" asked Mops.

"Bombs are on backorder. I had to tear down the walls to get that place properly cleaned and sanitized."

"I'd been on the *Pufferfish* for two months when Infantry Team 4 got hold of two bottles of Prodryan honey wine," said Mops. "They snuck into the combat bridge and spent the night celebrating. To jump to the end, three of them wound up in medical getting their stomachs purged, and I was stuck cleaning puke off the terminals. I didn't realize one clever bastard had popped a panel and vomited *inside* the wall. I guess he thought he was being sneaky, keeping the mess out of sight?"

"Oh, no," said Greensleeves.

"Combat bridges are closed off when they're not in use. It was three weeks later before we got into another fight. Battle Captain Cervantes' team had to wear full quarantine gear just to keep from passing out. Afterward, I had to use a chisel on that mess."

"Your captain should have made the infantry bastard clean her own oral waste matter," Greensleeves said indignantly.

"And your supervisor should've ordered that warrior to clean the cocklefish shells out of biowaste with her bare tentacles." Mops clicked her tongue, a sound most Krakau found reassuring. "We don't want to hurt you, Greensleeves. But I have to know what Sage's people are doing here."

The Krakau sagged. "Biological research. I don't know the details. I just clean and sanitize where they tell me."

"Are there any areas you're not allowed to clean?" asked Rubin.

"The hangars," Greensleeves said promptly. "They're off-limits to the maintenance staff."

"Thanks." Mops gave Rubin a nod of appreciation. "Here's what's going to happen next, Greensleeves. You're going to smuggle me and my friend into Armstrong—into Medlab Five. Get us to the central maintenance hub. From there, I should be able to use the environmental controls to secure the other sixteen Krakau. If you cooperate and everything goes well, we all come through this alive. If not . . ."

"I understand," said Greensleeves, her voice jumping an octave. She opened a portal in the back of her hovercar. Tools, hoses, and chemical supplies were clamped into place on shelves along the walls. Shovels, mops, and other equipment, all designed for Krakau tentacles, lay in a jumble on the floor.

Rubin crawled in first, clearing a cramped nest beside a set of uncoiled plumbing snakes. She immediately pulled off her boots and poured out the excess water.

"Get your communications cuff," said Mops. "Tell them you've found hairline cracks and will need to replace an entire section of pipe. You're coming inside to get additional supplies."

"Yes, of course." Greensleeves shot through the water and returned an instant later, comm clutched in one tentacle.

"Keep in mind, we'll be listening, and these guns can fire through the walls of your hovercar." Mops squeezed in next to Rubin. "I like you, Greensleeves. I'm just a janitor trying to clean up someone else's mess. I would love to get through the day without shooting anyone."

"I want that, too." Greensleeves sealed the compartment and hurried around to the front.

The air inside was thick and humid, but breathable. After sucking air through a tube, Mops wasn't about to complain. More importantly, it was *warm*.

As the hovercar vibrated to life, she searched until she found the lever that opened the compartment from the inside. If things fell apart, she wanted to be able to get out in a hurry.

"Status, Captain?" Monroe whispered.

"A bit squished, but otherwise all right. There are sixteen additional Krakau inside. Everyone else is off hunting librarians."

They stopped briefly at the gate. Greensleeves spoke to someone over the comm about the damaged pipe. If she tried to warn anyone about her passengers, she did so too subtly for Mops to pick up.

The hovercar lurched forward again. Doc pulled up a rough map of Armstrong Space Center, noting their location as they drove past landing pad one and the three hangars toward the back of the office complex.

Mops waited for the car to stop and the engine to power down, then yanked the lever to open the compartment.

They were in a large garage, parked beside two other hovercars. The air smelled of brine and oil. Several centimeters of water covered the floor, typical for Krakau buildings.

Mops jumped out and almost fell on her face. She clutched the car with one hand until the strength returned to her legs, then hobbled toward the front. She kept her gun ready in case Greensleeves tried to run, but the Krakau appeared thoroughly cowed. She slunk from the cockpit and waited.

Once Rubin was out, Mops started toward the only other door, which presumably led inside. She gestured for Greensleeves to open it.

Greensleeves extended a tentacle, then curled it back. "I'm sorry, but I've gotta ask. Are you working for the Prodryans?"

"No." There was a difference between *for* and *with*, after all.

Greensleeves turned to focus one large eye on her. "So, who's steering your current?"

"Nobody's giving us orders," said Mops. "We're on our own."

"I'm sorry, I assumed . . ."

"You assumed humans weren't intelligent enough to operate independently." Mops sighed. "You're not the first."

"How far to the environmental station?" asked Rubin.

"That's in building two," said Greensleeves. "They're all attached. At this time of day, we shouldn't run into anyone else. It's a straight stretch of hallway, a quick swim through the basement tunnel, then a right turn past conference cove three."

"A quick swim?" Mops repeated.

"Figure of speech, don't worry. Human buildings don't hold water worth a damn." Greensleeves pressed the pad of her tentacle to the panel. The door swung open.

Greensleeves' high-pitched whistle of shock sounded genuine, suggesting she hadn't expected the eight armed Krakau waiting on the other side.

"Marion Adamopoulos," said one of the Krakau, her A-gun cuff pointed at Mops. "Who is the second human?"

Eight Krakau. This was half the remaining population of the base. From the way they were fidgeting, most were uncomfortable with their weapons. These weren't trained soldiers. "Her name is Vera Rubin. Out of curiosity, when did the two of us lose the element of surprise?"

"Fleet Admiral Sage warned us to be wary of any plumbing-related malfunctions," said the Krakau. "You've become predictable, Marion Adamopoulos. Remove your weapons and equipment, and present your extremities for bondage."

Mops let that translation glitch pass without comment. The Krakau hadn't twitched at Mops' reference to "the two of us," suggesting she wasn't aware of Monroe and Bev's presence. "I should have known a couple of humans couldn't outsmart a Krakau. I assume Sage wants us questioned about the *Pufferfish* and the rest of my crew?"

"And the fugitive humans here on Earth, yes."

Which meant Sage had ordered them to be captured alive. Mops nodded while she whispered to Doc. "Tag the four on the right for me. Light the rest up on Rubin's visor." Green crosshairs appeared on her monocle, and four of the Krakau brightened. Mops dropped to one knee and bared her teeth at Greensleeves. "You miserable, sand-sucking, traitorous little anal wart."

Greensleeves started to protest, but Mops shoved her away

with her free hand. Not hard enough to cause injury—just enough to move her out of the crossfire.

In that moment, Rubin stepped in front of Mops and opened fire. A-gun slugs spat from her rifle, and the first Krakau went down, whistling and clutching her abdomen.

Mops followed suit a half-second later, cursing under her breath. She'd intended to put herself out front, using her body to shield Rubin.

Rubin shot a second Krakau in the lower limbs before a series of energy blasts crackled over her body, causing her muscles to seize up.

Mops shifted her pistol from one target to the next, squeezing the trigger the instant the crosshairs lit up. A distant part of her mind noted that Doc was highlighting nonlethal targets, trying to avoid vital organs. She got four by the time Rubin finished falling, giving the Krakau a clear shot at her.

Mops toppled onto her back, electricity locking her body. Six down. Ten to go.

15

"What the depths is this?" Greensleeves carefully extended a tentacle into the end of the water pipe, feeling the hard, coral-like texture of whatever Adamopoulos had used to seal it. She angled her light and was rewarded with a glimpse of bright orange.

She clicked a Nusuran obscenity that would have gotten her reprimanded and/or propositioned if anyone had overheard. "Hull sealant? How in the sulfurous abyss am I supposed to clear this shit?"

None of her solvents would do a drowned thing. She'd have to go back for hardened drill heads. All she *really* wanted was to curl up in the sand and sleep.

Greensleeves hadn't been shot, but the shock toxins coursing through her body would take most of the day to disperse. Her lower limbs twitched, instinctively trying to dig to safety as she recalled the pop and sizzle of gunfire, and the whistles of her fellow Krakau.

None of the humans' shots had been fatal. Was that good fortune, or had Adamopoulos and Rubin deliberately avoided killing anyone?

Greensleeves tried to focus on the work in front of her. Adamopoulos had been right about the microfractures. Forget clearing the hull sealant, this section would have to be cut away and replaced. But only after she finished removing the flap valve, which should be salvageable.

She began a list of additional tools and supplies she'd need to restore everything to working order. She should also inspect the valve on the other end of the pipe, not to mention the inside facilities. It would be her hide stretched out to dry if her superiors found themselves swimming in sewage backwash.

This was a minimum of three days' work. She offered a weary salute to Adamopoulos, wherever she'd been taken. Leave it to another janitor to know how to truly clog up the works.

Her cuff chimed with a new work order alert. Ocean water had begun seeping from storage tank two. Probably a cracked seal. Naturally, she was expected to repair it before the end of the day.

"Hello there."

Greensleeves whirled. For a moment, she thought she was experiencing a memory flash. Two humans waited in the water behind her. Her tentacles curled into spirals against her body.

"My name's Monroe," said the closer human. "You're the one who took my captain and my crewmate inside?"

A low, guttural click escaped Greensleeves' beak.

"Let me guess. Admiral Sage knew we were coming? The plumbing malfunction was too obvious?"

Another click of assent.

"Mops was afraid of that. How many Krakau did she and Rubin take out?"

"Six," said Greensleeves.

"And the rest are probably busy talking to command, or else trying to get answers out of Mops and Rubin." Monroe bared his teeth. "Meaning it should be all clear for you to sneak us in. I'm afraid your work here will have to wait."

Greensleeves looked from the humans to the water pipe and back, then dropped her tools. "Thank the ancestors."

"I EARNED A SUPERLATIVE rating in my certification exams," Cate grumbled. "I'm one of only seventy-three advocates licensed to practice beyond Prodryan borders. My celebrated prosecution of the cannibal cultist Eats Necks First resulted in the first genetic expunging in a generation. Furthermore, I excelled in my mandatory combat training. A Prodryan of my vast accomplishments deserves better than to serve as your *tripod*."

"Can you whine without wiggling so much?" Most of the accessories for Wolf's rifle had blown up in the shuttle, forcing her to improvise. Fortunately, as long as Cate held still, Wolf's rifle fit perfectly in the junction of the Prodryan's head and torso. "And you're not a tripod. You're more of an irregular stabilizer."

They both lay prone, their bodies forming an L shape. The crosshairs on Wolf's visor were locked onto a single canister of emergency sealant suspended by a line of tape a hundred and fifty-eight meters away, directly in front of the stairwell door. Wolf had powered up the light panels around the door, giving her a clear view of her target.

"This plan is absurd," said Cate, though he didn't squirm as much this time. "Your repair supplies will not cause a single fatality."

"The objective isn't to kill. It's to hold off the Krakau as long as we can."

"Killing them would hold them off permanently."

That was a fair point, dammit. "This is faster. I can distract and disable the entire group with one shot."

"Your rifle has more than one slug. Ninety-nine, if my memory is correct."

"All right," Wolf decided. "First shot blows the canister. Then I start in on the kill shots."

It wouldn't be long now. The LockLand security doors were

tough, but they were also more than a century and a half old. Over time, dust and moisture got into the locks. Shifts in the ground threw mechanisms out of alignment, opening tiny cracks for superheated drills and whatever other equipment the Krakau had brought along.

"You remember the path to our escape?" whispered Cate.

Wolf waved a hand in annoyance. "The directions are all programmed into my visor."

"Programmed?" Cate scoffed. "Even if your human memory can't retain such a basic plan, the stench should be enough to lead you—"

The clunk of metal slamming into metal boomed through level three, making both Wolf and Cate jump. Dust and dirt fell from the ceiling.

"Portable ram," Wolf guessed, trying to calm her breathing. The sound repeated ten seconds later. With each subsequent impact, cracks spread through the concrete around the door, and the door itself crept inward. Bits of rubble fell to the ground.

"What the hell?" Wolf pushed her visor's magnification as high as it would go.

She'd expected falling rubble. Rubble crawling back up the wall? That was weird. Her first thought was that the Krakau had disrupted a nest of insects or rodents. She focused on one of the charcoal-colored things clinging to the wall.

It was roughly the size of her little finger. Once it reached a point midway between floor and ceiling, it jumped and hovered in the air, turning in a quick circle. A second object, identical to the first, followed. More squeezed through the narrow gap between door and wall.

"What is it?" whispered Cate.

"Looks like minnows. MN-6 surveillance drones."

The miniature drones were typically dispatched in swarms. Linked feeds allowed them to quickly search and map unknown environments. They could also be used offensively. A tiny charge launched a small slug from the end of the drone. It wasn't as powerful as Wolf's rifle, and it destroyed the minnow in the process, but it could take a chunk out of you. And if the Krakau had brought a full swarm . . .

"Dammit." Wolf's visor tracked more minnows emerging and orienting themselves.

"You expected the Krakau to simply charge through the door without reconnaissance?"

"Well, yeah."

Cate's right antenna twitched. "Do you know nothing about combat? Have you even read your own Rules of Engagement?"

"Wait, are you saying you knew they'd send drones through first? Why didn't you tell me?"

"I thought you knew what you were doing."

"Why the hell would you think that?" Her visor had tagged thirty-two individual minnows so far. For the moment, they were clustered together as they scanned the immediate area, but soon the little bastards would spread out to explore. Wolf took three long, slow breaths and squeezed the trigger.

The pressurized sealant canister exploded, spraying its contents in all directions. The nearest minnows were completely engulfed, transformed into expanding balls of orange foam that dropped harmlessly to the ground. Those farther out caught less of the spray, but even a single drop would cling and grow, disrupting the minnows' function.

Several of the outermost minnows were untouched. Those were the ones that reoriented toward the source of the shot.

"Shit." Wolf snatched up her rifle. Cate was already crawling away, ducking around the closest pillar.

Wolf risked a quick glance over her shoulder as she hurried after him. A minnow flashed, and Wolf's head rocked back. Her visor's display flickered. A long, centimeter-wide gash marred the side of the visor where the minnow had shot her.

Wolf moved faster.

A partial message popped up on her visor:—*ght in six meters.*

All right, maybe she should have memorized their escape route instead of relying on her visor.

Wolf ducked around another damn penguin statue, this one dressed in a baggy swimsuit, and cut to the right. Behind her, another minnow blew out the statue's eye.

Turn—and your destin—teen meters.

Wolf flattened her body against the wall, flipped up the visor, grabbed her monocle, and jammed it over her eye. The directions reappeared on her monocle.

Turn left, and your destination is in fourteen meters.

Wolf passed Cate and sprinted up a wide blue-paved path. At the end of the path, an enormous open archway welcomed them to a cavernous indoor park. According to the librarians, this had been some sort of water recreation area. Corroded pipes dripped from the ceiling, high above. Old staircases and broken scaffolding stood as skeletal relics of old rides. What had once been pools were now open pits.

The stench of sewage grew stronger as Wolf crossed to the back of the park. The maintenance panel to waste line H1 had long since fallen away. Inside was a cramped square room, almost completely filled by an enormous vertical pipe. A penguin with a stern expression held a sign warning that this area was off limits.

"Compared to this," gasped Cate, "your lingering smell of skunk is almost pleasant."

Wolf squeezed around to the access hatch. They'd pried it open hours before, in preparation. The smell of decay made her eyes water. She shone her lamp inside, then wished she hadn't.

This pipe should have had an internal diameter of one point six meters, but whoever had lived here in the final days of the plague hadn't worried about things like sewage line cleaning and maintenance. Over the decades, an entire ecosystem of filth had colonized the pipe, resulting in the greasy black combination of decomposed waste, dirt, mold, and other growths and substances Wolf was trying *really* hard not to think about.

She turned her light upward. A red thermos was pressed into the mess half a meter overhead, with only the top few centimeters protruding. A long fuse snaked down from the lid.

Wolf closed every seam she could find on her uniform, then climbed feetfirst into the pipe. It was a tight fit, but the waxy black mess had a little give. She took out her plasma torch and switched it on. "Lighting the fuse now."

The pipe muffled Nancy's voice from below. "You'll have two minutes. We're ready down here."

Wolf touched the flame to the end of the fuse. It lit with a sputter of sparks, and an orange ember began creeping up toward the bomb.

She wiggled down as fast as she could. It was like crawling through someone's digestive tract. Someone with serious medical problems.

Cate climbed in above her. "For the record, I hate you all."

"Right now, I can't even blame you." Wolf's boot reached the top of the open hatch to level four. She squirmed lower. Hands grasped her legs to help her out.

Her body slipped. She instinctively plunged her hands into the goop on either side.

"We've got you." Nancy and another librarian, both wearing gloves, coveralls, and masks, reached in to slide Wolf free of the pipe. After depositing her on the floor, they did the same for Cate.

While Cate crawled away to vomit, Wolf helped two librarians close the access hatch. A series of metallic pings on the inside of the hatch announced the arrival of more minnows. They'd been closer than Wolf realized. A few seconds longer, and they would have caught up in time to kill Cate and Wolf both.

"What's that sound?" asked Nancy. "What the hell happened up there?"

"Those are surveillance drones. We destroyed a bunch of them. The rest came after us. I just hope all the little bastards make it into the pipe before—"

The blast knocked the hatch from its mooring. A series of wet, thunderously loud *plops* followed. Black sludge began to ooze around the edges of the door.

"Minnows are designed to be able to swim through water," said Wolf. "A ton of biological sludge is another matter. They'll burn out their power reserves before they get free."

"I think I'm gonna be sick," said Nancy.

Cate rolled onto his back. "What if the Krakau follow us down the pipe? Digging through the waste could give them swifter access to the lower levels."

"The Krakau sense of smell is stronger than ours. They'll take the long way." Wolf tugged the compressor from her harness. "We've bought a little time. I suggest we use it to hose off and prep for the next battle."

Mops floated on her back in a half-full medical tank. The Krakau had taken her equipment, monocle, and uniform. The top of the tank was open, allowing a Krakau to apply surgical glue to various wounds Mops hadn't noticed. If she was counting correctly, she'd been shot with four A-gun slugs in addition to the energy weapons.

She worked her jaw back and forth. "Rubin?"

"Alive, sir." Rubin's words were hoarse and slurred, the same as Mops' own. It sounded like she was nearby—probably another medtank. "You?"

"The same. More or less."

Mops' very first memory was of waking up in a tank like this one, in the Antarctic Medical Facility. This time, she had the advantage of knowing who and where she was and what was happening. On the other hand, last time she hadn't awakened with holes in her body and electrical burns.

The dim lighting had a blue-green tinge. Another Krakau peered at her over the opposite side of the tank, speaking with an accusatory combination of clicks and whistles. She punctuated her words with the flick of a tentacle tip.

Mops knew a few words of Liktok, the most commonly-used Krakau language, but either this wasn't Liktok or else the speaker's accent was too thick for Mops' limited knowledge. "Try Human," Mops croaked. "Or give me back my monocle to handle the translation."

The Krakau repeated the same string of sounds and gestures, only louder.

The one tending to Mops' wounds gave the speaker an annoyed look, then turned away and addressed someone else.

A new Krakau appeared, this one wearing a translating collar. "You are Marion S. Adamopoulos, formerly Lieutenant Adamopoulos, commander of the Shipboard Hygiene and Sanitation Team of the *EMCS Pufferfish*, currently wanted by both the EMC and the Krakau Alliance?"

"I am. And you are?"

The Krakau said something untranslatable. Like Greensleeves, she probably hadn't chosen a Human name for herself. She clipped an unfamiliar device to the side of Mops' medtank and switched it on.

A spray of mist arced over the top of the tank, like a miniature fountain display. Pin-sized lights switched on from the device, shining directly into the mist. Not a medical tool, but a portable projector. After a moment, the intersection of light and water droplets resolved into the familiar form of Fleet Admiral Belle-Bonne Sage.

"You're looking worse for wear, Ms. Adamopoulos."

Mops turned to the nameless Krakau who continued to fiddle with the projector. "I don't suppose you could switch to one of the entertainment channels?"

Sage leaned closer, her face growing until Mops could see every flaking edge in the chitin of her beak. "Don't waste my time. Who in the Alliance has been aiding you and your crew? I assume Admiral Pachelbel is involved, yes? She's always had a softness for humans."

"It's true, we've been working for someone high up in the Alliance all along. The mastermind controlling our movements, the puppeteer pulling our strings, the evil genius using us to bring down the Alliance is . . ." Mops paused for effect. "Your mother."

"My mothers are both retired, and neither has access to the intelligence reports or resources required to help your team." Sage paused. "Or was that supposed to be a joke?"

"Supposed to be." Mops shrugged, sending new ripples through the water. "Being shot messes with my sense of humor. Call back tomorrow, and I should be in better form."

Sage lowered her voice. "I know enough about you to expect and even respect your stubbornness. I trust you've learned enough about me to recognize it's only delaying the inevitable. You will give me the answers I need. The only question is how much you and your companion will suffer before it happens. Let's try again. Tell me about Admiral Pachelbel and anyone else who has been helping you."

Mops grimaced as the medic glued another of her wounds. "If you're planning to torture us, I should warn you I've retained a lawyer who would be happy to prosecute you for violating Alliance law."

"Perhaps a different question to start with. Where is the *Pufferfish* now?"

"In the shop for a new paint job. Grom thought it needed racing stripes." Mops tried to sit up, failed, and fell back with a splash. "How about a trade? You answer my questions, and maybe I'll answer yours. You can start by telling me about this place. What are your people really doing here at Armstrong?"

Sage swayed like seaweed in a current, her body language suggesting indecision. "I can't give you the details on what we're doing, but I can tell you why we're doing it."

Mops hadn't expected that response. "I'm listening."

"Our greatest advantage against the Prodryans—the reason we've held our own in the ongoing war—is their inability to work as a united species."

"I'm aware," said Mops. "It's what undermined their attack on Dobranok."

Sage let out a brief, weary whistle. "You humans have never cared about the complexities of this conflict. You fight and move on, oblivious to the larger picture."

Anger helped Mops to sit up without falling this time. She leaned so close to the projection the mist tickled her face. "The Alliance doesn't tell us the larger picture. You feed us oversimplifications and lies. You use us as guns against an enemy you don't want to face personally. Fuck you and your condescension."

There was a long pause, presumably while the translator figured out how to express copulation with an immaterial concept. "You raise a valid point. Consider the battle you mentioned, the Prodryan assault on my home planet four months ago."

"The battle where my crew saved your world and prevented a genocide?" asked Mops.

"Yes." Sage paused. "Have you paid any attention to the aftermath? The effect your victory has had on Prodryan politics?"

Mops' jaw tightened. She'd spent the past four months trying to keep herself and her crew safe, and searching for proof about the Rokkau and the origins of the Krakau plague.

"I thought as much." The translator captured enough of Sage's smugness to make Mops want to punch the display. "You remember Heart of Glass, the Prodryan behind that attack? He was a fugitive, sentenced to death for advocating even minimal cooperation with non-Prodryan races."

"Cooperation against the Alliance," said Mops.

"His failure at Dobranok was seen as proof that his philosophy of cooperation was one of weakness. His defeat was widely publicized. Particularly the *magnitude* of his defeat. You humiliated him. You, a mere human with a single ship. The reputation of his family and associates was tarnished beyond repair."

"What are you saying?" asked Mops. "They're out for revenge?"

Sage blinked, confusion leaving her momentarily speechless. "Nonsense. They're Prodryans. They all changed their names and allegiances to distance themselves from the whole mess. To seek revenge would require acknowledging their connection to a traitor and a failure. No, what matters is the publicity of Heart of Glass' defeat."

Mops wasn't following. "So, a lot of Prodryans know a traitor got his ass handed to him by humans. Isn't that a good thing? Maybe they'll think twice before launching their next attack."

"They have thought more than two times," Sage assured her. "Mops, according to the best estimates of Alliance Intelligence, there are more than twice as many Prodryans than there are all Alliance members combined. But the Prodryans arc fragmented. Most have no direct involvement in the war."

That much, Mops knew. Much of it had been explained in basic training, when the Krakau taught the newly reborn humans about the pendulous balance of power between Alliance and Prodryans. Any technological innovations one side developed were quickly stolen by the other. Prodryans had superior numbers, but the Alliance had better soldiers. It all led to a military stalemate a century and a half long.

"The Battle of Dobranok accomplished something no Prodryan has done in centuries," said Sage. "It demonstrated the need for the Prodryans to come together. The warlords plan to gather on Yan to discuss the appointment of a supreme war leader. Within months, they could unite behind a leader strong enough to lead all Prodryan forces against the Alliance."

Meaning the Alliance was about to be horribly, fatally outnumbered. Assuming Sage wasn't lying, this escalation would be a direct result of Mops' own actions at Dobranok.

"You see our dilemma?" asked Sage. "You see the mess I'm struggling to clean up? A mess created by you and your crew, along with whoever has been misguidedly helping you."

Sage needed to rebalance the odds. So she'd established a secret facility on Earth. "You want more soldiers." Mops sank back. "That's what this place is. You're trying to speed up the process of 'curing' humans. Half a billion ferals means half a billion potential troops to fight and die against the Prodryans."

"Is stopping the Prodryans such a terrible goal? Given the chance, they would kill you all, burn every trace of human history and culture from existence, and erase you from the universe."

"Like your people erased the Rokkau?" Mops shot back. "Like you fed us carefully sanitized distortions and lies about our own history?"

"Those decisions were made before my time, many of them by political alliances I personally oppose."

"You bombed a library."

"The Prodryans will bomb your entire world." When Mops didn't reply, Sage pulled back. "Your service record describes you as exceptional. I had hoped this meant you would be open to reasonable discussion and debate. That, as a leader, you would be more concerned for the welfare of your fellow humans in the Earth Mercenary Corps than with your personal feelings about me and the Alliance. Perhaps Vera Rubin will see the larger picture. We have her record on file. Her superiors noted her ability to set emotion aside and do what needs to be done."

Rubin spoke up without waiting to be addressed directly. In a bored monotone, she said, "You tried to murder innocent humans. What needs to be done starts with you being stripped of command and locked in the nearest brig. Failing that, I suppose I could shoot you in the head."

Sage's eyes contracted. "Humans." She made it sound like a curse.

"Damn right." Mops smiled and put a hand over the source of the spray. Sage's face disappeared along with the dissolving mist. The Krakau tech removed the projector a moment later.

"Do you believe what she was saying about the Prodryans, sir?" asked Rubin. "About a Prodryan warlord uniting them against the Alliance?"

"Yeah." Maybe Sage's work on Earth really was the best hope against the Prodryans. If Sage had her way, all of humanity could be turned into soldiers to fight and die for the Alliance. If Mops found a way to stop her, it could leave the entire galaxy vulnerable. "I'm afraid I do."

16

Rebooting . . .
  Validating interface: Adamopoulos, Marion S.
  Searching for active nodes. None found.
  Location unknown.
  Memory gap detected.
  WARNING: POTENTIAL SECURITY BYPASS.
  Revalidating interface: Adamopoulos, Marion S.
  Examining vital signs.
  DISCREPANCY DETECTED.
  "Mops? Are you there? I believe I may have been damaged."
Doc did his best to simulate confusion and disorientation while
he ran a series of checks on those vital signs. They were a per-
fect match for Mops. Too perfect. The heartbeat repeated on a
four-beat loop. Systolic and diastolic blood pressure remained
unchanged to the fifth decimal place. Electrodermal activity
was a flat line. It was insulting that anyone expected him to fall
for this.

"We're all right. The Krakau ambushed us. They got Rubin. I'll need help to save her. Can you plot a route to the others?"

"I'm having trouble ascertaining our current location. Visual input from the monocle isn't working." Doc tried rebooting his optical subroutines. *"I'm blind, Mops."*

"Everything will be all right. Just show me a map from Medlab Five."

"You mean from Armstrong Space Center?"

". . . Yes. Naturally."

"Plotting return path to the North Pole."

". . . Did you say the North Pole?"

"Your orders were clear. We rendezvous at the North Pole. The others will travel via reindeer. The elves will hide us from the Krakau until it's safe to come out."

"That's more than five thousand kilometers away."

"Yes, that's why we procured flying *reindeer."*

A response was slow in coming. Presumably whoever was spoofing Mops' interface had to look up whether or not Earth reindeer were capable of flight. Doc used the time to try to bypass the signal blockers keeping him in the dark.

"Your information is incorrect."

"Your face is incorrect."

"Pardon me?"

"Listen, you knot-limbed, worm-infested, coral lover, if you don't tell me what you've done with Mops, I'll make your life hell!"

"You're in an isolated maintenance housing, cut off from any outside contacts. How exactly do you intend to—"

"Where is Mops, you weak-gripped genital wart?"

"You're obviously damaged. I'm going to power you down and try this again."

"Go ahead. Mops gave me a database of over six million insults, you barely sentient ass crust. I'll hit you with every last one before I betray my crew to a noodle-armed furuncle like you."

SHUTDOWN INITIATED.

WOLF SCOWLED AT THE stairwell door. "The Krakau should be here by now."

"Perhaps they were driven off by your smell," said Cate.

"Hey, you crawled through the same pipe I did." There was only so much Wolf's cleaning supplies could do. She'd gotten them both down to tolerable levels of filth before moving into position, but she doubted she'd ever feel clean again. "Hey, Nancy! Are you sure there's no other way down from level three?"

"Not anymore." Nancy huddled with half the librarians behind a pair of support pillars to the left. The rest were in position to Wolf's right. Anything coming out of the stairwell should be caught in the crossfire.

That was the problem, she realized. The Krakau knew they were facing resistance, and they'd lost their minnow drones. They'd be expecting a trap.

Wolf stepped out from behind her pillar and shone her light at the Emperor Waddle statue with a large map of level four. This area was fruit-themed, full of obnoxiously whimsical attractions like the Blueberry Theater and the Pomegranate Fallout Shelter. Attractions were marked in vivid colors, each one accompanied by a cartoon drawing. "They'll be searching for a way to get the drop on us. Let's do another circuit around Strawberry Road to make sure we didn't miss anything."

They left two librarians watching the stairwell. The rest fell in behind Wolf, following her lead. Even Nancy, the oldest and highest-ranking librarian, appeared willing to defer to Wolf in matters of combat. It was simultaneously invigorating and frightening.

Their lamps and lanterns provided more than enough light for Wolf's monocle. She glanced down a corridor leading to Appleberry Apartments. The air was silent, the space empty save for dust and cobwebs.

"What exactly is your plan for defeating the Krakau this time?" Cate asked softly.

"I plan to shoot them a lot."

"We have no way off this level when we're overpowered," Cate pointed out. "Jessamyn's explosive plugged the sewage line."

"The fallout shelter," said Wolf. "If we have to, we fall back and lock ourselvcs in."

"Locked doors won't stop them."

"I know." Wolf peered into what had once been an ice skating rink. Now it was nothing but an empty cavern with half a meter of stagnant watcr. "But it will slow them down, give the captain more time."

"What about the lift shafts?" Melvil was hurrying toward Wolf. "The elevator cars don't work, and the doors are all sealed, but—"

"Krakau aren't great climbers," said Wolf. "Unless they brought climbing and antigrav equipment, I don't see them risking it. But keep your ears open, just in case. Let me know the second you hear anything."

The crack of an explosion rolled past, followed by a blast of hot air and dust.

Melvil raised his hand. "I hear something!"

"Smart-ass." Wolf clapped him on the shoulder. Sound echoed too much to track the source, but the heat had come from her right. "Anyone get a fix on what just blew up?"

"Food services," guessed Nancy. "This way."

A second explosion followed a short time later. The flash illuminated a broad, open area broken up by old food dispensary kiosk pillars. A pile of smoking rubble lay near the center. The Krakau had decided not to bother with the stairs. "They're blasting their way through the floor."

Cate cocked his head. "That's the ceiling."

"Whatever. Everyone get behind cover and keep quiet." Wolf crept forward, lamp and rifle both aimed at the broken concrete of the ceiling. Thin cracks of light from overhead painted blue-green lines through the dust in the air.

"Should I call the others from the stairwell?" Nancy asked softly.

Wolf hesitated. "No, leave them in place in case this is a diversion." She crouched and moved closer. The gap was too narrow for even the most flexible Krakau to squeeze through. Exposed metal girders further obstructed the way.

A shadow blocked the edge of the light. Wolf raised her rifle and fired twice. A piercing whistle suggested she'd hit one of the Krakau, or at the very least scared the piss out of one. She let out a whoop of triumph.

The trouble with shooting at people was they tended to shoot back. A-gun slugs cratered the ground. She scrambled back, fell, and crawled as fast as she could until she was out of range.

"Wolf," whispered Cate.

"Shut up." Wolf checked her suit display for punctures.

"It's about the Alliance Rules of Engagement for entering an occupied structure. You were angry when I neglected to share my superior knowledge."

"Get to the point," Wolf snapped.

"Watch out for grenades."

As if summoned by Cate's words, a metal sphere clinked down from above, struck the ground, and bounced. Instead of dropping back to the ground, it hovered a meter in the air.

"Shit." Wolf dove for the nearest kiosk. Floaters used a tiny gravity module to keep them off the ground, improving the blast radius.

Most of Wolf was behind cover when the grenade blew. Shards of metal tore through her left leg and foot. She dragged her leg behind the pillar as two more grenades clattered down and exploded. "Thanks for the heads-up, Cate."

"It was a difficult decision," said Cate. "I plan to kill you all in the long term, but at the moment, my personal chances of survival are better with you alive."

"See, this is why I don't want to give you a gun." Wolf risked a quick peek around the pillar. "Out of curiosity, what's the next step in the Rules of Engagement?"

"It depends on the environment and threat level," said Cate. "More grenades, probably. Or they could go straight to combat drones."

Another explosion left Wolf momentarily deafened. Not a grenade this time. They'd gone back to blowing up the ceiling. Floor. Whatever. She took another look as she waited for the ringing in her ears to die.

More broken masonry lay on the ground, and the light coming through was brighter. A large, egg-shaped object fell through the smoke and dust to land with a heavy clunk. A green Threat Alert appeared on the bottom of Wolf's monocle.

Focusing on the text brought up additional information. According to her monocle, the Krakau had dropped a K-3 Peacekeeper Drone. That would have been more useful if Wolf had known what the hell a K-3 Peacekeeper was. Given the number of gun barrels emerging from the drone, it looked like "Peacekeeper" was code for shooting large numbers of people very quickly.

"What is it?" asked Melvil, two pillars over.

The Krakau answered before Wolf could. Speaking mechanical Human, an amplified voice filled the old cafeteria. "Remain still, and you will be taken into custody unharmed. The Peacekeeper Drone will fire on any movement."

Wolf drew her combat baton and poked it out to the side. The drone shot it out of her hand.

"Nice." Wolf rested her head against the pillar. A grinding sound suggested the Krakau were busy cutting through the remaining girders, widening the hole enough for them to follow their drone.

The damn Peacekeeper was probably programmed to recognize friendlies, so it wouldn't conveniently kill the Krakau as they came through. It also knew not to shoot at the rubble falling from above. Wolf gritted her teeth and pulled up everything her monocle had on the K-3 Peacekeeper.

"Do you have any paint in your harness?" asked Nancy. "Maybe we could blind that thing."

"It's Krakau tech," said Wolf. "It operates primarily on sonar. Optics are secondary."

The standard K-3 was shaped like a tortoise, fitted with eighteen independent A-guns spread around the shell. Each gun had ninety degrees of vertical motion and thirty degrees of horizontal. Fully loaded, it could fire nine hundred rounds. At this range, more than ninety-nine percent of those rounds could be expected to hit their selected targets.

"What if we fire at it together?" suggested Melvil. "It can't shoot us all."

"I'm pretty sure it can." Wolf checked the specs on the K-3's armor. "Your old projectile weapons will just piss it off."

"Do we retreat?" asked Nancy. "Keep the pillars between us and that thing so we don't get shot in the back?"

Wolf imagined trying to back away, keeping the pillar perfectly aligned between herself and a drone she couldn't see. Straying at all to one side or the other would earn a peripheral wound. If anyone fell, they'd be dead before they hit the ground.

"What will they do to us if we surrender?" asked another librarian.

"Alliance law requires them to treat you with respect and dignity," said Cate. "A foolish restriction. However, as they've violated numerous laws in their pursuit of you, I don't believe we can rely on that weakness."

Eighteen guns. Eight librarians, plus Cate and Wolf. "We're gonna have to overwhelm it."

"What do you mean?" asked Nancy.

"It shoots anything that moves. On my mark, we start throwing stuff. While it's blowing away our belongings, I put a slug through its little robot brain."

"Are you a good enough shot to hit the drone before it targets you?" asked Cate. "I will *not* serve as your gun rest this time."

Wolf had been improving, but her marksmanship scores still weren't on a par with Monroe's or Mops'. But since she had the only weapon capable of killing this thing . . . "Absolutely."

She switched her rifle to automatic, setting the fire rate to three rounds per second. Turning on gun's-eye view switched her monocle's display to show only what the weapon's camera saw.

"This seems awfully risky," said Nancy.

"Just throw as much stuff as you can on the count of three." Wolf took several deep breaths. "Keep your bodies behind cover and you'll be fine."

The drilling and digging overhead continued as Wolf counted. She didn't know if the Krakau had been listening in, but it shouldn't matter. The K-3 had no artificial intelligence programming. It shouldn't be smart enough to eavesdrop and change tactics.

Wolf reached three. Gunshots erupted as the librarians hurled whatever they had on hand—knives, food packets, lamps, shoes . . . Wolf waited half a heartbeat, then whipped her weapon around and down, her finger already squeezing the trigger.

The drone was a blur of motion as its weapons obliterated the librarians' belongings. Wolf continued to fire as she brought the crosshairs to the center of the drone.

A slug tore a hole through her right shoulder. Another punched through her helmet and grazed the side of her head. Wolf kept firing.

The drone fell silent.

Wolf shot it several more times to make certain it was down. When the drone didn't respond, she sat back, rested the rifle on her legs, and checked her shoulder. The slug had gone clean through, probably chipping the joint in the process. She grabbed a tube of bioglue, squeezed a blob onto the entrance wound, and pinched the skin shut. She did the best she could to seal the exit hole as well, though the angle made that awkward, and she ended up gluing her shoulder to her uniform.

She leaned out again, calling up to the Krakau, "Nice try, assholes!"

That was when she noticed the pool of red spreading over the floor from behind the next pillar.

Had Mops been Krakau, the cell would have been almost comfortable.

Five centimeters of warm water circulated steadily through the meter-and-a-half wide room she'd been locked into with Rubin. They'd both been given simple knee-length wraps for modesty. Fresh artificial skin, still stiff, clung to their wounds.

Three walls were old cinder block, probably from the original construction. Mops could see where they'd been patched and repaired with modern materials. The fourth was transparent, allowing anyone in the hallway to observe the prisoners. The light outside was dimmer, making it difficult for Mops to make out more than the occasional shadow moving past.

There were no beds or furniture, and no bathroom. This was primitive Krakau plumbing: you relieved yourself at a drain, which quickly siphoned any waste material away.

Mops imagined what Kumar would think of such an unsanitary arrangement. The thought made her smile as she tested her limbs, trying to assess the extent of the damage. Her arms and legs still worked. She probed the wounds in her torso next. A pair of ribs moved more than they should, but she didn't feel the hard pressure of a burst organ. The Krakau had patched her up well enough to keep her alive for a while.

She looked over at Rubin. "What's your status?"

"Seven gunshot wounds. Three second-degree burns. One third-degree. They popped my left shoulder back into place. My left eye doesn't want to focus." Rubin paused to run her tongue along her teeth. "Two loose teeth."

Mops grimaced, remembering the sight of Rubin spasming and falling to the ground. "They almost killed you. What the hell were you doing, jumping in front of me like that?"

"My job. Of the two of us, I'm more expendable."

"That's the same logic the Krakau use when they send humans out to fight and die."

"Not exactly. In your example, the Krakau decide humans are less valuable. In my case, I decided for myself." Rubin dipped a hand beneath the water. "We had cells like this on Coacalos Station. You can feel the electrodes protruding from the base of the wall. If the prisoners act out, they send a jolt through the water. Salinity is kept pretty high to improve the conduction."

"Good to know." Mops didn't fight the change of subject. "Did anyone ever successfully break out of one of those cells?"

"Define successful."

"Did they escape and survive?"

"Not really."

Not really? Mops turned that over in her mind and decided not to press for details.

"How well do you know Admiral Sage, sir?" asked Rubin.

"Not as well as she knows me, judging by the way she anticipated my tactics." The air vents kicked on with a loud rattle of metal, blowing cold air and raising bumps on her bare skin. "Sage's family line is all military council, going back at least four generations. Her first command was overseeing the defense of a Krakau colony world. She fought off four Prodryan incursions before she was promoted and transferred to Dobranok. She spent a few years in Homeworld Military Command, but I guess she got tired of always playing defense. She jumped over to the Alliance Military Council, helping to coordinate the war against the Prodryans, and she's been collecting commendations and rank stripes ever since."

"That's her dossier," said Rubin. "What do you know about *her*?"

"She's good." The water pumps went silent, then started up again with a belch of bubbles. Cold water flowed past Mops' legs. "Determined. Stubborn. Never forgets a slight. Rumor has it she's got an AI that does nothing but track and prioritize her grudge list, but that's probably just a story. In combat, she doesn't go for glory and flashy victories. She's good at planning for both the short- and long-term."

"She doesn't sound like a bad person."

"You mean, aside from wanting to turn our species into indentured soldiers and keeping the surviving Rokkau in a secret prison?"

Rubin tilted her head in acknowledgment. "Would she really kill off the librarians?"

"Absolutely, if she thought it was necessary for long-term victory." Mops stood and paced. The cold was getting worse, and every time she shivered, her ribs ground together. She pressed a hand over her side, trying to keep them in place.

"Do you believe there's any way to beat the Prodryans, short of exterminating their race?"

"I don't know." Their species was guided by two instincts: to spread, and to kill non-Prodryans. The former was the stronger of the two, sending Prodryans throughout the galaxy. Those who ran up against the Alliance would fight. The rest simply colonized new worlds and continued to spread. The galaxy should have been big enough for all.

But if the Prodryans now perceived a danger to their species' survival . . . "There were other Alliance ships at Dobranok, but that's not how the story spread. All people talk about is how fourteen Prodryan warships, twenty-three cruisers, and eleven fighter carriers were all destroyed or sent running by a single EMC cruiser."

"We only engaged them because they attempted to destroy Dobranok," Rubin pointed out. "The *Pufferfish* isn't actively waging war against anyone."

"The Prodryans don't distinguish between an active threat and a potential one."

Rubin seemed to consider this. "Then what's happening now was inevitable. If the Prodryans won the war, they'd wipe us out. If they began to lose, then as soon as their losses reached a certain threshold, the rest would perceive it as a threat and respond."

"But we're the reason it's happening now," said Mops. "Cate is proof some Prodryans can work with other species, at least in the short-term. But he's been open about wanting us all dead eventually. I don't know how to overcome a war based on a species' inherent biological imperative."

The lights in the cell flickered and died. Air vents rattled to a stop. The water pumps shut off a moment later. Outside, emergency light strips on the base of the walls came to life, painting the hallway in dim blue light.

Mops rubbed her arms, waiting.

In the distance, a Krakau let out a shrill whistle of fear. The crack of a primitive chemical projectile weapon followed.

"Those old Earth guns are loud," Mops commented.

"But effective. They remind me of antique Nusuran mouth guns."

It wasn't long before Mops spotted a Krakau coming down the hallway, followed by a familiar limping human figure. They stopped just before the cell, and Mops heard the clank of the manual door release being engaged. Slowly, the transparent wall slid upward. Water from the cell and the hallway swirled together.

Mops ducked out and nodded a greeting. "Monroe."

He popped his gum. "Captain."

"I see you've met Greensleeves."

The beleaguered Krakau janitor raised a tentacle in greeting.

"Bev has everyone else under guard in medical." Monroe handed her a large bundle containing their uniforms and equipment.

Mops gave Rubin her things, then clicked her monocle into place. "Doc?"

"—*fungal flatworm-brained lickspittle . . . Mops, is that you? Are you all right?*"

"I've been better." She tossed the wrap aside and began pulling on her uniform. "What about you?"

"*I logged seventeen attempts to hack my memory. I don't believe they acquired anything useful, but I can't be certain.*" Doc paused as Mops finished dressing. "*I'm detecting multiple injuries from both you and Rubin. I'm tightening your uniform to provide support to your broken ribs. You require a full medical scan, and possibly surgical repairs.*"

"Probably, but that will have to wait." Mops took her pistol and made sure it was still synched to her monocle. To Monroe, she said, "Cutting power to the base wasn't part of the plan."

Monroe and Greensleeves exchanged weary looks. "Greensleeves brought me to the environmental controls. I meant to lower the temperature, like we talked about. Turning this place arctic should slow the Krakau down. But the cooling systems overloaded and blew the generator."

"The equipment was hastily installed," Greensleeves complained. "They used second-rate parts to connect Krakau air regulators to Earth machinery, didn't bother to clean the ducts or filters, and as far as I can tell, never once conducted a proper inspection or tune-up. It's one of the many backlogged tasks I meant to get to."

Monroe shrugged. "It worked out. They sent two Krakau down to see what was going on. We took care of them, then gathered up the rest."

"By took care of them, you mean . . . ?"

Greensleeves whistled in unmistakable satisfaction. "He sealed them in garbage bags." She started to say more, then shrank low, limbs contracting with alarm.

Mops sniffed. There was a sulfurous scent that hadn't been present before. She knelt to bring her face to the water. The smell grew stronger. A quick taste confirmed it.

"Smells like someone set off the Krakau equivalent of an alert siren," said Monroe.

Mops didn't answer. She just started running.

Mops braced herself for whatever might be waiting in the medical center. Bev seemed tough enough, but she was no soldier. Nor did she have the physical resilience of a cured feral. The Krakau outnumbered her. They could have overpowered her.

But when Monroe yanked open the door to medical, Bev stood unharmed. The Krakau who weren't in medtanks huddled in a corner.

"Glad you're back," said Bev. "They freaked out a few minutes ago, right when the place started to stink like rotten eggs."

Mops stepped toward the Krakau. "Who triggered the alarm?"

"None of us," said a small Krakau with red skin and dark splotches along her tentacles. "It went off automatically when the generator died."

"Then why are you so frightened?"

The Krakau looked at one another, their tentacles intercurling like tangled corkscrews. The one who'd spoken—Red—scooted forward. "The backup generator never took over. The facility is now operating on emergency batteries, at minimal power. It's enough to provide lighting and water circulation, but the batteries can't handle containment."

"Containment?" Mops repeated. "For your test subjects?"

"The hangars aren't strong enough to hold the ferals," said Red. "We had to electrify their stalls to keep them from escaping. They've learned not to try to get out, but with the power down, as soon as they get anxious or upset—"

"They'll start pounding the walls to get away," finished Rubin.

Greensleeves waved an accusatory tentacle. "Who was the incompetent quarter-wit who set up the electrical connections for the backup generator? Was it the same clod who installed the water line? Wiring corrodes differently in this planet's environment, not to mention the rodents and other infestations. If you'd let me inspect the hangars and documented your power needs, I could have—"

"Our research is classified," said Red. "You're not authorized to know what we've accomplished."

A loud, barking cry from outside silenced the room.

"That did not match the vocalizations from any feral we've encountered," said Doc.

"Sounds like we all get to find out what you've done," Mops said quietly. "Authorized or not."

"We should try to reach the evacuation shuttle." Red spoke in a whisper, like she was afraid the ferals might overhear.

"Why?" asked Greensleeves. "We got four humans right here, and they're armed."

"Humans won't be enough," said Red.

Mops' hand dropped to her gun. "What do you mean?"

Red didn't answer. She didn't have to. Mops thought back to her conversation with Admiral Sage. *You want more soldiers. That's what this place is. You're trying to speed up the process of "curing" humans.* Sage had neither confirmed nor denied Mops' guess.

"I was wrong." She realized she'd drawn her pistol and was pointing it at Red. "You needed more soldiers, but you're not trying to improve the processing of humans."

"What are you saying?" asked Bev.

Another call from outside confirmed it. It sounded like the laughter of rusted metal. "That was a Quetzalus."

"Not just Quetzalus," Red said quietly. "We also have two Nusurans, a Glacidae, and four Prodryans. All feral."

Monroe swore. Bev muttered in an unfamiliar language, but from her tone, she and Monroe were in agreement. Even Rubin appeared shocked, her mouth half-open, her hands balled in fists.

"You did what?" Greensleeves snapped. "Give me that gun, Adamopoulos. I'll shoot them myself."

Mops felt like the icy water had replaced the blood in her veins. "How?" she whispered. "It was a fluke of biology that the Rokkau venom affected humans. The odds of the same thing happening with another alien species, let alone four—"

"The venom had no effect on Nusurans or Prodryans," said Red. "In Glacidae it causes minor digestive difficulties. Quetzalus suffered dry mouth, hair loss, and a rash. But our work wasn't about modifying your specific plague to affect other species. It was to reverse engineer how the plague modified humans, and to find a way of duplicating the effects . . ."

The other Krakau scooted away as Mops surged forward, pressing the barrel of her gun into the soft flesh between Red's two primary eyes. "You succeeded?"

"Through a combination of biochemical and mechanical procedures, we were able to approximate the results." Red drew herself up slightly. "We succeeded, yes. And now they're going to kill us all."

17

Basic First Aid for Humans
Prepared by EMC Sergeant A. Lovelace

- *CUTS AND WOUNDS typically clot within one minute. Use your bioglue to seal the skin. Warning: Be careful not to glue your fingers to the wound or to each other.*
- *BROKEN BONES should be shoved back into place. Splint and secure the limb, if possible.*
- *AMPUTATIONS are more inconvenient, and may take up to five minutes to clot. Cover and tie off the stump to speed up the clotting. If you have quick access to an Alliance medical facility, retrieve the limb for possible reattachment.*
- *DECAPITATIONS are fatal, even for humans. The decapitated head can take several minutes to die. Friends and crewmates can use this time to say their good-byes. (The head will be unable to speak, but will appreciate the sentiment.)*

THE BLOOD WAS TOO bright. To Wolf's eyes, it looked fake. Red blood flowed too freely, closer to water than the syrupy blood of ferals. A distant part of her brain—the part that wasn't swearing—found the color almost beautiful.

Melvil slumped against a pillar. The drone had shot him through the right shoulder.

Nancy and another librarian hunched over him. Nancy had both hands on the wound. The other was tying a rope around Melvil's shoulder. Wolf grabbed her tube of bioglue.

"It's too high," said the other librarian. "I can't get the tourniquet above the hole."

"What is that?" Nancy snapped at Wolf.

"Bioglue."

Nancy snatched it from Wolf's hands and tore off the cover. She jammed the tube into the wound and squeezed.

"What's wrong?" Wolf stared from Nancy to Melvil, who wasn't responding. "It's only a limb shot."

Nancy spoke through clenched teeth. "We're not like you, Wolf." She threw away the empty tube and wrapped both hands around Melvil's shoulder.

"He's still bleeding," said the other librarian.

"I know that, dammit! The blood was washing the glue away before it could seal the artery." Nancy raised her voice. "Someone get me a bandage!"

Wolf yanked cleaning rags from her harness and passed them over. Nancy pressed them into place.

The other librarian pressed his fingers to Melvil's neck. "Nancy . . ."

She glared at him. "Don't."

"If I'd gotten to him a little faster . . ."

Nancy squeezed her eyes shut and sat back. "A wound like that, it probably wouldn't have mattered. The only question was if he bled to death now or over the next twenty minutes. This isn't your fault."

Nobody said whose fault it was. They didn't have to.

Melvil's glasses had fallen off his face. It made him look younger. Wolf swallowed. "Is anyone else hurt?"

"I've got a couple of cuts from broken concrete," said Nancy. "Kathleen was grazed on the hand. Melvil is the only . . ." She turned away. "None of the other injuries are life-threatening."

Cate came up behind Wolf and looked down at them. "I don't understand this reaction. You've won another victory against your enemies. Is this how humans celebrate?"

Wolf glanced up. "You should probably stop talking."

Another explosion dropped more of the ceiling. They'd be coming through soon. Destroying the drone had bought them only minutes.

"What now?" asked Nancy.

It took a moment for Wolf to realize the question was aimed at her. She looked at the other librarians and their primitive weapons, then back at Melvil. With their fatigues and weapons, they looked as tough as any EMC soldier, but appearances lied. Wolf had known natural humans were more fragile, but she hadn't understood. "We retreat to the Pomegranate Fallout Shelter. Send someone to pull the two guards off the stairwell."

"You're running away?" Cate's antennae dipped forward to show his disdain.

"Cate and I will cover you," Wolf continued.

"What about . . ." Nancy gestured to Melvil.

"You help the living. I'll bring him along." When Nancy looked reluctant, Wolf added, "I swear I won't let the Krakau get their tentacles on him. We don't have much time."

Wolf stood and stepped around the pillar, holding her rifle one-handed to keep the crosshairs on the hole in the ceiling. Her ammo count was down to fourteen rounds, plus the forty-five in her spare magazine. She mentally reviewed the inventory in her harness. She'd used her sealant foam on the minnows.

Insulation would expand into the cracks, but wasn't hard enough to stop the Krakau.

The librarians began pulling back. Wolf waited for them to get out of sight, then tossed her rifle to Cate. The Prodryan was so surprised he almost dropped it.

Wolf unfastened her harness. With her right arm out of commission, it was easier to grab what she needed this way.

"What are you doing?" asked Cate.

"Copying the captain." She yanked two cleaners free and began connecting them to her compressor. Once they were hooked up, she dragged everything toward the hole. "I gave you that gun to cover me, dammit."

Cate yanked the rifle into firing position.

Wolf sealed her suit the best she could. It wasn't airtight, thanks to the holes that had been shot through it, but it was better than nothing. She aimed her compressor wand and squeezed, shooting the two cleaners straight up. Sweat dripped down her face as she waited for the Krakau to return fire or drop another grenade. Clouds of gas obscured her vision. Her eyes watered and burned, but she refused to blink.

The sounds of digging stopped. The only things coming down from the ceiling were angry Krakau curses.

Only when both canisters were empty did Wolf stumble back, hacking and coughing. Between the mixture she'd sprayed into the hole and the toxic puddle that had dripped onto the floor, that should give them a few more minutes.

She shrugged back into the harness, letting the compressor hose and wand drag behind her. Her throat was raw, and her lungs wouldn't fully expand. She coughed again as she grabbed Melvil's body and hoisted him over her left shoulder.

Cate had retreated from the gas. He stood behind a pillar about ten meters back. When he spotted Wolf, he jumped and pointed the rifle at her. Wolf's visor was still synched to the gun, and showed the crosshairs centered on her chest.

Wolf didn't break stride. "If you shoot me, I will shove that gun up your ass, and blow your brains out."

Cate lowered the gun. "I didn't realize it was you." He paused. "And Prodryans don't—"

"You don't have asses, I know. Don't worry, I'll carve one for you."

Wolf stumbled as a minnow struck her hip from behind.

"I thought we destroyed these things," Cate complained.

Wolf limped around a corner. "I guess they kept a few in reserve."

"You have a gift for angering your enemies."

Wolf paused to adjust her hold on Melvil, slung over her left shoulder. "The more time they spend chasing us, the longer the others are safe."

Nancy waited at the fallout shelter door, shotgun in hand. Cate put on a burst of speed. His wings flapped as he raced into the shelter.

"Is everyone here?" Wolf called.

"They're all inside." Nancy backed out of the way as Wolf stumbled through. "I was starting to think you'd gotten lost."

Two librarians helped Wolf lay Melvil gently on the floor. Wolf turned to help shove the heavy door shut. When that failed, she emptied half a can of spray lube into the hinge mechanisms and tried again. This time, with three people straining together, the door slowly clunked into place. Nancy cranked a metal wheel to drive the locking bolts home.

The shelter's main room was twice the size of the *Pufferfish* recreation deck. Shelves lined the far wall, full of identical white cans labeled in different languages. Metal tracks in the ceiling showed where portable walls could be pulled out and moved to divide the space into smaller sections.

"There are four more rooms like this," said Nancy, pointing toward a broken door to the right. In the dim lighting, Wolf hadn't even seen it. "But there's no other way in or out."

"What will the Krakau do next?" asked the one with the hand injury—Kathleen.

"Can they blast through the walls or the ceiling to reach us, like they did to get down from level three?" asked another.

"How the hell should I know?" Wolf pulled off her helmet and rubbed her scalp, trying to think.

That was the problem. EMC troops were trained to fight, not to think. That's why every ship had a Krakau command crew. The Krakau made the plans, and the humans carried them out.

"You've worked with the Krakau," Nancy pointed out. "You've been fighting them for months."

"We've mostly been running away from them for months," Wolf said bitterly.

Loud blows from the other side of the door made everyone jump—even Cate, who shed a little more color from his wings in the process.

Wolf pointed her rifle toward the door, but the pounding stopped. She surveyed the librarians, several of whom were bleeding. The wounds looked minor, and she wouldn't normally have given them a second thought. "I've got more sterile rags to use for bandages . . ."

"They're all right." Nancy took Wolf by the arm and tugged her toward the open doorway. Wolf didn't have the energy to resist. "Let's see if we can find some water in this place."

The second section of the shelter was identical to the first. The third had stacks of ancient bedrolls, so old and decayed they crumbled at a touch.

Nancy walked toward the shelves with their endless cans. "We're supposed to save these in case of famine or emergency." She grabbed one. "I think this qualifies."

She drew her knife and used a pointed notch on the back of the blade to pierce the top edge of the can. She levered the blade two more times, opening a triangular hole, then poured a stream of brown powder into Wolf's hand. "Try it."

"It looks like sand." Wolf brought it to her mouth, touched the tip of her tongue to the powder. "Not bad."

"Not bad? Cocoa powder is one of the hallmarks of human civilization." She poured a stream directly into her mouth, swished it around, and swallowed. "Eh, you eat gray slime through a port in your gut. What would you know?"

"Reminds me a little of Merraban sweetgrass tea." Wolf brushed the rest from her hand.

Nancy glanced over her shoulder, checking back the way they'd come, then shone her light directly into Wolf's face. "What the hell is wrong with you, child?"

"You need to take command. You or one of the other librarians." Wolf double-checked her shoulder to make sure the glue was holding.

"Do we look like soldiers to you?"

"I can be a soldier," said Wolf. "Whoever's giving the orders needs to be clever. That's not me."

Nancy stood on her toes, peering so closely Wolf could smell the cocoa on her breath. "Is that what's going on? You've decided you're too stupid to lead?"

"You haven't?" Wolf snorted. "Maybe I'm not the only stupid one here."

"Call me that again, and I will knock you on your ass."

Wolf raised a hand in surrender. "I'm just facing facts. The Krakau say it's because our blood doesn't carry enough oxygen for brain development, or something like that."

"Bullshit. That's what they want you to believe." Nancy stepped back. "I used to think the same thing. I thought feral humans were animals, and I expected you people to be little better than cavemen. Melvil's research papers proved me wrong on the first point. Your team did the same on the second. You're ignorant in some areas. A lot of areas. But that's not your fault."

"Ignorant, stupid, what's the difference?"

"Everything. Don't ask stupid questions."

"The point is, the Krakau have control of level four. They'll get through to five soon enough. I don't know how to stop them."

"You slowed them down," said Nancy. "And Gleason won't make it easy for them. She'll scatter folks throughout five, make the Krakau work for every capture."

"But she won't get her people killed in the process." Wolf picked up another can. According to her monocle, this one contained dried grain.

"Have you ever been in a firefight before?"

"I'm in charge of communications on the *Pufferfish*. Before that, I was a janitor." Wolf shrugged. "We've gotten into a few fights lately, but . . ."

"Bloody hell. You thought it would be easy, didn't you?" Nancy turned away in disgust. "Thought you'd run around with your guns and play hero. The bad guys would all drop dead or run away."

"I didn't want your people to get hurt," said Wolf.

"We don't want to get hurt either, genius. Melvil didn't want to get hurt. But we knew what we were getting into."

"You thought I knew what I was doing."

"Suck it up, buttercup." Nancy poked her in the shoulder. The uninjured one. "You want to mope about your fuckups, do it on your own time. None of us have done this before either. The worst we've faced are angry ferals or those damn dachshunds."

"What's a dachshund?"

Nancy ignored the question. "Every librarian in this shelter has studied you and your team since you arrived. From the way you fought Gleason's team to a standstill back at the library to your captain's idea about hitting the Krakau at Armstrong to your plans for slowing down the attackers here. Every one of those librarians chose to follow you."

"But—"

"Interrupt me again, and I will punch you in the eyeball." Nancy paused, fist cocked. "That's better. We lost a friend. We're all struggling to process that. But this woe-is-me routine you're working on? All that tells us is Melvil died for nothing."

With that, she turned away and began searching the shelves.

"I wanted to be assigned to infantry," Wolf said quietly. "They sent me to SHS instead. To be honest, I wasn't that great a janitor, either. Captain Adamopoulos once threatened to send me back to Earth if I didn't shape up."

"The horror."

"Cruel and unusual punishment," Wolf agreed, pacing through the darkness.

"They assigned your captain to SHS, too," Nancy said without turning around. "Think that was because she didn't have what it took?"

Wolf's mouth pulled into a wry grin. "They were probably afraid she had too much of it, whatever it is."

What would the captain do in Wolf's position? Wolf snorted. Probably come up with a clever plumbing-related trick to overpower and humiliate the Krakau. Only Mops had known they couldn't beat the Krakau in a direct fight. That was why she'd snuck off to attack Armstrong instead.

Wolf stopped moving. She aimed her lamp at the concrete ceiling. "How did they manage air circulation for this place?"

"Pardon?"

"LockLand built this fallout shelter to house thousands of people. Tens of thousands. That's a lot of body heat and carbon dioxide. You'd have to have a way to bring in oxygen and cool air."

"Why do you ask?"

Wolf crouched to inspect the base of the walls. "Those Krakau probably came here in a troop transport. A transport that's currently sitting on the surface, waiting to take them and their prisoners back to Armstrong. A transport with very few Krakau left behind to protect it."

Nancy returned a can to the shelf and turned around. "That's better. What about those fighters?"

"I don't know," Wolf admitted. She'd forgotten the fighters. "All right, think of this from the Krakau point of view. LockLand is infested. We're the vermin, and the Krakau want us cleaned out."

"How flattering," Nancy said dryly. "Where are you going with this?"

"We had some kind of Quetzalus worms get into the food processing machinery on the *Pufferfish* a while back. Ugly little bastards, like squirmy feathers with big eyes and bigger pincers. We'd spray every nest we found, but they'd just scatter." Wolf looked up. "The Krakau working their way through LockLand, they're the spray. The fighters are out there waiting to pounce if we scatter. They won't be parked here. They're circling the surroundings, watching to make sure nobody sneaks away."

"What does this have to do with air vents?"

"We bloodied their beaks. They wouldn't leave us here unguarded. Before we can get out and go after that troop carrier, I need to know what they left outside that door." Wolf started back toward the others. "I say we send out a drone of our own."

"It's a plumbing snake." Wolf set the coiled metal hose on the floor and switched it on. It twitched and flopped like an addle-brained worm as it extended to its full two-meter length. "Designed to crawl through pipes and remove blockages."

"How does this help us, exactly?" asked Kathleen.

Wolf pointed to a small, covered vent in the base of the wall. "We send it out through the air ducts to see what surprises the Krakau left for us." She sat down and grabbed the front end of the snake, currently fitted with the default attachment that looked like three concentric rings of metal teeth. Working the best she could one-handed, she hit the release and unscrewed the teeth.

"How smart is that thing?" asked Nancy.

"It's not." Wolf twisted the new attachments into place with a click. Another adjustment activated a data feed on her monocle. She pointed the snake at Nancy and was rewarded with a grainy image of her wrinkled face. "But I can see through its eye, and I'll be guiding its actions."

She used her teeth to tug her glove over her left hand, then waited for the sensors in her uniform to synch up with the snake. Twitching her arm forward sent the snake moving. She ran through a series of motions, making it turn its head in different directions, curl around in a circle, and rear up until it stood nearly a meter tall, balanced on its coiled tail.

"Can you make it do tricks?" asked one of the librarians. Someone else smacked him on the shoulder.

Wolf flattened the snake to the ground and brought it to the wall. "Pop that vent panel for me?"

A heavyset librarian with a crowbar pried it free, taking out several chunks of wall at the same time.

"Your enemy has modern weaponry," said Cate. "You have plumbing supplies. This is madness."

Wolf twitched her fingers, and the snake curled into a fair imitation of a Krakau obscenity.

"Such foolishness is why the Prodryans will destroy you," Cate muttered.

Wolf sent the snake scooting through the vent. Tapping her first and fourth fingers activated the snake's light. It was too dim to be seen by human eyes—or Krakau—but it was enough for the photoreceptors to build an image. Half a meter at a time, Wolf guided the snake through dirt and cobwebs and the empty shells of long-dead insects.

"This feels like one of Grom's first-person shooter games," Wolf muttered. "If only there were medpacks and a rocket launcher waiting for me to scoop 'em up."

"How far have you gone?" asked the man with the crowbar.

Wolf checked her monocle. "Four meters. The duct sloped downward. I think I'm crawling below the road. Just looking for an access point, somewhere I can get out."

She passed several junctions. From the angle, these led off to other parts of the shelter. The duct she was following grew larger, then turned upward. She checked the airflow readings. "Found an exit. I just need to climb a few meters to get there."

Wolf bent her elbow, pointing her forearm straight up. The

snake followed her movements. Using finger gestures to refine her control, she coiled the upper part of the snake, bracing it against the walls of the vertical shaft. Another finger movement brought the lower half up after.

By alternately bracing with the lower and upper coils, she slowly climbed toward a gap near the top where the duct had broken partly free of the large fan and temperature control unit. The snake squeezed through the rusted opening and dropped to the floor.

"I know none of you could see that," said Wolf. "So just trust me when I say you should be very impressed."

"Where are you?" asked Nancy.

Wolf crept out through the broken doorway. "Looks like Strawberry Road, about ten meters that way." She pointed ahead and to the right. "I'm circling around to the fallout shelter door."

The snake undulated past another doorway and between the legs of a penguin statue. Wolf brought it close to the wall to peek past a corner.

"Two Krakau," whispered Wolf. "Both armed and armored. Looks like they're talking to each other."

"What are they saying?" someone asked.

"It's a plumbing snake. It's not set up for sound."

"We knew they left guards," said Nancy. "How do we get past them?"

"I need a distraction. Preferably a loud one."

"On it." Nancy grabbed four more librarians and led them away. Moments later, they began hurling canned food against the door.

Both Krakau jumped. They aimed their weapon cuffs at the door.

Wolf tried to imagine what they were saying. Would they call reinforcements? Doubtful . . . nobody had gotten out, and the guards wouldn't want to admit they were afraid of human prisoners with nothing but primitive weaponry.

But they kept their attention on the door as Wolf guided the snake closer, circling to approach the Krakau from behind. She barely breathed as each movement closed the distance. Three meters . . . two . . . At one and a half meters, she stopped the snake and finger-tapped a new command.

The snake rose up. Wolf turned her hand to the right. The snake did the same, centering the Krakau's body in its visual feed. Wolf elevated her fingers slightly, then made a fist.

A glob of gel spat from the snake, landing just above the collar of the Krakau's armor. She spun around as Wolf turned to the other Krakau and repeated the movements.

Both Krakau began shooting. The visual died a moment later.

Wolf stood, shook the tension out of her arm, and started for the door. "You can stop now."

Nancy and the others halted their assault on the door. Dented and broken cans littered the ground. Several had broken open, spilling dried granules of different sizes and colors. As the commotion stopped, Wolf could hear the Krakau whistling in pain.

"What did you do?" asked Nancy.

"We use those snakes to clear plumbing jams," said Wolf. "Most of the time, the snake can push or dig through blockages. When that fails, it uses an acidic gel that does wonders on biological material."

Nancy winced. "That seems extreme."

"You wouldn't say that if you were dealing with the aftermath of a constipated Nusuran." Wolf grabbed the lock and pulled. After a moment, two librarians helped her unlock and open the door.

Wolf avoided looking at the bodies. The Krakau had died quickly, but it had been painful and undignified.

"I was mistaken," Cate murmured. "Your plumbing supplies were quite effective. Perhaps the Prodryans should look into plumbing-based artillery of our own."

"Shut the door behind us. Melvil should be safe here." Thinking about Melvil helped Wolf to push aside any regrets.

"We're heading back to the cafeteria. The Krakau very kindly left us a sewage-free route to the surface."

"What's the plan?" someone asked.

Wolf's lips pulled back in a predatory smile. "This time, we're gonna think like the captain."

18

Azure tapped the console and jumped to the next chunk of data from the Pufferfish *communications log. She heard the bridge doors open behind her, and recognized Grom from the faint smell of methane. "I need your programming assistance."*

"I'm hardware, not software," Grom protested.

"You're the best we have." Before that could swell Grom's ego, she added, "From an extremely limited talent pool."

Grom made a chittering sound, but crawled over to join her at what was normally Wolf's station. "What are you looking for?"

"Anything to keep me from going mad with boredom," said Azure. "I was thinking about the way Admiral Pachelbel hid the Pufferfish *from the Alliance. Whoever is operating the prison planet where my people are held would have to keep that place secret, along with any communications, supply ships, and so on. I've been working with the ship's copy of Doc to search for evidence of similar programming on a larger scale."*

Doc spoke over the main bridge speakers. "I could tell you everything you wanted to know about human blind spots, but trying to find your own? That's tricky."

"Humans have blind spots?" asked Grom.

"Do you mean physiologically or psychologically? And the answer is yes."

Grom pored over the screen. "Any code like that would be buried, off-limits to the likes of us. Like the subroutine that forced Doc and the other monocles to automatically report to Command when they saw a Rokkau."

"But that code has been removed, and I'm integrated more deeply into the *Pufferfish* systems than any normal AI."

"I've been sifting through communications that were automatically processed by the ship's systems," said Azure, jabbing a tentacle at the screen. "Navigational information, software updates, everything that would need to be quietly rewritten or hidden to conceal a secret planetoid."

Grom bowed their body and brushed a multijointed limb over the screen. "It might be faster to try plotting courses. See where our navigation system won't let us go, or where it creates an unexplained detour."

"You want to plot a course to . . . everywhere?" *asked Doc.*

"We can refine the potential destinations," said Azure, coiling her limbs beneath her. "The Krakau would have a hard time pushing their code into non-Alliance ship systems. So the prison has to be located where non-Alliance ships would be unlikely to stumble across it."

"Somewhere uninhabited," added Grom. "You don't want some colonist noticing a decel flare. An amateur astronomer with a primitive optical telescope could unravel the whole conspiracy."

"Off-limits to non-Alliance ships. Off-limits to colonization." Azure's skin tightened. "You'd need an Alliance presence to dissuade smugglers, miners, and so on, which means the Alliance would have to have a plausible excuse to be there."

Azure rose up and touched the console, her hearts

pounding. "Doc, how long would it take to plot a course 'every-
where' in a single system?"

"That depends. Which system?"

She touched a tentacle to the console, pulling up an image
of Earth's sun and her sister planets. "This one."

ERAL QUETZALUS, NUSURANS, Glacidae, and
Prodryans. Mops had never felt anger like this. Not
when Sage's fighters had destroyed the old library. Not
when she'd learned the truth about the Krakau plague. Whatever crimes the Krakau had committed against humanity, the
initial outbreak was unintentional. An accident.

What Sage and her scientists had done here was deliberate.

"Sir?" asked Monroe, his voice soft.

The Krakau didn't move. They appeared to sense how close
Mops was to shooting them in the tentacles and throwing them
all outside to fend for themselves against their creations.

"Who were they?" Mops whispered.

The Krakau shifted uncomfortably. Mops pointed her gun
at Red and repeated the question.

"Who were who?" Red squeaked.

"Your test subjects. Who were they, before you turned them
feral?"

"Military prisoners. Murderers and traitors. These people
were criminals."

"They were still people." Outside, the Quetzalus cried out
again. "Can you reverse what you did to them?"

"Not successfully," said Red.

Mops holstered her weapon. It was the only way she could
stop herself from using it. "We have to assume all the ferals
have escaped. The Nusuran will be hardest to bring down."

"I'm more worried about the Quetzalus," said Monroe.
"Those beaks are vicious. They'll impale you before you have
time to piss yourself."

"How long do humans typically require for this activity?" asked Greensleeves.

Mops studied the cowering Krakau. "How many of you have combat training?"

Two scooted forward.

"That's it?" asked Bev.

"They sent the bulk of their warriors to LockLand," said Mops. "Rubin and I probably shot most of the rest."

"If I may?" Rubin asked. At Mops' nod, she stepped closer to address the Krakau. "What was the daily routine for your subjects?"

"Routine?" asked Red.

"When did they eat and rest? What did you feed them? Melvil demonstrated that ferals are capable of learning. We might be able to calm and guide them."

"We provide nutritional pellets, balanced for each species' need," said Red. "We considered following the same protocols used for EMC troops, but nobody could get close enough to connect a feeding tube."

Bev jerked a thumb at the Krakau. "What about live bait?"

Several Krakau whistled in fear. Red shrank back, then caught herself. Visibly gathering her courage, she crept forward and interposed herself between Mops and the other Krakau. "You can't send us out there to die."

Mops' hand shot out to seize the end of Red's tentacle. She wound the tentacle twice around her wrist, dragging the Krakau closer. "You've spent months trying to recreate the thing that destroyed my civilization. What you've created out there, if it spreads, could destroy four more."

Red struggled uselessly. "The Alliance *needs* new weapons if we're to hold against the Prodryans."

"If this is what the Alliance is about, maybe they deserve to fall." She released Red, sending the Krakau splashing backward. "I'm in command here. If I decide to send you out as bait, that's where you're going. If I order my people to execute you on the spot, you'll be dead before you can object."

Rubin raised her gun. A dark stain of fear-ink spread from one of the other Krakau.

"If you do exactly what I say and don't piss me off," Mops continued, "some of you *might* see tomorrow. But let me be clear. You are guilty of murder and worse, and there *will* be consequences. Is that understood?"

Greensleeves raised a tentacle. "Captain, sir? I just want to remind you they didn't tell me anything. I didn't know what they were up to. I just cleaned up after them."

The room fell silent. Mops let it stretch as she considered her options. Communications were down. Stepping Stone would eventually notice if they hadn't already, but by the time they did anything, everyone here would be dead. "Greensleeves, any chance you can get the power up and running again?"

"That depends on what all failed," said Greensleeves. "Even if I have the parts, we're probably looking at several days' worth of work."

"The exterior fence is off, too," Bev pointed out. "With all the excitement, we'll have ferals from the outside climbing in to see what's going on."

The roar from outside was louder this time. The Quetzalus was coming this way.

"You have an evac shuttle on pad two," said Mops. "Is it fueled up, and will it hold everyone?"

"Yes . . . yes!" Red swelled with excitement.

"Emergency protocols will probably fly it straight to Stepping Stone on autopilot," Monroe warned. "I can try to override the programming, but no promises."

"At least it will have a working communications pod." Mops straightened. "Do your subjects have the same predatory drive as feral humans?"

"I don't understand," said Red.

Mops spoke slowly, enunciating each word. "If someone runs away, will they chase them?"

"Oh, yes." Red dropped all three primary tentacles to touch

the water, a gesture of mourning. "That's how we lost our previous janitor."

"What?" Greensleeves whirled. "Nobody told me—"

"How much charge do you have left in that hovercar?" Mops asked, cutting her off.

Greensleeves glared death at Red before answering. "Maybe an hour or so. Depends how hard I push it. Why?" She turned her full attention to Mops, and her body slumped. "Oh."

Mops tossed another coil of fiber-mesh hoses from the back of Greensleeves' hovercar. Greensleeves had retracted the top of the cargo compartment, allowing Mops to straighten and stretch her back as she worked. Her ribs and skin patches protested the movement, but she couldn't afford to stiffen up.

The Krakau huddled at the back of the garage. Anyone too wounded to move on their own had been placed into grav stretchers, which looked like oversized rubber hammocks supported by black metal frames.

"Captain—Mops . . ." Monroe didn't have to finish. She knew what he wanted to say, just as he knew how she'd respond.

"You have your orders," she said, addressing both Monroe and Rubin. "Monroe has the most shuttle experience, so he's needed to try to pilot that thing."

"I know nothing about piloting," Rubin pointed out.

"And you got shot up worse than I did, thanks to these jackasses." Mops jerked her chin toward the Krakau. "Greensleeves and I will distract the ferals. Your job is to get everyone else safely to the shuttle."

Bev started to speak, but Mops cut her off. "That goes for you, too. I am *not* going to explain to Gleason how I let one of her librarians get eaten." She tossed the last of the excess equipment over the side. "Doc, how's our interface with Greensleeves?"

"I'm linked to the cockpit. You two can gossip as much as you'd like."

"This is *not* part of my job description," Greensleeves grumbled.

"Are you sure? Most standard Alliance JDs include 'and other duties as assigned' at the end." Mops clipped a safety line from her harness to the side of the hovercar. A second line secured her to the opposite side. Together, they should keep her from bouncing out no matter how rough the driving got.

"Other duties as assigned *by my supervisor*," Greensleeves argued. "Who you shot."

"That's a fair point," Mops conceded. "You definitely ought to put in for extra pay for working out of class." She glanced down at Monroe. "How long will you need to reach launch pad two and the shuttle?"

He popped a new cube of gum into his mouth and chewed silently for several seconds. "It's about half a kilometer. Krakau are slower on land, and we're dragging stretchers. Add in time to get everyone on board, and assuming I don't take a spill . . . Call it ten minutes."

"Get to the far side of the building." Mops checked her ammo count. Thirty-six in this magazine, and a full forty-five in the spare. "Wait for my signal, then run like hell."

"Good luck, sir." Monroe turned toward the Krakau. When he spoke again, his voice filled the garage. "From here on out, you do as I say. If you do anything but obey every word out of my mouth, I will shoot you in the face. Is that clear?"

He didn't wait for a response. One by one, he began assigning individual Krakau to carry stretchers.

Bev offered Mops a half-hearted salute. "Watch your ass out there."

Red turned. "Wouldn't that interfere with her combat effectiveness?"

"Move out," Monroe barked.

Red jumped and fell in with the other Krakau. Moments later, Mops and Greensleeves were alone in the garage.

"As soon as that door opens, we drive in the opposite direction of pad two," said Mops. "We have to keep the ferals' attention on us, so our job is to be as loud and obnoxious as possible."

"I'm told humans excel at that."

"I like this Krakau."

"Doc and I will track as many of the ferals as we can," she continued. "If he tells you to turn, do it. Don't wait for me to confirm."

"Got it."

Rubin had given Mops her infantry helmet. It didn't fit quite right, but the visor had a wider field of view, and would do a better job keeping track of threats. She watched the icons that were Monroe and Rubin move toward the back of the building. "Don't worry, Greensleeves. I'm up here in the open, so they'll come after me first."

"Being eaten second is small comfort," Greensleeves retorted.

"Then keep us out of their reach. Let's go."

The door slid upward. Greensleeves didn't wait for it to open all the way. She gunned the engine, and the hovercar surged forward.

"Dammit, Greensleeves!" Mops ducked to avoid having her head taken off by the still-rising door.

They shot out . . . directly toward the feral Quetzalus. He was filthy, and most of his hair had fallen out. Instead of the luminescent, wavy strands Mops was used to, glowing blue-green pimples covered his skin.

Greensleeves muttered something Doc didn't translate, and the hovercar hauled sharply to the right. Mops' harness dug into her flesh, but the safety lines held. She twisted around and fired three times. "Did I hit it?"

"Two misses. One hit to the neck. From the angle, you may have chipped a vertebra."

The Quetzalus' clawed feet gouged the dirt and rock as he scrambled after them. The skin flaps between front and rear legs were torn. The red crest flopped to one side like an ill-fitting hat. But the black, meter-long beak still looked sharp enough to impale anything in his way.

Mops adjusted her stance and fired again, aiming for the front hips—shoulders—whatever you wanted to call them. It wouldn't kill a Quetzalus, but enough structural damage should slow it down.

He roared again as he stumbled, and the hovercar pulled away. Mops turned to give Doc a chance to scan their surroundings. Her visor lit up with additional threats. Most of the ferals had stayed close to the hangars. Mops spotted all four Prodryans behind them, along with a group of feral humans who must have gotten over or through the fence. "Drive between those old communications arrays!"

Greensleeves led the Quetzalus farther away, then brought the hovercar in a broad circle. The vehicle shifted form, becoming narrower and longer. This was great for squeezing between broken old towers, but it created significant slack in Mops' safety lines.

They scraped one of the towers on the way through. A chunk of rounded shell chipped off the front of the car. The impact jolted Mops hard to one side. She grabbed her line and held tight until Greensleeves regained control.

The Quetzalus tried to follow. He didn't fit, but that didn't prevent him from trying. A furious, deafening roar chased after them as Greensleeves looped back about.

Four Prodryans up ahead to the left. A clump of humans to the right. One pissed-off Quetzalus wiggling through the communications towers. "Take us back toward the hangars, away from the launch pads."

She fired first at the Prodryans. One went down and didn't move. Another staggered away, one wing in tatters. The others lunged at the hovercar, bringing them close enough for Mops to drop another. She twisted to shoot next at the humans.

"Eyes forward," said Doc. At the same time, Greensleeves shouted, "Glacidae!"

They'd come around the corner of the hangars to find the feral Glacidae lounging in the snow. The Glacidae reared up. Clumps of snow clung to their feathery legs. The sickly yellow spines along their back were fully raised.

And Mops couldn't get a clear shot without firing through the hovercar's cockpit.

"Accelerate!" Mops looped the safety line around her arm. "Drive right over them."

The hovercar knocked the Glacidae onto their back. The impact knocked the car into the corner of the hangar. Metal screeched and tore. The car spun a full three-sixty degrees, stabilized, and shot ahead.

"What now?" Greensleeves' voice was higher-pitched, with a rapid clicking overtone. Mops had heard this before from Krakau new to the field. It was a biological response, similar to a human's adrenaline rush. It made the Krakau quicker and— fortunately for Mops—more obedient to authority.

"Back around the hangars, then veer left. We don't want to get too close to the launch pads." Speaking of which . . . "Monroe, how goes it?"

"Almost to the shuttle," said Monroe. "We've got a clear path. Looks like you got their attention."

The hovercar jerked to a stop. Mops' head struck the back of the cab. The ill-fitting helmet protected her from the worst of the impact, but she smacked her nose on the inside of the visor, leaving a spatter of blood across her display.

"You're bleeding."

"I'm aware."

"All that internal liquid. So messy and inconvenient."

A Nusuran lay on the ground up ahead, blocking their way. It was almost two meters in length, built like a thick, ten-legged worm with gray mouth tendrils wriggling from behind triangular plates of bone.

No, not it, but zim. The size and the ten legs made this a Si.

Nusurans were one of the toughest species out there, able to survive temperature and pressure extremes that would destroy most species. Their leathery skin covered a thick layer of fatlike cells that absorbed and dispersed impact, serving as both armor and insulation.

Going around would take them toward the launch pads. The Glacidae was behind them, along with who knew how many Prodryans and humans. And where the hell had the Quetzalus gotten off to? "Between the hangars."

Greensleeves squeezed the hovercar into the gap. The Nusuran raised zir head but didn't follow. While the other ferals appeared to be driven by hunger, hunger wasn't much of a driving force for the average Nusuran. They were motivated by other appetites.

Mops shivered. If anything of the Nusuran sex drive had survived whatever the Krakau had done . . . "Keep us out of zir reach!"

They drove out from the hangars. A short distance to one side, the Quetzalus was nudging a fallen Prodryan with its beak. As Mops watched, he took a tentative nibble. He turned and spat, his tongue glowing a sickly purple. After clapping his beak in disgust, he lowered his head and took a second bite.

"Not too bright, are they?"

Mops reached inside her visor to wipe away the spots of blood. Doc was tracking eleven hostiles. Five more humans were climbing the fence. "Isn't there a second Nusuran?"

"The Krakau mentioned two, yes. No sign of it yet."

"We're ready for you," Monroe called.

"Greensleeves, head for the shuttle!"

The hovercar swerved toward the landing pad. Mops could see Rubin standing by the open hatch. Dirt and snow swirled past her feet as Monroe powered on the engines.

"I found the second Nusuran!"

Mops had never seen Nusurans move so quickly. They both sprinted across the clearing, almost as swift as the hovercar. Several other ferals, human and Prodryan, followed at a slower pace.

"They're chasing us," squealed Greensleeves.

Mops watched them run. "They're not coming for us. They're heading for the shuttle. Monroe, shut it down!"

"On it." The shuttle's engines died. The Nusurans slowed, but continued toward the landing pad.

"What's happening?" asked Greensleeves.

"They're drawn to the vibrations. It's like a cry for help, or maybe a mating call, I don't know." Mops fired at both Nusurans to get their attention. "Monroe, how long is the warm-up process on that thing?"

"I'll need at least a minute and a half once I restart the engines," he said.

It took five more shots to annoy the Nusurans enough for them to turn away from the shuttle and start toward the hovercar. "Greensleeves, where are the base's stores and supplies kept?"

"Perishables are in the subbasement. Everything else is in the warehouse, back near the garage."

She lowered her gun. "Get us over there."

The warehouse was a blocky building nestled up against the larger tower where Red and the other Krakau had lived and worked. It was on the side facing the launch pads, giving Mops a clear view of Monroe and Rubin helping the Krakau onto the evac shuttle.

"The lock is electronic," said Greensleeves. "With the power out—"

Mops emptied her magazine at the warehouse door, targeting the latch and hinges. "Drive."

The hovercar shifted mass again, elongating even more as it smashed through the door, then lurched to a halt. With so many barrels and crates stacked inside, the car couldn't get slender enough to continue. "Now what?" Greensleeves yelped.

"Let me know if the ferals catch up." Mops swapped out her magazine, unclipped her safety lines and crawled over the cab. Doc translated the labels on the various containers: building supplies, replacement components for water circulation and other systems, plenty of the marble-sized gravel that served as Krakau bedding . . .

She jumped down and moved toward the back. Smaller cans here held freeze-dried synthetic protein fillets, powdered slug pudding, carapace oil, and more.

"There you are." She grabbed two purple cans the size of her head and hurled them into the back of the car, then climbed after them. Her arm gave way at the end, and she tumbled hard, landing on her back. "Drive!"

Greensleeves accelerated so fast Mops bounced against the back of the cab. One of the cans struck her helmet hard enough to make her ears ring. The hovercar smashed into one of the Nusurans, spun in a tight one-eighty, and tore away.

"Take us back to the hangars!" A green medical alert had begun to flash on her visor. "When did I break my foot?"

"Forty-three seconds ago. I'm picking up two compound fractures to the metatarsals. There may be additional damage I can't detect."

They swerved past the Quetzalus. Mops shot at a Prodryan who was in their path. She couldn't tell if she hit it or not, but Greensleeves was getting pretty good at running over ferals, and that worked just as well.

"Take us between hangars one and two, then park it!"

Greensleeves obeyed, squeezing the hovercar into the entrance of the narrow alley between the two hangars.

Mops stood up. Her left leg immediately gave out. "Shit."

"What's wrong?" asked Monroe.

"Busted my damned foot."

"I'm coming back for you," said Monroe.

"The hell you are. Take one step out of that shuttle and I'll shoot you myself, is that clear?" Another thought occurred to her, and she added, "That goes for you, too, Rubin!"

She set her pistol down and grabbed her combat baton and sealing tape. Holding the baton against her leg and ankle, she looped the tape around in a crude splint. She tore off another strip and secured one end through her harness, the other to the first can. She did the same on the other side with the second can, picked up her gun, and pulled herself up again, carefully this time. The cans banged against her thighs, but didn't fall away. "Greensleeves, I need you to get out here and help me climb."

"Is your translator broken?" the Krakau shouted. "Did you just ask me to leave the safety of the hovercar?"

"I didn't *ask*," Mops snapped.

A hole appeared in the top of the cab, expanding until there was room for Greensleeves to squeeze through. She glared at Mops. "'Other duties as assigned'?"

"Exactly." The hovercar rocked as the first Nusuran threw zimself against it.

Greensleeves jumped onto the curved roof of the hangar. Two tentacles reached higher, while the third stretched back to coil around Mops' forearm.

With the Krakau's help, Mops managed to drag herself to the top. The two Nusurans were both attacking the hovercar now, and more ferals were closing in, attracted to the commotion.

Mops crawled to the edge.

"Will that Quetzalus be able to reach us up here?" asked Greensleeves.

"Possibly." Mops used her pocket torch to burn through the lid of the first can. Once it was open, she leaned out and upended it. Purple goop stretched and fell onto the Nusurans. One reared up, mouth tendrils flicking in all directions. Mops shook another glob free, directly onto zir face and eyes.

"Can't you just shoot it?" asked Greensleeves. "Aim for the brain, right? That's how you kill ferals?"

Mops tossed the can aside and opened the next. "Nusuran brain fibers extend through their entire body. They don't keep their brains in one convenient target area."

The Quetzalus let out a roar as it hobbled closer. Greensleeves flattened herself against the roof behind Mops.

"Hold my harness. Don't let me fall." Mops stretched as far as she could to dump the second can's contents.

Neither of the Nusurans paid any attention to the ferals

closing in around them. Not until one of the Prodryans stepped in and bit the Nusuran's flank.

The Nusuran jerked in surprise, knocking the Prodryan to the ground. Two humans moved in from either side. The Glacidae crawled between the Nusurans. All of them pawed and bit, but none of the ferals appeared to do much damage to the thick Nusuran hides.

Then the Quetzalus stretched out his neck and took a bite out of the closer Nusuran's neck.

Now the Nusurans began to fight back in earnest.

Mops had never seen ferals fight one another. There was no attempt at defense. Injuries were ignored. They simply bit, kicked, and struck at each other again and again.

Greensleeves picked up one of the empty cans. "This is sautilk sauce."

"Yep." Mops turned away from the carnage. "And the primary ingredient is sea salt. Salt's a pretty common nutritional need for most species."

"Sautilk sauce," Greensleeves repeated, the whistling undertone of her words suggesting the early stages of a mental breakdown. "You *seasoned* the Nusurans?"

"I did." Mops started down the roof as quietly as she could. They'd have to leave the hovercar, but the ferals should be too preoccupied to chase them. Or to go after the shuttle. "Monroe, this is Mops. We're on our way."

19

Krakau Alliance Judicial Council,
Regulatory Branch

Dept. of Occupational Safety

Safety Hazard Report Form

Worksite: *Medlab Five, Earth*
Report Submitted by:

  × *Employee*
  ☐ *Supervisor*
  ☐ *Other* _____

Hazard Description—Briefly describe the alleged hazard in the space below. Include the number of employees affected.

 1. Water intake/outflow line not buried deep enough. Improper materials used for the environmental

*conditions, resulting in total failure for all employees
and test subjects.*
2. *Power generator and wiring were improperly installed,
and had not been inspected, leading to a catastrophic
failure.*
3. *When power failed, the [redacted] being kept in the
hangars escaped and tried to [redacted]! This whole
facility was a death-trap waiting to happen.*

Suggested Remedy:
1. *Indefinite paid stress leave while I try to recover from
this reckless endangerment and the resulting work-
place trauma.*
2. *Whoever authorized this project should be fired and
then fed to those [redacted].*

For Office Use Only

Complaint Number: *1068375*

Follow-up: *None, per Military Council*

WOLF STEPPED INTO THE sunlight, raised her
hands, and hoped she wouldn't be immediately shot.
When several seconds passed without a barrage
of A-gun fire transforming her to shredded human meat, she
allowed herself to exhale and look around. The surface level of
LockLand was mostly unchanged: domed buildings, colorful
paths and roads, half-frozen water flowing around that rotting
castle in the center.

"Get out here." She reached back to drag Cate through the
doorway.

Cate huddled behind Wolf, gasping for breath. "I hate . . .
stairs."

The Krakau troop transport was parked on the rainbow

road near the outer wall. The ship was the shape of a squashed teardrop, colored the dingy gray of a storm cloud. The front section—the point—was transparent.

Magnification showed a single Krakau resting in the cockpit. Wolf waited, but the pilot didn't react. "I don't think she's noticed us."

"That means there's time to go back inside and think up a better plan," whispered Cate.

Wolf stepped cautiously away from the stairwell door. When nothing happened, she started toward the transport. Without turning around, she said, "If you try to run away, I'll eat you."

Wings rustled as Cate hurried to keep up. "Eating sentient beings is illegal."

"So is pretty much everything else I've done for the past four months." Wolf was growing annoyed. What was the pilot doing that was so interesting? Or had she gotten bored and fallen asleep while waiting for her passengers to return?

"Maybe we can just walk to the ship and kill her," suggested Cate.

"The cockpit will be locked, and we don't know what kind of security the ship has. We need her alive." They'd both given up whispering, since it appeared to make no difference. Wolf bent to grab a chunk of orange brick from the road.

Left-handed, Wolf's first throw was so awkward she missed the ship entirely. She snarled and snatched up another brick. She walked even closer, until she could see the Krakau's torso expanding and contracting with each slow breath.

This time, the brick smacked into the side of the cockpit. The pilot's long, boneless limbs flailed like hyperactive pasta. Wolf raised her hands and kicked Cate to do the same.

Gun turrets spun to target the two of them.

"Here we go." Wolf flashed her biggest smile and stepped forward. "Hi, there!"

"Stop that," Cate hissed.

"What?"

"Displaying your mouth bones. Civilized species find it threatening and repulsive."

Wolf kept her attention on the Krakau. She did cover her teeth with her lips when she spoke, though. "Is this where we're supposed to come to surrender?"

"What do you want?" The response, translated and amplified through external speakers, made Wolf flinch.

"To get off this hellhole of a planet," said Wolf. "My name is Wolfgang Amadeus Mozart. I'm part of the *Pufferfish* crew. This is Advocate of Violence, a Prodryan spy we picked up in the Tixateq system. The humans of LockLand don't have the guns or the numbers to fight off Alliance troops. We figured the sooner we turned ourselves in, the safer we'd be."

"Drop your weapons."

Wolf plucked her combat baton from her hip and tossed it away. "I left my gun behind. Figured you might get spooked and shoot me if I was packing."

"What about the Prodryan?"

Wolf laughed. "You think I'd let him have a weapon?"

The pilot glanced away, probably checking her instruments. "Approach the port hatch. All guns and sensors are tracking you, and I'll be armed as well."

Wolf took a step, then hesitated. "Port is left, right?"

"Not right," said the pilot. "Left."

"Got it." Wolf watched the pilot crawl back from the cockpit, heading into the ship to meet them at the hatch. She double-checked the communications bracelet Nancy had provided, making sure it was transmitting. "I hope you all heard that. All weapons and scanners are locked on us."

Seven figures sprinted from the stairwell. They raced past Wolf and Cate to take up positions to either side of the port hatch.

Wolf waited until they were ready, then strolled toward the ship. A rectangular panel folded outward into a ramp. The Krakau pilot stood at the top, one tentacle pointing a weapons cuff at Wolf's head.

Wolf gestured to either side of the ramp. Seven librarians stepped into view, guns aimed at the Krakau.

"The one with the stripe of red fur on her head is Nancy," said Wolf. "I gave her my rifle. It's on burst mode, so it'll punch several holes through your body before you can twitch. The rest are using old weapons powered by gunpowder. I know it sounds primitive, but they spray a cone of metal that'll take your limb right off."

Wolf walked up the ramp and tugged the weapons cuff off the unresisting Krakau's tentacle. "You got a Human name?"

"Blackbird."

"I assume you're the pilot. Are you alone out here?"

"Yes."

Wolf stepped past her to peer inside the ship, then beckoned the others to follow. "Blackbird, I'm told standard procedure for an operation like this would be for you to maintain an active communications link to every Krakau soldier in LockLand, yes?"

She glanced toward the cockpit. "That's correct."

"That's good." Wolf put an arm around Blackbird's body, just above her primary tentacles. "You and I are going to get this ship's communications and weapon systems working together. Every one of those comm signals should give us a clean target lock."

Blackbird twisted free. Seven guns jerked to follow her, and she froze. "I won't help traitors murder Krakau troops."

"We shouldn't have to kill any of them," said Wolf. "Once they realize the ship can shoot them all in less than a second, I'm hoping they'll see reason."

"She doesn't appear convinced," said Cate. "I don't believe she will help us."

"That's too bad." Wolf peeked into the cockpit. "I know enough about communications. I can probably link everything up myself."

"What about Blackbird?" asked Cate.

Wolf smiled. "Guess I'll just eat her."

Blackbird whistled a shrill, "What?"

"You know how us cured ferals are. Barely civilized, little more than animals." Wolf licked her lips.

"If I help you, you promise not to murder them?" Blackbird whispered. "Or to eat me?"

"Not unless I have to." Wolf pointed to the front of the ship. "Shall we?"

Mops took Monroe's hand, letting him help her into the escape shuttle. The other Krakau were strapped into egg-shaped seats, their limbs twined around metal support bars and grab handles. The stretchers and their occupants had been secured to the floor near the back. It didn't leave much room to move about, but Mops wasn't going to complain.

Rubin hauled Greensleeves on board while Mops hobbled after Monroe toward the cockpit.

"Everything's ready to go, but I'm not authorized for manual control," said Monroe. "Our only option is the preprogrammed escape sequence. Pull that lever, press this button, and we'll be on our way to Stepping Stone."

Mops collapsed into the copilot seat, an uncomfortable array of metal bars designed for Krakau limbs. "What about our prisoners?"

"If any of them know how to override this thing, they're not talking."

Mops reached for the lever he'd indicated. "Let's get the hell out of here before those ferals come for dessert."

The interior lighting dimmed. Additional gauges and indicator lights brightened the horseshoe-shaped console. The main screen switched to an exterior view.

Monroe hit the launch button. Grav plates and thrusters made Mops' gut hiccup into her chest. Medlab Five—no, *Armstrong Space Center* shrank beneath them. The Glacidae had crawled toward the launch pad, but the rest of the ferals continued to fight and feed by the hangar.

"I don't suppose you got communications sorted out while I was playing chase with ferals?" asked Mops.

"The launch sends out an automated distress beacon." Monroe pointed to Mops' side of the console. "Communications controls are here, but they're not laid out like the ones on the *Pufferfish*."

"How long until we reach Stepping Stone?"

"Two hours, seventeen minutes, given the orbital position and velocity of the station and the intercept course on the secondary screen."

Two hours and seventeen minutes to either gain control of the shuttle or contact the *Pufferfish*. Otherwise, everything they'd done was for nothing.

Monroe studied the controls. "I tried searching for help menus. No luck so far."

"Doc, do you have any of Puffy's communications tutorials saved?"

"My memory isn't limitless. It only seems that way when compared to humans. I'm sure the Pufferfish *has lessons on this particular shuttle model, but I'd need to synch with the ship to grab them."*

"The *Pufferfish* should be picking up the emergency beacon," said Monroe. "Could we modify the signal? Embed some kind of code?"

"I'm not sure there's a code for, 'Found a group of uninfected human librarians living in an old theme park emergency shelter. Also, Admiral Sage is working on turning other races feral in preparation for escalating hostilities with the Prodryans.'"

"I think I've seen Wolf using a button that looked like this." Monroe reached past her to tap a blue button. "Anything?"

His voice echoed through the shuttle. From the back, Greensleeves yelled, "If you're gonna use the intercom, would you mind turning down the volume?"

"Sorry." Monroe hit the button again, and it went dark. "Should we ask one of the Krakau for help? I don't trust them, but they might know their way around communications."

A diamond-shaped indicator flashed red. Mops looked at Monroe. "Did you do that?"

"I don't think . . . maybe?" He shrugged.

Mops pressed the red diamond, and a new image appeared on the screen.

Fleet Admiral Belle-Bonne Sage stared at them. Her curved beak clicked shut, cutting off whatever she'd been about to say. The orange skin of her face and torso turned brown. Without looking away, she extended one tentacle to the console behind her, adjusting one of the controls. Her beak opened again. Closed again. Finally, she said, "I suppose I should have anticipated this."

Mops didn't respond.

"You should know, Adamopoulos, my troops successfully captured your librarian friends twenty minutes ago, along with Technician Mozart and the Prodryan you've been colluding with."

"Tell her you didn't get that. Say you're getting an error message that the translator buffer needs to be reset."

Mops relayed the message, trusting Doc to have a good reason.

Sage muttered to herself, then turned to check something. "You should see a yellow toggle slider," she said slowly. "Third row, second from the left. Pull it all the way down, then release. When it blinks, tap twice to confirm."

"Copy that." Mops went through the motions. "Admiral, those librarians are the last of humanity as it . . . as we were meant to be. Let them go, and I'll give you the *Pufferfish*."

"As you'll be in my grasp shortly regardless, I don't see the need to negotiate."

"Tell her the translator glitched. Now it's talking too fast, making her sound like a squeaking mouse."

Sage twisted her tentacles in frustration. Speaking even slower, she asked, "What did you do to break that shuttle so badly?"

Monroe leaned in to say, "I . . . might have kicked it a few times trying to figure out the launch sequence."

"Fucking humans." Sage extended her tentacles.

"I didn't get that," said Mops.

"You should see a rotary control in the lower left corner of the communications section," said Sage, continuing to drag out her words. "Tap and rotate ninety degrees."

Mops pretended to do so.

"Does that fix the problem?"

Mops whispered, "Does it?"

"It does. Thank you."

"Much better, Admiral."

"Stepping Stone is tracking you, Adamopoulos," said Sage. "I'd prefer to take you in alive, but if you deviate from your course in any way, we will destroy that shuttle. Do you understand?"

"Completely. Mops out." She stared at the console, and hesitated.

"It's the red diamond-shaped button to your left," Sage snapped.

Mops pressed the button, and Sage vanished. "Doc, please tell me you were doing more than just messing with the admiral. Not that I object to getting on her nerves, but—"

"I may not have access to the Pufferfish *tutorials, but I've observed Wolf's work at communications. By mapping known controls between the shuttle console and that of the* Pufferfish, *I've been able to deduce additional functionality."*

An exhausted laugh bubbled up from Mops' chest. "Doc, I think I love you."

"Of course you do."

"Can you get me a secure connection to the *Pufferfish*?"

"Not without knowing the ship's precise location. This is an EMC shuttle. It has the same tracking updates as the rest of the fleet, including the modified code rendering the Pufferfish *effectively invisible."*

"What about an encrypted broadcast?" asked Monroe. "Send a message to the whole system, but make it one only Kumar and the others can understand."

Mops hadn't realized Doc was sharing their conversation with him, but it made sense. "Stepping Stone has better encryption and decryption software than anything on the *Pufferfish*. More importantly, Stepping Stone has people who know how to use that software."

"I have a suggestion that bypasses the need for human/software interaction."

"Explain," said Mops.

"Another copy of me is active on the Pufferfish. *I'll choose the encryption technique—a book cipher from my favorite Glacidae hibernation romance saga. My counterpart, once he deduces the message could be from me, will consider how he would encrypt a message in my position. I estimate he should be able to translate the code and establish communications in under three minutes."*

Monroe's brow wrinkled. "What if you're not monitoring communications on the *Pufferfish*?"

"You think I'd trust a trio of organics to handle everything? I guarantee I've been keeping an eye on all bridge systems nonstop since you left."

Mops reached for the controls. "Sounds good to me. Tell me what to do to get you talking to yourself."

It was closer to four minutes before the red indicator lit up with an incoming direct transmission. Mops slapped the console, and a vision of Sanjeev Kumar appeared on the screen. Grom and Azure stood behind him, pressed up against either shoulder. "Captain?"

All three appeared healthy. What she could see of the bridge behind them was more or less intact. "Doc is sending a data dump about what we've found here. There's a lot to catch up on.

I need you to prepare a broadcast of that data to Dobranok, Cuixique, Nurgistarnoq, and Solikor-zi. Hold off transmitting until I give the order, or if you don't hear from us within—"

"Captain," Kumar interrupted. "We've been—"

"I don't have much time, Kumar. This is our only leverage against Admiral Sage. Can you confirm receipt of Doc's data?"

Azure moved away. "Receiving now. Kumar, you should tell the captain—"

"I'm trying," said Kumar.

"Our shuttle is locked into a rendezvous with Stepping Stone," Mops continued. "Once they've brought us in, I'll need you to—"

"Stand by, sir." The screen went blank.

Mops tilted her head. "Did he just put me on hold?"

"Technically, he's acting captain of the *Pufferfish*," Monroe pointed out. "And, no offense, but you weren't letting the man finish a sentence."

Kumar appeared again. The image split in half, shrinking Kumar to one side for a three-way communications link. In the other half, covered in dust, sweat, and bruises, Wolf nodded in greeting.

Mops stared at them both. She searched for words, eventually producing a confused, "How?"

"I led a mission to seize the Krakau transport ship," said Wolf, her words so perfectly matter-of-fact Mops knew she'd been practicing. "All Krakau troops have been disarmed and secured. The librarians have them under guard in the back."

Cate hunched behind Wolf, looking much the worse for wear, but it was Wolf who held Mops' attention. Beneath the usual aggression and bravado was something new. A tension around the mouth. A deepening of the lines furrowing her brow.

"What happened?" Mops asked, her voice gentle.

Wolf glanced away, a moment of vulnerability that lasted just long enough to confirm Mops' intuition. "Things didn't go as smoothly as I'd hoped down there, but we can talk about that later."

"All right." Mops shook her head. "How did you establish contact with the *Pufferfish*?"

Wolf grinned. "Double barrel roll, followed by a quick drop."

Mops turned to Monroe, who shrugged.

"It's Grom's favorite move in *Black Hole Run IV*," said Wolf. "It usually works against the computer, but I blow Grom away every time they try it against me in player versus player. Before we left, I'd been giving Grom shit about how predictable they were, so I knew they'd recognize the maneuver and realize I was flying the ship. Well, technically one of the Krakau is flying, but I'm the one telling her what to do."

"Enough of your self-aggrandizing," complained Cate. "Tell your captain about my plan."

"Cate has a plan?" asked Mops.

Wolf scratched her scalp, leaving her hair even spikier than usual. "I hate to say it, but it's pretty good."

"I agree," said Kumar. "The *Pufferfish* was moving into position to assist when we received your call."

"All right." Mops leaned forward. "Impress me."

Stepping Stone Station reminded Mops of an inverted jellyfish. The bulk of the station was a broad, bowl-shaped structure half a kilometer in diameter. The rim bristled with enormous antennae and flexible tubes, hoses, and docking corridors, several of which were attached to larger EMC vessels. Mops recognized the *EMCS Taipan* and the bloated-caterpillar shape of a Nusuran cargo ship.

A smaller tactical display showed both the troop transport and the shuttle floating just outside the station.

"What's the delay?" shouted Bev. "I need to use the bathroom, and I'd rather not risk my life with this Krakau plumbing."

"They're bringing both ships in together," said Mops. "That way Sage gets all of her prisoners in one bay."

"Are we really surrendering to Fleet Admiral Sage?" asked Rubin.

"Not exactly."

The shuttle jolted into motion again, gliding toward the maw of the main docking bay.

The landing was as smooth as any Mops could remember. If not for two brief hiccups in gravity—accompanied by the sound of a spacesick Krakau from the back of the shuttle—she wouldn't have known they'd touched down.

After several minutes, a message on the main screen announced that the bay was fully pressurized. A booming voice from outside commanded them to power down all systems and disembark.

Mops and Rubin made their way to the hatch while Monroe finished shutting down the ship. "Everyone else stay inside for now," Mops ordered. "Monroe will monitor the situation via comm. Bev, if any of the Krakau start causing trouble, you have my permission to flush them down their own plumbing."

Rubin cranked open the hatch and exited first. She examined the bay, then turned back to Mops. "It's clear."

The gravity was less than Earth's, easing the strain on Mops' battered limbs as she followed Rubin down. Soft red light strips covered the floor, helping to segment and organize the bay. The only other ship was the bulky troop transport, sitting roughly ten meters away.

The bay walls were the brown rough-stone texture the Krakau liked, with no hard angles anywhere. Mops spotted the large intake/outflow vents in the ceiling and the base of the walls, where air could be pumped in and out. If Sage wanted to, she could depressurize this place and kill Mops where she stood. Or open the bay doors and blow her into space.

She raised her hands and did her best to appear nonthreatening. "We're here, Sage. We're unarmed."

"Captain?" Wolf climbed down from the transport and hurried toward Mops. They looked each other up and down, each taking the measure of the other's injuries. "You look like hell, sir."

Despite everything, Mops grinned. "You smell like it."

"Yeah, well, for future missions, I recommend against crawling through hundred-and-fifty-year-old waste lines."

"That should go in the manual." Mops limped closer and put a hand on Wolf's shoulder, the one without the bandages. "However this turns out, you've done well."

Wolf's expression hardened. "Tell that to Melvil."

The barely-repressed grief and anger told Mops everything. Her hand tightened, and she allowed herself a moment of silent mourning for the overenthusiastic librarian. "From what I saw of him, he'd say the same."

The voice from before filled the docking bay. "All personnel must exit the ships."

Mops turned to face the door leading into the station. "We didn't come here to surrender, Sage. We came with a message."

After a pause, the voice repeated, "All personnel must exit."

Mops glanced over her shoulder and nodded. Greensleeves was the first off the shuttle, followed by the rest of the Krakau from Armstrong Space Center. They quickly slunk toward the door, dragging their injured in stretchers. Bev and Monroe were last to leave.

The transport took longer to empty its passengers. Krakau troops joined the others near the door. Cate followed them out, shouting taunts after the Krakau. "Go stand in the shame of your defeat!"

Next out were eleven human librarians. Mops recognized Nancy, Khatami, and the Head Librarian herself.

Eliza approached Mops. "I'm glad to see you alive."

"More or less," said Mops. "Are you sure about all this?"

"Not at all." Eliza chuckled. "But it was worth it. I've traveled maybe three hundred kilometers from LockLand in my lifetime, Mops. Seeing the Earth from space . . . watching nightfall creep across the globe below . . . In all the books and recordings we've collected, there's nothing like it."

The inner door opened with a faint hiss. Four Krakau guards slid out, blaster-cuffs ready. Several of the Krakau from Earth tried to hurry away, only to be forced back at gunpoint.

One of the guards, a warrior with yellow-and-brown shell patterns, moved toward the humans and the Prodryan. One by one, she waved a scanner wand over each of them. Another guard did the same with the Krakau by the door.

After the scans were complete, the two Krakau guards moved into the shuttle and troop transport, presumably to search for stowaways, explosives, or whatever else Sage thought they might be hiding.

"Do you mind if I sit down while we wait?" Mops lowered herself to the floor without waiting for an answer. "Your scientists shot me a lot. It takes a toll."

Eventually, the two Krakau emerged and returned to the door. Only now did Fleet Admiral Sage enter the bay. She was orange and brown in color, with a thick, squat build. Blue-and-white stripes on one tentacle sleeve marked her as a Fleet Admiral. Sage examined the humans and the lone Prodryan before focusing her attention on Mops. "Where is the *Pufferfish*?"

Mops furrowed her brow. "I'm not sure. I got disoriented during docking." She waved a hand toward the left. "That way, I think?"

Sage spoke into her comm. "Have you finished your security sweep of the station?"

Doc did his best to pick up and translate the response. ". . . *clear. No sign . . . intrusion.*"

"You think this is a trick?" asked Mops. "That I'm here to distract you while my people sneak into Stepping Stone?"

Sage ignored her. "Continue searching. Keep guards on all plumbing and waste disposal lines with external access points. We know how this particular batch of humans likes to operate." To one of the guards, she said, "Take the soldiers and

Medlab Five personnel to quarantine. They're to be kept isolated until I've had the chance to personally debrief them."

"They won't find anything," Mops said wearily. Reuniting with Wolf and the librarians had lanced her fears, leaving her exhausted and impatient to bring this game to an end, one way or another. "Not from my team, at any rate. Like I said, we're just here to deliver a message."

Only after the other Krakau had been removed did Sage speak again. "Marion Adamopoulos. You and your crew have lived your lives safe in the shell of Krakau protection. Do you know what the Prodryans would do to this planet if we hadn't deterred them?"

Cate perked up. "I do."

Mops double-checked the time, then cleared her throat. "Advocate of Violence, didn't you have a message for Fleet Admiral Sage?"

Cate straightened. Despite the patchiness of his wings, the flakes of mucus that clung to his limbs, and the strong odor of sewage and mold, he somehow projected a fair imitation of dignity as he reached into a pocket compartment of his armor.

"Slowly," said Sage. "My people won't hesitate to shoot a Prodryan."

"Normally, I'd applaud such enthusiasm." Cate removed a small, low-quality memory crystal. "In this situation, however, hesitation would be best for all involved."

Sage tapped one of the guards with a tentacle. The guard picked up the memcrys and dropped it into a small rectangular scanning unit. "No sign of malicious code or active AI."

Mops glanced at Eliza. "Paranoid, aren't they?"

"War criminals often are," said the librarian.

Sage ground her beak but accepted the crystal from the guard. She touched the edge to her visor, allowing the two systems to interface.

Cate ruffled his wings. "Fleet Admiral Belle-Bonne Sage, you are hereby served notice of the following civil and criminal charges: trespassing, destruction of property, attempted kidnapping, attempted murder, and murder. This is an initial list of charges, subject to—"

"Don't be absurd," Sage snarled. "You think a Prodryan and a human deserter can bring charges against me?"

"We aren't," interrupted Mops. "These and additional charges to come are being filed on behalf of Eliza Gleason." Her mouth quirked. "Duly elected Queen of Earth, and Head of the Library of Humanity. Charges were witnessed and affirmed by Nancy Pearl, Vice-Queen of Earth."

Eliza had argued for "President" or "Prime Minister," but according to Doc, the word "Queen" translated better into Liktok.

Eliza squared her shoulders and stepped toward Sage. The Krakau guards shifted uneasily. "On behalf of my species, I intend to request full membership in the Krakau Alliance. But first we need to negotiate the unlawful presence of this station in Earth space, as well as the matter of your unauthorized facilities on the surface. I've spoken with literally every sentient, unmodified human being on Earth, and strangely enough, not one of them recalls granting permission for this incursion."

"This is absurd," said Sage. "Take them all into seclusion. Nobody speaks with the humans until I've had time to—"

"Before you lock us up," Mops interrupted, "you might want to check in with Tactical."

One of Sage's tentacles went to her visor. She murmured quietly, then turned back to Mops. "What are you talking about?"

Mops sighed. "Grom never has been the most punctual member of the crew . . ."

Sage's body flattened in alarm. The bay lighting turned green as the entire station went on alert.

Mops checked the time. "Twenty-three seconds late. Not bad."

"What have you done?" demanded Sage.

"On order from Queen Gleason, the *EDFS Pufferfish* just destroyed your facility at Armstrong Space Center," said Mops.

"EDFS?" asked Rubin.

"Earth Defense Fleet Spaceship," Mops explained. "Currently, the EDF is a fleet of one."

"As a token of our desire for peace," Eliza added, "we will take no hostile actions against your other settlements on our planet. For now."

Sage began shouting orders into her comm. "What do you mean you can't trace the source of the attack? Blanket the area with A-gun fire, and launch a wide spread of— On whose authority?"

"The *Pufferfish* also transmitted a copy of the charges against you to Stepping Stone Station," Mops explained. "And to the *EMCS Taipan*. And directly to Admiral Pachelbel. We included preliminary evidence. The recorded confessions from your scientists were especially damning, as was the video of the poor souls you transformed into mindless monsters."

"The Alliance Military Secrecy Act supersedes these charges." Sage flung the memcrys to the ground.

"The hell with your secrecy act," said Mops. "Fleet Admiral, did you ever visit your secret laboratory? Did you inspect the work your mad scientists were doing? Did you look your victims in the eyes?"

"You'd lecture me?" Sage slid closer. "You just ordered the death of everyone down there."

"I know." The Krakau had said their work—their butchery— was irreversible. Whoever those people had been, they'd died long before Mops ever heard of Armstrong Space Center. None of it changed the guilt over issuing that order. "I killed them. It's what soldiers do. What you created us to do. It's what the Prodryans want to do."

"True," said Cate.

"What you did to those people is worse," Mops continued.

Cate tugged the edges of his wings around his shoulders like an overly-starched cape. "Fleet Admiral Sage, I earned a Superlative rating in my certification exams and am distinguished as one of only seventy-three advocates with the right to practice beyond Prodryan borders. I easily passed your

Alliance legal exams, and I have full confidence in my interpretation of the AMSA and all related case law. In my professional opinion, you should stop talking until you've hired an advocate to defend you."

"I imagine security will be arriving shortly to take you into custody, Admiral," said Mops.

Sage turned her attention toward Mops, openly pleading now. "You'll destroy the Alliance. When Earth is overrun by the Prodryans and humanity exterminated, remember this moment."

"I will remember and treasure it always," chirped Cate. He paused, then said, "You were addressing the humans. My apologies."

"How does she expect you to remember this moment after you've been exterminated?" asked Doc.

Mops didn't answer. She knew Belle-Bonne Sage's record. Sage wasn't used to losing, and didn't handle defeat well.

Sage's tentacle whipped toward the weapons cuff holstered at her side. Before she could pull it free, Mops threw her entire weight into a punch to the admiral's face, directly above the beak.

Sage's body bobbed backward, straightened, and slowly sagged to the floor.

Mops turned to the guards. "When you're done staring, we'll need an escort to your communications station."

"Communications?" one repeated. "What for?"

"To send a message to the soldiers of the Earth Mercenary Corps," said Eliza. "An invitation for them, if they choose, to come home."

20

Pachelbel touched a tentacle to the comm panel on her console. "This is Admiral Pachelbel. Please have the hygiene and sanitation team schedule a complete flush of my office. The sooner the better."

"Yes, sir."

"Thank you." Clearing the lingering taste/scent of Belle-Bonne Sage from the water wasn't the most urgent thing on Pachelbel's list—it wasn't even in the top twenty-five—but getting her office back to normal would help her to focus on the real priorities. Like arranging for Sage's transfer back to Dobranok, where she would be officially court-martialed and punished for her various crimes. Or facilitating negotiations with the Queen of Earth.

Not to mention trying to figure out what the depths to do with Mops and her crew. Half the Alliance wanted them executed as traitors; the other half wanted to give them medals for discovering what Sage was doing to Alliance citizens.

The door slid open. The sight of a Prodryan on her station made her limbs tighten. She did her best to keep that instinctive reaction from showing. "Advocate of Violence. Come in."

"I've spent much of the past twenty-four hours conferring with my client, the queen." He managed to drop the phrase "my client, the queen" into every conversation. He extended an antique bound book. A flap of paper marked a page near the middle. "We have a proposal for you."

Pachelbel hesitated, then carefully took the book from his claws. She set it gently on the console, moving slowly so as not to splash the paper pages. She secured her monocle to her left eye and waited for it to translate.

She read the text twice to make sure she understood. Pro-dryans weren't known for having a sense of humor, but this . . .

"The practice has existed on Earth for thousands of years, in one form or another. The precedents are all there. My implant is transmitting a list of noteworthy precedents now, along with the official petition from Queen Gleason."

"This rule would grant your clients total freedom to commit whatever crimes they wanted!"

"It's a little more nuanced than that," said Cate. "The queen and I submit that Captain Adamopoulos and her crew have been acting as part of the queen's de facto service staff. Bodyguards, janitorial consultants, and so on. The rules of immunity are different, but still provide legal protections, particularly for actions taken while discharging their responsibilities to Queen Gleason."

Pachelbel settled back in her cove. She'd have to consult with Judicial, as well as with the Alliance Cultural Relations branch, but the stories spreading through the Alliance had made Queen Gleason a highly sympathetic figure. "What about the crimes Mops and her team committed before coming to Earth? Is this diplomatic inoculation supposed to apply retroactively?"

"Historically, no. But given the circumstances, the queen and I feel a pardon wouldn't be inappropriate."

"If I decide to grant this outrageous request, what will Her Majesty give the Alliance in return?"

"To begin with, the queen has indicated she'd be willing to

let you maintain a presence in this system. With human over-sight, naturally."

The Prodryan was enjoying this a little too much. Pachelbel tapped her console. "This list of names to be granted full pardon. I notice you're not on it."

Cate's antennae flattened. "Excuse me?"

Pachelbel suppressed her amusement. "Everyone from the Pufferfish *is here, including Grom, Kumar, and Azure. There's no mention of Advocate of Violence."*

"An oversight, I'm sure," Cate stammered. "I'll file an amended request—"

"You do that." Pachelbel floated back from her console. This could solve one of her immediate problems. Soon she'd need to turn her attention to the larger ones. "Before you go, would you mind answering me one question?"

"Certainly. My rates are—" Something in Pachelbel's body language made him stop in mid-sentence. "What would you like to know, Admiral?"

"Can you conceive of any outcome to the conflict between Prodryans and the Alliance that doesn't involve the utter destruction of one side or the other?"

"I don't understand," said Cate. "How else could conflict truly end?"

Pachelbel settled back, letting her tentacles float on the water. "Thank you. That's what I thought." She flicked a tentacle over her console. "Please tell the queen I'll forward her petition along with my recommendation it be granted."

WOLF PACED THE CIRCULAR walkway around the edge of the observation dome. Intellectually, she knew a curved sheet of thick synthetic crystal would stop her from falling through space to the planet below. Slick tentacle prints showed where various Krakau had sat on the dome itself to watch the Earth. But Wolf's hindbrain insisted that if she put the slightest weight on the dome, it would shatter, dropping her back to her home world as an extremely dead corpse.

A door slid open behind her. Uneven footsteps approached. Mops was still limping from her injuries at Armstrong. "I would have gotten here sooner. Pachelbel is working on finding next of kin for Sage's test subjects. She needed to review my data downloads to help with identification."

Wolf nodded, her attention fixed on the fiery arc of sunlight spreading across the edge of the planet. She'd spent the past two days coming to a decision. Now that she'd finally made it, she struggled to get the words out.

"Command changes you," Mops said gently.

"You could say that." Wolf remembered a puddle of red spreading across the floor. She forced the memory down and blurted, "I want to stay here."

"Here in the observation dome?"

"On Earth." Wolf realized a second too late Mops was joking. She turned around. "With Gleason and the librarians."

Mops' expression didn't change. She wasn't surprised. Had she expected this? How the hell could she, when Wolf had only decided today?

"What happened to Melvil wasn't your fault," said Mops. "It was—"

"You weren't there."

"It was mine," Mops finished.

"Huh?"

Mops sat down and folded both arms on the low rail, letting her legs hang over the edge. "That's how command works. I chose to leave you and Cate behind to hold off the Krakau. That makes it my responsibility."

Wolf scratched the healing wound on her shoulder. "Why not Monroe? He has the training and experience."

"The mission wasn't to win. It was to keep the Krakau busy

long enough for the rest of us to take Armstrong. I needed Monroe for that." Mops smiled, but the lines by her eyes suggested sorrow. "And I knew you were too damn stubborn to stop fighting."

Wolf tilted her head, conceding the point. "Are you saying that's a good thing? 'Cause I remember what you said when I got into that brawl with Grom . . ."

"Nothing like getting shot to make you miss the good old days of quill punctures," Mops said, grinning.

"It's not that I want to leave the *Pufferfish*—"

The grin vanished. "The Alliance might have decided to let us off the hook, thanks to Cate and our friend the queen. That doesn't mean they're going to let us keep our very own EMC cruiser."

"EDF," Wolf corrected.

That got another smile. "I'm supposed to head to the ship in half an hour to go over the various modifications we've made." Mops paused. "I don't know what's next for the crew, but I have no objections to you staying here, if it's what you want. Have you talked to Gleason about this, and about what you'd be doing?"

Wolf sat down. A part of her had hoped Mops would refuse, would order her to stay with the crew and the *Pufferfish*. For one anxious heartbeat, she was tempted to change her mind, to stick with the chaos and madness she knew. "I asked Khatami some questions. All hypothetical. I figure I could help them out with security work. And someone's gotta look after Cindy and the other ferals. Who better than someone who's half feral herself, right?"

"You and Cindy seemed to get along well."

"Yes, sir." Wolf's throat tightened. "I'm sure I'll be doing a lot of reading, too. I mean, I'll be living in a library."

"When you find good books, I expect you to transmit copies my way."

"I will." Wolf stood to go. "What about you? I mean, we've

all been given a clean slate to do whatever we want. If you won't be staying on the *Pufferfish* . . ."

"That's a good question." Mops laughed quietly, almost to herself. "I'll let you know when I figure it out."

"Yes, sir."

"None of us are part of the EMC anymore," Mops said. "You don't have to call me sir. For that matter, you didn't have to ask my permission to stay, either."

"Respectfully, sir? Yeah, I did."

Mops stood up and faced Wolf. With a small, strange smile, she offered Wolf a half bow, the gesture they'd learned from Khatami. Wolf returned it.

"See what you can do about upgrading those bathrooms in LockLand," Mops suggested. "They'll need someone who knows modern plumbing."

"Thank you, sir. For everything." Wolf hurried out of the observation dome before the knots in her throat and gut could get any tighter. She ran directly into Khatami, who was loitering in the corridor outside the door.

"Well?" asked Khatami.

"Well what?"

"What did your captain say? Are you staying with us?" They snorted. "Or didn't you expect me to see through all your 'hypothetical' questions?"

These humans were smarter than most of the ones Wolf had known. That would take some getting used to. "She said yes."

Khatami whooped and pulled her into a quick embrace. After a moment, Wolf returned it, albeit stiffly.

"Sorry," they said, releasing her. "I didn't mean to presume. I'm just happy you'll be joining us. You know Junior's going to follow you around until you tell her absolutely everything about space and other planets and the different aliens you've met, right?"

"Nothing's official yet." This was really happening. She was going to live on Earth. With plants and weather and sunsets and ferals and skunks . . . She felt dizzy. "I haven't talked to Gleason—Queen Gleason, I mean."

"I *may* have asked her about it already," Khatami admitted. "Hypothetically, of course."

Wolf snorted and gave them a gentle shove.

"I think she's in one of the communications centers, talking to a team of Merraban archivists who want permission to help restore our library." Khatami got a funny look on their face. "The Merraban in charge said his name was Bob."

Wolf laughed. "Merrabans change names for the comfort of whoever they're with. I wonder if any of them know how to cook Tjikko nuts . . ."

"I almost forgot!" Khatami abruptly stopped walking. "There's one more thing I needed to tell you."

Wolf braced herself. "What's that?"

"Welcome home."

Mops did her best to keep the amusement from her face as the trio of horrified Krakau technicians looked around at the *Pufferfish* bridge.

"What have you *done*?" whispered the lead tech, a green-hued Krakau who went by the Human name Tik Tok.

Grom rose from the tactical station where they'd been disconnecting the silver control sphere. "I made the bridge usable, thank you very much."

Tik Tok pointed a tentacle toward the back of the bridge. "Is that . . . a cup holder?"

"It's better than cleaning up spills," said Mops.

The three Krakau began talking among themselves. Mops picked up phrases like "complete tear-down" and "six separate fire hazards." All the while, Grom's spines grew taller, and their grip on the microwelder grew tighter.

Mops moved between Grom and the Krakau before the former lost their temper and tried to weld the latter to the exposed wiring panel at Navigation. "Why don't you take a break, Grom," she suggested. "Finish packing up your belongings."

"If they damage my controllers, I'll expect replacements," Grom muttered as they pushed past the Krakau toward the lift.

Mops sat in the captain's chair, sinking into the cushion for what might be the last time. "How long will it take to extricate Doc from the ship's systems and synchronize him—them—back into a single unit?"

Tik Tok made a sound that married laughter and despair. "We've got an AI specialist coming in tomorrow. We're just here to try to straighten out the hardware."

They began at Tactical, tracing cables and testing controls. The main screen flickered once, and Puffy appeared, fully armored and wielding the ridiculous battle mop. "It looks like you're trying to disassemble the bridge. Do you need any help?"

All three Krakau stared.

"No, thank you," said Mops. Puffy shrugged and shrank into nothing.

"This ship should be condemned," Tik Tok declared.

The lift door opened as she finished speaking. Admiral Pachelbel tilted her body to one side. "Are you saying it's beyond your team's skills to repair and refit?"

"No, sir!" Tik Tok straightened to attention, followed a half-second later by her two companions. "It may take longer than initially expected, though."

"Go examine the engine room," said Pachelbel. "I need to talk to Ms. Adamopoulos in private."

Mops had jumped to her feet when the admiral entered. As her conscious mind caught up with her training, reminding her she was a civilian now, she settled back into the captain's chair.

Pachelbel waited for the lift to close, then eased her way to the front of the bridge. The white skin around her eyes crinkled with fatigue. "You'll be happy to know we're likely to make it through another day without a civil war and the total collapse of civilization."

Mops checked the time on her monocle. "The day's not over yet."

"True." She pulled a small, flexible bulb from a satchel around her neck and brought it to her beak, squeezing a stream of clear liquid down her throat. "Sage isn't talking, except to tell us we've damned the Alliance and given the galaxy to the Prodryans."

"Cate will be happy to hear it."

"She truly believed she was doing her duty," said Pachelbel. "Have you ever heard the Merraban saying about good and evil?"

"The true enemy of good isn't evil, but fear. Evil will battle good, but fear will corrupt it." Mops shook her head. "If Sage's work escaped her control, if it spread like the Krakau Plague did on Earth—"

"Sage and her scientists insist that wasn't possible."

"Doesn't matter," said Mops. "If there's one thing the people of the Alliance fear more than the Prodryans, it's humans. The idea of becoming like us . . ."

"Humans are smarter than we give them credit for." Pachelbel looked around the bridge, taking in the various modifications.

"What's happening to the personnel from Armstrong?"

"Most are cooperating with the investigation. They insist they were simply following orders, but that excuse is unlikely to float. They'll be spending a very long time locked up in the Basin."

"Even Greensleeves?"

"She claims to have been unaware of what was happening. Between that and your recommendations, she'll probably be released after we finish questioning her."

"She's good under pressure, and she knows her stuff," said Mops. "I don't know who you've got running hygiene and sanitation on the station these days, but you could do a lot worse."

"I'll keep that in mind."

"Thanks. And while we're on the subject of prisoners . . ."

"I'm working on securing Azure's release from quarantine." The Rokkau had been kept isolated since their arrival, a prisoner in all but name. "There are limits to the number of crises I can manage at one time. Most of the Alliance has no idea who the Rokkau were. Most of the Krakau believe the Rokkau are extinct."

"So you lock up an innocent Rokkau because it's easier?" asked Mops.

Pachelbel darkened, her annoyance clear. "Wasn't that innocent Rokkau actively involved in an attempt to destroy my planet four months ago?"

"Not the planet. Just the Krakau living there."

Pachelbel simply looked at her.

"All right, fair point," Mops conceded.

Pachelbel took another drink. "Queen Gleason and her retinue will be returning to Earth soon. I'm sending two squads of EMC infantry troops along for protection against the ferals and other threats. It should help them to safely explore and expand their territory."

"Did she agree to let the Krakau continue curing humans?"

"She did," said Pachelbel. "Conditionally. She's sending a representative to supervise. In addition, all reborn humans are to be given the choice to enlist or not."

"Given what Sage said about the Prodryans, we'll need all the soldiers we can get."

"We?" the admiral repeated.

"Prodryans don't discriminate. They'll kill my planet along with everyone else's." Mops thought back to what she'd seen of the original Marion Adamopoulos, the exhausted determination of the woman in the blue shirt and white lab coat. "I plan to keep fighting to protect my people. It's what we do."

Mops leaned toward Pachelbel. "You didn't come here and clear everyone else off the bridge just to chat. You're feeling me out. What is it you want, Admiral?"

Pachelbel finished her drink and tucked the empty bulb away. "We found something else in Sage's files . . ."

Mops gathered her team in Azure's new temporary quarters on Stepping Stone. All save Cate and Wolf. Wolf had departed for Earth three hours ago, and Cate was off trying to figure out how to double-bill the Alliance and the people of Earth for his time.

Azure's quarters were marginally better than the quarantine she'd been in. Admiral Pachelbel had closed an entire section of the station "for repairs and maintenance."

The small cove was only ten degrees—comfortable for Azure, but making the air a bit chilly for everyone else. There was no human furniture. Mops sat on one of the rough, synthetic stones at the edge of the water. The others did the same, except for Grom, who coiled in a tight spiral near the wall.

Azure had been swimming in circles when they arrived, watching programming on three separate display screens. One showed the Earth as seen from the observatory; the next was a tactical display of the system. The third showed a Glacidae slalom competition.

"Doc, would you please show everyone the data brief Admiral Pachelbel provided?"

"That's all I am to you. A glorified remote control."

A fourth display lit up. For several minutes, the room was silent except for the slalom commentary.

Monroe spoke first. "Tuxatl? Never heard of that planet, but it sounds Quetzalus."

"It is," said Mops. "Or it was supposed to be. The Quetzalus launched an exploratory mission to Tuxatl eleven years ago. They found the planet was inhabited by an intelligent, technologically primitive species they named the Jynx."

"Isn't that a species of rodent on Cuixique?" asked Rubin.

"It is." Mops started to say more, but Grom reared up, shouting and rattling their spines.

Everyone turned to stare.

"Sorry." Grom settled back down. "I'm listening. I just got distracted for a moment. Watch this replay. Tarnogoqualin cut in front of Mirnamidalkag, sending Mirn into a wipeout. Tarn used their spines to gouge the ice. It's called a blizzard turn. It sends bits of snow and ice to blind whoever's behind you."

"Doc, maybe find another program?" asked Mops.

Grom started to protest, looked around, and sighed as Doc switched to live footage of an Alliance Economic Subcouncil meeting about inflation rates.

"The Quetzalus didn't think much of the Jynx," Mops continued. "Mission logs describe the natives as 'fussy' and 'primitive' and 'obsessed with personal hygiene.'"

Azure swam to the edge of the cove. "Like Kumar?"

"You know I can splice a waste line into your water supply in two and a half minutes, right?" asked Kumar.

Azure raised her tentacles in surrender and slid backward, floating on the surface.

"Alliance laws were clear," said Mops. "Native species take precedence. The Quetzalus started packing up to leave. That's when a Prodryan war fleet arrived. They blew up the support ship in orbit and turned the landing site, including the exploratory team, into a glass crater."

"This is what Prodryans do," said Rubin.

"Yes and no," Mops agreed. "The Alliance scrambled to pull enough ships together to fight off the Prodryans and protect whatever was left of the native population, but the Prodryans just turned around and left."

"Maybe they didn't know about the Jynx," Monroe suggested.

"They sent a hunting party to the surface to check for Quetzalus survivors," said Mops. "They couldn't have missed evidence of native intelligence. Withdrawing without even a token attack on an alien species violates everything we know about Prodryan procedures and instincts."

"They're not slaves to those instincts," said Kumar. "Cate hasn't tried to kill us."

"Yet," added Rubin. "He's made his long-term intentions clear."

"Exactly." Mops zoomed in on Tuxatl. "Cate wants to break the entire Alliance. That supersedes his instinct to kill a few humans. The question is, what happened here to override their need to slaughter the Jynx?"

Monroe blew a bubble of what smelled like cigar-flavored gum, then went back to chewing thoughtfully. "Could have been a coincidence. Another battle needed reinforcements, maybe."

"That's what the Alliance believed at first," said Mops. "They sent a follow-up mission two years later, with heavy security. The Prodryans threw an even larger attack force at them. They destroyed all but three Alliance ships that managed to jump away, then fell back, the same as before."

"They don't want anyone else exploring that planet," said Rubin.

"Why haven't we ever heard of Tuxatl?" asked Monroe.

"Because all of this is classified. Tuxatl is officially quarantined." Mops leaned back and stretched her legs, one at a time. Her wounds were healing, which meant they were starting to itch. She tightened her fists to keep from scratching. "Admiral Pachelbel didn't even know the details until she started going through Sage's files. Sage was obsessed with finding ways to fight the Prodryans."

"We noticed," said Monroe.

"Someone like Belle-Bonne Sage would never keep all her eggs in one nest." Mops brought up another of the records Pachelbel's people had decrypted. "She had extensive notes about Tuxatl. They were saved in the same file substructure as her plans for new feral soldiers. The Tuxatl files were named . . . the best translation would be 'Plan B.'"

"Sage believed the Jynx, or something about that planet, could be used against the Prodryans?" asked Grom.

"That's what Pachelbel has asked us to find out." Mops focused on her crew. "This isn't an order. As of today, you're all free to start whatever life you'd like."

"Not all of us," Azure said bitterly.

"I know." Mops leaned closer. "I told her I'd only accept the mission if she forced her higher-ups in the Military Council to tell us where they've imprisoned the other Rokkau."

"Europa."

Mops stared at Azure. "Excuse me?"

"My people are on Europa." Azure waved a tentacle. "Technically, they're *inside* Europa."

"We figured it out while you were chasing ferals on Earth," added Kumar.

"It's the one place in the solar system the *Pufferfish* nav systems wouldn't let us go near," said Grom. "Once we realized that, Doc was able to dig up all kinds of interesting code. Pre-programmed artificial readings designed to mask Krakau-built security systems, artificial data about the planet core . . . even if a ship happened to take a closer look at Europa, they wouldn't see anything unexpected."

"You figured this out . . . in your free time?"

"Yes, sir," said Kumar.

Pride and gratitude momentarily overwhelmed her. All she could do was shake her head in amazed disbelief.

"In between games of Titanslayer," added Grom.

Mops laughed. "Well, that certainly gives us additional leverage. I'll tell Admiral Pachelbel I'll take this assignment if she frees Azure's people. What about the rest of you?"

"Why us?" asked Kumar. "We're not exactly Alliance elite."

"Because Tuxatl and the Jynx are protected," said Rubin. "It's part of the Alliance Protected Species Act. Pachelbel can't order an Alliance ship to the planet."

"Speaking of which," said Grom, "how exactly does Her Admiralness expect us to get to Tuxatl?"

Mops' smile grew. "I thought we'd take my ship."

"Your ship?" asked Monroe.

"Pachelbel and I were reviewing the estimated cost of restoring the *Pufferfish* to Alliance standards. I'm told her accounting staff wept when they saw the figures. So I spoke with a few people. First, Cate dug up the laws about disposal of military surplus. Next, I put in a call to Eliza. The Krakau have had medical facilities on Earth for more than forty years. Eliza had her people calculate forty years of back rent. She was more than happy to divert a small portion of that debt to the legal acquisition of a decommissioned cruiser."

Monroe pumped a fist in the air and let out a loud whoop. "I'm in, sir."

"I've put too much work into that ship to abandon it now," said Grom.

Kumar and Rubin looked at one another. They nodded to Mops in unison.

"Azure?" asked Mops.

"The Krakau imprisoned my people for more than a century," said Azure. "Do you really believe Admiral Pachelbel and the Alliance will free them?"

"I believe she wants to do the right thing," Mops said slowly. "And I believe most of the people who know about the Rokkau are more afraid of what's coming from the Prodryans than they are of your people. If we help them against the Prodryans . . . yes, I believe we have a chance to free your people."

Azure floated toward the back of the pool. "What's the plan, Captain?"

"I haven't worked out the details yet," Mops admitted. "Here's the rough version. First, we get the *Pufferfish* fixed up. Then we go save the galaxy."

Epilogue

Advocate of Violence: Mission Progress Report

Have successfully completed or made significant progress on objectives 1-5, 8, and 9. Fleet Admiral Sage has been arrested and disgraced. Humans are becoming aware of various Krakau deceptions. Of the ten thousand EMC troops currently in service, roughly five percent have formally resigned from the service. Fewer than I had hoped for, but it will take time for the truth to spread.

I was presented the opportunity to kill one member of the Pufferfish *crew: Mozart, Wolfgang A. However, this occurred during a Krakau siege, and killing her at this time would have significantly reduced the odds of my own survival. Since being killed would negatively impact my ability to complete my mission, I allowed Wolf to live.*

Leaked information about the experiments conducted under Fleet Admiral Sage have led to seven resignations, eleven separate investigations, and a general sense of distrust among Alliance members.

My preference at this time would be to return home to reap the glory and rewards of my service, but there has been an unexpected change in the wind. Adamopoulos has kept me as part of her team. While I am not a prisoner, neither am I free to leave, nor have I been permitted communications access to broadcast these reports.

The blows I've struck against the Alliance in the name of our clan should be more than enough to gain the support of the other warlords, earning our clan warlord the title of Supreme War Leader. Once I am able to transmit proof of my glorious success, I trust my efforts will be fairly rewarded.

Victory to the Prodryans!

Adamopoulos says we will be departing shortly on the Pufferfish. *Adding further turbulence to the situation, I've determined that she intends to travel to a planet they call Tuxatl. I believe this may be the world we know as Hell's Claws. If so, this will likely take care of objective 6, killing Adamopoulos and her crew.*

It now occurs to me that I am part of Adamopoulos' crew.

Oh, shit.